MATO

Andrew Clare

Yamato

Andrew Clare

Kurodahan Press
2013

YAMATO
Copyright © 2013 Andrew Clare

FG-JP0038L
ISBN: 978-4-902075-53-3

KURODAHAN PRESS
Kurodahan Press is a division of Intercom, Ltd.
#403 Tenjin 3-9-10, Chuo-ku, Fukuoka 810-0001 JAPAN
www.kurodahan.com

Dedication

To the memory of Yoshitada Yamaguchi

16.11.1913–11.10.1947

JAPAN: 1953

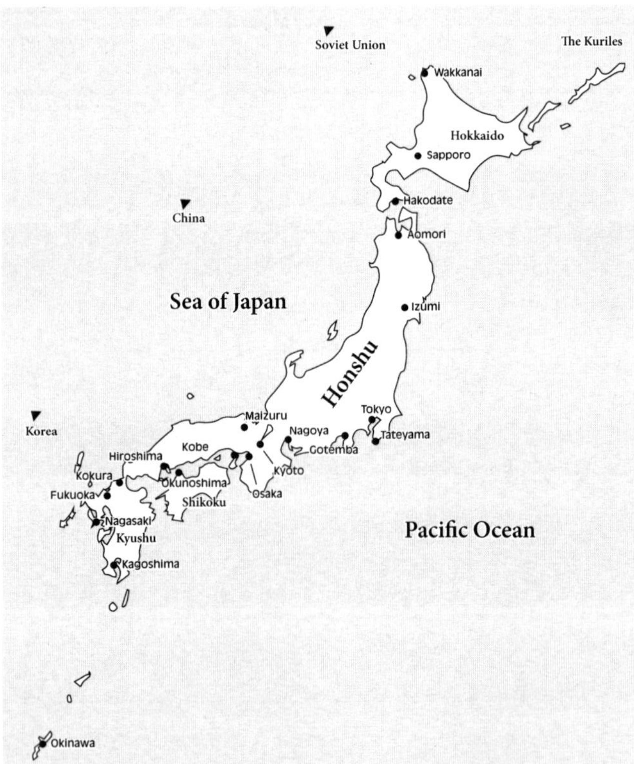

Soviet Union
The Kuriles
Wakkanai
Hokkaido
Sapporo
Hakodate
China
Aomori
Sea of Japan
Izumi
Honshu
Tokyo
Maizuru
Korea
Nagoya
Tateyama
Kobe
Gotemba
Hiroshima
Kyoto
Kokura
Okunoshima
Fukuoka
Osaka
Shikoku
Nagasaki
Kyushu
Pacific Ocean
Kagoshima
Okinawa

Yamato

"Under the circumstances, the danger of a proletarian revolution in Japan is beyond doubt and arises from fundamentally the same sources as in other countries—from the domination of monopoly capitalism. The survival of feudalism in Japan, sharpening as it does the antagonisms of interests between the peasantry and the landlord class, creates the danger of revolutionary peasant movements and thus creates conditions for the support of a proletarian revolution by a peasant war."

Writings of Leon Trotsky, 1937–1938

Prologue

Sugamo Prison, Tokyo: November 7, 1944

The Russian sat in silence listening to the soft words of the Buddhist priest. A better life would await him following reincarnation. His impassive eyes stared vaguely at a narrow shaft of light that filtered into the dank concrete cell through a small oblong aperture set into the outer wall. A solitary candle on the bedside ledge had almost expired, its flame flickering and dancing as the soft wax dissolved, clinging to the last few moments of life.

"Had it all been worth it?" the priest had asked. He thought so. His efforts and self-sacrifice would undoubtedly contribute to the winning of the ideological battle. He had no regrets. Were he to have his time over again, there was nothing he would do differently.

Footsteps came closer. Closer. Closer . . .A large key was inserted in the heavy lock. The Russian flinched, his body stiffened and his nail-less fingertips drummed nervously on the tabletop. The solid metal door was pulled open, bringing with it the rank smell of poorly ventilated, overcrowded cells. The time had come.

The priest motioned toward the door. The Russian nodded, resigned to his fate. He stood with difficulty, straightened his ripped jacket and hobbled in the direction of the corridor. His face was barely recognizable, bruised and swollen from repeated beatings. The light from the corridor was unbearable to his unaccustomed senses and he squinted, raising a hand to shield his sensitive eyes.

Two guards moved to his flanks and supported him by the arms, guiding his broken body along the window-less corridor. A small but compact prison officer, with an uncomprehending, brutal face, led the way; the priest brought up the rear, eyes downcast, concentrating on the uneven floor surface. How many desperate souls had walked this way . . .

Dull, yellow, phosphorescent lighting fizzed and crackled quietly overhead. Dark, nascent forms hovered in the gloom on either side of them—looking on with feigned insouciance—their own fate reflected in what they saw. The party made its way around a right-hand bend and then slowly, painfully, down the short flight of worn stone steps that led to the chamber below.

A thin stream of reddish brown water trickled down a narrow channel in the wall, spreading out vein-like into a myriad of smaller channels lower down. Rusting pipes chased one another across the crumbling ceiling.

The door to the room was already open, and a cool draft blew up the stairwell. The Russian dipped down to allow his six foot frame to pass under the lintel.

He straightened and stood rooted to the spot as his eyes came level with the wooden platform in front of him. Despite the cold, sweat soaked through his shirt and ran down his forehead. He shuddered, sucking in cold stale air through cracked, ochre-colored teeth. And then his resolve renewed itself. He raised his head, threw his shoulders back and thrust his chest forward. He brushed aside his escort and stood upright—proud and unrepentant, waiting for the command.

The prison officer took a pace forward, crisply pulled out a file from where it had been clamped under his left arm, opened the enclosed order and perfunctorily read it out to those assembled before him. The pronouncement was short: The condemned was to be hanged by the neck until dead.

The same emotionless voice barked out another command, but, before the guards could respond, the Russian had raised a hand indicating that he would climb the platform without assistance.

He focused on the rope that was waiting for him and, with great effort, dragged one foot up in front of the other until he reached the top of the short set of wooden steps. The guards joined him and quickly bound his hands behind his back. A black hood was produced, but the Russian, stubborn to the last, shook his head vigorously and shouted,"Nyet!" The noose was tightened, and the knot slipped snug behind his left ear.

One of the guards came back down the steps and joined the others below. The remaining guard took a step backwards, felt for the lever and without hesitation pushed it forward. The trapdoor opened, and the deadweight plummeted—coming to a sudden and violent stop. The priest looked away, fingers curling around his rosary.

The short life of Richard Sorge, journalist, diplomat, and supreme spy of the Soviet Union, had come to an end.

One

Tokyo, Japan: March 26, 1953 (eighth year of the Occupation)

A curious, unearthly mist drifted irresolutely across the glassy water of the Imperial Palace moat. A gentle breeze rippled the surface and brought with it a taste of the coming storm. Opposite, the gray granite of the Dai-Ichi Insurance building, headquarters to the Supreme Commander for the Allied Powers in Japan, seemed bigger and more imposing than ever against the backdrop of the darkening sky.

Special Agent Ralph Carnaby of the CIA took a sip of strong black coffee, eased back in his worn leather chair and peered out the window of his sixth-floor office into the gloom that was Tokyo.

A shadow fell across the room. He looked sideways to see dark menacing clouds rolling in from the east. The windows were flecked with rain, and the roar of a C-119 Flying Boxcar carried on the wind as its huge hulk climbed begrudgingly into the air. *Yet another consignment of cannon fodder bound for Korea.* He screwed his eyes tight shut and wished like hell he were someplace else.

The phone rang. He placed his half-empty coffee cup down on the desk and snatched the receiver up from its cradle. It was Dan Morita, phoning in from the Ops room two floors below.

"Ralph?" Morita sounded breathless. "I've just had a report from downtown. Looks like we've got a homicide in the Bay area . . ."

"For chrissake, Dan, it's fifteen minutes to the end of our shift," *and I had a date tonight,* thought Carnaby.

"Sorry to ruin your evening, Ralph, but it can't wait. It's one of our guys."

The younger man tried his best to sound apologetic, but he could tell from Carnaby's voice that he was annoyed.

"Okay," said Carnaby reluctantly. He checked his wristwatch and said, "Have a car ready in five. Let's do this thing as quickly as we can. You can fill me in on the details on the way." He slammed the receiver back down. He knew he was being unreasonable, but this had happened all too often of late and he was growing tired of the way the "establishment" constantly seemed to be interfering in his private life. He exhaled forcibly, gripped the edge of the desk and levered himself upright. He crossed the room in two great strides, reached for his mac and turned the light off as he went through the door.

He ran into Morita in the lobby, and they went toward the rear exit together, bumping shoulders in the narrow corridor. "By the way," he said, breaking the uneasy silence, "why are we involved in this at all? A routine homicide, that's a matter for the MPs, isn't it?"

"I should have told you before."

"Told me? Told me what?"

"It was Donaldson that made the call."

"Donaldson?" Carnaby stopped and stared at Morita, confusion spreading across his face. Donaldson—the youngest and newest member of the team. The twenty-five-year-old rookie who just couldn't seem to do anything right. "What the hell was he doing down there?"

"Well," began Morita, looking away, "seems he was in the neighborhood and just happened to be walking by when the MPs showed up."

"But I thought he lived out Tachikawa way."

"He does. I think he was on his way to that strip joint down by the bay entrance."

"Jesus. At that time of day?" Carnaby pinched the bridge of his nose. "And you agreed we'd go and take a look?"

"Donaldson said he felt a little uneasy about it and . . . "

"For chrissake, Dan. We get enough crap served to us on a plate without you volunteering for more."

Morita held his hands up in mock surrender. "I know. I know. I just had a gut feeling, that's all. You know, a lieutenant in the US Army committing suicide. That sort of thing doesn't happen anymore, Ralph."

"Suicide? I thought you said 'homicide.'"

"I did. That's the weird thing. Donaldson said the MPs seemed dead certain it was suicide almost as soon as they'd gotten there."

"So it's suicide." Carnaby sighed heavily. "What the hell's wrong with that guy? Who was he anyway, the deceased, I mean?"

"I don't know. He was only found an hour ago. They claim not to have a positive ID yet."

Carnaby pushed the door open with his shoulder. "You know, it's amazing that anything gets solved with all the bureaucratic bullshit that goes on around here."

The car was parked in the motor pool. Morita climbed in the driver's side and Carnaby went round the passenger side and tilted his head skyward. He pulled on the door handle and the heavens opened. Lightning danced in the sky as an electrical storm held sway over the elements. Rain lashed the windscreen mercilessly, and the wind buffeted the black Buick as it struggled to turn onto Hibiya-dori. They cruised up the wide street, jockeying for position with two rickshaws as they scurried down a side street searching for cover. Over to the left, the Peace and Hope Memorial stood sentinel-like before them. The two-hundred-foot granite structure soared precipitously into the heavens, its arms outstretched like a crucifix—cradling a bronze dove in each hand. Still caged in scaffolding, the angelic figure was meant to symbolize everlasting peace—a commitment on the part of the Japanese to respect the American-designed war-renouncing constitution and never again embark on a war of mass destruction.

Carnaby allowed himself a wry smile as he recalled the heated debate in the State Department about what a huge waste of money this whole project was. Even as the finishing touches were being applied, Prime Minister Yoshida had secretly agreed to America's demand for limited rearmament and authorized the creation of a hundred-thousand-strong "police reserve"—a pseudo-military organization whose function was to guard against communist-backed revolution.

The memorial's epiphanic presence gradually receded into the background, its great form enveloped in a curtain of swirling mist and rain. They crossed the Sumida on Eitai-dori and, before long, turned onto the coast road and left the city lights far behind. Carnaby groped around inside his jacket and pulled out a crumpled pack of Lucky Strikes. He struck a match and looked up at Morita. "Do you mind?"

"Hell no. Go ahead if it makes you feel better."

He applied the dancing flame to the tip of his cigarette. He drew on the filter deeply, extinguished the match and exhaled, filling the car with smoke. He looked round and raised his eyebrows. "What's on your mind, Dan? I've never known you so quiet."

"Oh, I just feel I've kind of screwed up your evening. That's all. I should've taken the call and gone out myself."

"Forget it, Dan. It's not your fault. It comes with the job. You know that as well as anybody."

"Yeah, I guess so." Morita looked visibly relieved. "What were you planning on doing anyhow?"

A half-smile appeared on Carnaby's face. "Nothing much. I had a date fixed up with some broad I met at the Foreign Correspondent's Club a couple weeks back. Perhaps just as well. I get the feeling she just wanted to pump me for information on the Repatriation Program."

"You kidding?" said Morita, taking his eyes off the wet road for a second.

"I wish I was. That's all she talked about at the club and again when she phoned to confirm the date." He took a couple of short puffs of his cigarette, wound the window down a fraction and let the wind whip the butt from his fingers into the filthy night.

"Professional women . . ." Morita muttered under his breath, moving his head from side to side.

"What was that?"

"I said 'professional women.' They make me nervous as hell!"

"Yeah, maybe I ought to lower my standards a little—that way I might get to enjoy myself for once."

They looked at each other. Carnaby began to snigger and then they both lost control and roared with laughter.

Twenty minutes later they turned off the coast road and entered the dockland area. It was a foul night. Mist from the Arakawa River swirled and eddied around the dimly lit harbor entrance, intermittently obscuring the prow of a tug boat moored at the quay. The vessel's tightly strung canvas awning sang in the wind, and a solitary gull cried out from amidst the squall above.

Yamato

As the Buick slowed and rounded the corner of the gloomy pre-war apartment block, one of the few areas not to have been razed by the incendiary bombing raids at the end of the war, the car's headlights picked out a group of uniformed figures standing next to a military police jeep. A tall, gaunt figure broke from the group and loomed out of the mist toward the car as it came to a halt.

"Shit," said Carnaby, recognizing the limp. "It's Lorimer and his henchmen."

Lorimer, or Captain Harry Lorimer to be precise, had picked up a shrapnel wound eight years earlier during "Operation Olympic," the landing on southern Kyushu which had proved necessary following the failure of the atomic bombings of Hiroshima, Nagasaki and Kokura to produce unconditional surrender by Japan's High Command.

"Better late than never, hey, Carnaby? Well this is a pleasant surprise. I wasn't expecting to see you here at this time of night."

"Cut the wise cracks, Lorimer. What have we got?"

"A suicide," replied Lorimer in his characteristic self-assured manner. "No doubt about it. Sorry to disappoint the two of you, but it looks as if you've made the trip for nothing." There was a clear challenge in his voice, as if he were letting Carnaby know that he considered the presence of the CIA to be an encroachment on his territory.

"Yeah, well, I'll be the judge of that," said Carnaby, winding the window up and opening the car door. He rolled the collar of his overcoat up and turned toward the dull facade of the building, motioned to Morita to go ahead and followed Lorimer up the concrete steps and in through the open door.

The body lay sprawled across a mahogany desk, head twisted to one side revealing a small reddish black hole an inch or so below the right temple. The exit wound was much bigger and the wall behind was a frieze of mottled crimson. The barrel of a Browning M1911 service pistol protruded from behind an intricately woven wicker waste paper basket. A half-empty bottle of Rodnik vodka stood opened on a low occasional table, and on top of the desk an upturned glass whiskey tumbler had spilled its contents over a single sheet of writing paper. Underneath the congealed blue ink the opening words "My dearest Emma" were barely visible at the head of the page.

"Who was he?" asked Carnaby laconically.

"His name is . . . " Lorimer paused as he opened his notebook. "Or should I say *was* Harvey Brice. Lieutenant, US Army Counter Intelligence Corps. We're still making inquiries, so I can't really add much more at this stage I'm afraid."

"Excuse me, sir." Donaldson appeared from behind the photographer with a buff-colored folder clasped in his hands. "It looks like he was involved in the Pacific War research project. You know—the thing General Brannigan is in charge of."

Carnaby raised his eyebrows. "Brannigan's mob? You mean as in Major General Charles Brannigan?"

Lorimer gave Donaldson a withering look and held his hand out for the folder.

"I thought he retired years ago."

"Far from it," said Lorimer trying to be helpful. "He no longer heads up G2's Counter Intelligence section, but he's a long way off throwing his hand in. As your colleague here has so helpfully pointed out, he runs the research project in the old Posts and Telecoms building. They're writing the history of the Pacific War. Pure propaganda, of course."

"Of course," muttered Carnaby turning away and scanning the room. His eyes came to rest on two objects hanging from hooks on the wall, a *biwa* and a *koto,* traditional stringed instruments of the Heian Court. He plucked at the nearest one and winced at the sound—alien and discordant to his unappreciative senses.

"So, that's all you have on him right now, huh?" he said, glancing toward the unfinished letter. "What about 'Emma'? Do we know who she is?"

"Girlfriend, wife, sister—who knows? At this stage, it's pure conjecture I'm afraid." Lorimer appeared apologetic and added, "We can of course find out, if necessary."

"Yes, do that," answered Carnaby, narrowly avoiding falling over the photographer, who had suddenly assumed a squatting position while he screwed a new flash bulb onto his camera.

"Look, Carnaby," began Lorimer, "I don't want to sound unhelpful, but isn't it obvious what's happened here? He was a lousy closet communist. The screw had turned. He felt the pressure and this was the only way out. I mean, for chrissake, we've all seen enough of this back home since McCarthy got in on the act. This is a classic case. All the signs are here. Why else is he living off base in this fucking shit hole?"

"There could be any number of reasons," answered Carnaby firmly.

"Oh, come on. Open your eyes. Look around you. It's like Stalin's private *dacha*." He waved his arm theatrically and indicated all the Russian 'objects' in the room: books, a nest of dolls, postcards from Moscow. "And what about that bottle of vodka?" he resumed. "That's not the kind of cheap crap you pick up on the black market."

"Hey, come on, guys, we're on the same side here." Morita cut in and tried to diffuse the growing tension. Carnaby was senior, but technically he was outside of his jurisdiction, and Morita knew for sure that Lorimer could make things difficult for them if he decided not to cooperate.

Carnaby was a born sceptic and had learned through bitter experience not to take things at face value. He took out a cigarette, lit it and drew deeply on it, filling his throat and lungs with bitter smoke. Rain drummed on the windows, clattering the opaque glass panes in their ill-fitting wooden frames. A picture on the wall suddenly caught his eye. It was a sepia photograph of the Kyushu landings almost a decade ago. For an instant he was back on the beach at Kagoshima with the 11th Airborne Division, crouching low on his haunches behind a bullet-ridden sand dune, staring at the body of the G.I. slumped next to him—torso ripped apart by a mortar shell, its face contorted with pain, frozen with fear in death.

Lorimer slammed two hefty volumes down on the desk. The sound of leather binding smacking the polished wooden desktop brought Carnaby back from his reverie. He extended his right hand and turned the two books around so he could see their titles. The first volume was Lenin's *The Development of Capitalism in Russia,* a classic Marxist text which appeared on the list of dangerous books regularly scrutinized and updated by every good Kempeitai military police officer. The second, *An Analysis of Japanese Capitalism,* was a work by the Japanese Marxist writer Moritaro Yamada. Yamada had been placed under house arrest for the duration of the war for his part in espousing the virtues of communist ideology and propagating the collective Marxist conviction that capitalism was but one stage in history which would inevitably be transcended. He was executed in the fall of 1944 as a traitor.

Carnaby recalled that, during the subsequent purge, seventeen members of the Cabinet Planning Board had been arrested for promoting similar "progressive" left-wing policies, long considered by the Thought Police capable of undermining the political status quo. Possession of books such as these, without good reason, was still a serious offence.

"What did I tell you?" said Lorimer with an air of superiority. "He was a goddamned Commie."

Carnaby ignored the remark. "I want your people to go through this place with a fine-toothed comb. If you find anything, and I mean *anything* at all, I want it in my office by 09:00 tomorrow. Clear?"

"Oh, absolutely," replied Lorimer with more than a hint of sarcasm in his voice.

"Donaldson?"

"Yes, sir?"

"I want you to assist Captain Lorimer here. It will be your job to make sure nothing is overlooked."

He clapped Donaldson on the shoulder and then made toward the door, but stopped short of going through it. "By the way, who found him?"

"The landlord, Mr Kobayashi. He's sitting out in the corridor." Lorimer gesticulated toward the gloom. "He says he had just returned from the mah-jongg parlor around 18:30 when a gunshot rang out from the rear of the building. He went straight down the corridor, tried the door and when he saw this he panicked and telephoned the police."

"Is that it?"

"That's it," confirmed Lorimer with a nonchalant shrug.

"Dan, come here." Carnaby lowered his voice and grabbed Morita by the elbow, steering him through the doorway. "Why don't you stick around a while and see if you can get anything useful out of the landlord. He might talk to you. You can hitch a ride back into town with your 'friends.'"

Morita was dumbfounded. "You mean you're gonna leave me here? With *him*?"

"It was your idea, buddy—dragging me out here so I miss my date. You owe me for this—big time." Carnaby smiled. He *was* beginning to enjoy himself after all. "We can talk about this in the morning."

He didn't wait for the reply. He turned and strode down the corridor, checking his gait momentarily to take stock of the landlord, whose dark squat form was sitting on an upturned packing crate, flaccid face half buried in his hands.

He took a final drag on his cigarette, dropped the butt and screwed it into the gravel with the sole of his patent leather shoe. *Poor bastard,* he thought. *How many more do we have to lose for the sake of this goddamned country?* He climbed wearily into his car, swung it round, tires kicking up spray from the asphalt, and disappeared into the inhospitable night.

Two

Carnaby had arranged to meet Morita at Ochi's coffee shop at around 09:30, but he had too much on his mind and decided instead to head straight over to the Police Kendo dojo in Ichigaya Ward where Morita trained most mornings, and wait for him to finish. The prohibition on the practice of martial arts had officially ended in 1947, although, as Morita had once confided in him, in reality the tradition had been carried on in secret throughout the early years of the Occupation.

"Ohayo gozaimasu." The secretary recognized Carnaby and greeted him in customary fashion for the time of day, indicating with a wave of the hand that it was okay for him to go up to the practice hall unaccompanied. It was as if in climbing that short flight of wooden stairs, he had been transported back two centuries to feudal Japan. Ahead of him, he could hear the shrill, staccato *kiai* or battle cries of the practitioners piercing the more regular sound of bamboo colliding with bamboo and the rhythmic, almost hypnotic beat of a *taiko* drum.

He had timed it just right. The swordsmen, each dressed in protective armor, moved back three paces—like the parting of the Red Sea. Another beat of the drum and they knelt down in neat rows, placed their bamboo practice swords to the side and removed their helmets.

At the head of the line, dignified and sombre in appearance, stood the teacher, or *sensei.* Strength is a deceptive quality. It means different things to different people. The *sensei* may have been in his sixties, but he was tall and lean, with broad muscular shoulders; and he had the calm, steely eyes of the warrior. He was clad simply in a blue cotton jacket and *hakama,* the wide, pleated skirt of his samurai ancestors.

The drum was silent now. The *sensei* advanced slowly, and then, without warning, whirled and pirouetted in the center of the dojo, his bare feet gliding effortlessly across the polished cedar wood floor. The sword transformed itself into a silver streak of light in the air around him as he dispatched his imaginary foe. Each cut, refined and perfected on the field of battle over the course of half a millennium, and at the cost of countless lives, was designed to locate and sever those arteries least well protected by the opponent's armor—between the neck and shoulder guards, under the armpits, and between the inner thighs—all areas where protection had been sacrificed in favor of mobility. Once cut, it was an ineluctable truth that the lifeblood would flow out, unstoppable, within a matter of seconds.

Carnaby, spellbound, watched this age-old ritual in contemplative silence.

The *sensei* was performing the final *kata* or sequence of pre-arranged cuts, parries and thrusts of the Omori School of swordsmanship. He stopped dead. His steely eyes remained focused on the mid-distance. *Zanshin*—continuing awareness. And then, with a barely audible sound, he resheathed the blade.

The *sensei* relaxed, his sword now safely held in his left hand, and surveyed the faces of the young practitioners before him. Morita was at the far end of the front row, his handsome features glistening with sweat.

"Tanaka! What were you thinking of during that last practice sequence?"

Tanaka's eyes blinked as he thought hard about the question. His chest still heaved from his exertions. After several seconds he looked up and said, "To be—to be as forceful as possible, *sensei*."

The *sensei* gave him a reproachful look. "That's no good. Get rid of all thinking."

"Get rid of all think . . ." Tanaka unconsciously began to repeat his teacher's words.

"The great Rinzai Zen priest Takuan taught that a swordsman should abandon all thoughts of survival in combat. This is not a position of indifference or of neutrality but of transcendence. The swordsman should strive to achieve the state of *munen* in which the mind becomes like the deep water of a lake: its surface calm, its placidness capping depth. From *munen* comes a flowing mind and body; life and death become one in a state of no-thought. Moreover," continued the *sensei,* "when one enters the state of *munen* the sword is elevated from its role of a weapon with which to take human life, *satsujin no ken,* and becomes an instrument that gives life, *katsujin no ken. Satsujin no ken* identifies the sword with the annihilation of things that stand in the way of peace, justice, humanity, while *katsujin no ken* identifies the sword with the annihilation of the ego-self."

The action having stopped and not understanding anything the *sensei* was saying, Carnaby drifted off into his own reverie. His thoughts turned to the things Donaldson had sent over from Brice's apartment the day before. As a rule, he never took work home with him. But the box had arrived late and he'd been tied up in meetings all day so he took it with him anyway.

He arrived home shortly after 19:00, poured himself a bourbon and sat down with the box on the dining room table in front of him. He looked at it for a few seconds, took out a penknife and cut the tape. Beads of sweat had begun to form on his brow as he opened the lid and peered in at the contents. A bulky manila envelope lay on top of two books he guessed had to be the Marxist texts Lorimer had discovered the previous night. He fished out the envelope, broke its seal and, having pushed the box back to make space, emptied the contents out in front of him.

'There must be something here. There has to be,' *he told himself as he cast his eye over the strange assortment of objects: a diary, a small tarnished brass key, what appeared to be a church service pamphlet issued by the Russian Orthodox Church in Chiyoda ward just a few blocks away, and a small bundle of letters neatly tied with a single piece of green ribbon and on top a label with the words,* "Emma Correspondence."

The accompanying letter from Lorimer was predictably unhelpful:

"As expected, nothing much yielded here. Note the church leaflet! Need I say more? Maybe it will be your Pandora's box.

"Let me know if you need further assistance.

H. Lorimer."

"Assistance!" more like goddamned hindrance, *Carnaby had thought to himself contemptuously.*

He fingered the objects disconsolately. The letters gave off a faint scent of lilac. He didn't like the idea of reading someone else's love letters, so he shut them away in a drawer. He would read them later—if nothing else gave him what he was looking for.

The key was well-worn, of the sort that went with an attaché case or, perhaps, a gymnasium locker. Otherwise there were no distinguishing marks, no clues as to what it might lock or unlock.

He replaced the key, picked up the diary and began flipping through its yellowing pages. It was last year's edition, and a number of pages for the months of November and December were missing, leaving in their place lines of jagged paper—as if torn out and disposed of hurriedly. Other entries had been obliterated. He held the defaced pages up to the light, squinting in a fruitless effort to discover what was written beneath the swathes of blue ink. Impossible. The thin parchment had almost been scored through. It reminded him of the war years and the heavy-handedness of the censors. The way those goons deleted things had always struck him as being completely arbitrary. It was as if they derived some sort of perverse pleasure from rendering a perfectly innocuous letter incomprehensible to its intended recipient. God knows Laura had certainly found it irritating. It was hard enough knowing your mail was being scanned by strangers in the first place. He wondered if Emma had felt the same. He wondered if she even knew that Harvey would not be writing to her anymore.

He lit a cigarette, filled his lungs with smoke, then let it out slowly and watched it spiral upwards toward the air vent. He drained his glass, stood up to get a refill and then remembered the folder containing Brice's military record that he'd picked up on the way out the office. He put everything back in the box and hefted it over onto a low sideboard near the window.

He returned to the table, rummaged around in his briefcase and pulled out the military record. He sat down again, untied the cord, snapped the file open and pulled out a slim "regulation green" file. He repositioned his desk light and began leafing through the pages. The file was full of the usual standard narrative: Name, rank and serial number. Details of his next of kin, his education and basic training. He had been an above-average shot, consistently scoring high marks on the range with both pistol and carbine. Under the column headed 'Distinguishing Marks and Characteristics' it was noted he was left-handed and had a mole on his right forearm. There was a column indicating his medical history and inoculations for foreign service. Nothing out of the ordinary there. Under the heading "Awards and Decorations" was listed a citation for bravery and a recommendation for the Legion of Merit for excep-

tionally meritorious conduct during the Kyushu landings. Finally, there was a handwritten note in the remarks column stating that he was fluent in Russian and Japanese.

Aside from the last two entries, the record could have belonged to anybody. He pinched the bridge of his nose. He had a dull throbbing migraine. He slugged his second glass, walked to the window and opened the curtains. It was dark, and the city lights winked at him from all directions. God, he had never been so frustrated. Common sense told him it was a straightforward suicide case, but he had a bad taste in his mouth, and it sure as hell wasn't the whiskey.

"*Rei! Arigato gozaimashita.*" The class bowed in unison and thanked the *sensei* for his teaching.

Carnaby was jerked back into the present and instantly sat up, as if he'd been caught napping. Morita stood and noticed him sitting half in shadow in the corner. He nodded and walked over.

"Very impressive."

"He's quite something, isn't he?" agreed Morita. "So what's on the agenda this morning?"

Carnaby gave him a plastic smile. "When did you last go to church?"

Behind them, the swordsmen were filling wooden buckets with water and then racing each other on all fours the length of the *dojo*, hips high, pushing cloths and cleaning great swathes of the wooden floor. Cleanliness and purity were virtues encouraged by the indigenous Shinto gods.

A light rain had begun to fall. The Nikolaido, Holy Resurrection Cathedral of the Russian Orthodox Church, was a sprawling mass of Byzantine architecture, semi-derelict from years of neglect and totally out of character with its newly constructed sterile concrete surroundings.

Carnaby placed one hand on the heavy, studded wooden door and pushed. It swung inwards, creaking on its rusting hinges. The air was heavy with the smell of kerosene. They edged their way in past an intricately carved marble aspersorium standing on a rough-hewn stone plinth, and entered the nave. Dust lay thick on the terracotta-tiled floor, and in the corner, the shattered remains of what once must have been a magnificent glass chandelier glittered and peeped out from under a threadbare blanket. A gust of wind whipped about a large sheet of canvas stretched across a gaping hole in the masonry near the rear of the apse.

They moved further into the nave. The inner sanctuary of the church was in a much better state of repair. The dust on the floor seemed to stop where the rows of pews began. Candles had been placed in recesses in the wall at intervals of five feet or so, and the beautifully painted faces of a row of icons appeared alive in the flickering candlelight.

Carnaby suddenly started at the snick of a door latch, spinning on his heels in the direction of the noise. Forgetting for an instant where he was, Morita instinctively reached inside his jacket.

"Leave it! For God's sake," hissed Carnaby under his breath.

A bundle of dark robes shuffled unsteadily toward them, a broom handle clasped in its right hand. An old bearded man with a sallow complexion peered at them out of myopic, rheumy eyes. "Welcome to the house of God, my friends." The kind old face spoke. "I am Metropolitan Vladimir of the Orthodox Church."

The old man finished his introduction and extended his right hand. The dark interior of the church accentuated the whiteness of his emaciated arm. Carnaby shook the proffered hand warmly.

"I hope you don't mind this intrusion, Father." He hesitated, unsure whether he had used the correct form of address. "My name is Carnaby, and this is my colleague Morita. We're investigators with the Occupation authorities." He glanced sideways at Morita, who acknowledged his introduction with a smile and slight nod of the head.

Carnaby looked the old man in the eyes, unsure of how he would react. "Father, did you know Lieutenant Harvey Brice?"

A sparkle of life came to the priest's eyes. It was but an instant. His face clouded over again, as if he knew what he was about to hear.

"I'm afraid Lieutenant Brice was found dead at his apartment on Saturday evening. He appears to have committed suicide." Carnaby broke the news as gently as he could.

Tears welled up in the old man's eyes. He was silent for a moment, lost in his own thoughts. His hands trembled as he transferred his weight to the broom. He coughed and cleared his throat, looked up through moist eyes and spoke calmly. "I thought it strange that he had not come to see me." He gazed far off into the distance. "He would come here every Sunday, without fail. I do not suppose he was truly a believer." He struggled to find the right words. "You see, he was a linguist. His Russian was really very good. It was a chance for him to practice his language, and it was my opportunity for a little company."

"I realize that this has come as a great shock to you, Father, but we need to ask you a few questions."

"I understand," said the priest quietly.

"Have you any idea why he would have taken his own life?"

The old man took a deep breath and regained his composure. "To be sure, he was troubled by something during the last few weeks. But he did not like to talk about his work. I could sense he was not entirely happy. But on the other hand, he was so very much looking forward to going back home." The priest swallowed hard and then continued. "He talked a good deal about his fiancée, Miss Forbes. They were going to be married in the summer. He was very excited about it all."

"There was some suggestion—" began Carnaby, hesitating.

"That he was a communist." Morita cut in, supplying what he considered to be the missing words.

Carnaby gave him a stern look.

The priest closed his eyes and shook his head emphatically, "No, no, no. Nothing could be further from the truth. I can assure you. He was—how do you say?—a true patriot." Sensing a look of doubt in his interlocutor's eyes, he added, "If you are concerned about my allegiances, they are to no one but the church. My own country forsook me long ago."

"I'm sorry, I didn't mean to—"

"It is alright. You have your inquiries to make."

Morita tried to make up for his slipshod comment. "When Lieutenant Brice attended church, did he ever fraternize with the other members of the congregation?"

"Not to my knowledge. He would arrive early, usually. We would talk for about thirty minutes, and then he would leave promptly at the end of the service."

Carnaby looked around the church uncomfortably. "It can't be easy living and working here?"

"No, that is true," answered the priest, "but then it never has been. I survive. The church receives a modest stipend from the

Soviet embassy here in Tokyo. Oh, but please do not misunderstand me. I am not on the Soviet payroll. That is not to say I have not been approached in the past to act as—how shall I describe it?—a conduit for information. It is more to do with national pride—being seen to present a unified front. It is important to the Russian embassy to assist us financially even though our ties with the mother church have been severed."

Carnaby thought he detected a lingering note of bitterness in the priest's voice. Conscious that they were running short of time, he resumed the conversation. "Tell me, Father, how long have you been here?"

The old man tilted his head toward the mullion windows, as if deep in thought. "Let me see now. I came here in the summer of 1920 to escape the Bolsheviks. A great many of my colleagues had been persecuted following the revolution. I was lucky. I managed to hide in the catacombs of the Glinsky Hermitage for two years. I had some savings, and, when the opportunity presented itself, I came here under the patronage of the great Metropolitan Sergei." He described a cross on his chest with his forefinger and momentarily closed his eyes before continuing. "I have lived through periods of great change. The Great Kanto Earthquake of 1923 was responsible for that." He waved a hand casually in the direction of the gap in the roof. "It used to be a bell tower. And as for the chandelier and the rest of the debris you see about you, that is the work of your B-29s during the war—March 10, 1945, to be precise. I shall never forget it."

Carnaby shot an uncomfortable glance at Morita.

"Sadly, the great Metropolitan Sergei passed away in September of the same year, and I have been here alone since then doing what I can to continue his work. Of course, ideologically, Stalin is—was, I should say—opposed to all that we stand for. And as for the Americans, well, as you know, freedom of religious belief is something to be encouraged, is it not?"

Carnaby smiled. They had drawn a blank and it was time to leave. He thanked the priest. "Oh, by the way, Father, if anything does occur to you," he said, massaging his neck with his right hand, "I'd be very grateful if you would call me at my office." He tore a page out from his notebook and jotted down his details before handing it to the priest.

The old man took the note, folded it carefully and tucked it inside his robes. He followed them out of the church with his gaze. *May God watch over you, my son.*

"What do you think? Is he on the level?" said Carnaby as the car pulled away from the parking bay.

"Seemed pretty genuine to me. But then I'm no expert on priests."

"Yeah, I know what you mean. Hey, how 'bout we grab a cold beer and a bite to eat?"

"Sounds good. I'm famished. I know a good charcoal grill a couple of blocks from here."

They sped back along Hongo-dori in the direction of the office. The drizzle had stopped, and the sun's rays had begun to dry up the sidewalks. Clouds scudded across the sky. Carnaby's mind was racing. Something just didn't add up, something that had been on his mind all night. He drummed his fingers on the dashboard. And then it hit him—the report. "Jesus! The report!" His thoughts took on verbal form and escaped from his mouth in a half-strangled expletive.

"The report?"

"Brice was goddamned left-handed. It's down there clear as day in his military record." Carnaby felt his chest tighten and adrenaline start to flow. "He was a left-handed shot! Why would a left-handed man shoot himself in the right side of the head?" He didn't wait for an answer. "We'll have to skip lunch. Step on it, Dan. We've got an autopsy to arrange."

Three

It was a cold afternoon in Bletchley. Snow lay thick on the ground, and a biting March wind blew across the playing fields and howled through the quadrangles rattling the window panes.

Bletchley Road Junior School was like any other pre-war English school in the area—large, gray, imposing—a wonderful example of late Victorian architecture; and yet its appearance was as dismal and forbidding as could be in midwinter.

The pupils of Form 3c, a mixed class of twenty-six eight-year-olds, were doing their best to concentrate on the last class of the day—copperplate handwriting. The subject: today's news. Apart from the sound of twenty-six steel nibs scratching across twenty-six sheets of poor quality writing paper, an eerie silence had descended on the classroom.

Emma Forbes, the form mistress, was sitting at her desk, momentarily lost in thought, taking this rarely offered opportunity to gaze wistfully out of the large sash windows into the distance. Since the beginning of the year her thoughts had turned increasingly to her wedding day. It was still almost four months off, but preparations had already begun. A date had been agreed on with the vicar of St. Mary's and entered into the church appointments register. And, after several lengthy consultations with family and friends, the organist, and finally the vicar himself, she had decided on the order of service and choice of hymns. She would walk up the aisle to the strains of "Praise My Soul the King of Heaven," a magnificently rousing hymn and her favorite since childhood days.

The wedding reception was going to be at the Pavilion in the park. Harvey had wanted a small private affair, but she had protested bitterly. She, for one, intended only to do this once in her lifetime, and she was determined to do it in style, and hang the expense! It seemed like all her friends had already married before her. And here she was older than all of them at 28 and only just about to do the same. And not only that, most of her friends already had babies. Some of them had two.

Emma felt she had some catching up to do. She was conscious that she was discussed by her friends and had even overheard Jane Tate, whom she had considered one of her better friends, discussing her quite candidly with the vicar's wife and saying how long-distance relationships could never last. Emma was upset at the time, but in her own mind she knew it would work out. Harvey was too decent to run out on her.

Aunt Clarice, the self-appointed head of the family, seemed to have taken it upon herself to do most of the organizing and, amongst other things, had offered to make the wedding dress, despite a bit of a falling-out between them several months before over the suitability of Americans as husbands.

Aunt Clarice could be so pompous at times. Having lost both her sons in the war, one could, Emma was forced to concede, understand her point of view. "What's wrong with a good old English boy? You won't go far adrift with one of your own kind," she would say reverently. Her aunt had only met Harvey once before, and she had obviously taken an instant dislike to him, casting aspersions on his Roman Catholic upbringing, and, on more than one occasion, seeing fit to comment on his "unorthodox" table manners, and in particular his habit of tucking his napkin into his shirt collar at mealtimes. "And the way he uses his fork in his right hand to stab at his food and chase it round the plate."

Such comments had been made in a light-hearted but nevertheless mocking tone of voice and clearly with the intention of hurting Emma's feelings. And Emma had taken them as intended and was furious at her aunt's condescending behavior. Over the last few months however, the anger and frustration had given way to feelings of mild irritation, and her aunt seemed to be making an effort to smooth things over and patch things up. Perhaps she was impressed by Emma's fortitude and commitment to a man she had barely seen in six months and who lived and worked half way round the world.

Emma smiled. Her aunt was incorrigible, but there was little sense in arguing and making matters worse so close to the event. And in any case, she couldn't afford to have her wedding dress made by a professional seamstress what with saving for a new house and everything else they would need.

She wondered what Harvey was doing at that precise moment. She placed both elbows on her desk, cradled her chin in her hands and closed her eyes tight shut and tried hard to imagine. Japan was eight hours ahead, which meant it was half past eleven at night. Maybe he was already asleep and dreaming of the wedding too. Or maybe he was sitting up and reading one of his favorite Russian novels.

It was only three months until his discharge. She could hardly wait, she was so excited. She hated wishing time away, but she was sure she would simply die if the day did not arrive soon. She was unusually weary today and wanted to get home and write a letter, something she had done religiously every week for the past six months.

She wound her finger round a tendril of shiny brown hair that had fallen down from her plait. She glanced at her wristwatch: five minutes to go. "Alright, children, finish your news at the next full sentence please. It's almost time to go home."

The bride-to-be returned to the schoolteacher of the present. She moved away from her desk and continued to issue instructions, "When you've finished, pass your writing to the desk at the end of your row."

The end-of-school-day bell sounded, and the predictable classroom cacophony erupted.

"And don't forget to put your names at the top of your work," she added, in her best teacher's voice, designed to rise above the din of desk lids slamming and chair legs scraping the parquet floor.

As she moved from one row to the next, collecting in the sheets of paper, she noticed little Johnny Jenkins, looking wan and utterly forlorn. She guessed his news would be about how his daddy had taken him to see the trains at Bletchley Station or played with him in the park at the weekend. In reality he had been killed off the Korean Peninsula six months before while serving as a midshipman aboard a Royal Navy minesweeper. It was so unfair. The Second World War had been over eight years now, and ordinary people were surely entitled to a little happiness and security, having endured so much. She was desperately sorry for little Johnny and his mother, who was left with three little ones to provide for.

She lined the children up and filed them out into the yard where they were collected by parents with smiling, happy faces. All except little Johnny. His sullen-faced grandmother grabbed his hand roughly and half-dragged the poor boy in the direction of the school gate.

Emma returned to the classroom and quickly cleaned the blackboard. She scooped up the pile of children's work, thrust it into her briefcase and went out through the door into the dark, narrow corridor. She would normally stop by the staff room with the class register, but today she wanted to be alone with her own thoughts. So instead she pulled her thick coat on and trudged out into the snowbound playground and headed up the hill toward the main road. A couple of children skipped past her, going in the opposite direction, singing, "Red, white and blue, the Queen's got the flu, the King's got the tummy ache and don't know what to do."

At the crown of the hill she paused to get her breath. A short convoy of army trucks snaked along the road, their thick studded tires churning the dirty snow into slush. She hitched her briefcase strap further up her shoulder, glanced in both directions and crossed the road, being careful not to slip on the steep grass verge on the other side. Once across, she climbed over a stile cut into a low dry stone wall and came out on a country lane which ran parallel with Newton Road. This route was not as direct as the main highway, but it was quieter and much prettier and Emma always chose it on days like this when she preferred her own company.

The snow-capped trees were beautiful in winter, and the low boughs of the beech trees seemed to reach down and beckon her onward up the hill. Two startled wood pigeons swooped overhead, coming to rest on a heavily laden branch sending snow cascading to the ground. A puffball of icy particles blew back up into the air, the tiny crystals filtering through the patchy dusk sunlight. It was so magical. Emma loved winter, even when it dragged on as long as it had this year. Everything was so crisp and fresh and pure. People were too busy these days, the pace of life too frantic. Nobody ever took the time simply to stop and gaze and wonder for a few moments at their natural surroundings. She made a mental resolution to do this more often, and once Harvey was with her, to spend as much time as they possibly could together in the countryside.

She smiled to herself, but then, noticing how the evening was drawing in, decided to hurry home and have something warming to eat and settle in for the night. She covered the last half mile, which was relatively flat, much more quickly, and, despite the cold, she was perspiring as she turned into Beechcroft Road.

She saw the police Humber from a distance of about two hundred yards, and at first, probably due to the failing light, had thought that it was parked outside the adjoining semi-detached house. As she drew closer however, she realized that it was actually parked nearer the side of her own house, and she felt a sudden rush of panic. Was her mother alright? Had something awful happened to her pregnant sister? Her imagination beginning to run away with itself, she quickened her pace, clutching her briefcase tighter into her side.

She reached the wrought-iron gate at the end of the small front garden, pushed hard and went on up the path. Salt crunched under her leather-soled shoes. A shadowy figure appeared in the bay window and then disappeared just as quickly. She felt her chest tighten as she reached out for the door handle. Something wasn't right. She had a sense of deep foreboding. Her heartbeat quickened as she fought to remain calm. She kept telling herself there would be a rational explanation.

Before she had a chance to turn the handle, the door opened inwards. Emma's eyes opened wide, staring, disbelieving. Her mother stood in the porch in floods of tears, arms outstretched beckoning, her whole body quivering uncontrollably.

Emma shouted, "Mother! What is it? Tell me what's happened!" Her voice was desperate, probing, searching for any kind of clue. Her mother's arms wrapped around her, embraced her and pulled her inside, hands caressing her hair.

Unable to contain herself any longer and being in no fit state to break the news gently, it all came blurting out, "It's Harvey. He . . . he's dead."

Emma was stunned. It was several seconds before her mother's words registered their full impact. Tears welled up in her eyes and she spun around, frantically looking for someone who would say it wasn't true, that there had been some awful misunderstanding, or even that it was some sort of ghastly joke.

The policeman hovered uncomfortably in the kitchen doorway. He was young and himself close to tears.

"Please," she pleaded, turning in his direction.

But he cast his eyes down and muttered something that sounded like "I'm very sorry."

And then she saw the telegram hanging limply from his hand. She darted forward like a thing possessed and snatched it from him. Moving into the light she stared in horror at the typewritten message:

SCAP Official Wire
Date: March 28, 1953
Time: 10:30 (local time)
Subject: Lt. Harvey Brice, US Army Intelligence Corps
INFORMATION FOR NEXT OF KIN: ATTENTION: MISS EMMA FORBES

"We regret to inform you that Lt. H. Brice was found dead in his apartment on March 26, 1953. The cause of death was suicide. Please accept our condolences."

Emma's world collapsed before her very eyes. A kaleidoscope of images flashed through her mind: dancing with Harvey at the Bletchley Officers' Ball, boating with Harvey in Oxford, Harvey waving goodbye from the window of the train as it pulled away from Bletchley station.

Waving goodbye forever.

She closed her wet eyes and slumped to her knees on the threadbare carpet.

Four

The doctor donned his protective clothing and fastened the hood securely so that it formed an airtight seal around his mask. He entered the laboratory by the airlock, walked over to the incubator, inserted his hands through the rubber-lined apertures and continued his unfinished work. Another consignment was nearing completion. His hands trembled—but not through want of experience. They were sinister hands. Hands that held a dark and terrible secret.

Around the mainland, five more nervous men carried out the same thankless task.

On the other side of the city, Ralph Carnaby had arrived at the pathology department of the Roosevelt Memorial Hospital in Chiyoda Ward. The hospital was used exclusively for the treatment of US Army personnel—even when there were empty beds and the local Tokyoites were in dire need of medical attention. It was like the 'Allied Car' on the subway, virtually empty during rush hour, while the Japanese were packed sardine-like into the adjoining carriages. It used to bother him at first, but now he hardly noticed it. In the early days of the Occupation the majority of the patients were convalescents, recovering from the trauma of the battles fought on islands like Saipan, Iwo Jima and Okinawa, or from the delirium of strange tropical diseases contracted in the jungles of Leyte and Sarawak. There had been a quiet spell in the mid- to late '40s, but for the last two years all 250 beds, the theatre trolleys and the makeshift cots had been taken by the wounded, the dying and the dead of MacArthur's holy crusade on the Korean Peninsula.

He had had occasion to come here twice already this year, and it was still only March. Not a very auspicious start to the year. He opened the double-swing doors and was met head on by an outward rush of cool air. The autopsy room was acrid with the smell of surgical spirit—like a kind of miasma. He disliked places like this intensely. How anybody could do this kind of work and keep sane was beyond him. The only consolation was the pathologist, Tom Gregson. He was a real pro, not one of those morose types with a ghoulish sense of humor. Gregson had a razor-sharp intellect, and Carnaby trusted his judgment implicitly. Some said he was the most eligible bachelor in town, but the downside for any interested member of the fairer sex, as far as he could see, was his almost puritanical work ethic.

He looked around him. It was like the obligatory autopsy scene in some second-rate detective story: a tiled floor sloping gently to a shallow drain in the middle; an assortment of surgical instruments: saws, braces and the like, hanging from pegs on the wall; and of course, the steel-topped concrete slab. The only thing missing was the body. He was spared the sight of Brice's mauled corpse. He had purposely arrived late, confident that the whole procedure would be complete by the time he showed up.

The pathologist came out of a small door in the far wall, drying his hands on a paper towel. "Ralph! How the hell are you?" He greeted Carnaby as if he hadn't seen him in years.

"Just swell, Tom." He took out a cigarette. "Do you mind?"

"Hell no. Be my guest." Gregson screwed up the paper towel and tossed it into the trash can. He looked up at Carnaby. "Lieutenant Brice is quite a popular guy. You're his second visitor today."

"What?" Carnaby raised his eyebrows, surprise registering in his voice as he loosened his necktie.

"Captain Spicer. Know him?"

"No. I've never heard of him. What did he want?"

"He's from Personnel over at HQ. Said he'd gotten wind of the autopsy from the MPs and wanted to know why it was necessary. He ranted on about how we shouldn't be causing the relatives any further distress by stopping him from shipping the body back stateside. What's going on, Ralph? There's nothing unusual about performing an autopsy where the deceased died in suspicious circumstances. As a matter of fact, I'd say it's pretty much routine."

Carnaby was gazing out the window and noticed Gregson looking in his direction, waiting for an answer. "I, I don't know what's going on Tom. What did you tell him anyhow?"

"I saw red and gave him a real mouthful. I asked him just who the hell he thought he was coming in here unannounced and telling me how to run my morgue. I'll be damned if he was going to pull rank on me. I've been doing this for the better part of ten years and with no complaints. Until now that is."

Carnaby tried hard not to smile. *Same old Tom Gregson.*

Gregson wiped spittle from the corners of his mouth. "Once I'd calmed down a little, I basically told him the same as I'll tell you—that it doesn't look like suicide to me. Strange thing is, he didn't seem to like my conclusions. Said he was surprised the autopsy had been authorized in the first place and would have thought I had better things to do with the number of our boys coming back injured from Korea. I mean Christ, Ralph, I don't pick them. I just check them in and do the job."

Carnaby nodded and said, "So, after you'd explained your findings, what did he do?"

"Nothing much. He insisted on seeing the authorization. I showed it to him. It's down here in black and white." Gregson rapped the document with his open hand.

"So what did he say then?"

"Nothing much. Just kept going on about you being too junior to authorize it—that you should've had your boss sign off on it."

"Aspin? He wouldn't have any gripes with it, that's for sure." Carnaby cupped his jaw and rubbed his stubbly chin with the palm of one hand while he thought. "What I don't get is why in God's name did Lorimer tip Personnel off in the first place?"

Gregson sighed. "Sure beats the hell out of me, Ralph." He moved back a step and smoothed his well-groomed hair.

"I mean, surely they—and the relatives for that matter—are just as keen as anybody else to wrap this thing up once and for all." Carnaby frowned and rubbed his eyes.

"You should take some leave. You look beat. This case getting to you?"

"I wouldn't say that. I'm just getting too goddamned old for this game, that's all. It's about time I went back to the US and took on some of the responsibilities I've been shirking for the past few years."

"You and me both, Ralph." Gregson knew exactly how his

friend felt. He had felt that way himself a number of times. But his work was the here and now, and deep down he knew he would never go back to the States, not to settle at any rate. "Anyway, listen Ralph, I think your hunch may have proved right. Come over here."

He led Carnaby over to a laminated table in a corner of the room and scooped up a half-finished report. "Two things. First of all, the wound is consistent with a 9-mm slug. Whether or not it came from *the* Browning is a question you need to put to your ballistics people. The interesting point is, however," Gregson paused while he checked his notes, "it doesn't appear to have been fired at point-blank range. In a suicide case, the skin immediately surrounding the entry wound is invariably peppered with gunpowder. There was only a slight deposit on Brice's skin."

"Are you suggesting someone just crept into his apartment and shot him from the side while he sat at his desk?"

"Well, stranger things have happened. In any case, that's for you to find out. Maybe the shooter just waltzed in there, warned Brice not to move and then plugged him from the hip when he was a couple of feet away. Remember, Ralph, the entry hole was a couple inches below the temple. It would be difficult to hit the spot without aiming carefully."

"I follow you. But you said there were two things."

"Yeah, that's right," he answered, hardly able to contain his excitement. "It's the vodka. It was half empty, right?"

Carnaby nodded.

"Well, get this. He didn't drink any of it. There were only residual traces of alcohol in his blood."

"But maybe, maybe he only had a mouthful before he was shot and then knocked the glass over as he fell forward onto the desk."

"Yeah, maybe," said Gregson adjusting his glasses, "but you'd expect a much bigger deposit. Now obviously it was the shot that killed him, right?"

Carnaby nodded again.

"The point is," he resumed, "I think whoever shot Brice attempted to pour the liquor down his throat only *after* he'd done it."

"You mean to make it look as though he had primed himself for it?"

"Exactly. Dutch courage—call it what you will. If you were going to shoot yourself—God forbid, you'd have a skinful first, wouldn't you? Well, anyhow, his windpipe had closed up, muscles stopped working. It wouldn't go down and must have come gushing out again. His clothes stank of it when he arrived here. The small quantity I found in his blood sample would have been slowly absorbed through the soft fleshy part of his inner cheek."

"Why is it I get a permanent uneasy feeling with this case?" Carnaby placed both fists on the tabletop, leaned forward and looked sideways at the pathologist. "So, assume Brice did not commit suicide but *was* shot by someone else at around—what time did the landlord say? 18:30?—while he sat at his desk writing a letter to 'Emma.'Besides confirming my gut reaction, we're no further on. Is there anything else you can give me, Tom, anything at all?"

Gregson linked his fingers behind his back and began pacing up and down, eyes cast down, focusing on the irregular blood spots spattered on the tiled floor surface. He cleared his throat, "Well, not from a forensic evidential angle. There are no signs of a struggle—no contusions, abrasions or bruises, other than the ones around the gunshot wound, and I'm satisfied they occurred as a result of the bullet entry."

"And there was no forced entry, at least according to the MPs," said Carnaby dryly.

"Right. There's some slight discoloration in the center of the forehead, but that's consistent with the victim slumping forward onto the desk surface." He leaned against the wall, one hand in his pocket and tapped his teeth with the stem of his pipe. "From a purely speculative point of view, seems to me he knew his killer." Gregson paused while he tamped tobacco into the bowl.

Carnaby gestured for him to go on.

"No struggle. No forced entry. I might be jumping to conclusions, but it looks to me like whoever plugged Brice was invited in. Maybe they were talking, reminiscing about old times and then, just when Brice was relaxed, *Bang*!" Gregson raised two fingers in the air and aimed them at Carnaby like a gun, making a popping sound with his cheeks.

"Yeah, it's possible," said Carnaby. "Come to think of it, other than Brice's desk chair, the only other chair in the room was the lounger, near the door. The angle would have been about right. But wait a minute. The gun was Brice's. How the hell did the killer get hold of it?"

"It could have just been lying around, you know, Ralph. I don't pack a piece these days, but when I used to it would turn up in the strangest of places—under the bed, by the bathroom mirror, stuffed down the side of the sofa, hardly ever where you'd expect it to be."

"Yeah. It's possible," said Carnaby doubtfully, "but it takes some balls to pick a gun up and use it not knowing if it's loaded." He glanced at his watch. "Anyway, Tom, I've gotta get going or Aspin will have my ass. I've been summoned to a meeting with the legendary Major General Charles Brannigan."

"Okay, Ralph. Better you than me. It was good seeing you again. You look after yourself and don't leave it so long next time." The pathologist's sense of humor was as deadpan as ever.

Carnaby punched him playfully on the shoulder, turned to leave and then stopped and looked back. "Do me a favor, will you, Tom? Keep this thing to yourself. I mean, just put the facts down in your report, leastways until I figure out what's going on around here."

"You got it, Ralph." Gregson smiled adding, "Call me if you need anything."

"Yeah, thanks."

He emerged onto the bright sidewalk, pushed his neck back in his collar and breathed a deep sigh of relief. Soaking up the winter sun he felt human again.

'Ya-ki imo-o!' A sweet potato vendor turned the corner pushing his cart carrying two large pans, steam billowing from underneath the lids. A couple of street children or *charinko* were squatting by the goods entrance playing rock-paper-scissors. Both were filthy and shoeless, and both were crowned with a matted tangle of coarse black hair—the legacy of a country ravaged by war, of dreams and lives shattered, a legacy shared by thousands of other orphans who eked out a meager existence in the countless cardboard shantytowns that littered the capital.

They looked up as Carnaby approached. "Haro. Haro. You got gum, Mister?"

He grinned. He reached in his pocket and produced a handful of loose change. He held out his hand. *"Dozo."* The children beamed and took the money and then began squabbling over how to divide it.

He moved off and stopped further down to cross the street. He looked back. The two waif-like children had dashed across to the vendor and were triumphantly holding aloft large foil-wrapped baked sweet potatoes, dancing and whooping with joy. Carnaby smiled to himself then turned and walked quickly away.

Five

Spring: Bletchley

Emma sat on the settle in the living room, with the warm spring sun streaming through the windows onto her back, leafing through her diary.

16 April 1953

Arrived in Washington for Harvey's funeral. Met at the airport by Michael and Caroline. Floods of tears all round. I felt so sorry for them losing their only son. The funeral was very moving, as expected. I had no idea Harvey had so many friends. There must have been two hundred or more squashed into that little church. His sister, Bethany, made a lovely speech—full of warmth and compassion—largely anecdotal, mainly childhood memories about growing up during the Great Depression, and how Harvey always wanted to help people, make a difference to those less fortunate in the world.

I felt full of admiration for Michael and Caroline. Neither is young, and they stood there and hugged and kissed and shook hands with all who attended to express their condolences. The strain was evident on Caroline's face, but she conducted herself in such a dignified manner. I wish I could be more like her—elegant and refined, even in the face of such sadness. I felt a little abandoned at times. People didn't know me, but after all, it was their day. Their grief must be just as strong as mine. Oh, Harvey. Why has this happened? I am completely lost without you. I must be strong, at least for Michael and Caroline's sake. But who will be strong for me?

26 April 1953

I spent today brooding over the recent past again. It is as if I exist in a perpetual state of suspended animation. My legs are leaden. I must pull myself out of it. After much thought I have resolved to . . .

Suddenly the doorbell rang. She snapped her diary shut and pushed it under a cushion—away from prying eyes.

She went to the dining room and peeped round the net curtains. It was her sister, Lucy. She dabbed her eyes with her sleeve, went quickly to the door and let her in. "Sorry, Luce, I was just having a nap in the back," she said as she embraced her sibling.

"That's alright. Hey, have you been crying again?" Lucy brushed Emma's fringe away from her face and looked at her forlornly.

"I'm fine now."

"Really?"

"Yes, honestly." Emma gripped Lucy's forearms, as if to reassure her. "Come on through, I'll make some tea."

"I'll make it, you sit down."

Emma laughed. "I've been sitting down all day. If I don't get up soon and do something my legs will atrophy."

"Alright, you win." Lucy giggled. "We'll both make it. It's a silly thing to argue about anyway. Is Mother out?" she asked following her sister into the kitchen.

"Yes. She's gone to see Aunt Clarice. She won't be back until after six."

Good, thought Lucy. It wasn't often they got the chance to sit and chat like sisters do about intimate things. Mother was such a prude, and these days it was difficult to have any sort of meaningful conversation with her in the same room, even if she wasn't actually taking part.

They carried the tea through on a small silver tray. Lucy kicked her shoes off, reclined on the sofa and sipped her tea. "The flower room is beautiful, isn't it? It hasn't changed a bit in all these years," she said, setting her cup and saucer down on an inlaid mahogany occasional table. A well-thumbed copy of last month's *Housewife* magazine lay next to the coaster, its cover featuring an exclusive on Princess Beatrix of Holland and "The Hidden River," the first part in a new serial story by Storm Jameson.

Emma smiled. The "flower room" had been a term of endearment since their childhood. The walls were covered in dried, pressed wildflowers, clustered together in wooden frames according to genus. Their father had been a keen gardener and was passionate about protecting and encouraging Britain's natural flora, which he had thought were becoming increasingly endangered in meadows due to so-called "advances" in farming techniques, particularly with increased demand during the war years. Emma and her sister had themselves both played a small part in this process working as 'land girls' on nearby farms.

On the facing wall, Emma's favorite by far were specimens from the daisy family (*Compositae*): sunburst yellow goldenrod, corn marigold and elecampane, oxeye daisy, purple coltsfoot and feverfew, and the more muted colors of the butterbur, yarrow and cottonweed—more muted, but equally attractive in their own way; and, of course, there was the ubiquitous cornflower, peerless when it comes to vivid blue, immortalized by the poet John Clare when he wrote, "*. . . the corn bottles crowding their splendid colours in large sheets over the land and 'troubling the cornfields' with destroying beauty.*" On very bright winter days, when it was snowbound and too cold to venture out for long, Emma liked to gaze at this wall, and then, once the images were fixed in her mind's eye, stare just for a moment directly at the sun, and then screw her eyes tight shut. She would be instantly and magically transported in time and place—lying amidst the grass in a flower-festooned meadow on a languid summer's afternoon, her senses intoxicated by the scent of pollen carried on the cool breeze as it sifted through the bird infested hedgerows, and the indescribably splendid spectacle of thousands upon thousands of long-stemmed flowers bobbing their delicate heads, as if in greeting.

"You look well," said Emma, dreamily. "How are you feeling?"

"A little tired I suppose. I haven't had much of an appetite for the past few weeks, and I haven't been sleeping too well either."

"Well, it certainly doesn't show. I can't believe you are going to be a mother soon. It's quite ridiculous. You realize that, don't you? You look far too young."

"That's nice of you," said Lucy, distractedly.

Lucy was evidently looking after herself: her thick golden hair neatly piled up on top of her head and held in place with a slender silver hairpin; her face, a little fuller than usual, with its soft lines and big bright eyes—still full of youthful curiosity, and her lips pretty in Max Factor pink. Lucy had always taken care of her looks. Even during the austere war years when luxury goods were simply unobtainable, her appearance was immaculate—improvising mascara with burnt cork and subtle shades of lipstick with a variety of vegetable extracts and other household ingredients.

There was only three years between them, but looking at Lucy made Emma feel acutely aware of her age. She could almost feel the youth ebbing out of her, and with it, her good looks and her dreams for the future.

"I was wondering," said Lucy, breaking the silence, "whether you fancy a trip to London at the weekend. I've got a couple of tickets for the Festival of Britain."

"Oh, I don't know. You would have more fun there with Robert, I'm sure."

"Nonsense. And in any case, Robert has to be in the office on Saturday—year end and all that."

Emma forced a smile. "It wouldn't be much fun with me the way I am at the moment."

"But that's the whole point, silly. It will take your mind off things. Get you out of the house for a while. A change of scenery is always a good idea when you have things on your mind."

"Well . . ."

"Oh, go on, do say yes! It sounds fantastic. There was a full page write-up in *The Times* yesterday. There's the Dome of Discovery, which is supposed to be fascinating, and a huge Ferris wheel. And we could have lunch at Zach's Glass and Steel Café. Apparently the food is excellent and reasonably priced. It would do you a world of good, don't you think?"

"But what about you? Do you think it a good idea going all that way so close to your due date? And what about the rides? You won't be able to go on anything that goes faster than a high street tram."

"It's only a few hours on the train, and in any case, there's lots more to do besides the rides, you know." She unconsciously placed both hands on her middle and stroked her bump.

"How is baby anyway?" asked Emma.

"Oh, just fine. He's a real wriggler. That's for certain. Little devil keeps me awake half the night!"

They both laughed. Emma played with the cushion frill and looked down at the carpet. She thought of the baby that she had so badly wanted with Harvey, of what could have been but now never would be.

"Are you alright, Sis?"

Tears slipped from Emma's eyelids, and she groped around the sides of the sofa for her handkerchief.

"Sorry," she said, her voice muffled through the cotton veil, "that was selfish of me."

Lucy sidled up to her sister and put her arm around her shoulder, leaned forward and kissed her on the cheek. "Don't be silly. Of course it's not selfish. You're upset, and you are probably going to carry on being upset for a good deal longer."

Emma sighed and clenched her small fists, knuckles turning white. "But it's a month now since it happened, and . . . and yet it's all I think about day and night. I feel as though it's eating into me, as if there will never be a way out."

"That's just not true, Emma. Time is a great healer. You have to experience grief, and if it takes a year—or two years—then you just have to accept it. It would be pretty strange if you didn't feel the way you do. I mean, look at Mother. She was traumatized for years after Father's death."

"But she's different," snapped Emma. "She's determined to be miserable. Father died eleven years ago and she still can't accept it. Won't accept it. Won't even discuss him."

"I know she can be difficult," said Lucy softly.

"*Difficult*?" Emma said sarcastically. "That's a complete understatement. She is totally inaccessible. She's just not equipped emotionally to come to terms with her own grief let alone talk to me about mine. Why only last week, we were sitting in here just like you and I. On this sofa, in fact. I was trying to explain to her how I felt at Harvey's funeral, and you know what she did?" asked Emma rhetorically. "She just got to her feet—I mean while I was in mid-sentence—and walked out of the room. I found her in her bedroom, sitting on that old sea chest of Father's, clutching his photograph to her chest and sobbing uncontrollably."

Lucy cast her eyes down, taking in the paisley design on the worn carpet. With a barely audible sigh she looked up. "Emma, I know it's not easy living with Mother. But I think you can be a little hard on her at times. She had been with Father for nearly twenty years when she lost him."

Emma tilted her face up. "I know. Which is why I would expect her to appreciate what I'm going through."

"People," began Lucy, "are not all the same. They are products not only of the generation in which they were born but also of their own particular circumstances and experiences."

"Well, of course," said Emma, wiping a residual tear from her cheek, "but eleven years is a long enough time to come to terms with something, and it's not as if she hasn't had any support. We've both been there for her to lean on, and . . ."

"Hey, come on, isn't this absurd? Let's not fall out over this. All I'm saying," continued Lucy, trying not to sound exasperated, "is that it must have come as a bitter blow for Mother, especially as she hadn't seen Father for two years, when news came from France that he had been killed. Two years of living in hope that he would return. It really is no wonder she just, well, retreated into her own world."

"I really don't see how it is any different to my situation, Lucy. I haven't seen Harvey for nearly seven months." She shrugged her sister's arm from her shoulder and pushed away from her, as if realizing for the first time that she would never see him again. "You're right when you said it's not easy living with her. She can never put herself in somebody else's shoes. She only thinks about herself and her own problems. You never actually have a conversation with her. There is no interaction. It's like having a completely separate discussion." Emma paused and then said, "Maybe I should move out."

"What do you mean?"

"You know, find my own digs somewhere. Give us both some breathing space."

"But Mother would be so lonely without you."

Emma linked her fingers together and stretched her arms up toward the ceiling. "She would cope. She *was* expecting me to move out after the wedding in any case."

"But seriously, Emma, it would be an unnecessary expense, and Mother does so much for you and—"

"I'm a big girl now and quite capable of looking after myself," she said testily.

"Oh, for goodness' sake, Emma," snapped Lucy. "There's no need to take that tone of voice with me. I wasn't implying that you don't know what you are doing or that your responsibilities are here with Mother. I'm just worried, that's all. I suppose it's my condition. I worry about lots of things at the moment. I want you to be safe, and I think the company is good for you."

Emma scrutinized her nails for a second, frowning.

Lucy looked long and knowingly at her sister. "There's more to it than that, isn't there? It's Harvey, isn't it?" She paused, unsure of how to say it, and then, "You don't believe it was suicide, do you?"

A deeply perturbed expression crossed Emma's face. She nodded slowly and raised her eyes. "I just keep going over and over it in my mind. And what I really don't understand—can't understand—is why? Why would he take his own life? It makes no sense at all."

Lucy saw that her sister was trying hard not to cry again, and said, with a voice full of tenderness and regret, "It really is difficult to believe it has happened. There's so little concrete information coming back from over there. It's almost as if it's a conspiracy."

"I'm sure I would have known if anything had been wrong. It was only a month ago when he managed to call on the telephone, and he sounded his usual cheerful self. Said he was so looking forward to his discharge and coming back here to . . . be . . . with . . . me." Her voice trailed off, and her eyes filled with tears again as she fought to control her distressed breathing.

Lucy pulled her in still closer and caressed her arm. "What about his letters?"

"His letters?" Emma looked up quizzically through her knitted brow.

"Yes," said Lucy. "I mean, was there anything in any of the letters you received since the call which would suggest something was the matter?"

Emma bit her lip and gazed at the fire. "Not that I can recall. Then again, it's hardly surprising really. His mail was still being censored—working in intelligence the way he did. He would know not to write anything out of the ordinary." She paused, then added, "But maybe I'll read through them once more, just to make sure, when I'm feeling up to it." She stood and walked slowly and deliberately over to the window. She tapped the barometer and stared far off into the distance—out toward Whaddon Chase. Dark clouds loomed low in the eastern sky. Rain was on its way. "Lucy." Emma turned to face her sister with a determined look about her. Behind, the sky had turned a curious shade of cobalt. She cleared her throat and said, "I have something to tell you."

Six

Major General Charles Brannigan had a lavish office in the former Posts and Telecommunications Building, another imposing edifice of late Meiji Period restoration architecture. Like most of the buildings commandeered by the Occupation authorities, the Posts and Telecommunications Building fronted Hibiya-dori, facing, at a respectful distance, the Imperial Palace.

Carnaby climbed the stone steps and returned the guards' salutes as he went through the large revolving door. Having checked the interior plan next to the elevator, he made his way through the labyrinth of interconnecting passageways toward Brannigan's office.

The final corridor brought him out onto a broad hallway in the building's east wing. The hallway, redolent with the smell of freshly cut lilies, ran parallel to a rectangular inner courtyard. It was said that the former War Minister, General Anami, used to indulge his favorite sport, archery, along its length, using the exposed buttress end of an ancient wooden beam as his target.

The worn red carpet gave way to a polished parquet floor as the hallway opened out onto a wide reception area. Brannigan's secretary was tucked neatly behind a large oak desk, which threatened to dwarf her already diminutive stature, with a telephone glued to her ear, scribbling the caller's details down on a pad in shorthand.

He hovered in front of her, his coat draped over his right arm, rocking slightly on the balls of his feet. He cocked his head back and stared at the unfurled Stars and Stripes hanging limply from the wall above. The secretary was coming to the end of her call. "No, of course I won't forget, sir. I'll have the general return your call just as soon as he is free." *Pause.* "You're welcome sir." *Pause.* "Thank you. Goodbye."

Carnaby cleared his throat. The woman replaced the heavy Bakelite receiver and looked up at him through pretty hazel brown eyes, her left hand going unconsciously to her well groomed hair. "Can I help you, sir?"

"Captain Carnaby. I have an appointment with the major general."

She opened the appointments ledger and checked the entry. "Ah yes, Captain—a 15:30 appointment." She looked at her watch: 15:15, and then looked up again with a slightly perturbed expression.

"Is there a problem, ma'am?" he asked.

"No, no. It's just that, the general has a very tight schedule."

He spared her further embarrassment. It looked as if she was having a tough day. "It's okay. I can wait," he said, smiling.

The phone rang, and she picked the receiver up again and reached for her pencil. Brannigan's voice boomed, more from the double doors behind her, than from the receiver. "Where in God's name is Carnaby? I'm due on the other side of town in thirty minutes." "He's what?" "He's here now? Then why didn't you tell me?"

"He's only just this minute-"

"I don't care what he's only just this minute done. Send him in, will you? I haven't got all day."

She held the receiver between index finger and thumb, a couple of inches from her ear, as if it was somehow something altogether too distasteful to contemplate.

Carnaby smiled again. "So, does that make me early or late?"

The secretary lowered her voice and tried to return the smile. "Your guess is as good as mine."

He knocked on the heavy door and went straight in. He had decided there was no point in being intimidated by this man.

"Captain Carnaby? Do come in. Have a seat and make yourself comfortable." Brannigan spoke in an affable manner, rather like a doctor attempting to put his patient's mind at rest before imparting some terrible prognosis. "Would you like one?" He proffered a mahogany box filled with expensive-looking Havana cigars.

"No, thank you, sir. I'm really trying to give them up," Carnaby lied, removing a stack of old *Fortune* magazines from his chair onto the floor.

"Pity. I find smoking in moderation a great antidote to anxiety. Not that I suffer from too much of that around here—if you get my drift." Brannigan smiled insincerely, guillotined his cigar and applied a match to it. He sucked in a large quantity of smoke, swilled it around in his mouth and blew it out again, producing a small smoke screen between them. "I don't believe we've ever met, Captain."

Carnaby's eye wandered for a moment and came to rest on a marble bust of a young man with a shock of neatly parted wavy hair and heavy, strangely handsome Germanic features.

"Pardon me, sir?"

"I said, I don't believe we've ever met."

"No, sir. I don't think we have."

"Which is kind of strange," he continued, transferring his cigar to the other side of his mouth, "because I think I've run into just about everyone else in the CIA at one time or another. Maybe you just work harder than the others and hide yourself away in your office. Or maybe you're out all the time investigating suicides and the like." Brannigan gave him a knowing look and chewed on his Havana.

Carnaby felt his eye being drawn back to the bust.

"Richard Sorge," said Brannigan through the haze.

"Excuse me, sir?"

"I said, Richard Sorge. You *were* looking at the bust, weren't you?" Brannigan had a smug expression on his corpulent face. "It gets 'em every time. You'd expect to see Roosevelt or Truman sitting up there all high and mighty, now wouldn't you? Not me. No, sir." He paused while he took another long draft on his cigar. "Nope, I just hate convention for convention's sake, if you know what I mean."

Carnaby didn't, but he nodded anyway.

"It was a gift from old Jacob Malik, the Russian ambassador himself. A sort of peace offering really. In recognition of our tacit wartime cooperation, for want of a more appropriate way of putting it. Sorge—the greatest goddamned spy of the twentieth century, posthumous hero of the Soviet Union."

Carnaby risked a furtive glance at his watch while his superior droned on. *Christ* he thought, *there's no stopping the man.*

"You've gotta admire men like him. They risk everything for their cause. And they get away with what they do for as long as they do out of sheer audacity. They rely on their innate intellectual superiority and supreme confidence to pull it off. They can see the danger that's headed their way, but they regard it with reckless impunity. A sort of fatalistic attitude, I guess. We helped install him here in Tokyo during the war. As a Russian spy of course. But in those days we didn't consider the long-term effect of what we were doing. We were prepared to try anything to undermine the Japanese war effort. No one gave any serious consideration to events that led to this so-called 'Cold War' that we're supposed to be fighting at the moment, even though the signs were there for everyone to see way back at the Yalta Conference." He gestured over his shoulder with his thumb. "He caused one hell of a stink among the Japs. Until he was caught that is. Poor bastard was hanged over in Sugamo Prison in '44. Still," he paused to catch his breath, "I don't suppose you have the time or the inclination to listen to an old goat like me lecture you in history."

Carnaby was about to say how, come to think of it, he had come across the name once before, when Brannigan leaned forward and brought his meaty fist down hard on the desktop. "Now tell me, Captain, just what in tarnation is going on here?"

He hesitated, momentarily confused by the abrupt change of subject. "You mean with regard to the Brice investigation, sir?"

"You're goddamned right I mean with regard to the Brice investigation."

"Well, sir," he began, "to tell you the truth, we are not convinced that Lieutenant Brice committed suicide. You see—" Carnaby stopped mid-sentence. Brannigan was grinning and jerking his head from side to side as if he didn't believe a word he was hearing. After a few seconds he looked up, his great fat cigar still clamped between thin lips. He gestured expansively with both hands, slowly placed them behind his neck and stretched back in his creaking leather chair.

"I don't buy it, Carnaby. You've got to ask the question: Why? He was the nicest, least offensive kid on the block. Now you tell me what motive anyone would have for killing him? It just doesn't make any sense, now does it?"

"I agree, sir. It doesn't make any sense, at the moment. But then neither does taking his own life. It seems to me he had every reason to go on living. He was due to get out of the army in June and planned to go to England and marry his sweetheart,

Emma Forbes. By all accounts he was besotted with her and—" he was about to say "he wrote her every week" but for some reason, perhaps guilt at having read some of the letters, he checked himself and instead lamely said, "And in any case, there was no suicide note."

Brannigan sniffed derisively. "Captain Lorimer informs me that Brice had begun writing such a note to his fiancée but that perhaps he could not bring himself to finish it."

"With respect, sir, that's mere speculation." Carnaby struggled to control his rising temper. "Captain Lorimer had no grounds to form that kind of a conclusion. There was little more than an address and an opening line on the page."

"But wasn't it soaked through with whiskey?"

"Vodka, sir. Russian vodka."

"So, it would be pretty hard to say exactly what was and what wasn't written underneath. Wouldn't you agree, Captain?"

"From where I was standing, sir, it was patently obvious that it was just another of Brice's weekly missives to Emma Forbes."

Brannigan smiled. "What was it you said a moment ago about *speculation*?" He added particular emphasis to the last word, as if to drive the point home.

Calm down. For chrissake, calm down. Carnaby silently admonished himself. Brannigan was still sharp, despite his advancing years. He had to be careful not to give away more than he intended.

"In any case," continued Brannigan, "it's not entirely unknown for someone to end his life without leaving any clues as to why he did it." He lit a second cigar and dropped the spent match into the base of a six inch howitzer shell that served as an ashtray. "Do you recall having heard of General Kades' adjutant, back in '47?"

Carnaby shrugged, but his superior went on regardless.

"Colonel Jim Morrison. Brilliant strategist. Adviser to Kades for the best part of ten years. A prince of a guy. He was all set to succeed the general. And then what happens. One afternoon in early September he goes up to some retreat in Karuizawa and blows his brains out. Totally out of the blue. No suicide note. No signs of depression beforehand. No nothing. No Colonel Morrison. To this day, nobody knows why in hell he did it. Face it, Carnaby, it happens. Hell, nobody likes it, but it is one of the unfortunate consequences of war."

Carnaby adjusted his backside in the uncomfortable wooden-backed chair. He considered telling Brannigan what he had learned from Tom Gregson, but then thought better of it. He didn't want to get him in trouble, and the way this meeting was going he was rapidly reaching the conclusion that some things were better left unsaid. He had come here intent on asking Brannigan all the questions, but it was clear that Brannigan was calling the shots. He was in control of the interview, and Carnaby felt distinctly uneasy about it.

"Did Lieutenant Brice seem, well, depressed at all in recent weeks, sir?"

The older man considered the question briefly and then answered, "We've all been very busy lately, trying to meet the deadline for this infernal publication." He slapped his open hand down on top of an untidy pile of loose papers. "To be frank, Captain, he did seem a little down. But most people do from time to time. Maybe if I had realized earlier, I could've talked to him, maybe even arranged early discharge on medical grounds."

"Do you think," Carnaby leaned forward in his chair, "he might have gotten someone's back up, sir? You know, talking all the time about leaving the army and getting married. That kind of talk can start to rile someone if their own situation isn't going so good."

"Like I said, Captain, he was the nicest kid around," Brannigan said impatiently. "If he'd had any enemies, I'd have heard about it, sooner or later.

Carnaby ran his fingers through his hair and tried a fresh approach. "Would it be possible to talk to some of his former colleagues? Maybe someone working with him day to day could put their finger on something, something that might give me a break in this case."

Brannigan stubbed his cigar out and closed his eyes. "I doubt it would do any good. I saw him as much as most. Fact is resources are a little stretched at the moment. Speaking of which, I think you worry too much about what goes on around here. There must be dozens of unsolved internal security cases that you could devote your obvious talents to more profitably. This is, as I'm sure you'll appreciate, a matter which the military police are best equipped to handle. Captain Lorimer has his critics, and his methods are at times a little antiquated, but you should give him due credit. He's much smarter than you think. What's more, the MPs are prepared to see this incident for what it is and not go off on some fanciful wild goose chase."

Carnaby could feel it coming, even though it had never happened to him before.

"Now don't take this personally, Captain. I appreciate all you've done to help, but I really must insist that you turn this case over to Captain Lorimer and have no further involvement after today."

Carnaby opened his mouth, but Brannigan silenced the beginnings of a protest with a raised hand. He rocked forward and stared across the desk, his dark emotionless eyes boring holes in Carnaby's head. "Look, Carnaby, I'll level with you. There's more at stake here than you could possibly imagine." He grunted and stood up, with surprising ease for a man of his age and size, and walked over to the window and peered out the slats at the palace moat. A group of schoolchildren, all dressed in sailor uniforms, were lined up in neat rows having their photograph taken in front of the Nijubashi Bridge. He turned back to face Carnaby. "What I'm about to tell you is classified, top secret. Totally off the record. It must not go beyond these four walls. Do I make myself clear?"

Carnaby nodded and gave Brannigan his full attention.

"Compiling the official history of the Pacific War isn't the only thing we do here." He leaned his ample backside against the edge of his desk and folded his arms. "As a professional soldier who has spent most of his life in the service of his country, naturally I cannot pretend I wasn't utterly dismayed by the destruction of the Imperial Japanese Armed Forces at the end of the war."

"But, General, that was surely central to the occupation policy, I can't see how -"

Brannigan looked irritated as—Carnaby was beginning to realize—he did whenever he was contradicted or interrupted. "Captain, do you mind?" He fixed him with another of his deathly stares. Carnaby settled back down in his chair and cupped his hands together while Brannigan paced backwards and forwards in the confines of the small room.

"Disarming Japan to the extent we have done was one big fucking mistake from start to finish. No doubt about it. All it's succeeded in doing is increasing our exposure to the risk of a Commie invasion. And if that happens," he looked skywards, "then God help us. The shit will really hit the fan." Carnaby noticed the veins running across Brannigan's forehead were beginning to swell and stand out the more excited he became. "And, as for those goddamned faggot liberals in the Pentagon, they think they're smart as hell. You know what they say? No? Well, I'll tell you. They say our hands are tied because of Article 9 of the Constitution and that in any case Japan has a two hundred and fifty thousand-strong 'militia' to deal with communist insurgents. They're full of shit. Have you seen that so-called 'militia?'" he said, rhetorically. "Why it's little more than a gendarmerie. What we really need is an anti-Soviet military alliance. We need to be able to mount a preemptive strike, if necessary. Article 9 should never have seen the light of day."

Carnaby tried to remember the gist of Article 9. He had read it once, in the *New York Tribune*, as he recalled, soon after the Constitution came into force in the spring of 1947.

Designed to prevent the Japanese from acquiring and maintaining war potential, Article 9 had been inserted into the American-designed new Constitution at the eleventh hour:

> *Aspiring sincerely to an international peace based on justice and order, the Japanese people forever renounce war as a sovereign right of the nation and the threat or use of force as a means of settling international disputes.*
> *To accomplish the aim of the preceding paragraph, land, sea, and air forces, as well as other war potential, will never be maintained. The right of belligerency of the state will not be recognized."*

"Of course, it's full of loopholes." Brannigan's voice phased back in. Carnaby looked up. His superior was frowning. "Are you listening to me?"

"Yes, sir, of course."

"As I was saying, the Pacific War history project isn't really what we're about. At least it's not our main purpose. Since the end of the war, we have been working on putting in place a network of demobilized officers throughout the Japanese mainland, officers who are willing to assist in the organization and deployment of a nationwide militia. They all have one thing in common: a deep-rooted distrust, even hatred, of communism."

Carnaby tried not to look surprised, but his face must have

betrayed his feelings.

"Oh, don't worry, Captain. It's all above-board, approved by the president himself." Brannigan picked a sheet of paper up from his desk and dropped it into Carnaby's lap.

It certainly looked like an official memorandum.

"As you are no doubt aware, Captain, at this point in time, upwards of eighty five percent of the Japan-based US occupation forces are over in Korea with their backs against the wall, fighting the last quarter for good old Uncle Sam. There's no denying our boys are taking one helluva beating. The North Koreans are a bunch of tough motherfuckers. And confident too, especially with all that indirect support the Russkies have been giving them." He walked over to a small drink cabinet and took out a bottle. He unscrewed the top and poured himself a slug of neat bourbon. "Of course, the problem we have over here," he resumed, draining his glass, "is that due to a lack of foresight we have effectively prevented ourselves from rearming Japan—and at the very time we need this country as our ally. No one is prepared to take the blame and admit we screwed up on Article 9. Japan is about the only country around here that isn't communist."

Brannigan craned his neck back while he thought for a moment and then continued his relentless diatribe. "You know, I get sick and tired of all these people in the press at the moment bitchin' about the millions of bucks we're having to spend to reconstruct this goddamned country. The way I see it, if we established a full-scale military alliance with the Japs, investment from the big industrial combines and arms procurement would act to stimulate the economy in any event."

Carnaby seriously doubted the logic behind this theory, not to mention the legal implications involved, but he kept his opinion to himself.

"Anyhow, to get to the point, Captain, this whole operation is of paramount importance to our government's communist containment strategy out here in the Pacific basin region. It *must* be kept under wraps until the time is right to make an official announcement. And that means we don't want any unnecessary publicity." He moved back around his desk and, gripping the armrests with his big hands, lowered his bulk into the mottled leather chair. Linking his fingers together he looked down his nose at Carnaby. "So you see, Captain, why it is that I am more than a little concerned about the extent of your inquiries into Lieutenant Brice's suicide."

"With all due respect, sir, I didn't ask to be involved. But having been brought into the case, intentionally or otherwise, I've just done what I've always done."

"Which is what?"

This time it was Brannigan's turn to interrupt.

"Try to figure out the inconsistencies. You know, sir, those little things that don't quite add up."

Brannigan had one of the spent matches braced between index finger and thumb, exerting just enough pressure to make the slender, tapered stick of wood bow outwards without snapping. His eyes remained fixed on the match. "And have you found many of these *inconsistencies*, Captain?"

Carnaby took a deep breath. "Enough to suggest that the circumstances surrounding Lieutenant Brice's death warrant further investigation."

The match snapped in two with a splintering sound. Brannigan's eyes lifted and stared unblinking at him.

The telephone rang, breaking the tense silence. It was the secretary out in the lobby phoning through to say Brannigan's car was waiting to take him to his next appointment.

Brannigan grabbed his coat and briefcase and strode purposefully toward the door. He put his right hand on the brass door knob and looked down at Carnaby. "I think we understand each other, Captain. I don't think there will be a need for us to meet again. Have a good day."

The door banged shut and Carnaby aspirated heavily, letting his shoulders fall forward and kneading his temples with the palms of both hands. A migraine stabbed at his eyes. He felt like he'd just gone fifteen rounds with Jake LaMotta.

That night he dreamed he was still in Brannigan's office, facing the desk and peering through the fug of tobacco smoke. Brannigan was hunched, facing the desktop and moving his head from side to side. Slowly he lifted his head, and as the haze cleared it wasn't Brannigan's face that stared back at him but a heavyset, handsome face with Germanic features. The head was still now, but its right index finger was pointing and wagging from side to side, reproachfully, like a metronome. And then out of the corner of his eye he caught sight of the marble bust, pale in the cold blue winter sunlight. It was Brannigan's head. Severed at the shoulders and rocking gently to and fro with its eyes screwed tight shut and mocking Carnaby with silent laughter.

Seven

Kobe—a city of hustle and bustle and a million lights. One of those lights now blazed beacon-like from the vista windows of the US Consulate guardroom. Inside, two world-weary G.I.s busied themselves preparing for the long morning ahead on the graveyard shift.

Frank Sinatra's "Sweet Lorraine" phased in and out as the younger man tried desperately to tune in the start of the New York Yankees ball game.

"Goddamned lousy reception."

"Yeah." The pug-faced sergeant nodded in agreement and continued stirring his coffee with the end of his pencil. "Still, nothin' beats seein' the real thing, huh? You goin' to the game on Saturday?"

"I might just do that. Got nothin' else planned." The younger man lit a cigarette, inhaling deeply as he considered the idea. "It ain't exactly Yankee Stadium, but what the hell? The Japs play a pretty good game these days. How about you Ged? What're you plannin' on doin'?"

Pug-face set his drink down clumsily, spilling black coffee, and moved away from the table with a wide grin across his leathery face. He reached back and pulled out a wad of notes from his back pocket. "Payday. Don't ya just luv it? Why, I'm gonna get myself a pretty li'l Jap girl and have me one hell of a good time. *That's* what I'm plannin' on doin'."

"Gonna get yourself laid, huh? Don't you ever think of nothin' else, Ged?" The younger man beamed and took a slurp of coffee.

"Nope. Can't say as I do. At my age you've gotta make the most of it. Don't see no sense in savin' my dough. You sure as hell can't take it with you when you go. I'm gonna blow every last cent and have a real good time. Just see if I don't." Pug-face, obviously feeling the need to elaborate and justify his profligate lifestyle, continued. "I mean, take Al Fraser, for example. You know Al, don't ya?"

"Sure I do," replied the younger man. "I bumped into Al at the PX only yesterday."

"Well, as I was sayin', he's been runnin' round with that floozy Yumiko or Yoshiko—whatever her goddamned name is—for months now, and she just takes advantage. And Al, he's too good-natured to notice it. Sure, he wines and dines her and buys her expensive presents and all, but she just takes him for a ride. I've seen her over at Merrill's bar a heck of a lot recently, and with a different guy on her arm every time. Know what I think?" said Pug-face rhetorically. "I think he should dump that fucking bitch pronto."

The younger man nodded furiously and then raised his eyebrows as if he was expecting more.

Pug-face looked distractedly out the window and tried to remember the point of the story. Suddenly something caught his eye. "What was that?"

"What was what?"

"I could've sworn I saw a flashlight out there."

"You know what I think?" said the younger man, cramming half a Hershey bar into his cavernous mouth. "I think you're paranoid."

The sergeant moved his big pudding face closer to the window and looked long and hard into the gray night. "Yeah, I guess you're right." He turned around and then remembered what he had been leading up to before he had interrupted himself. "Anyhow, to get back to what I was sayin' . . . I prefer my relationships to be at arm's length and on my terms, with no strings attached. You see what I'm sayin'?"

The younger man nodded again.

"That way," continued Pug-face, "no-one gets hurt, and I still get to have a great time."

He fanned the notes out and put them to his bulbous nose. "Aw, I just luv the smell of dough."

The younger man roared with laughter and shook his head vigorously. He glanced at his watch and, trying not to choke, said, "H—hey, Ged, it's almost two. You're on in four hours.

Shouldn't you be thinkin' of turnin' in?"

Pug-face sighed heavily. "Yeah, I guess you're right." He rubbed his face with his bear-like hands then peeled his shirt off and flung it onto the bunk in the corner of the room. It reeked of stale sweat. His white, flaccid belly sagged like a deflated balloon over his webbing belt. He stretched, yawning as he did so, and then scratched his sides with both hands. A long puckered scar curled menacingly around from his side and across his abdomen. He got it at Iwo Jima in '44 fighting the Japs hand to hand. The younger man had seen it dozens of times before, but the brutality of it still shocked him. It had been an Arisaka bayonet, 1897 Pattern.

Ged knew that because, after he had pulled it out of his side and pummelled the Jap's brains in with the butt of his carbine, he had kept it and looked it up afterwards in an old military manual. He had even managed to identify the triple-circle mark of the Nagoya Arsenal, clearly stamped on the ricasso. He'd since sent it back to his folks in North Carolina to look after for him until he returned home.

Pug-face took another swig of coffee and wiped his mouth crudely with the back of his hand.

The younger man eyed him with interest and suppressed a smile. There were times when he thought Ged was more primate than human. He couldn't help feeling sorry for the poor bitch who would have the pleasure of his company at the weekend.

"Somethin' funny?" Pug-face caught his stare.

The younger man flushed and stammered out a reply. "Naw. I—I was just imaginin' old Al Fraser's face if he knew his sweetheart was runnin' around with a whole bunch of G.I.s as soon as his back's turned."

"Yeah. Wouldn't that be somethin'?" Pug-face smirked, slung a towel over his shoulder, picked his wash bag up, and went off in the direction of the washrooms.

Other than the guardroom at the front, the US Consulate building was quiet and basked in the moon's silvery swath of light—like one of Utagawa Sadahide's post-modern *Ukiyoe* wood block prints.

The building had stood in its present location at the foot of the Rokko Mountains for almost 150 years. It had originally been used as an outpost for the Pearl River Trading Company, one of the few foreign concessions granted by the Shogun during the 250-year period of *sakoku*—self-imposed isolation. The US government took up official residence in 1931, and, apart from an unfortunate but brief interlude between 1941 and 1945, had been there ever since. The only thing marring the building's otherwise elegantly refined colonial appearance was the newly-erected steel mesh fence, wrapped tautly around its perimeter and crowned with a tangle of glittering razor wire.

A cool breeze sifted through the bamboo.

Below, five human forms crouched in the darkness, blending into the dense backdrop of the bamboo grove. The leader checked his wristwatch, raised a gloved hand and moved silently forward with his accomplices close behind.

He knew the guards' routine. He knew their names. He knew that they were lazy, especially so since the new fence had gone up three weeks earlier. He knew they never altered the time of their patrol and that after midnight they seldom ventured out of their cosy guardroom at all. He knew all of this, and more, because his agents had told him so after six weeks of relentless and painstaking surveillance. (*And what had the guards to fear? The only entrance was at the front, and the downstairs windows were secured with steel shutters.*)

Two of the men, clothed in black from head to toe, extended a bamboo ladder against the fence. The smaller of the two then scurried up the ladder, the soles of his split-toed *tabi,* rubber boots, gripping each rung in turn. Once at the top, he pulled out a thick canvas sheet, laid it across the razor wire, unwound a knotted rope attached to the top rung and dropped it over the other side of the fence. Each man in turn climbed up to the top, slid his back across the canvas and descended the rope before dropping noiselessly into the consulate's compound. The last man up—the "brake man"—dropped from the top and used the rope to bring the ladder up and over the canvas and down on the opposite side. The ladder was then transferred to the nearside wall of the building and braced while the locksmith unrolled his tool roll and selected a small crowbar which he then applied deftly to the second floor window shutter. He effortlessly slid the sash up, hooked one leg over the sill and levered his lithe frame through the window opening. He reappeared seconds later and proffered a hand down to the leader.

Yamato

Although it was after midnight, timing was crucial. They had to be in and out within thirty minutes. Nothing could be left to chance. Reliance could not be placed on the ineptitude of the guards. They each knew their roles well. The two subordinates moved out into the hallway ahead of the others and took up positions at opposite ends of the floor—one overlooking the wide sweeping staircase while the other secreted himself in a small upstairs bathroom which had a window above the main entrance.

The leader and the remaining two men walked slowly but confidently down the hallway and stopped in front of a heavy wooden door with "Restricted Access" written in bold red letters across its front. The leader hesitated before pulling a neatly folded plan from his inside pocket. He crouched and shone a pencil torchlight onto the creased paper. He looked up at his accomplices and confirmed it was the right room with a slight nod of the head. He stuffed the plan back inside his jacket, stood up and stepped back to allow the locksmith space to apply the skills of his trade.

To his amazement the room hadn't even been locked. The leader shook his head in disgust. He found it all the more difficult to understand how Japan could have lost the war against men such as these. But then, of course, they were now Japan's allies. They had grown accustomed to their indolent lifestyle—at Japan's expense—and lost their appetite for war, losing with it the sharpness and awareness they once possessed.

Having located the safe, the locksmith went to work immediately. He produced a specially adapted stethoscope from his waist bag, inserted the two rubber ends into his ears and placed the metallic surface of the amplifier against the smooth metal surface of the safe door. He readjusted his kneeling position and then began turning the dial, first to the right and then back again, his brow furrowed in intense concentration.

The lock's tumblers clicked and dropped into place one by one and within a couple of minutes the door was open. The locksmith went to his pre-arranged position by the door while the leader and the fifth member of the group, the photographer, laid the safe's contents out on a nearby tabletop.

The leader shone his pencil light from one object to another, picking them up carefully, and replacing them on the tabletop. "This is it!" Excited at his find, he inadvertently raised his voice and then instinctively contracted his neck, narrowed his eyes and looked from side to side. He held the book firmly in both hands and scrutinized the front cover, passing his stubby fingers over the embossed eagle as if reading Braille. He opened the cover, and there in bold black lettering was confirmation of what he had come to find: *M-209 Encryption Code,* the key to deciphering the US Navy's encoded radio traffic in the Pacific basin.

Wasting no time, the photographer skipped around the table and dragged a green-shaded desk lamp across with him. He switched it on and positioned the book directly under its light, moved in closer and hunched his shoulders as he peered through the camera's tiny viewfinder. He would need to work quickly; there were twenty-five pages of narrowly spaced code. If the lighting wasn't exactly right and the camera was not held rock-steady, the photograph would blur. Just one indistinct character would potentially be enough to derail the whole mission.

A door banged noisily downstairs. The leader, now by the door, froze like a statue and darted a glance down the hallway. The lookout was crouched down behind a large glazed vase, with slender bamboo shoots growing out of its middle. The leader peered the other way toward the small upstairs toilet, where his second lookout was positioned. Nothing.

Tension filled the air. A second passed. Then two. They heard the sound of the toilet flush and then the cistern filling up again. The pug-faced sergeant, having finished his nightly ritual, trudged sleepily down the corridor back to the guardroom. He pushed against the swinging door with one great hairy shoulder, sucking in his stomach as he struggled to do up his fly. And then he was gone.

Upstairs, all was quiet. The contents of the safe had been replaced, and the door of the room pushed to, but not locked. Outside, five diminutive figures climbed back over the fence and disappeared into the gently swaying bamboo as Frank Sinatra's honeyed voice crooned softly on the breeze.

Eight

Colonel Aspin's office was on the same floor as Carnaby's but at the opposite end of the corridor and occupied a large corner location, the extra space being a privilege of rank.

Unlike most of the CIA's senior crowd, Aspin was pretty easygoing, ready to share a joke, and always seemed to be there to offer words of encouragement when needed most. He was also an eternal optimist, and his good-natured manner was highly infectious. Tall, lean, and with a distinctive shock of blonde hair, he was extremely popular with the other agents. Known for his paternalistic, caring approach to management, his door was invariably left open, and he encouraged his team members to drop by if ever anything was troubling them.

"Ralph, how are you? Seems like days since we last talked." Aspin spotted Carnaby even before he'd had a chance to knock. *He's as sharp as they come*, thought Carnaby, even on four hours sleep a night. "Come on in and pull up a chair."

Carnaby closed the door behind him and sat down. "Thanks, Mike." Aspin encouraged the use of first names. "To tell the truth, I've been a little tied up for the past few days."

Aspin gave him a knowing look and smiled mischievously. "I heard on the grapevine that you've been creating quite a commotion over this Brice affair. The MPs are mad as hornets."

Carnaby sighed heavily and massaged the back of his neck with his right hand. He looked up. "Don't tell me—Lorimer?"

"Right first time. He's really got it in for you this time. He's even lodged an official complaint."

"Goddamn. Are you serious?" he said, his voice edged with incredulity.

"Afraid so. And because it's gone through official channels, I can't ignore it," said Aspin, adding under his breath, "much as I'd like to."

"I just don't get it," said Carnaby, slapping both hands down on his thighs. "I mean, sure, we've never exactly hit it off. Ever since the Bullion Affair we've hardly had a good word to say about each other."

The Bullion Affair. Just before the Americans landed in November 1945, the Japanese central bank dumped millions of dollars' worth of gold bullion into the mud flats of Tokyo Bay to prevent it falling into the hands of the enemy. The dumping ground was discovered following the interrogation of a senior Japanese officer in one of the Imperial Army's engineering divisions. Captain Lorimer, or Lieutenant Lorimer as he was then, was in charge of security during the subsequent recovery operation. When the bullion was returned to the bank's vaults, it was found to be light to the tune of a million dollars. While there were never any official accusations, and nothing was ever proved, Carnaby, who at the time was a junior officer attached to the OSS (the predecessor to the CIA) had made some cutting remarks about the level of security at an evening function held at the American Club. Lorimer had been sitting behind him and heard every word.

"But hell, Mike, I'm not trying to play the bad guy here."

"I know, I know," said Aspin sympathetically. With exaggerated care he squared off the edges of some papers he had been working on, placed them neatly in his in-tray and stood up. He scratched his chin, walked to the window, and gazed out at Tokyo Station's grand red brick entrance. As always, it was thronged with a multitude of busy commuters, now trying desperately to fight their way through a procession of placard-toting Communist Party supporters demanding a subsistence-level wage and an increase in the rice ration. He fingered a wilting aspidistra—its broad leaves turning a papery yellow from too little water and too much exposure to direct sunlight. "Damn Commies, they get more militant by the day." He turned around again and folded his arms across his chest. "By the way, what did Brannigan have to say?"

"Brannigan?" repeated Carnaby, a thought suddenly occurring to him. "Say, you don't think he put Lorimer up to this, do you?"

"Possible," said Aspin, doubtfully, "but unlikely, I'd say. Brannigan's far too busy to get involved in anything like this. Besides, why would he? As far as he's concerned, the MPs have jurisdiction. Lorimer does things by the book, and that's the way Brannigan likes it."

"You're telling me," said Carnaby, casting his mind back to his meeting the day before. "He also likes the sound of his own voice—that's for sure. I tried to explain my thoughts on the case, but it was clear from the start he wasn't interested. Wasn't prepared to cooperate. He thinks the homicide theory is nothing but a cock-and-bull story. 'A fanciful wild goose chase,' to use his words. According to him, Lorimer's department is doing the job just fine. He basically doesn't want me actively pursuing this investigation any further."

"And you think it worth pursuing?"

"I do," said Carnaby, "although it seems I'm about the only one around here who thinks that way."

"Listen, Ralph," said Aspin, with an uncharacteristic look of concern on his face, "I can stick my neck out for you so far, but when the likes of Major General Charles Brannigan become involved, then it's time to tread very carefully. Very carefully indeed. Do you understand what I'm saying?"

Carnaby nodded.

"You've probably noticed he's very proprietorial when it comes to the people under his command. He likes to deal with them as he sees fit. The job he's doing out here isn't exactly top priority any more. But he has Douglas MacArthur's favor, and *that*," said Aspin, emphatically, "well, that counts for a lot in this neck of the woods—a heck of a lot. What he wants, to be perfectly frank, he gets. They go back a long way, and MacArthur trusts his judgment, even now."

He paused briefly to collect his thoughts. "The other thing that isn't exactly common knowledge," he continued, thrusting his hands into his pockets, "is that Lorimer once saved Brannigan's life—took a bullet for him in the Philippines."

Carnaby sighed and threw his hands up in frustration. "So what are you saying, Mike? We've gotta put the whole thing on ice for fear of pissing off the likes of Lorimer?"

Aspin sat down again and examined his well-manicured fingernails. He placed his elbows on the desk, laced his fingers together as if in prayer, and looked down his prominent nose at

Carnaby. "That's not what I'm saying, Ralph." He spoke in measured tones. "What I am saying, though, is that we have to keep a low profile on this one. We can't be seen to be devoting too many resources to it, that's all. Having said that, if you happen across something during the course of your investigation, then of course, you should let me know about it. But any information you do uncover we're gonna have to share with Lorimer."

"And let me guess," Carnaby said, feeling suddenly deflated. "If Lorimer still wants to make things difficult for us at that stage and Brannigan supports him and orders us to stand down, we'll have no choice but to comply."

"That's about the size of it. To be honest, Ralph, it beats me why you're so caught up with this case." He studied Carnaby's tired face—the deep lines on either side of his nose and the dark shadow of stubble forming under his chin. Either he hadn't had time to shave that morning or he hadn't been to bed at all the night before.

"You know, Ralph, I don't remember the last time you took any leave. You work much too hard. Don't take this the wrong way, but why don't you take off for a week or so? Don't you still have that place in Hawaii?"

Carnaby felt a sudden pang and shuddered. He leaned back in his chair and gripped the armrests tightly. He had bought the place on the cheap two years before the war broke out. It was a small but new two-bedroom apartment overlooking the sea. He and Laura spent as much time as they could there—surfing, sunbathing, making love by moonlight. In fact, they had been there a week before the Japanese bombed Pearl Harbor. It held the happiest of memories for him. He hadn't been back there since she died. Instead, he paid a monthly maintenance fee and had a small-time real estate management company periodically visit the place and keep it in good repair. He knew it would make more sense to sell. But somehow he just couldn't bear to part with it.

"To tell the truth, I wouldn't know what to do with myself any more. I've been on my own for so long now."

"You don't see Beth any more?"

Carnaby looked at the floor.

"Sorry, Ralph, I didn't mean to pry."

"No, it's okay. We see each other occasionally. But, well, you know how it is. I'm busy. She's busy."

"Yeah, sure. I understand."

Carnaby knew his boss had his best interests at heart and was only trying to be helpful. He strongly suspected that Aspin was behind Dan's frequent attempts to hook him up with the latest in a long line of available young women.

A strange quiet seemed to fill the air. Later, when Carnaby reflected on the day's events, he was reminded of stories he had heard about animals suddenly becoming silent moments before a major earthquake or other natural disaster as if they somehow knew, intuitively, that something was going to happen.

Aspin glanced at his watch and said, "Well, I gotta get going." Just then an almighty explosion rocked the room, and the two of them were hit by a shower of fragmented glass and masonry as the window blew in.

"*Jesus fucking Christ*!" shouted Aspin, launching himself under his desk.

Carnaby had somehow managed to shield his face with his upraised arms, but had been thrown sideways by the blast and was now sitting, somewhat dazed, in the middle of the floor with the contents of Aspin's in-tray raining down on him like giant snowflakes.

"You okay?" cried Aspin as he grabbed Carnaby by the arms and hoisted him to his feet.

"Yeah, I guess so. I can't hear too well, but otherwise I think I'm fine," he replied, brushing plaster dust from his clothes.

Black smoke and glowing embers billowed up past the window cavity. On the street below, a wooden handcart loaded to overflowing with wastepaper and corrugated cardboard had caught fire and was engulfed in a raging ball of flame.

It was pure chaos everywhere. People and sirens were screaming. The carnage, for what was subsequently found to be a relatively small bomb, was incredible. There were at least a dozen demonstrators lying in the road—some motionless while others who were missing limbs writhed in agony and screamed uncontrollably. A middle-aged woman dressed in winter kimono and shawl groped about blindly, one hand over her blistered eyes, the other flailing in the air in front of her while she cried out for help. "*Tasukete*! *Tasukete*!"

A couple of quick-witted MPs, who happened to have been walking alongside the Central Post Office, had dashed over, pistols drawn, and were standing over what was left of the bomber—a charred torso exposing a ghastly tangle of slippery entrails. There were sudden, percussive shouts of "Back! Back! Get back!" as the MPs realized there was a second bomb that hadn't gone off.

An Eighth Army armored car rumbled into view through the rapidly dispersing cloud of smoke and took up position on the far side of the shattered remnants of the Communist Party procession, its heavy-caliber machine gun panning backwards and forwards scanning the crowd.

"What a goddamned mess," said Carnaby, holding a handkerchief to his nose. "The second time in as many months."

"Of course," spluttered Aspin, having inadvertently inhaled a fresh gust of smoke, "this is what happens when the *responsible* press circulate rumors that the emperor is to be indicted as a war criminal. God help us if that does happen. The shit will really hit the fan then."

The bombs were already going off in Carnaby's mind as he considered that prospect.

They both stood rooted to the spot for several seconds and stared at the bizarre scene unfolding in front of them. It was surreal; everything seemed to be happening in slow motion. It was like watching a slightly-out-of-focus piece of wartime movie footage.

"Come on," said Aspin, patting Carnaby on the back and breaking the spell. He ushered him toward the door. "Bomb attack or not, you have a briefing to give downstairs, and I, more importantly, have a swimming gala to attend at the American Club."

"Swell. Sounds like fun," said Carnaby, crunching glass underfoot as he turned to leave.

"Actually, I'm dreading it. Keep this to yourself, but I'm on the panel of judges for the GI Wives in Swimsuits Beauty Parade." Aspin puckered his face as if sucking on a bitter lemon.

Having seen some of these "beauties," albeit fully clothed, Carnaby could well understand his boss's predicament.

They went down the stairs together, flattening themselves against the stairwell wall every few yards as teams of emergency repair workers and medics made their way ponderously between the floors. Aspin waved goodbye and carried on down to the first floor, and Carnaby emerged onto the landing of the fourth and went into the Ops Room. The five agents under his charge were already there, standing in line with hands in pockets, facing the windows, resembling a group of errant schoolboys urinating into a ditch.

"Nice way to finish up the day," said Carnaby, attempting to inject a little levity into the situation. He removed his jacket and loosened his tie. The room was stuffy and he was already starting to perspire. He came around the front of the desk, placed his palms on its surface and, locking his elbows, swung himself up and back into a sitting position. He smiled at the five men, who were now sitting attentively in a row in front of him. Donaldson had turned white as a sheet and looked as though he might disgorge the contents of his stomach at any moment. He was the only one of them who hadn't been in the Pacific War. He had received a draft notice as a seventeen-year-old in October 1945, but the war had ended before he was due to leave the United States.

Carnaby cleared his throat. "In view of what has just happened outside, I'll keep this meeting short and to the point. Colonel Aspin has a more pressing engagement, and can't be with us this afternoon." He suppressed the sudden urge to smile. "You may smoke if you wish to."

Ted Groves took out a crumpled pack of Old Golds, shook one out for himself, and then offered the pack to the others. "Smoke, anyone?" Groves was the group's lucky charm, not that they were particularly superstitious. He'd been hit six times in the right leg by a *Nambu* light machine gun on Tarawa in December 1944, and twice in the left leg that time while dug in on Okinawa in May 1945. Then, six months later, he had taken a pistol shot in the left forearm while clearing houses in southern Kyushu just before Japan surrendered. And last, but by no means least, six months ago he had been stabbed twice in the stomach by a yakuza mobster while trying to mediate a truce between two rival gangs, both of whom were hell-bent on occupying the same territory in Nihonbashi, the heart of the black market district of central Tokyo. He had more holes in him than the proverbial pincushion.

"Okay, everyone," continued Carnaby, "listen up. I only have two items I want to mention this afternoon, and then I'll let you go and get cleaned up."

He peered down at his clipboard and flipped the cover sheet over. "First off, I'd like an update from you on the Repatriation

Program. Ted, is there anything new we should know about?"

The Repatriation Program. In the final days of the Pacific War the Soviet Union captured nearly three million Japanese soldiers. Most were transported to Stalin's labor camps, known as *lagers*, many of which were located deep inside Siberia. All the detainees were subjected to a systematic regimen of Marxist-Leninist indoctrination for the duration of their captivity. It was estimated that there were still some one hundred thousand detainees awaiting repatriation at the end of December 1952.

One particularly successful indoctrination strategy employed by their Russian captors involved the publication of a Japanese language newspaper called the *Nippon Shimbun.* Having been deprived of all reading material for the first year of captivity, many of the former Japanese soldiers were only too eager to 'volunteer' to assist as members of the editorial staff on the publication of the newspaper. Under the supervision of Russian officers fluent in Japanese, volunteers used former Kwantung Army printing presses brought back from Manchuria after the Japanese surrender. The articles were, without exception, scathing attacks on US Occupation policy in Japan and even accused the Americans of murdering radical Japanese critics who were opposed to what they were doing.

Candidates for repatriation were selected on the basis of how well they had "converted" to communism. Repatriation itself was conducted over a period of about a month from the time the detainees left the labor camp until they boarded the ship for Japan. The Ministry of Internal Affairs was known to have set up an intermediate screening camp at Blagoveshchensk for the specific purpose of rooting out those candidates who had been poorly indoctrinated. A scandal had come to light late in 1952 when accusations were made in the Diet that the General Secretary of the Japan Communist Party, Kyuichi Tokuda, had written to the Soviet authorities and instructed them not to repatriate certain reactionary POWs but rather only those whom the authorities were sure had become true communists.

In response to this worsening state of affairs, SCAP had ordered the strengthening of debriefing operations at the various screening centers in Japan, principally at the largest center at Maizuru on the northern seaboard of Honshu. Notwithstanding these efforts, it was clear that large numbers of repatriates (or *aktivs* as they were known in Russia) had subsequently joined the Japan Communist Party and were actively engaged in spying on behalf of the Soviet Union. The activities of the *aktivs* however did not stop there. Of more particular concern to the CIA in recent months was the increasing involvement of these *aktivs* in illicit money-raising operations. The CIA had achieved a major breakthrough at the beginning of the year when, acting on a tip given to them by one of their informers, they had exposed a chain of unlicensed brothels in western Honshu and a number of districts in Tokyo. It transpired that all the hotels were managed by former repatriated officers of the Imperial Army. The individuals concerned were arrested and their bank accounts frozen, thus denying the Russians twenty million dollars in funds which would otherwise have been used to oil the machinery of the Soviet anti-capitalist propaganda machine.

"There's not a whole lot to report on the hotel front, Ralph," said Groves, looking up. "It seems like we scared them real good. Everyone's run for cover."

"That figures," said Carnaby, lighting a cigarette and tossing the pack back to Groves. "Let's keep an eye on it and see what develops. Okay. Anything else?"

"Yeah," replied Groves blowing out smoke. "Our man in Shinjuku, Yasuhiko Aramaki, confirmed this morning that the Ikebukuro branch of the JCP will be taking a leading part in the rice riots later this month."

"Do we know when exactly it'll be?"

"Afraid not. It seems as though they're waiting for another local branch to confirm its participation before they settle on a date."

"Let me know as soon as you hear anything more on that, Ted. We're running out of time to organize a proper 'reception.' That it?"

"I guess so. Oh," said Groves, slapping himself on the forehead, "I almost forgot. According to Bob Finn over in Legal, a hooker from one of the brothels we closed a couple of months back is planning on suing us. She claims we took away her livelihood and . . ."

Donaldson jerked suddenly and sprayed a mouthful of black coffee over his neatly pressed trousers as he lost control and guffawed, "She must be friggin' crazy!"

"I don't doubt it," quipped Groves, looking at the younger man as one might regard an irritating child. "I wasn't suggesting we ought to be concerned, simply that you might like to be forewarned so as not to be caught off guard when the reporters get wind of it and start asking awkward questions, as they surely will do."

"Boy, she must be really dumb." Donaldson still didn't get it.

Groves continued, a flicker of impatience registering on his face. "She's hired some hotshot showcase trial lawyer from Osaka. Finn says he trained at a top-notch litigation firm in New York before the war. He's known for representing the underdog in high-profile cases. Finn reckons he's been on some kind of personal crusade ever since the first batch of war criminals was hanged last year. He reckons that he was behind the string of appeals that prevented their execution back in '48."

"Well," said Carnaby thoughtfully, "I don't know how they plan on arguing against a SCAP directive." He had been a lawyer before the war—a general practitioner in a small provincial office in Fresno. All this was a far cry from the real estate and wills practice he had at one time been so familiar with.

"I asked Finn the very same thing," said Groves. "He said his guess was that this lawyer might fight her case on the grounds that it's unconstitutional for SCAP to ban private brothels while the Japanese government openly sanctions 'rest and recuperation salons.'"

"Good grief. Okay, Ted, I guess we'll know soon enough. Thanks for the heads-up. Since it was my name that made the newspapers last time, I daresay I'll be fielding the calls from the press corps." He chuckled to himself and added, "You know, I can't imagine this lady will find too many character witnesses out there."

The laughter gradually subsided, and Carnaby gripped the edge of the desk and leaned forward slightly.

"As I said at the start, I don't want to keep you guys too long. Before you go, however, I just want to talk about protocol with regard to the Brice investigation."

Dan Morita looked up, suddenly paying more attention.

"It appears there have been some complaints from the MPs that we are poking our noses in where they're not wanted. Well," he said, clearing his throat and squinting up at the yellow lighting, "as I always say, that's the thing that we do best."

A peal of laughter echoed through the room. He smiled and nodded appreciatively, and then motioned with his hands for quiet. "Having said that, this time there are other, more influential, parties who agree with them. To come to the point, we are no longer continuing the Brice investigation on an official footing."

Murmurs of disapproval broke from the agents.

"However," he fixed each of them with his steely gaze, "and this is strictly off the record, by the way. If you do find anything, don't fill out an Ops report. Or if you do, don't file it. Just come see me and give me an oral account of whatever it is you've discovered."

The agents looked at each other with raised eyebrows.

"I know what you're all thinking, and I do appreciate it's unorthodox. But believe me, this will save us a lot of heartache in the long run." Carnaby could hardly believe what he was saying. He could just picture Aspin's face if he got wind of it. "Alright everybody, that's about it for today. Thanks for showing up, and I'll see you all bright and early in the morning."

They all filed out, except for Dan Morita, who stayed behind.

"Is there something you want to talk about, Dan?"

"No, not really, Ralph. I'm just concerned about you. That's all. You look beat lately."

"Funny," said Carnaby, "that's what Aspin said too." He twisted and broke his cigarette butt in a cheap tin ashtray bearing the inscription "Made in Occupation Japan—Enjoy Life!" He brushed some shreds of tobacco from his trousers and looked up. "To be honest, I feel dead beat. Still, what can you do?"

"Listen, Ralph. There's this great hot spring resort over at Gotemba, not far from Atsugi Air Base. I was just thinking, we could take a jeep and a case of beers and have ourselves a real relaxing weekend."

Carnaby hadn't the heart to stop him, even though he knew what was coming.

"As a matter of fact," continued Morita, right on cue, "I know a couple of girls working over in Education. I'm sure they'd love to come along."

Carnaby was already smiling and shaking his head. "Dan, I appreciate your concern, but I'm just going to have a quiet weekend at home, try and catch up on my sleep. Old guys like me need to do that from time to time."

"Okay, Ralph," laughed Morita. "Maybe some other time."

"Yeah, sure. Let's do that. Only, maybe leave out the girls."

This time they both laughed.

"Well, I guess I'd better go see what state my office is in. If it's anything like Aspin's, it'll take an hour or two to clean up. I'll see you in the morning."

"No, you won't," he said with a broad grin. "Have you forgotten? I'm doing the raid on that gambling joint in Funabashi with Kobayashi and Wheeler."

"Oh yeah, I had forgotten. Say, isn't that Brice's neighborhood?"

"Yeah, now that you mention it, that's right. You still got him on your mind?"

"Looks like it. I can't seem to shake it. Anyway, if I don't see you tomorrow, then have a good weekend. Let's catch up on Monday."

"Let's do that, Ralph. And take it easy."

The door closed behind him with a metallic snick. There was a faint pattering, as if a distant audience was applauding. It had begun to rain. He started to pull on his jacket when he noticed the corner of a letter he had received that morning sticking out of the inside pocket. He tugged it out and examined the white envelope. His name and address were printed on the front and it was postmarked May 1—one week ago to the day. He broke the seal, slid the letter out and opened it on his lap.

The message was typewritten, and short, very short: "If you close any more clubs in Tokyo—you die."

Nine

It had rained all night, and it was still raining now. The damp cold was irresistible. Dan Morita sat huddled in the passenger seat of the garbage truck, hands pressed together and tucked between his thighs for warmth. The cab heater rattled and coughed but produced no heat. He was dressed in typical laborers' clothing—thick, quilted over-jacket concealing his Browning service pistol, blue canvas trousers tucked into split-toed rubber boots, and a cotton headband knotted untidily at the back. The finishing touch—his own idea and one he was particularly pleased with—was a partially smoked, rolled cigarette, carefully placed behind his right ear.

A Japanese policeman, similarly attired, occupied the driver's seat, his head lolling in an ungainly manner as he dozed—a thin silvery thread of saliva trailing from his moist bottom lip.

Morita screwed his face up and peered out at the rainy sky, just beginning to lighten on the horizon. *What* had *he done to deserve this*? he thought, his eyes following the wipers back and forth across the windscreen. He tensed his muscles and shivered involuntarily. Yawning, he checked his wristwatch—05:25—five minutes to go.

Around the corner, a block away, a Toyota SB light truck, bearing the logo "Kuroda & Co., Shop Outfitters and Decorators" was parked by a loading bay, lights doused, engine purring softly. It was an ordinary truck of the kind that could be seen at any time of day and on any highway in Tokyo. Its cargo, however, was far from ordinary: six well-armed policemen clad from head to toe in riot gear, two large steel battering rams, a selection of freshly greased bolt cutters, and one particularly well-built German shepherd dog—for the moment muzzled and quiet.

Two hundred yards further down the road, agents Kobayashi and Wheeler, both forensic accountants by training, sat in the relative comfort of a dark blue Toyota sedan, pouring each other hot coffee from a flask and working their way through a pack of Chesterfield cigarettes.

Morita glanced cautiously out the window into the distance and surveyed the object of their early morning excursion. The shop, although large, was shabby and nondescript and seemed to be held in place by the two rather more substantial buildings on either side. A signboard in dire need of repainting hung across the window: "Tanaka & Co., Ltd. Tailors: Quality Suits Since 1912." As expected at this unearthly hour, the shutters were still closed and padlocked. The lights were off, and other than a mangy black cat patrolling the sidewalk in front of the shop's entrance, there was no sign of life.

The shop was, in fact, a tailor's. But it was also a front for a fairly sizable gambling and loan shark operation run by the Maruyama-gumi yakuza organization. It had been under surveillance for the last two months, and it was suspected that a substantial portion of its illicit profits were spirited away and used to finance the activities of one of the more violent extreme right-wing groups in Tokyo, the Imperial Blood Oath Society.

Morita looked at his watch again. One minute left. He shot a sidelong glance at his sleeping partner. "Hey, Kimura, wake up. This isn't a damned picnic, you know!" He accompanied his admonishment with a swift and stinging slap to the thigh.

Kimura sat bolt upright and wiped his dripping mouth with the back of his hand. "S—sorry, boss."

"Get ready. Thirty seconds and we go," said Morita, reaching for his two-way walkie-talkie. He switched it on, cupping his free hand around the mouthpiece. "Coronet 1 to Coronet 2, come in, over."

A crackling sound came over the airwaves followed by an acknowledgment. "Coronet 2, receiving your signal strength 5, over."

"Coronet 1 to Coronet 2, standby, thirty seconds to go." He held his watch up to his face and silently counted down the seconds, sweat trickling in rivulets down his back. Ten seconds, nine—he could feel the adrenaline start to surge—seven seconds, six, five—and then suddenly he saw something. "Fuck!" he hissed, fumbling for the transmitter switch. "Stop! I repeat, stop!" He slid down in his seat, grabbing a handful of Kimura's jacket sleeve and dragging him down too. He flipped the switch again and whispered, "Wait for my signal, out."

In the distance a dark shape shuffled unsteadily along the sidewalk in the direction of the shop. Morita couldn't make it out clearly because of the distorting effect of the rain. "Kill the wipers," he rasped.

Kimura's hand shot out, too quickly, and inadvertently caught the horn, sending a shrill blast through the early morning air.

"Shit! What the hell are you doing?" Morita held his breath, biting his lip so hard he could taste blood. Kimura was a big guy—two hundred and thirty pounds and five feet eleven. He had been the heavyweight judo champion of Shibuya Ward three years running, and he was a real asset in a brawl. But there were times—and this was certainly one of them—when Morita thought he was lacking in the common-sense department.

The figure stopped about a hundred yards away, its head, cowled in some filthy material, bobbing backwards and forwards with short jerking movements, like a rodent sniffing the air for signs of danger.

Several tense moments passed and the bundle of rags moved off again, carrying what looked like a sake bottle in its left hand. It slowed as it reached the front of the tailor shop, and turned slowly to face the door. There was a small step up onto the porch. The vagrant hesitated, looked to his left and right, and stepped up out of the rain. Morita's hand went unconsciously to the grip of his pistol. The vagrant transferred his weight from one foot to the other and then back again as he tried to undo his fly. Swaying like a somnolent drunk, he slowly bent down and placed the sake bottle on the ground, straightened up, and continued his unfinished business.

After what seemed like an interminable length of time, he picked the bottle up and stepped backwards, staggering suddenly as he misjudged the step. He paused to get his bearings, took a swig from the bottle and then, much to Morita's horror, raised it high above his head and dashed it against the wall of the adjoining store.

Morita cringed and closed his eyes, sinking lower into his seat. What with the garbage truck horn and the sound of the breaking glass, if there was anyone in the tailor shop, it would have to be an absolute miracle for them not to have heard anything.

Morita slowly took his hand away from his eyes and, craning his neck, looked at his surroundings. There was no sign of the vagrant and, more importantly, no sign of any movement in the shop. The rain had probably drowned out the noise. He heaved a deep sigh of relief and thanked his lucky stars for the inclement weather.

"Okay," he said, as much to himself as anybody, "let's try again." He plucked the radio out of its webbing cradle and re-established contact with the truck. Watches were synchronized, and the countdown began again, this time for real—"Five, four, three, two, one: Go! Go!"

Morita checked the rearview mirror. Seconds later the truck came into view, careering round the corner, its front fender dipping low as it slowed to take the curve. Kimura punched the gear stick forward and released the clutch. The garbage truck lurched forward, picked up speed and tucked in behind the truck as it sped past them and down the deserted strip of wet road. The Toyota's taillights glowed as it aquaplaned to a gliding halt outside the tailor's shop. The tailgate dropped, and its formidable cargo spilled out onto the sidewalk.

By the time Kimura had pulled up, the padlock had been ripped off and discarded, and two burly policemen were already busy smashing their way through the wooden door. The force was so great they ripped the whole doorframe out.

Morita ran in after the riot team, sliding back the action of his pistol. Inside, all hell had broken loose. A tall, iron brazier had been upended, spilling its contents across the polished wooden floor of the central corridor. Shards of glowing charcoal were scattered dangerously close to a *fusuma* sliding paper door. From upstairs, Morita could hear a crashing sound, followed by confused shouts and then the unmistakable almost comforting voice of one of the policemen barking out commands. "Stop! Or I'll shoot! Hands on your head!"

Somewhere from the back of the store came the sound of people running frantically and then more confused shouting as they realized the rear entrance—their only possible means of escape—had been sealed from the outside. They turned back, running headlong into four waiting policemen and Hachiko, the German shepherd. More confusion and shouting ensued, this time punctuated by a great deal of excited growling and barking, ending in a bloodcurdling yell as Hachiko's teeth found their mark.

Morita moved slowly and cautiously along the corridor, his pistol held out in front of him, index finger poised over the trigger. He stopped just short of the brazier, now making a curious low hissing sound as if groaning under its own weight, and carefully slid open one of the paper doors. Behind was a traditional Japanese room of sixteen tatami mats, still smelling strongly of cheap watered-down whiskey from the previous night's entertainment. In the corner was a small *tokonoma* decorative alcove housing a calligraphy scroll with the Chinese characters for 'filial piety' in black ink and in front of it a shallow blue porcelain bowl containing seven slender red willow branches, artfully arranged so as to look, when viewed from the side, like a small tree with a single trunk.

Down the center of the room, in a straight line, was a long, narrow strip of white linen. On top of the linen, and spaced out at more or less equal intervals, were three mah-jongg boards, each covered with intricately carved ivory counters. The gambling party had evidently gone on late into the night, and the areas surrounding the boards were still cluttered and untidy with guttered candles, ashtrays filled to overflowing with cigarette butts, and half-empty glasses.

Morita stepped back into the corridor and lowered his gun arm as he closed the door. He had just started to move off again when suddenly a revolver appeared through a gap in the paper door opposite. The gun loosed off a wild shot that splintered the lintel behind his head and sent him sprawling for cover on his stomach. A second bullet ricocheted off the rim of the brazier and whistled past his ear with a high-pitched whine. He had fallen awkwardly, landing on top of his pistol. He couldn't free his arm without exposing his back to the shooter. He somehow managed to squirm toward the brazier, being careful not to actually touch it. He risked a look over the top and was just about to pull his gun free when the shooter was propelled bodily through the partly opened *fusuma*, a look of abject terror on his face. Kimura had bulldozed the gangster from behind and come crashing through the flimsy paper door. In one fluid series of moves, he grabbed his winded quarry by the crotch, lifted him into the air as if handling a sack of feathers, turned him upside down, and slammed him headfirst like a pile driver into the hardwood floor. There was a satisfying thud accompanied by a short groan. The gangster lay motionless, a steady stream of dark red viscous liquid oozing out of his crushed nose. Kimura kicked the gun away from the body, sending it skittering across the glassy surface of the corridor.

"Jesus, Kimura," said Morita, staring at the widening pool of blood, "I think you've killed him!"

Kimura beamed with delight, clearly satisfied with his own handiwork. "Don't mention it, Boss." He reached down and grabbed a hank of loincloth, and hauled the body back through the smashed doorframe.

Morita stood up and dusted himself off, shaking his head. He never could understand Kimura. Still, he thought to himself, with a faint smirk, he shouldn't be too hard on the big guy. It wasn't the first time, and surely wouldn't be the last, that he'd got him out of a sticky situation.

Meanwhile, things had quieted down at the back of the shop. A procession of five handcuffed gangsters made their way along the gloomy corridor, escorted by four policemen. Hachiko brought up the rear, skipping forward excitedly, nuzzling bare legs, and then dropping back again—as if herding stray sheep toward the narrow gate of a moorland pen. He seemed to have formed a particular attachment to the last of the captives, who was limping badly and trying unsuccessfully to stem the flow of blood from a deep wound in his left buttock with the loose end of his stained loincloth.

Morita looked up, smiling cynically as he holstered his unused pistol. "My, my. What *do* we have here? The most suspicious bunch of tailors I've ever seen, that's for sure." He laughed hoarsely and slapped the lead policeman on the shoulder. "Good work, Takahashi. Keep them in the large tatami room and watch them closely." He scrutinized the line of wiry, tattooed bodies as they filed into the room, adding, almost as an afterthought, "Oh, and put a couple of your men to work fixing up the shop front. And remember: nobody in or out without my say-so."

He turned around to see the remaining two police officers frog-marching a small, bespectacled old man down the stairs. He was all of five feet nothing in his bare feet, which were bicycling furiously in midair as he protested his rough handling. "This is an absolute outrage! I demand you call my lawyer! I'll sue you for harassment and bodily harm!"

"This is Mr. Tanaka," said one of the policemen, dumping him unceremoniously on the floor. "We found him hiding in a closet upstairs, waving this thing in our faces." The officer produced a short, razor-sharp dagger known as a *tanto.* In one glance, Morita's expert eye took in the detail. The blade, approximately twelve inches in length, had a slight curvature—but not too much—designed for thrusting rather than cutting, edged with a beautiful but simple temper mark of undulating clouds. Devoid of unnecessary embellishment, it was undoubtedly the work of Sukesada Osafune, a master swordsmith working in Seki, present-day Gifu Prefecture, in the early Muromachi Period, about five hundred years ago. *Perfect,* he thought, with a contented smile.

"So," he said, reluctantly transferring his eyes from the blade to Tanaka's wrinkled face, "caught in possession of *and* attempting to use an edged weapon as defined under Cabinet Order 334 of 1950. Are you quite sure you still want to sue us, Mr. Tanaka?"

"It was self-defense," spat Tanaka, his claw-like yellow fingers working frantically to refasten the frayed cotton sash around his quilted winter kimono. "They threatened me with firearms," he added, scowling up at the policemen with a supercilious look.

Morita put his hand in his pocket and fished out a folded sheet of paper. He shook it open and thrust it toward the old man's face. "Ever seen one of these before? It's a warrant to enter premises forcibly. We are authorized to carry and use weapons as necessary." He waved the sheet of paper in the air. "I can get a copy for you if you like."

Tanaka shrugged sulkily and continued his ranting and raving.

"Okay, fellas, would you mind showing Mr Tanaka through to the office? I have a few questions I'd liked to ask him," he said, adding under his breath, "once he's calmed down, that is."

There was a noise from the store entrance behind, and Morita turned to see the two accountants stepping gingerly over the threshold, hoisting their raincoats up and trying to avoid skating on the pieces of charcoal still lying on the floor.

"Come on in, boys. I'm afraid you've missed all the action." He couldn't help teasing the two middle-aged pencil-pushers.

"That's very kind of you," replied Wheeler in perfect Japanese.

Joe Wheeler was an anomaly. He was one of the very few foreigners, known as gaijin, or outsiders, who felt completely at home in Japan. Born to missionary parents just after the turn of the century, he was raised and educated in Japan. In those days, with his parents away from home so much spreading the Gospel, he spoke more Japanese than he did English. With his father's encouragement, he studied economics at Tokyo Imperial University and went on to qualify as the only non-Japanese licensed chartered accountant in Japan. He returned to America following the outbreak of war in November 1941, where his language skills were put to good use in cracking high-level encoded communiqués originated by the Japanese high command to their various overseas attachés. Like so many of his contemporaries, when the war ended, he found he was unable to settle down in America and decided instead to return to Japan and take up his current assignment with SCAP.

They went through into the office, where Tanaka had already been securely handcuffed to a wooden desk chair. He was looking a little more subdued now and sat slumped in the chair with a sullen expression.

Morita asked one of the police officers to fix them some coffee, turned to the large desk in the corner, and showed the accountants what they had found.

Kobayashi picked up one of the four large accounting ledgers and leafed through the first few pages. "Doesn't look too bad," he said optimistically.

"Wait a minute," said Morita. "We also found this." He bent over and, grunting with the effort, dragged a large wooden box from under the desk. Loose-leaf accounting entry sheets spilled out of the box onto the floor. He stood up, massaging his lower back with the heel of his right hand. "There's also another, smaller box behind that one."

"Ah," said Kobayashi, looking crestfallen, "in that case, we could be in for a long day."

"Well, we'd better get started," said Wheeler, pulling up a chair and looking at his watch. "I'd like to get out of here before nightfall."

"Maybe the loose-leaf stuff is what they don't want the auditors to see. You know—the double-entry accounts that show their gambling revenues," said Morita, raising his eyebrows and trying to be helpful.

"Yeah, maybe," muttered Wheeler, thrusting his hand into the larger of the two boxes and pulling out a fistful of yellowing parchment-like paper, "although something tells me otherwise. This looks like it relates to the tailoring business." He paused, and then started to smile. "Would you believe it?" he said, his smile getting broader by the second. "This particular entry is dated 1927!"

He was laughing openly now, and Kobayashi had begun to join in. "These accounts . . . are . . . twenty six . . . frigging years old!" They were both sitting there wheezing and gasping for breath.

"I'm glad you guys think it's funny," said Morita, adding sardonically. "I didn't know accountants had a sense of humor."

"Oh," said Wheeler, still struggling to control himself, "this is priceless, absolutely priceless."

Morita looked over his shoulder as Takahashi brought the coffee in and noticed Tanaka trying to wipe tears from his eyes with the shoulder of his kimono.

"You think it's amusing, do you, Mr. Tanaka?"

Tanaka blinked a couple of times, trying to focus through wet eyes, all the while smiling at Morita and shaking his head.

"What kind of a goddamned filing system is this anyhow?"

Tanaka had stopped smiling now. He gave Morita an icy stare, and said, "My filing system is perfectly adequate *and*, I might add, has been so for the past forty years. The ledgers contain the current accounts as well as those for the last three years."

"And the box of crap in the corner?" said Morita, starting to lose patience and waving his arm in the direction of the accountants.

Tanaka breathed heavily. "As your colleagues have discovered already, those boxes contain out-of-date records going back, I shouldn't wonder, to the incorporation of the company in 1912. I had started to sort through them yesterday."

"Listen, Mr. Tanaka," said Morita, placing his hands on his hips, "I'm starting to get a little tired of this. You know why we're here, don't you? Why don't you save us all a lot of trouble and tell us where the *other* accounts are?"

"The *other* accounts?" repeated Tanaka, his eyes narrowing.

"Do I have to spell it out for you? I'm referring to the accounts for the gambling and loan shark operation run by your yakuza friends."

"I don't know what you're talking about."

"I'm talking, Mr. Tanaka, about the bunch of scumbags we've got tied up across the hallway over there." He tried to keep his voice even.

Their eyes met briefly; then Tanaka looked at the floor. He spoke slowly and deliberately. "I lease part of this building. The identity of the landlord is neither within my control nor any of my business. I pay my rent on time and, in return, the landlord allows me to have quiet enjoyment of the premises for the purposes of carrying out my business."

There was a sudden fleshy, slapping sound as Morita put his hands together and clapped. He stared at Tanaka, his expression devoid of any emotion. "That was a flawless performance. You really should be on stage, you know that?" He stepped sideways slightly, without moving his eyes, and lifted a chair with his right hand. He positioned it in front of Tanaka, back to front, and straddled it, supporting his chin on the curve of the backrest.

"You make a lousy liar," he said, a half-smile appearing on his face. "I found out from publicly available records that the ownership of this property changed hands just twelve months ago. Your new landlord, Kitahama Realty Corporation, is owned one hundred percent by Maruyama Trading Company. Their president and chairman is Kenji Maruyama. Does that name sound familiar to you?"

The older man coughed explosively. There was a short, uneasy silence as he fumbled for words.

"Here," said Morita, matter-of-factly, "let me refresh your memory." He stood up, took out a large white envelope from his jacket pocket, and moved around from the chair. He broke the seal, extracted two black and white photographs, and dropped them neatly onto Tanaka's lap. The photographs, both taken from a discreet distance, showed a well-dressed man, in his late fifties going into the entrance of the tailor's shop. He was powerfully built, although the muscle was beginning to run to middle-aged fat. His hair was well-groomed, steely gray, and neatly parted on the left side. He had an intelligent almost gentle face—surprising for one suspected of having ordered the deaths of more than two hundred rival gang members over the last five years.

"Well? I guess you're going to tell me you've never seen him before, aren't you?"

"No," said Tanaka, coughing again, "this gentleman bought a suit from me a month ago. But his name is Suzuki, not Maruyama."

Morita laughed hoarsely. "And I suppose you can recall the names of all your customers, can you?"

Tanaka closed his eyes momentarily and let out a long sigh. "I don't do off-the-peg suits. This is a small shop and everything is made to order."

Morita was irritated now and began pacing the room. He stopped suddenly, and squatted down in front of the chair. "Tell me, Mr. Tanaka, what do you get for playing your part so well? A kickback on rent payments every month? I want to know where those accounts books are."

"I told you, I *don't* know. Why don't you ask the *scumbags* next door?"

"Don't get cute with me, you piece of shit!" screamed Morita. It was then that he lost control. Lurching forward, he grabbed hold of Tanaka's face, his well-muscled fencer's hand applying immense pressure, twisting and squeezing, like the jaws of a vice. He pressed his face up close, and snarled, "How would you like to look like this permanently?"

Tanaka's eyes were bulging out of their sockets and darting nervously from side to side. He was having difficulty breathing and, with his hands still fastened to the arms of the chair, he was beginning to panic.

Morita suddenly looked toward the door and shouted, "Takahashi!"

The sound of running footsteps was heard, and then the door slid open. "Yes, sir?"

He let go and stood up. Tanaka gasped, like a diver breaking the surface for air. His shoulders heaved as he tried frantically to force oxygen into his laboring lungs. Morita looked back at Tanaka. "I will ask you one last time. Where are the accounts books?"

Tanaka was slumped forward, his breathing still erratic. In between short, panting snatches of breath, he whispered, "I . . . don't . . . know."

"Takahashi. Undo his cuffs. I want you to take Mr. Tanaka down to the docks." The burly policeman knelt down and removed the handcuffs. "Oh," added Morita, "and you'll need something heavy." He pointed through the open door at the brazier. "That should do."

Tanaka, who had turned very pale, spluttered, "What are you doing? You can't do this! You can't—"

Morita ignored him and carried on giving instructions. "Take the radio with you and call me as soon as you've done it."

Tanaka started screaming hysterically as the policeman yanked him to his feet and out of the room. "I can't tell you, I can't—they'll kill me!"

A couple of police officers lifted the brazier, carried it outside and hefted it into the back of the truck. The engine kicked into life, and they sped off on their short journey.

Wheeler looked up. "You know, Dan, you scare the hell out of me sometimes."

Morita chuckled. "You find anything yet?"

"Nope. It's all pretty routine so far."

"Say, Dan," said Kobayashi, turning away from the desk, "why *don't* you question those guys next door? Can't see no harm in doing that."

Morita sat down on the chair vacated by Tanaka. "Oh, we will, Kobayashi. All in good time. The guy that Kimura comatosed," he said, jerking his thumb over his shoulder in the direction of the corridor, "turns out he's the senior guy. Takahashi says he's still out cold. As for the others—I doubt they'll know anything."

A few minutes later, the truck arrived at the docks. It pulled into a deserted parking bay, came around in a half-circle and then backed up to the seawall. The tailgate was kicked down with a crash. Two of the policemen fastened a pair of handcuffs to Tanaka's ankle. Then they took a length of rusty chain and wrapped the other end several times around the brazier, which was now balanced precariously on top of the wall. It was high tide. A flock of gulls arced and wheeled in the air above.

Takahashi dragged Tanaka to the edge of the truck. He looked out and shouted, "Hey, Imai. Can you see the depth marker?"

"Yes, sir. It says eighteen feet."

Takahashi smiled. "Time to get wet."

Tanaka screamed and clutched madly at Takahashi's arm with his bony hands. "Stop! Stop! I'll tell you."

Takahashi placed his boot against the side of the brazier. Tanaka screamed again, "No! They're behind the *kamidana*!"

"Thank you," said Takahashi politely, suddenly extending his right leg.

"No!" Tanaka let out an ear-piercing cry as he watched the chain race over the edge, clouds of red rust spraying into the air. The brazier plunged into the sea below with an almighty splash, dragging the chain behind it. Only then did he realize he was still sitting in the back of the truck, the handcuffs hanging impotently from his ankle.

Takahashi and his officers fell about laughing.

"You bastards!" shouted Tanaka. "You *fucking, fucking* bastards!"

Takahashi walked around to the cab and put a call in to Morita. "Behind the *kamidana,* sir."

Kamidana—the word for the small, wall-mounted Shinto shrine, commonly found in Japanese homes, the symbolic link between modern-day man and the nation's atavistic religious beliefs.

"*Kamidana,*" Morita mouthed the word to himself, savoring its sound in his mouth. "I know!" He jumped to his feet and ran out of the room and into the tatami room opposite. He knew he'd seen it. Along the wall from the decorative alcove, about six feet up, was a simple shrine constructed of pine. It had seated effigies of the emperor and empress in ceremonial costume and some ceramic jars containing rice wine and *sasaki* leaves. He placed a hand on either side and pulled. Nothing. He tried pushing up, and the whole thing slid off the wall. It was lighter than he thought, and he lowered it easily to the floor. Behind was a cupboard with a simple latch. He lifted it and threw open the double doors. "Gotcha!"

Four ledgers, just like the others, were stacked on the middle shelf, one on top of the other. He lifted them down and carried them back into the office. "Say, fellas. I've got a little something for you."

The afternoon dragged. Tiredness pressed down on his shoulders like a ton weight. All he wanted to do was sleep. Meanwhile, the accountants painstakingly worked their way through the columns for loans: borrower's name, address, date of loan and amount loaned, interest rate, repayment schedule, and further action taken. They were looking for any of the people they knew were connected with the Imperial Blood Oath Society.

Morita went out for a bowl of noodles, and came back thirty minutes later. The day stretched ahead of him. He whiled away the time in looking around the shop, questioning the gangsters which, as he thought, proved to be a waste of time, and exchanging gossip with the police officers.

Around 16:00 he thought he'd better show some interest and check on the accountants' progress. He made his way back down the corridor to the office. Wheeler was standing in the doorway, looking like he'd seen a ghost.

"You are just going to love this," he said slowly, emphasizing each word. He led Morita by the sleeve over to the desk and slapped his hand down on the open ledger. "Take a look at the third entry from the bottom."

Morita dropped his head forward.

"No! Wait," said Wheeler, grinning like an excited schoolboy playing a game. He covered the name and address column with his big freckly hand. Morita squinted and read the other columns: December 26, 1952; 3.6 million yen; 10% compound annual interest; twenty four monthly repayments of 150,000 yen plus interest; repayments one month in arrears (February 2, 1953).

Wheeler smirked and slowly removed his hand. Morita stared for a long time, disbelieving. "Well, I'll be damned."

The name was written in *katakana,* the phonetic alphabet used to render foreign words and names into Japanese: habii buraisu. *Harvey Brice.*

Ten

Carnaby took the coast road south out of Tokyo. It was pretty much deserted, save for the distant headlamps of a car on the horizon, the beams playing like searchlights across the black sky.

He stared blankly through the windscreen, all the while his mind working to figure out who this morning's caller was and who, presumably, would be waiting for him at the fisheries building this evening.

The caller had seemed harmless enough, a Japanese woman with reasonable English and a bizarre smattering of American slang. She said she had information about who was sending him death-threat letters. She was scared and didn't trust the police, which is why she wanted to meet somewhere out of town. When he asked her how she knew to contact him, she had answered that she preferred not to say on the phone.

He was exhausted and couldn't think straight. Other than the fact that his name had appeared in the newspapers in connection with the club closures and SCAP's general crackdown on gangland activities, he couldn't imagine why he was being singled out like this. He couldn't help feeling he was walking straight into a trap. He hadn't even arranged proper back-up. He'd simply scrawled a note on a pad on Dan Morita's desk saying where he was headed and to send in the heavy mob if he didn't show up by 22:00. Christ, he didn't even know if Dan would be returning to the office tonight, or if he did whether the note gave sufficient details as to his whereabouts.

He suddenly realized he hadn't driven along the coast road since that fateful night two months ago when Brice's body had been discovered. His mind drifted back to the case.

It just didn't add up. What possible motive would anyone have for bumping Brice off? By all accounts he was a mild-mannered introvert with an impeccable record. He simply wasn't the type to get involved in anything that wasn't completely on the level. He was the archetypal clean-cut, honest, all-American hero. Everyone he'd spoken to who knew him was of the same opinion.

The more Carnaby thought about it, the more he felt it had to be connected with the work he was doing before his move to the research project in November of the previous year. Otherwise why would he have bothered moving so close to being discharged?

He looked at his eyes in the rearview mirror. They were dark, like bottomless wells. For some reason he couldn't quite put his finger on the Brice case had awakened something inside him, something he hadn't felt in a good many years—that sense of adventure and purpose that he used to feel starting out on a new case as a rookie agent all those years ago. There was some point to what he was doing, to his very existence in Japan. He was tired of spending his days busting black marketeers and conducting endless security checks on a bunch of old-fart communist sympathizers, whose days were numbered anyway.

And there was something else. Something he wouldn't admit to Dan, or to anyone else for that matter. He felt a moral obligation to Emma Forbes. It meant something extra to him, doing what he was doing, as if he somehow owed it to her. He had never met her, but having read her letters he felt he knew her intimately. Maybe it was guilt at having done so that drove him on and fueled his desire to find the killer.

He began to think of what Dan had said to him a few days ago: "Don't get too emotionally involved. This is just like any other job Ralph. You need a clear head to see you through it."

He muttered to himself. Dan was right, of course. The problem was that it wasn't just like any other job. He *was* emotionally involved, whether he wanted to be or not. It was all the more surprising since he had never considered himself the emotional type.

Suddenly he felt the gravity push him back in his seat as the car struggled to negotiate a tight bend. An image of Laura flashed in front of his eyes, and realizing he was going recklessly fast on the narrow coast road, he eased off on the gas pedal and turned his attention to driving again.

Thirty minutes later he turned off the road and saw the neon sign dead ahead: "Amano Fisheries." The entrance was unmanned and the barrier fixed in the upright position. He dimmed his headlights as he came through the front gates and downshifted to allow time to take stock of his surroundings. The moon was nearly full, and he could make out the buildings quite clearly, so he doused his lights completely. He braked and slowly brought the car to a halt.

To his left was a low wall which ran all the way along the perimeter and up to the main buildings. The quayside and the sea itself were on his right, and between the car and the main buildings lay a large expanse of open ground. He guessed this area was used by trucks to maneuver into the loading bays where they would receive their cargo of fresh fish bound for the thousands of small restaurants in and around Tokyo. He suddenly felt exposed and decided to park out of sight behind the perimeter wall. There was a narrow opening two thirds of the way along, and he aimed for it, all the while scanning the area for any sign of life.

He made a U-turn so the car was facing the gap in the wall. He killed the engine and stowed the ignition key securely in his inside jacket pocket. He leaned to his right, exposing his shoulder holster, pulled out his .38 and made sure it was loaded. He knew it was, but it was the habit of a lifetime. There was no shortage of stories about well-seasoned agents whose lack of attention to such details had cost them their lives.

He holstered the weapon again, readjusted his jacket and climbed quickly out of the car. Careful not to make a noise, he gently pushed the door to, leaving it slightly ajar for a quick getaway.

He turned toward the group of buildings, cupping his hands to his mouth at the same time and breathing warm breath onto them. Jesus, it was cold. A light breeze blew gently in from the vast expanse of the Pacific. Three seagulls arced and wheeled in the distance as if waiting for the trawlers to return and spill their catch onto the quayside. The weather was calm for that time of year, especially for that area, which was on the edge of Tokyo Bay and lacked much of the natural protection the bay itself afforded.

He shivered, drew his jacket snugly around him and thrust

both hands deep into his pockets. There didn't appear to be a way up to the buildings from behind the wall, which made him uneasy since there was no alternative to going back through the gap and walking round the front—in full view of whoever was waiting for him. It was risky, but what else could he do? He couldn't just skulk behind the wall all night freezing to death in the hope that the caller would find him.

He chewed on his lower lip for a second before deciding he would look far less suspicious if he acted naturally and simply walked straight up to the entrance. He moved forward through the gap and then suddenly froze. A slightly built, shadowy figure moved quickly across the open ground to his front and disappeared behind one of the outbuildings.

He felt his heartbeat quicken. He crept forward and then, hugging the wall, broke into a gentle trot. Once level with the outbuilding he darted across and skirted around it anti-clockwise, all the time keeping the building between his back and the entrance to the fisheries building.

He came full circle so that he was looking straight at the main entrance. It was then that the door opened. The shadowy figure stepped out onto the top step and flashed a perfect set of white teeth in his direction. It was a woman dressed in a short black jacket and dark *monpe* trousers. She wore a dark scarf around her shoulder-length hair. She was probably in her early to mid-forties but well-groomed and very attractive.

She waited a second, smiled again and then turned and disappeared back inside the building.

"Dammit." He swore out of pure frustration.

He strode across the open patch of ground, up the steps and opened the flimsy door. He put his head around the door and peered into the ill-lit corridor. A strong scent of perfume lingered in the air. He didn't recognize the brand, but it was very distinctive—almost sweet, like rose petals. And expensive too, he figured.

He looked around wondering which way to go. There were a number of options, none of which gave him any clues as to which way the shadowy figure had gone.

He turned right, headed cautiously down the corridor and stopped at the first door. The sweet perfume had dissipated and been replaced by the less pleasant smell of brine and rotten fish. He turned the handle and pushed, but it was locked so he moved on to the next door. He pushed again, and this time the door opened with a low creak. He groped around for the light switch and turned it on. A single bare light bulb was suspended from the grimy ceiling by an old length of cord-bound electrical flex which looked as though it might snap at any moment. The bulb gave off a dim, yellow light—just enough to make out the room's contents. There was nothing unusual to be seen. It looked like a storeroom with a miscellany of tools, trolleys, drying racks and other paraphernalia used in the fisheries industry heaped untidily against the back wall.

A couple of faded posters hung on the wall to the right. One of them depicted three workers, presumably fishermen, punching the air in a gesture of solidarity. Unionization. Collective assembly. All rights enshrined in the new constitution. Yet another shining example of the way the Japanese were wholeheartedly embracing American democratic principles.

He snorted at his own cynicism.

There was a table in the middle of the room constructed of rough-hewn timber planks and held together by a series of wooden pegs. On top were two tins of black pitch, some brushes and an old, rusty oil lamp. Other than that there was nothing of any interest. He turned the light off and closed the door.

He was about to continue down the corridor when he noticed a faint glow coming from the opposite direction. Retracing his steps he carried on past the main entrance to the other end of the corridor. A wooden stairway led up to the floor above. He placed one foot tentatively on the bottom step and slowly transferred his weight onto it. The wood was, despite its appearance, sound, and he padded quickly up the remaining steps onto the second floor landing. The glow, now much brighter, emanated from what looked like a small office and the door had been left conveniently open.

He pulled his gun out and edged nervously toward the opening. He took a pace forward into the office, half expecting to be greeted by the same attractive woman he had seen outside. The room was empty, and he couldn't help feeling disappointed. He slipped the gun back into its holster and breathed a sigh of relief. Despite the cold, he could feel sweat running down his back.

For a fisheries office, the room was lavishly done out with paneled walls and a mock Tudor fireplace. There was a silver carriage clock and a rack of tobacco pipes on the mantelpiece, and he guessed the room's occupant must be the company president or someone of similar status. The decor was at odds with the traditional Japanese ideal of artless simplicity, which he had grown to like, and the whole atmosphere reminded him of pictures he'd once seen of Sherlock Holmes' Baker Street residence in London. A row of framed photographs, all depicting the same well-dressed man, caught his eye and he moved over and picked the largest one up. The well-dressed man was flanked by twenty or more small, bowlegged Japanese men. All looked exhausted and undernourished, and all were poorly dressed. A large passenger-cargo ship was moored in the background. He could just make out the name on the prow, written in roman letters: *Koan Maru*. The well-dressed man had his arm around one of the smaller men in a welcoming almost paternal manner. Just for a moment, but only a fleeting moment, he thought he had seen the smaller man somewhere before. But then he dismissed it. Hell, he hated to say it, but they all looked the goddamned same anyhow. He set the frame back down on the shelf.

He lit a cigarette and thought about sitting down and waiting. After all, it was another ten minutes until the agreed-upon meeting time. But he was restless and agitated by the cat-and-mouse game he was being forced to play. He quickly looked round the room once more, stubbed his cigarette out in a large green ashtray on the president's desk, and went out of the room headed in the opposite direction from the way he had come. Halfway along the corridor was a small recess and another set of stairs leading up to the next floor. He strained his ears and listened, his senses alive to the slightest sound. Nothing. He stepped back into the shadows and looked up the stairwell as it alternated between light and dark from the neon light outside.

Light, dark. Light, dark.

A moth flew out of the dust-speckled light, unsure of its destination, drawn first one way and then the other by the intermittent beam of light.

He heard a floorboard creak. Thinking it was the elusive woman, he smiled to himself and stepped out into the corridor.

Bang! An ear-piercing crack shattered the calm evening air and screamed down the corridor.

He took the shot full on in the left shoulder. He reeled, and the impact caught him off balance, spun him around and slammed his body into the wall behind. The strength went from his knees, and he slid down to the ground. He bared his teeth in a grimace and instinctively moved his uninjured right hand up and probed the wound. He felt a warm sensation as blood flowed freely from his shoulder.

"Son of a bitch!" He spat the words out venomously. A wave of nausea came over him, and he fought to suppress it, pushing air into his laboring lungs. Using his elbow, he eased himself back into the recess under the stairs—the only cover available—and fumbled around for his gun, all the time looking down the corridor for any sign of his assailant. His vision was blurred, and the velocity of the shot in the building's close confines had affected his hearing badly. He knew for certain that if the shooter came at him now in his disoriented state he was a goner.

He finally managed to free his pistol from its ill-fitting shoulder holster and pointed it in the general direction of the doorway at the end of the corridor. His left arm was lifeless and hung impotently at his side, as if detached from his body. It ached like a bastard.

There was silence.

He took a deep breath, mustered what little strength he had left, and pushed himself into a standing position, his hand on the rough-paneled wall for support. There was a whiff of gunpowder. Gradually his head cleared, and he staggered out into the corridor again. As he approached the doorway he heard a faint metallic chink coming from downstairs. Without thinking, he lurched through the opening, gun raised and yelled, "I'm coming for you, whoever you are!"

He faltered and collapsed against the banister, the sudden rush of activity sending pain knifing through his shoulder and chest. He blew out in exasperation and silently chastised himself for having given his position away.

A door banged, and Carnaby heard the sound of running footsteps outside.

"Shit." He guessed the shooter was making a run for it. Summoning all his reserves, he rushed down the stairs, taking them two at a time, ran along the short stretch of corridor, burst through the outer doors and went sprawling to the ground on his stomach.

The wheels of a dark, shapeless car spun and kicked up dirt as it sped away toward the highway. He squeezed the trigger and discharged a round. The slug hit the back of the trunk somewhere low down, but his attacker was clean away. He dropped his forehead to the ground and let out a long slow groan.

He was feeling weak now, his vision badly distorted. He got to his knees and stood up—too quickly. Blood rushed to his head, and he thought for a second he would pass out. He had to get to Dan Morita. Dan would know what to do.

He staggered forward, opened his gait and quickened his pace, striding toward the wall and his car. His shoulder throbbed, and blood coursed down his jacket sleeve, leaving a trail in the dirt behind him. A drum beat mercilessly inside his skull, and his vision began to blur again. He staggered sideways groping blindly for some means of support that wasn't there. His head swam, and blackness closed in quickly as he collapsed in a heap across a cluster of garbage cans, scattering them like ninepins.

The neon sign blinked innocuously above his inert form, the light playing across his crimson-soaked jacket. The sky above was clear and filled with a million bright stars—a sure sign of a cold night ahead.

Eleven

Carnaby dreamed he was on a whirligig at the midnight fair—spinning round and round, faster and faster, bright dizzying lights rushing past his eyes in a blur of color. The other riders were laughing and shrieking with delight. He wanted it to stop and let him off, but instead it carried on in ever-widening circles. His horse seemed to be going much faster than everyone else's, and he had to grip the pole with all his strength to avoid being thrown to the ground. The ride operator, who was dressed as a Pierrot clown, sat there, motionless, with a malevolent smile plastered on its Parian white face, all the while regarding his increasing discomfiture. Its hand, with its freakishly long, slender fingers, hovered above the brake handle. The gentle breeze, which had been so pleasant, now became a raging gale, conspiring with the clown to unseat him from the saddle. He was giddy and nauseous and desperately wanted to get off, stagger away, lie down and sleep. *Stop it. Please, for God's sake, stop it!* His grip slackened, unable to resist the intensifying centrifugal force, and his hands moved to his head and covered his eyes. He peeped through his fingers to see the clown's smile stretch still wider across its face, like a great red gash, and then its hand dropped suddenly. There was an almighty screeching noise as the brake was applied. The ride stopped instantly, and he was catapulted headlong off the horse's back—tumbling through space to land on his back with a thud in the middle of the fairground. Lights flickered unforgivingly all around him, and a face—familiar, he thought—peered down at him. It was saying something to him, but he couldn't make out what. He tried to sit up on his elbows, but his shoulder hurt too much. He tried to focus, straining his ears to pick up the indistinct sounds.

"How are you feeling?"

An angelic vision gazed down at him: blonde, shoulder-length hair, attractive face, dressed in white robes. "Can you hear me? How are you feeling?"

The lights had stopped flickering now, and his head was no longer spinning. He opened his eyes fully, blinked, and stared up. "Beth?"

She nodded, tears in her pretty blue eyes, and massaged his arm lovingly.

"I thought for a moment I was in heaven."

"You very nearly were. You were very lucky, you know."

He tried a second time to prop himself up on his elbows but collapsed again onto the hospital bed. "My shoulder hurts like hell."

"Don't try to move. Not just yet anyhow." She moved to his side and stroked his hair tenderly, leaning over him as she did so.

He hooked his good arm around the small of her back and gently pulled her closer, noticing the subtle scent of perfume behind her ear. She lowered her head and closed her eyes. Their lips touched, and then she quickly pulled away as a metallic, rattling noise sounded from the corridor behind them. A hospital orderly walked past, wheeling a steel trolley, laden with towels and bedpans.

They looked at each other and laughed.

"You know, Beth, you look great. We should do this more often," he said, still smiling.

"Yeah, we should. But not here, not like this."

He looked about him, slowly taking in his new surroundings. "How long have I been here?"

"You've been unconscious for two whole days. Dan Morita found you and brought you in late Friday night."

Good old Dan, he thought, *I knew he'd come through.* "I'm dying for a cigarette," he said, wincing in pain as a sudden spasm gripped his shoulder.

"I'll bring you some later," said Beth, with a smile.

He tucked his chin into his chest and tried, with some difficulty, to look down at his immobilized shoulder. "So, what's the prognosis, sister?"

She smiled at the sarcasm and mopped his brow with a damp

compress. "Doctor Ellis will be along in a half hour. You can get the specifics from him then." Her eyes followed the contour of his arm down, and stopped on the splint taped to his side. "It seems the bullet lodged itself in the muscle of your shoulder, cut through some ligaments, and chipped the bone. The doctor said it could have been a lot worse. Apparently it's healing very well, although you're going to be laid up for a while. What we were really concerned about was the amount of blood you'd lost. We gave you a transfusion as soon as you arrived, but it was only late last night that your condition stabilized."

She was gripping the bed linen with her small fists, knuckles turning white. He noticed for the first time just how tired she looked—dark shadows under bloodshot eyes. "You didn't stay all night on my account, did you?"

She laughed, and then turned her face away, biting her lip.

"Hey, easy," he said, reaching out and caressing her slender back. "I'm as strong as an ox. It'll take a helluva lot more than a little piece of lead to put me out of action for good."

She turned back toward him with tear-filled eyes. "I was so worried about you, Ralph. I honestly thought you might not pull through."

"Hey, like I just told you—"

"Yeah, like you just told me," she cut in, with a frightened look, "you're strong as an ox." She lowered her eyes for a moment and then looked him full in the face, gripping his right hand with both of hers. "Ralph, I'm scared. I know you've been in some scrapes before. I mean, it's part of your job, isn't it? And I appreciate that. But this . . . this is somehow different." She leaned back and looked long and hard at his arm. "This was deliberate, calculated. Somebody has singled you out. I talked to Dan and—"

He raised his eyebrows and frowned slightly.

She continued. "Well, he agrees. There have been some pretty strange things going on lately."

"Listen, Beth, I know how you must feel, and I'm touched that you're concerned. I gotta admit I'm still trying to figure it out myself. But I don't want you to worry yourself too much. Just trust me."

"I just don't want you to get hurt, that's all. I couldn't bear it if anything happened to you—"

"*Nothing* is going to happen to me, Beth."

She stared at him with a harsh look in her eye. "It's all very well saying that, but what if Dan hadn't got your message? What if he hadn't made it out there Friday night and found you? What if . . . " Her voice trailed off, timorous. Tears were rolling down her cheeks, leaving wet streaks across her makeup. "You know what the doc said?" she blurted. "Another hour and you wouldn't have made it."

He pulled her head into his chest and stroked her neck, whispering to her soothingly. "Come on, Beth, it's okay. I promise you I'll be more careful from now on."

There was a firm knock, and the double doors swung open.

"Ah, Doc," he said, easing Beth up from his arm.

She stood up, wiped her eyes quickly and pushed a few trailing hairs neatly back behind her nurse's cap. "Sorry, Doctor," she said, eyes downcast, as she sidled past.

"Don't worry about it, Beth. You've had a long day," said Ellis, watching her leave the room. He looked round and raised his eyebrows. "How do you manage it, Ralph?"

"Manage what, Doc?"

"You know—breaking the girls' hearts even when you're unconscious!"

Carnaby laughed, trying to make light of it. "Yeah, sure. I think you've been working her too hard, Doc. She got all emotional on me."

"She works hard alright. There's no doubt about that. But, seriously, I think she still really cares about you, Ralph." Ellis adjusted his glasses with his forefinger, sliding them back up the bridge of his nose. "She could've gone home yesterday, once you were off the critical list. But she chose not to. Instead she sat here next to you, right through the night, watching you, waiting for you to come around."

"To be honest, Doc," said Carnaby, grunting with the exertion of trying to lift his backside clear of the bed and get his circulation going again, "I don't know why we stopped seeing each other in the first place."

"I always did think you were a good match," said Ellis softly. "Anyway," he continued, changing the subject, "it's good to see you making a recovery. Even I was starting to get a little concerned at one point." He took hold of the patient chart, which was suspended by a cord from the end of the bed. "Well now, that's looking a whole lot better. Your blood pressure is back up, almost to normal. No sign of any infection either. Tell me, how do you feel?"

"Like a million bucks. I keep getting jolts through my shoulder, but I guess that's understandable. And I'm feeling pretty groggy still. Otherwise, not too bad, all things considered."

"The grogginess will pass as the anesthetic wears off. We had to go easy on the painkillers, but we can let you have another dose in a few hours. Provided there are no complications, Ralph, you should be out of here in a week."

"Great," replied Carnaby, visibly relieved. "I can just imagine the paperwork that must be mounting up on my desk while I've been away."

"Now hold on there, cowboy. I said out of *here*. I didn't say anything about going back to work. You may be making a good recovery, but you are going to need at least six weeks rest and recuperation before you can even think about resuming your regular duties."

"Six weeks?" Carnaby pushed his head back into the pillow and sighed heavily. "Are you serious, Doc? What on earth am I gonna tell Aspin? He's already overworked as it is."

Ellis had raised a hand in the air, as if to silence any further protests. "It's already taken care of. Aspin stopped by early this morning. He said you should take it easy. Oh, and he also said to tell you that when he suggested you go on vacation for a week or two, this is *not* what he had in mind."

They both laughed again. Hell, thought Carnaby, why not? After all, it *had* been a while since he'd taken any real time off. Longer, in fact, than he cared to remember. And if his boss was happy about it, then he would be crazy not to take advantage.

"By the way," said Ellis, "I meant to ask, what happened to you anyway?"

Carnaby stared at the wall opposite—white: a blank. And then he remembered. "To be honest, I'm not entirely sure. I was set up. Walked straight into a trap."

"That's too bad," said Ellis sympathetically.

"Still," said Carnaby, "I guess I should consider myself lucky. This is my first visit here in seven years—as a patient that is."

"Yeah," chuckled Ellis, "I wish I could say the same for some of your colleagues. Groves was here this morning, that's the second time this month."

"He was?"

"Yeah. He got into a brawl last night with some New Zealander. Tried to land a haymaker on him, but the guy ducked and he hit a supporting pillar instead. His hand's swollen up like a goddamned balloon."

"Wonder what that was all about," muttered Carnaby.

"Oh, the usual."

"Girl trouble?"

"You got it." Ellis adjusted his glasses again and beamed. "Anyway, Ralph, I'll look in on you later today. Meanwhile, try and get some rest."

"I'll do that, Doc. And thanks for patching me up."

Ellis pulled the door open, paused and then looked back over his shoulder. "Oh, and if you do need anything, press the red button on the panel there. The nurses' station is just down the corridor."

Carnaby settled back and probed his left shoulder, just as he had done when he took the bullet. He sure could do with some painkillers. He tried closing his eyes, but this only brought the spinning sensation back and made him feel sick again. He looked lazily across at the bedtable and noticed yesterday's *Nippon Times* lying folded on the glass surface. His head was throbbing, and he didn't really feel like reading anything. He tried closing his eyes again, but his senses began to reel. Feeling listless, he picked the newspaper up anyway and gazed disinterestedly at the front page.

It was dominated by a blurred photograph of two men, each clad from head to toe in mountaineer's clothing and holding the flag of the United Kingdom, standing on top of a snowcapped peak. The caption read:

> Everest Conquered! Edmund Hillary, British mountaineer and explorer, and his Sherpa guide, Tenzing Norgay, are the first to reach Earth's highest point: the 29,000-foot summit of Mount Everest in the Himalayas. The two climbers set out on the last leg of the ascent, entirely unaided, and reached the top at 11:30 a.m. yesterday. With this unprecedented feat, one has to wonder what challenges now remain for the world's best mountaineers.

He snorted. Those guys must be nuts.

The bottom half of the page was devoted to a summary of the order of service for the coronation of Queen Elizabeth II, scheduled to take place in London's Westminster Abbey the following week. He skimmed the description, cocking his head to one side, like a confused cat, trying to make sense of the eons-old ritual of installing a new British monarch on the throne.

> Then shall the Orb with the Cross be brought from the Altar by the Dean of Westminster and delivered into the Queen's right hand by the Archbishop, saying, 'Receive this Orb set under the Cross, and remember that the whole world is subject to the Power and Empire of Christ our Redeemer.'
>
> Then shall the Queen deliver the Orb to the Dean of Westminster, to be by him laid upon the Altar . . . .
>
> Then the people shall rise; and the Archbishop, standing before the Altar, shall take the Crown into his hands, [St Edward's Crown] and laying it again before him upon the Altar, he shall say: 'O God the Crown of the faithful: Bless we beseech thee this Crown, and so sanctify thy servant ELIZABETH upon whose head this day thou dost place it for a sign of royal majesty, that she may be filled by thine abundant grace with all princely virtues: through the King eternal Jesus Christ our Lord. Amen.'
>
> Then shall the Queen go to her Throne, and be lifted up into it by the Archbishops and the Bishops . . . and the Archbishop, standing before the Queen, shall say: 'Stand firm, and hold fast from henceforth the seat and state of royal and imperial dignity, which is this day delivered unto you, in the Name and by the Authority of Almighty God, and by the hands of us the Bishops and servants of God, though unworthy. And the Lord God Almighty, whose ministers we are, and the stewards of his mysteries, establish your Throne in righteousness, that it may stand fast for evermore. Amen.'

Carnaby lowered the paper and blinked two or three times. He was beginning to think that all Britishers were eccentric as hell. Not that he knew any personally. His headache seemed to have gotten worse. He kneaded his forehead with the middle knuckle of his index finger and then turned to the shorter stories.

There was nothing of particular interest, just the usual hotchpotch of one-line items. The ship *Takasago Maru* had brought back six hundred repatriated Japanese soldiers who had been held captive by the Soviets since the war. On approaching the docks at Maizuru, a number of passengers were heard to shout: "We are entering enemy territory!" This was followed by a bracing rendition by the former POWs of the "Internationale" and a communist youth song.

A train had been derailed at Kurihama, near the US Navy base in Yokosuka, and a large consignment of ammunition, including several boxes of mortar tubes and other supplies, had gone missing. On the Korean War front, fighting between Chinese-backed North Koreans and American troops was intensifying south of the 38th Parallel. More troops were to be mobilized, leaving only a reserve force in Japan. And in Tokyo's Kita Ward police had surrounded the home of a psychologically deranged unemployed man, who was holding his wife and two children hostage, demanding payment of dismissal compensation from his former employer.

The world has gone completely mad, he thought, tossing the newspaper onto the counterpane. He stared into space, and gradually tiredness got the better of him.

He slept for a few hours. And when he awoke, he found a different sort of vision staring down at him.

"Dan!"

"Ralph. How are you?"

"How am I? Pleased to see you, that's how I am." He hoisted himself up, but then crumpled back into the pillow in pain.

"Hey, take it easy."

"Yeah," he replied, "I keep forgetting about this." He peered down at his bandaged arm.

An ambulance siren wailed from somewhere below, and a brace of startled pigeons fluttered like confetti outside the window.

"How 'bout some coffee?" Morita indicated the steaming cup on the glass-topped table. "Doc said it was okay. And you can have some real chow starting tonight."

"Swell," said Carnaby, lifting the cup from the saucer, "I'm famished." He took a mouthful. "Boy, that sure does taste good."

The two men looked at each other, long and hard, like long-lost brothers suddenly reunited.

"I really owe you this time, Dan," he said, replacing the empty cup.

"Forget it, Ralph. That's what partners are for."

Carnaby was shaking his head slowly from side to side. "Naw. This time I really screwed up. Seems you found me just in the nick of time."

"Yeah," said Morita, pulling up a chair. "I gotta admit I was scared shitless when I found you. You'd damned near froze to death—never mind the gunshot wound."

There was another short silence, as if they both realized for the first time just how close a call it had really been.

Morita asked, "So, are you gonna tell me what happened?"

Carnaby recounted the events of that night, being careful not to leave anything out. When he'd finished, he sat back, satisfied, and tired.

Morita folded his arms. "And you have no idea who might have been behind it?"

"Like I said, I can only think it's connected with the letters I've been getting these last few weeks. Although, having said that, I can't imagine what good they think that'll do. Even with me out the way, it's not as if the investigations and raids are suddenly going to stop."

"But then, you said it yourself, Ralph—it's your name that was in the newspapers."

"I don't buy that crap. Come on, Dan, think about it. I might be leading the investigations on the ground. And I'm the fall guy they like to wheel out in front of the press every time there's a public relations problem, but I'm sure as hell not responsible for allocating resources and deciding which programs get implemented and which don't."

"Okay, so maybe it's some crazed individual with a score to settle."

"Yeah, maybe," he said, starting to smile.

"What's so funny?"

"I was just thinking—maybe it's that hooker Groves was going on about."

"Yeah, anything's possible," said Morita, swiveling on his chair and pulling out a large buff folder from his briefcase. "Anyway, I thought I'd take a drive out there tomorrow morning and snoop around a little. Seems odd to me that this woman you saw was able to get into the fisheries without breaking the locks. And, I mean, why did she choose that place anyway?" He placed the folder on his lap and stared at Carnaby with a smug expression. He untied the cord and smiled.

"Now what's funny?"

"The raid, Friday."

"The raid? Oh yeah, I meant to ask how it went. Did you find anything?"

"You could say that." Morita pulled out a sheaf of papers. "Hot off the press. Just got this from the Allied Translators and Interpreters Service." He handed it to Carnaby. "It seems our mysterious friend, Harvey Brice, had himself a little cash flow problem."

Carnaby's eyes were wide like saucers. "Jesus, well I'll be . . . "

"Yeah. That's just what I said."

"Three point six million yen. What's that? About ten thousand US?" Carnaby whistled. "That's a heck of a lot of dough to be owing the mob." He suddenly found a new lease on life, and pushed himself into a sitting position. "A month in arrears—goddamn. Do we know if they collected?"

"Nope. We grilled the front man, Tanaka, but he swears that collections are handled by the mob. All he does is book the loans. Personally, I think he's full of horseshit and knows more than he's letting on."

"What about Maruyama?"

"A few of his people were there, mainly low-life gofers. The one person that might have been able to tell us something—well, the poor guy had a run-in with Kimura and got his face mashed for his trouble. He's all wired up and can't talk right now."

Carnaby sat back again and gazed into space. "What beats me, Dan, is why on earth Brice needed a ten-thousand-dollar loan in the first place."

"Yeah, and something else," said Morita. "The yakuza don't normally advance money without taking some kind of collateral up front."

"Collateral?" repeated Carnaby. "But what would Brice have had of any value?"

"Search me." Morita shrugged.

"And if they had collateral, why would they bother killing him?"

"You know, in all my time working out here, I've never once come across anything like this—I mean, a non-Japanese getting mixed up with mob business. It just doesn't ring true."

"Well, there's a first time for everything, I guess." Carnaby scrutinized the accounts extract again. "This guy Tanaka—where is he now?"

"Back at the compound."

"Will he cooperate?"

"I doubt it if Friday was anything to go by. He's a tough nut to crack."

"I don't get it. He's already in it up to his neck."

"He's scared. And he should be too. Maruyama's a ruthless son of a bitch."

"Can we set up a meeting?"

"With Maruyama?" Morita cracked his knuckles and made a noise like air escaping from a tire. "We could," he said, with a hint of reluctance in his voice, "but I'm not sure where it gets us."

"It seems to me we've got nothing to lose."

"The point is, even if he is responsible, there's no way in hell we'll be able to pin it on him. They'll close ranks. There'll be a dozen or more guys prepared to take the rap. And while the fall guy's doing time, his family will be looked after. I've seen the police reports—two months ago, at the Parisian Grill in Ginza, Maruyama got into an argument and gunned down a man in cold blood in front of the whole goddamned restaurant. He was picked out of a lineup by four witnesses. But guess what? Within a week all four of them had retracted their statements."

"On what grounds?"

"Oh, you know—'on reflection, it *was* pretty dark in there'; or 'I'd had more than I thought to drink and I'm not certain who shot who.' A couple of days later, one of Maruyama's stooges turns himself in, full confession, the whole works. He wasn't even there for chrissake." Morita paused, and pinched the bridge of his nose. "And that's a case where Maruyama did it himself, which almost certainly wasn't the case with Brice."

"I know what you're saying, Dan," said Carnaby, his expression suddenly serious, "but we've got to start somewhere."

"Okay," he said softly, "I'll see what I can do. But it may take time to arrange. It's not like you can just pick the phone up and make an appointment."

But Carnaby wasn't listening any more. "Well, well . . . " he muttered, his eyes fixed on the single sheet of paper.

Suddenly without warning, the doors opened and a large, matronly woman came bustling into the room preceded by her piercing Scottish tones. "Visiting time is over, young man," she said, without so much as looking at Morita.

"Sorry, ma'am, I didn't realize—"

"No, of course yer didn't, dear. That's what they all say, even though it's written quite clearly on the door." She pushed between Morita's chair and the bed just as he was trying to stand up and reached her ample arms out to plump up the pillow. "Come on, lean forward a little will yer now? Are you still here, young man?" she said as she backed into Morita, now making for the door.

"Just leaving, ma'am," he blurted as he stumbled sideways.

He raised his eyebrows and made a suggestive face at Carnaby. "Take it easy, Ralph. I'll drop by soon with an update."

Carnaby fixed his eyes on the bedspread and concentrated hard so as not to start laughing. "Yeah, see you, Dan. Thanks again."

Twelve

The doctor sat cross-legged on the tatami floor of his bedroom, a smoldering cigarette hanging from the corner of his thin-lipped mouth. Weeks of relentless work and worry were beginning to take their toll. His 55-year-old face was a mass of wrinkles, his eyes bloodshot and sunken. He gripped the newspaper as if it were his death warrant. He stubbed out his cigarette in a small crystal ashtray, as if doing so would somehow erase the main story from the front page. He slumped back onto the thin cotton futon and closed his eyes. But the headline was imprinted like neon in the blackness: "War Crimes Tribunal—Phase Two: Names of indicted to be made public soon."

As he drifted off to sleep, the newspaper fell to the floor and his limp hand flopped down to his side. Before long his eyelids began to twitch and he sank deeper into the ephemeral void of the past. It was the same dream. The inexorable march of time had failed to remove it from his subconscious.

He was standing on top of a small mound. He looked skyward, checking for rain. Cumulus clouds were beginning to form like giant cotton balls on the horizon. Rain would be disastrous; the half-life of sarin was reduced virtually to zero in wet conditions, rendering the results of any experiment meaningless. He returned his gaze to the piece of open ground in the distance. He was in a pensive mood.

Fifty wooden crosses were embedded deeply in the parched, russet-colored earth describing a large circle with a diameter of almost a hundred meters. The marutas *had been tied to the crosses with ropes drawn tightly around their wrists and ankles so that the coarse hemp bit deeply into parchment-thin skin—leaving behind angry purple weals. Each* maruta *wore a steel helmet, and about their necks hung heavy oblong metal plates, necessary protection against the exploding projectile which would presently be lobbed into the center of this unfortunate congregation. The whole scene resembled some sort of strange pagan ritual. It would have been mildly comical, except for the fact that the fifty human beings were about to be sacrificed in the name of scientific progress—a necessary evil if Japan were to furnish itself with an effective biological and chemical warfare capability.*

The doctor parted his lips slightly, as if tasting the air. Around him a dozen or so lightly clad personnel scurried about, frantically trying to finalize preparations for the experiment while the weather remained stable.

Medical orderlies, wearing drab white overalls, busied themselves arranging swabs, ampules and hypodermic needles, while army NCOs broke open sealed containers and began distributing protective clothing to those that would be observing from the mound.

An army photographer, straining under the weight of his equipment, planted his right foot firmly on top of the perimeter sandbags, splayed the legs of his tripod and carefully attached the heavy camera. This was to be no simple exercise in propaganda. The film was to be used for analytical purposes only. There had been strict instructions from the high command to suppress the release of all such information, and only that morning there had been cause to execute a number of idle peasant bystanders lest news of experiments like these leaked to the outside world.

"Kurouchi!" *The doctor shouted in the direction of the burly sergeant.* "Is everything ready?"

"Yes, sir." *Kurouchi, his face impassive, stood bolt upright and barked out his reply.*

Those personnel surplus to requirements moved off in single file down an adjoining gully and disappeared into the dark entrance of the bunker.

The doctor, alone now except for an orderly and Kurouchi, pulled on his rubber gloves, fastened his mask and readied his binoculars. He took a deep breath and raised his hand in the air.

Kurouchi loaded a large red flare cartridge into the Very pistol's lightly-oiled glistening chamber, snapped it shut and pulled back the hammer. He raised his arm and squeezed the trigger. The flare soared upwards before exploding with a staccato crack, sending out a radiant burst of white-hot magnesium light.

A few seconds passed, and then a dull report carried on the light morning breeze as a mortar fired in the distance. And then silence, save for the barely perceptible sobbing of the teenage boy on the nearest cross, and the low, rhythmic purr of a lorry engine to the rear.

The doctor shot a furtive glance toward the wind sock and then looked forward again, just in time to see the mortar shell erupt, sending up a pall of dirty gray smoke as it did so. The shell contained a reduced charge—just enough explosive to release its deadly contents without causing injury to the marutas. *The smoke quickly dispersed allowing the doctor to train his binoculars on the face of each victim in turn. He felt a surge of adrenaline as he waited for the gas to make its presence known. One or two had already succumbed to the smoke and hung motionless. They were the lucky ones. Those surrounding them began to twitch and tug spasmodically at their ligatures.*

The doctor licked his lips excitedly, wiped the lenses of his binoculars, and put them to his eyes once more. The experiment was progressing well, and the agent was already attacking the central nervous system of certain individuals. Before long they were all convulsing violently. Unable to resist the spasms, their bodies twisted and writhed, forming grotesque shapes against the horizon. Several of the marutas *had begun to cough up blood and one individual—a fine strong specimen—had wrenched his bloody wrists free and lay prostrate over the oblong metal plate, his ankles broken under the weight. His back suddenly arched as he retched violently, discharging the contents of his stomach into the gelatinous pool of blood which oozed and suppurated in the sandy earth about his head.*

All was still. There was a stench of death in the air, and carrion birds wheeled and turned in the sky above.

The doctor checked his watch and quickly scribbled a note in his ledger. His only regret was that he was unable to dissect the corpses immediately. He was forced to wait at least thirty minutes before he could begin drawing blood and weighing organs. Who knew what processes occurred during that vital initial period? This was all far removed from biological experimentation where diseases such as the plague could be implanted and fostered in the comfort of the laboratory and where the marutas *could be dissected while still alive in order to produce the best results. Such luxuries were impossible in the Spartan environment of the field hospital.*

Half an hour later, two NCOs, still dressed in protective clothing and with bayonets fixed, marched a half-naked farmer down to the patch of open ground. If he remained standing, they would know that the gas had dispersed and the area was safe. This human canary was the doctor's idea, and he smiled at his own ingenuity.

The doctor looked over the corpses as they were cut down and gave instructions to the orderlies. As he bent down next to the body of a middle-aged man and removed the metal plate from his chest, a dark, menacing cloud passed over the sun. He stood and turned as if to leave. Suddenly, from behind him there was a loud rushing noise like air escaping from a deflating balloon. The doctor spun around and tripped, falling untidily onto the outstretched legs of the dead man. Its torso rose from the ground and sat up, arms outstretched. The body slumped forward onto the doctor with talon-like fingers groping for his throat. He recoiled and instinctively pushed the head back—revealing the most hideous expression of mute anguish.

The screaming inside his head brought him round, head swimming as he came to the surface gasping for air. He sat straight up with the sweat-soaked sheet wrapped around his shoulders and back like a shroud. His eyes opened wide and he let out an ear-piercing scream: "Anda!"

Thirteen

Carnaby sat in the lobby of the hospital, waiting for Beth to show up. It was five days since he had been admitted—the longest five days of his life. His shoulder was still painful, and he had trouble moving it too far in any direction. Still, the monotony of the place not to mention the food—was driving him to distraction, and he had decided it was time to leave. Beth was taking a short vacation and had volunteered to stay with him a few days and help him settle back into his apartment.

He checked his watch. She was late. The lobby was teeming with people—nurses pushing wheelchairs, doctors and medical personnel checking notes and conferring in corners. The whole place was a hive of activity. He had barely moved out of his small private room when hospital staff began removing the table, chairs and wardrobe and filling the space with two more beds. The war in Korea was getting worse—that much was plain to see.

He looked around and thought he saw her. But when the woman turned in his direction it was somebody else. He placed his right hand on his knee and pushed himself up from his chair. He sauntered over toward reception, stopping once or twice to avoid hurrying bodies and again to give way to a slow-moving and stony-faced nun, who looked as though she might have just administered the last rites to some poor soul.

"Pretty busy around here." Carnaby smiled at the young orderly manning reception and pulled out a pack of cigarettes. "Say, Mac, do you have a light?"

"Sure thing, sir," replied the orderly, his face impassive.

Carnaby leaned forward while the orderly applied a match

to his cigarette. “Thanks,” he said. He stuffed the pack into his trouser pocket and started to make his way back over to the waiting area when he spotted Beth skipping down the stairs at the far end of the lobby. She looked so young and energetic, he could have wept. She’d changed out of her uniform and had on a brown, calf-length skirt and fur-lined leather jacket. The jacket was open at the front and revealed a tight fitting white blouse with pretty sequins down the front. Her breasts were full and bounced slightly with each step as she came toward him smiling.

“Sorry I’m late,” she said, coming to his right side and threading her arm through his.

He kissed her on the cheek. “You look great, as usual.”

“Thank you. So do you. Your arm okay?”

“Oh, it’s felt better. But I guess I’ll survive. Listen, it’s getting late. Why don’t we grab a cab as far as the intersection at Ochanomizu. We can pick up some groceries from the store there and walk along the river to my place.”

“Sounds like a great idea. You know Ralph, I’m so looking forward to a quiet few days. Just the two of us.”

“Me too.” He kissed her again and they dived through the revolving doors together and out into the late afternoon Tokyo sunshine.

The cab dropped them at the intersection after a fifteen-minute ride. The store was closed to undergo a repaint job, so instead they bought a box of beautifully presented sushi from a street vendor. The fish was fresh and the colors vibrant. The pink, fatty meat of the tuna, or *toro,* contrasted with the hard steely-blue of the mackerel and the vivid red of the sea bream. Most of the Americans Carnaby knew didn’t particularly care for Japanese food, especially the raw variety, and avoided it as much as possible. But he seemed to have acquired a taste for it, probably, he guessed, the result of his friendship with Dan Morita more than anything else.

They crossed the road and descended a long flight of stone steps that led down to the riverside path. An old, cadaverous man was sitting on an upturned bucket close to the bridge support, just enough in the shadow so the fish wouldn’t see him. He was clutching a slender bamboo rod in his bony hands. He didn’t move, even when they drew level with him. His ‘kingfisher's' eyes were fixed on the spot where the line disappeared into the still, greenish water.

Along the edge of the leaf-choked path ran a narrow rain gully. It wasn't windy, and yet the leaves seemed to move every now and again.

"Look!" squealed Beth pointing excitedly.

Carnaby squatted down and, using a twig, brushed aside some of the dead leaves. Underneath, dozens of tiny mice scurried about looking for cover.

"Aren't they just the cutest things you've ever seen?" she said.

He smiled and they continued arm in arm along the path.

They rounded a corner and crossed a narrow road. A black GI, easily six feet four and powerfully built, walked casually toward them hand in hand with a young Japanese girl. She was waif-like, wore an indecently short skirt, and teetered along in a pair of badly scuffed stilettos. Her makeup was smudged. The 'morning-after look,' he thought, except it was four o'clock in the afternoon. As they passed, the GI nodded slightly, and Carnaby smiled knowingly.

They walked on and crossed another, wider road and came out in a much smarter neighborhood flanked by ginkgo trees and new apartments built for the increasing ranks of affluent middle-class workers. Beth took the lead and went first, holding the gate open for Carnaby to come through with the box of sushi.

"You still remember the way," he said, closing the gate behind.

"Hey, come on. It's not so long ago, is it?" She laughed as she pirouetted up the short path.

He grinned and patted her on the backside. She squealed, playfully, and headed into the entrance to the apartment block. His place was on the third floor. The elevator was out of order so they took the stairs. Having been bedridden for the better part of a week, his legs ached. He was out of shape—he had to admit it—and by the time he reached the top of the stairs he was damp with sweat and breathing heavily.

He sensed it even before he saw it. They came out onto the landing to find a shaft of dull sunlight coming from his open door. Tension filled the air.

"Shh! Wait here." He passed her the box of sushi and drew his pistol from inside his jacket.

Alarmed, Beth grabbed his jacket sleeve. There was a short

silence as she looked anxiously into his face.

"It's okay. I'll be back," he said, gently shrugging her off. He walked forward slowly, his gun sticking out like an antenna in front of him.

"Be careful," she whispered insistently.

He reached the open door and peered round, paused to let his eyes adjust, and then slipped into the room.

A minute or two later he reappeared, looking thoroughly annoyed. "It's alright. There's nobody here now."

Beth heaved a sigh of relief and threw herself at him, wrapping her arms around him. He winced at the impact to his shoulder, but clenched his teeth and didn't say anything.

She buried her face in his neck and looked over his shoulder and surveyed the wreckage in the room behind. "Oh, God. What a mess."

He turned slowly, put his arm around her waist and guided her across the threshold. It looked like a bomb had gone off and vaguely reminded Carnaby of the scene in Aspin's office a couple of weeks before. Debris lay everywhere. Exploded silk cushions littered the floor. The curtains had been torn down and lay draped over the sofa—like the sloughed-off skin of some gargantuan predator. His mahogany writing bureau, an antique left to him by his Great Aunt Celia, had been upended, its drawers smashed and splintered. A sea of paper and other items of stationery were strewn across the room. A lithograph, "Icarus," signed in pencil by Matisse, had been rudely punched out of its frame and lay crumpled in the corner. It was no great work of art, but he had been fond of it. He had bought it at a painting exhibition in Los Angeles shortly after returning from Japan in the winter of 1945. It had been the first decent picture he and Laura had bought for their new Fresno home.

They moved cautiously from room to room in stunned silence. Everywhere he looked, his possessions had been desecrated. Even the austere Japanese room had not escaped the onslaught—the tatami mats had been pulled up and stacked lengthways against the walls. A vase lay smashed where it had stood in the *tokonoma.* A hanging scroll had been pulled down and trampled underfoot.

Beth embraced him again and then pulled away slightly and looked searchingly into his eyes. "But *why*?" she said, in a barely audible voice. "Why are they doing this to you, Ralph?"

She was close to tears again now. He caressed her hair and said quietly, "I don't know, Beth. I don't know."

"Well," she said, lowering her eyes, "we can't stay here tonight."

A slow waltz played softly in the background. They held each other tightly, cheek pressed against cheek, eyes closed, and moved slowly in the middle of the room. He squeezed her waist and nuzzled her ear. Their heads turned and they kissed, long and hard, tasting the brandy on each other's tongues. They were both aroused now and wanted each other desperately, passionately. Her fingers slid up his shirt, probing his muscular chest, working to undo his buttons. She peeled it back from his shoulders, taking care not to hurt him, pressed her face against his torso and tasted his masculine saltiness. The shirt dropped to the floor. They embraced again then parted slightly. She took him by the hand, pouting, teasing, and led him through to her bedroom.

He looked at her, longingly, moved his hand slowly to her blouse and stroked her breasts. Her buttons came undone easily. He slipped his hand inside and around to her bra strap and fumbled uselessly with one hand. She smiled, faintly amused, teasing again, and then reached behind with both hands and released the clasp. His hand returned—to bare skin this time—fingers circling and kneading while they kissed. He slowly and methodically moved his mouth down her face, tugging at her bottom lip and kissing her chin, progressing down to her slender neck, and then swiftly down to her waiting breast. He secured her by the waist while his tongue worked vigorously, licking, circling, probing her areola with short stabbing actions. Her nipple responded, hardened, and stood erect in his mouth. Her hands went to his waist and undid his trousers.

He pushed her back onto the bed. She lifted her knees up and slid off her pants, pulling him down on to her. Their bodies entwined, joined and became one. They moved together, slowly, for a while, and then she gently rolled him onto his back and began licking him again. She arched her back and straddled him, eagerly guiding him into her. They rocked and groaned together. The pace quickened and became more desperate. The low groans had become gasps of pure ecstasy as they both approached climax. And then, suddenly, his head lolled sideways on the pillow and he let out a small sigh. Just as he thought the moment had come and he began to taste that metallic sensation under his tongue, the life force gave out. He tried to concentrate, massaged her sweating breasts with his palm, thought sexy thoughts. But it was no good. There was a mental block. She carried on moving, gyrating, and then she too realized.

She stopped, still panting, and hung her head down. Then she looked at him. "Is it me?" she whispered.

He stayed silent and continued staring at her bedroom wall. A mobile was moving slowly, casting spellbinding patterns on the wallpaper.

"Ralph?" she said, stroking his damp hair.

"No," he said, without moving his head. "It's not you, Beth." He turned and looked at her. "It's not you at all. You are so very attractive."

She leaned forward and lay on him, pushed her face into his warm, pulsating neck, and watched her tears stain the pillow.

The painkillers had started to do their work. His eyelids flickered, and fatigue carried him away.

Laura is radiant in red taffeta, he, clean-cut and handsome in khaki dress uniform. The band is playing a selection of Glenn Miller's favorites, and the wine (of which there seems an endless quantity), a gift from liberated Provence and left over from the V-E celebrations several months earlier, produces a pleasantly soporific effect. Uncorked bottles lined up on the benches, set free from their incarceration in French cellars, seem to be saying, "Come on. Try me. Let me work a little magic on you tonight."

Tower Theater: the official Fresno County V-J party. All around are smiling happy faces, heads bobbing in enthusiastic conversation, the clinking of glasses and scraping of cutlery on porcelain plates. The wind is getting up; a storm is brewing. The atmosphere is buzzing, euphoric—Japan has been floored and is down for the count. The war is a million miles away. It belongs to another age, another time, and, while rationing continues in war-ravaged Europe, everyone here, from the mayor on down, is determinedly having a whale of a time.

He glances dreamily across to the next table, raises his glass and nods occasionally at the faces he recognizes. People seem somehow much older than he remembers. Jeff Stimson and his wife Dottie are there, wearing pink party hats and putting on brave faces.

They have lost two of their three sons on the beaches of Saipan and Iwo Jima, and her fleshy arm is locked in a tight embrace around her only remaining son, Teddy, as if she means never to let him go again.

The Ewings are also there with their two boys safely returned home, both of whom are now very much drunk and making the most of sitting opposite Clara Flattely's buxom twin daughters. They are eighteen years old with flaming mane-like red hair and look predatory with their bright red lipstick, rouge and extremely revealing low-cut frocks. He allows himself a wry smile, and subconsciously wishes he was their age again. God, how time flies.

At the end of the table, staring vacantly into space, sits Dave Cosby, fresh off the boat from the Philippines, only to learn that his fiancée had been killed a week earlier in a freak accident at the local munitions factory. The shock is obviously setting in. The poor guy is completely oblivious to the conversation going on around him.

So many lives, so many loves, touched, affected and changed forever by a war which has come to an end almost as abruptly as it had started. He has been back almost a month and yet he feels strangely detached from it all. The majority of the revelers had not been there. In fact, the majority of those that had been there were still there—guarding Japanese captives in camps which had once housed the emaciated bodies of allied POWs or as part of the initial post-surrender occupation force or simply waiting for orders to be cut for their return to the US.

The incessant chatter of two elderly and very portly women carries across the soft rhythm of the band, which is now playing Gershwin's "Rhapsody in Blue." "Now let me see . . . no, no, I don't believe I do . . . oh, but wait now, yes I remember him perfectly now—and would you believe it . . . "

He grins and reaches his arm across the space between the salt cellar and water decanter and squeezes her forearm affectionately. Suddenly the music goes up a beat and picks up pace and couples begin swarming across the dance floor from all directions. The floor reverberates to the beat. A pair of teenage lovers, uninhibited and drunk as much with joy as alcohol—start a chain reaction by dancing on the tables. Soon, all the youngsters are up there—tapping, kicking, stomping, slamming, wheeling, gyrating, linking hands, now moving apart, now together, pelvis grinding pelvis. Wine is flowing, appetites are growing. The air is charged with sexual energy.

"Shall we?" he asks, raising his dark eyebrows. She nods, still smiling, then stands and comes round to the head of the table. He takes her by her slender arms and leads her into the surging, pulsating crowd. The music is too fast, but they don't care. They are reborn, teenagers again—vital, lustful, head over heels in love.

The music comes to a climactic end with a staccato drum roll. The revelers slowly drift back to their seats and charge their glasses. The afternoon's host springs up on stage and plucks the microphone from its stand. "Good evening, ladies and gentlemen," he says, in time-honored fashion. "Please put your hands together and give a warm welcome to our special guest, Mayor James Alderman."

Rapturous applause. Flashbulbs explode in unison like a string of dull firecrackers. A ruddy-faced man in his late sixties rises from his seat at the head table, whispers something to his wife, who smiles demurely in response, and makes his way, a little unsteadily, to the podium. He blinks two or three times, dazzled by the glare of the bright stage lights, and surveys his half-invisible audience. Outside, the wind is really getting up and rain pelts the windows. He mops his brow, somewhat theatrically, with a white handkerchief, and takes possession of the microphone.

The applause subsides.

The mayor clears his throat and begins to speak extempore, without the customary sheaf of notes, his broad smile exuding confidence.

"Thank you, all. Thanks for that warm welcome. It truly is great to be here again with you good people. It seems like only yesterday I was up here giving the same speech after the war in Europe came to an end."

Applause.

"I wonder if I'm the only person here today who has managed to sample all three varieties of wine so kindly donated by our French cousins."

"No!" comes a shout from the audience, followed by peals of laughter.

"Seems like they'd have given you a better seat at the head table."

More laughter and applause.

"Now I know you folks haven't come here today to listen to me state the obvious, and you want to get on and enjoy the party. So

I'll keep it short and to the point. First of all, I'd like to say that it is indeed a great honor to be with you people who have served America and who love America. I'd like to thank each and every one of you for your faithful service to God and country."

Applause.

"Now we all know why we are here today. We finally beat those Japanese warmongers and made them pay for what they started at Pearl Harbor some four years ago now."

Applause.

"Just recently, my attention has been drawn to some left-wing newspaper articles—published here in our own state, unbelievably—which seek to criticize our government's decision to use the atomic bomb on Japan. They say it was immoral and irresponsible, particularly since a bomb with such destructive capability cannot possibly have been confined to military targets. Well now, let me tell you, it really galls me to see articles of this nature appearing in our own newspapers, especially after the sacrifice this country has made these four years. I feel sorry for those people who are so misguided they feel compelled, for whatever reason, to write such untruths. May God have mercy on them.

"I would like to remind you of the words of our own beloved President Truman, following the use of the atomic bomb on August ninth. He said, and I quote, "We have used the bomb against those who attacked us without warning at Pearl Harbor, against those who have beaten and executed American prisoners of war, against those who have abandoned all pretense of obeying international laws of warfare. We have used it in order to shorten the agony of war, in order to save the lives of thousands and thousands of young Americans.

"I would like to emphasize that last sentence, folks—that the bomb was used "in order to save the lives of thousands and thousands of young Americans." In looking around this assembly today, ladies and gentlemen, I am only too aware of the sacrifices that have been made by each of you on behalf of this country. I know in the audience somewhere are Jeff and Dottie Stimson. They lost their two sons, Eddie and Sam, only in the last few months of the Pacific War. Their youngest son, Teddy, thank God, is alive and well and here with us tonight. Also, Bill and Deborah Reagan over in the corner there, they lost one son, Tom, on D-Day eighteen months ago and are now waiting to hear word on their other son Joe, missing in action since the battle for Okinawa. Our

prayers are with you both.

"And of course there are many others who I know have similar stories to tell, each one as tragic as the next.

"This state, like many others, has seen thousands of its young men killed in the Pacific Theatre. Now as far as I'm concerned, if using the atomic bombs resulted in saving the life of just one of our boys and allowing him to come home safe, then it was justified. Issues of morality don't even enter into it."

Applause.

"In closing, ladies and gentlemen, I would just like to say that our men and women in uniform have done and, let us not forget, continue to do, the work that they have been called upon to do. It is thanks to their courage and your support here at home that the world is now a more just and better place to live in than ever before. Thank you for having me here today. May God bless you all, and may God continue to bless America."

Standing ovation, and all raise their glasses in a toast to the United States of America.

The lights are lowered, and the band begins to play a slow, romantic waltz. He steers her by the elbow back through the crowd for a final dance. They embrace and move slowly with the music. He kneads her lower back with his strong fingers, and gently pulls her hips in toward his. The air is scented with her perfume. She feels him aroused and buries her face in his warm neck. Tonight, she knows, she will succumb to his every desire.

The lights come on and the music stops abruptly. They remain, for several moments, entwined in the middle of the dance floor, still lost in their own dreams. They open their eyes and smile knowingly at one another. They leave quickly, shaking hands and exchanging brief words with the mayor on the way out. Behind them, on stage, a middle-aged woman takes up the microphone and begins to sing Irving Berlin's "God Bless America." He leads her by the hand as they weave in and out of the rows of parked cars, until they reach their own.

The car parked next to theirs, a 1942 Chrysler New Yorker, bounces and rocks and a high-pitched female voice comes panting out of the open side window.

He looks at her longingly over the hood, and then they climb in. The motor turns, whines and then catches, spluttering into life. He turns his head, and a young pale girl's face, with soft lines around her sleepy eyes, appears in the window of the Chrysler only to be pulled down again by an anonymous hand a second later.

The car turns off the road onto the main highway, and they speed off into the Fresno countryside. Most of the road is unlit and shrouded in darkness, but he has driven this way hundreds of times before the war and knows it well. He looks sideways, places one hand on her thigh and sends her one of his trademark smiles. She reciprocates, and, relaxed, allows her thighs to part slightly.

Black storm clouds gather above, lightning darts all around, and heavy rain begins to sheet down on them. The road ahead stretches out like a vast river. Torrents of water race them downhill, the roadside ditches being too shallow to cope with the deluge.

The road winds on through a valley and woodland. He swerves left and left again. Through the sparse coppice to the right, he sees occasional headlights from cars traveling in the opposite direction. The car produces a strange metallic humming sound as it passes at speed over an iron cattle grid and then plunges into a dip, over a disused railroad crossing, and bounces up the other side spraying gravel over the grass bank. Sheep, huddled together under a clump of trees, sheltering as best they can from the worsening storm, bleat madly in protest as the car passes them by.

Visibility is dreadful. Driving rain lashes the windscreen, and a vicious crosswind coming off the low lying fields to the right plays havoc with the steering. She pulls herself upright, and, ever so gently, so as not to cause offense, moves his hand from her thigh and positions it back on the steering wheel.

The sky has grown darker. He frantically wipes at the condensation that is building up on the inside of the windscreen. He shoots her another "don't worry, darling" kind of sideways smile, always playful and confident. The car comes round a sharp corner, sharper than he remembers it, too fast. Tires scream on wet asphalt. He applies the brakes and feels the rear end lose purchase and slide away from him. The car begins to spin violently out of control. She brings both hands up to shield her face and screams as the vergeside fence rushes up to meet them. The bonnet plows through the flimsy barrier and the car plummets over the edge, turning over and over on its side. Sparks fly as metal collides with rock.

The car stops abruptly, and with it, the screaming. It is on its roof at the bottom of a ravine. The passenger door hangs off its hinges like a dislocated jaw. Barely conscious, he gropes about in the dark for the door handle. Blood trickles down the bridge of his nose from a gash on his forehead. His legs are numb.

"Laura. Laura!" His futile cry is carried away by the wind and muffled by the blackness of the night.

Carnaby is jerked back into the present—sweat-soaked, wide-eyed and panting.

Fourteen

Carnaby was dressed in formal evening attire and feeling very ill at ease. He was riding in the back of the department's black Buick, en route to the British Embassy to attend a celebratory function in honor of the coronation of Queen Elizabeth II, which had taken place in London the day before.

He tugged at the collar of his hastily-rented suit and stared out the window at the rain with a sour expression. If the truth were known, he hated events like this. All those stuffed shirts and people putting on airs and graces. It wasn't his scene at all. In fact, it was his boss, Aspin, who had received the invite. But at the last minute, he had, very conveniently Carnaby had thought, been called away from Tokyo on business for several days. He had asked Carnaby to go in his place and act as the CIA's official representative. He recalled Aspin's very words from the telephone conversation they'd had that morning: "I appreciate you're still on sick leave, Ralph, but I'm sure you can manage this. I guess you've got more time on your hands than the rest of us right now. Matter of fact, you might actually enjoy it. It'll do you good to get out and meet people. And of course, you'll be carrying out a very important role as representative of our organization."

He stifled a yawn with the back of his hand. He looked at the driver in the front mirror and said, "Hey, Davenport, slow down will ya? I'm in no hurry to get there."

Davenport laughed good-naturedly. "Sure thing, sir."

He looked out of the window and patted his jacket pocket to make sure the invitation was still there. It was. Unfortunately.

After completing a long, slow loop of the Imperial Palace—

time enough to settle his grumbling stomach, the car turned onto Uchibori-dori, and the perimeter wall of the embassy came into view. The embassy itself was an impressive structure; even Carnaby was forced to concede that. The original red brick building built in 1872 had been completely leveled by the Great Kanto Earthquake of 1923. In its place stood a splendid building constructed of limestone blocks with pillars topped with intricately chiseled stone tulip bowls. The embassy was a popular landmark with Tokyoites—not least because of the beautiful cherry trees growing in and around the grounds.

Davenport dropped him off on the sidewalk a few feet from the main gate. As he walked up the gravel drive he briefly considered waiting until the car had disappeared from sight and then going and killing time in some local bar until it was time to be picked up again. After all, he reasoned, how would Aspin know? But he decided that would be churlish and instead strode purposefully up to the main entrance, being careful not to step in any of the numerous water-filled potholes.

Security was predictably tight; he counted fifteen British soldiers around the gate alone, and there were probably more inside. In addition, there was the usual group of MPs, who were currently engaged in putting some awkward questions to a brace of Russian army officers, all of whom were splendidly decked out in full dress uniform and sporting more medals between them than he ever remembered seeing before.

He showed his invitation and ID and was waved through the gate with surprising ease, leaving the Russian crowd behind complaining bitterly about the discriminatory treatment being meted out to them and how it was an outrage that subjects of the Soviet Socialist Republics were being hounded like common criminals. He smirked and headed toward the main building.

Once inside, he deposited his coat in the cloakroom and then went through into the ballroom. A string quartet occupied a small stage toward the back of the room and was playing Beethoven's String Quartet No. 5. It seemed the British ambassador, Sir Henry Coaldrake, had already given his welcome speech—words to the effect that it was a great occasion and a superb opportunity for members of the British Commonwealth Occupation Force to get to know their American cousins and the representatives of the other members of the Allied Council. And he had not forgotten a toast to the new monarch: "God save the Queen!" There were some benefits to arriving late after all, thought Carnaby. Doubtless if and when the Russian party were allowed in, they would complain bitterly that the ambassador's speech had been given in their absence.

Four extremely grand chandeliers hung from the ornate ceiling, and they would have given out a fair degree of light had they not been dimmed in order to create just the right sort of 'ambiance.' He looked around and surveyed the sea of heads in the gloomy half light. A waiter walked past him balancing a silver tray loaded with champagne. He took a glass and casually walked down the wide marble steps to the dance floor.

Seeing nobody he recognized, he made for the comparative safety of the refreshments area. There were already a number of individuals propping the bar up, most of whom, like him, had that certain hunted look about them. He held the slender stem of the elegantly fluted glass in his right hand and leaned his hips square on against the edge of the bar. His left arm, although much better now, was still extremely stiff, especially when trussed up in tight fitting clothing. He moved it jerkily, like a mechanical prosthetic limb, and placed it on the bar alongside his right arm. He took another sip of his champagne and gazed into the wall-mounted mirror to his front. The music had changed to a slow andante, and a number of English gentleman-types led their wives by the hand and began pushing them like mops up and down the parquet dance floor. Suddenly there was a commotion over in the corner and he noticed the Russians entering the room from a side entrance, still gesticulating madly. He smiled, and then catching sight of his haggard face in the mirror, looked away.

A couple of already very tipsy middle-aged duffers were in full swing discussing the availability or otherwise of the evening's debutantes. Their plummy drawl seemed to carry above the general din going on around him.

"Well, what do you make of her?"

"Damned fine filly, I should say."

"Yes, yes, I know that. But what I mean to say, Carruthers, is do you think she would be up for it?"

"Up for it? What *are* you thinking old chap?"

"A dance, of course. What on earth did you think I meant?"

"Not sure really. But is she wearing a ring?"

"I don't know. But what does it matter? I mean, a pretty young thing like that—if she chooses to come here alone, well, it's rather her lookout, wouldn't you say?"

"Yes, quite. Well, there's only one way to find out. Why don't you pop the question? Go on—ask the gal. She can only say no."

Carnaby shook his head, drained his glass and set it down on the bar again. Christ, he felt out of place. Like the proverbial fish out of water—deracinated, struggling to survive in an unfamiliar environment. He was just about to turn and wander off in search of distractions anew when he became aware of someone approaching from behind.

"Hello, stranger."

He screwed his eyes up and peered at the dark form as it came closer in the mirror. The amorphous shape gradually gained perspective and then suddenly appeared in sharp relief. He let out a cry of delight: "Gloria!" And then his enthusiasm died a little as he caught sight of her official press corps tag fastened to her lapel. "Don't tell me you followed me all the way out here to get the lowdown on the Repatriation Program?" He laughed out loud and turned to face her.

"Life's a bitch, don't you think? You've gotta make a living somehow. And anyway," she added, with a boyish grin on her not unattractive face, "I figure you kind of owe me for standing me up last time round."

He had to smile at that one. He liked her no-nonsense way of talking. He knew straightaway where he stood with her. Which was refreshing after dealing most of the time with Japanese, who were invariably indirect and evasive in the extreme.

"Buy me a martini?" She beamed, taking out a pack of cigarettes and offering him one.

"The drinks are free, aren't they?"

"Uh-uh." She shook her head, removed the cigarette and blew out smoke. "Only the champagne. Everything else is strictly cash up front."

"Damn," he muttered, pulling out his wallet. "So much for British hospitality."

He bought two martinis and another pack of cigarettes. They clinked glasses.

"Cheers," she said, her eye going to his redundant left arm. "Here's to health and happiness. Talking of which, I hear you got shot up pretty bad."

He looked surprised. "Boy, news sure does travel fast."

"It's a small world. You find out who did it?"

"Nope," he replied, matter-of-factly. He thumped the butt of his cigarette on the back of the pack and placed it between his lips. He fished around in his pocket for a match, but she beat him to it, cupping one hand around the incandescent flame.

"Thanks," he said drawing in a lungful of smoke and staring beyond her into the distance.

"Oh, I get it," she said, a little testily. "You're not at liberty to talk about it. 'I scratch your back, you scratch mine'—ever hear that expression?"

"Sure I have. But what exactly can you do for me?" he replied, tossing the ball back into her court.

"You'd be surprised, Ralph. Surprised at what I see and hear but am told by the press club I'm not allowed to report."

"Such as?"

Without taking her eyes off him she drew on her cigarette, the tip flaring provocatively in the half-light. She folded her left arm across her middle and supported her right elbow in the palm of her hand. Tilting her head slightly to one side, she smiled coquettishly at him.

"Oh," spluttered Carnaby, "now *I* get it. Don't tell me—you're not at liberty to talk about it, right?"

She laughed and looked down at her feet, and described little circles with the toe of her shoe as she chased a flattened cigarette butt around the floor.

"Listen, Gloria," he said in a conciliatory tone, "to be perfectly frank, I don't know for sure who is responsible. My hunch is it was someone connected with the yakuza or maybe the Korean gangs—someone wanting to publicly register their disapproval of SCAP's interference in their affairs."

"But why pick on you?"

"Oh, come on," he snorted, "is your memory that short?"

"You talking about the club closures?"

"You're damned right I'm talking about the club closures."

"Just what the hell are you insinuating?"

"You remember, don't you? My name—appearing across the front page of your newspaper three months ago."

"Now hold on there, mister. It may have been my paper, but that information was passed to us by your press department bona fide for publication. Besides which," she added defensively, "it wasn't my goddamned article."

There was an uneasy silence as they both stared at each other—at a standoff.

He was the first to buckle. He breathed out heavily and let his shoulders sag. "Look," he said in a low voice, "I'm sorry. I didn't mean to blame you. I'm just a little tired, that's all." He looked at her and smiled hopefully. "Friends?"

She chewed her bottom lip and took a deep breath. Just as he thought he'd blown it and she would walk away, she smiled back at him. "Friends." She swilled the remains of the ice around in her martini and drained the glass. Her eyes wandered lazily back to his arm. "It was Amano Fisheries, right?"

"Pardon me?" he replied, momentarily confused by the change of subject. "Oh yeah. That's right. What of it?"

"I guess you checked it out. Afterwards I mean."

"Yeah, sure. One of our guys went out there right after it happened and questioned the owner. He said he had no idea why it had happened on his property."

"And you buy that?"

He shrugged. "No reason not to."

"I did a little poking around."

You're good at that, he thought, smiling attentively.

"You know that that place is inside the British occupation zone, right?"

"I didn't, but please go on."

"Well, it turns out it's just inside their jurisdiction. When I arrived here tonight, I got talking to some British major—Danby I think his name was. I was asking him whether the Brits are involved in the repatriation program—"

"You asked him *that*?" cut in Carnaby, unable to hide the incredulity in his voice.

She turned the corners of her mouth down dismissively. "Sure, why not? You have to be thick-skinned in my business. Anyway, he seemed happy to talk—after I'd plied him with a few drinks that is. He told me that up until two years ago Amano Fisheries had been used as a disembarkation point for repatriated Japanese soldiers shipped via the Kurile Islands. The Brits had an interrogation and resettlement center over at Tateyama."

He felt a sudden hot flush. "You said up until two years ago. So what happened then?"

"He didn't really know, although he said he got the impression that 'you Yanks'—to use his words, wanted to centralize and control the whole operation through Maizuru and that Amano was only a small-scale operation used for overspill."

"Is that it?"

"Yeah. He got a little nervous after that. Kind of had that look on his face as if to say 'God, I've told you more than I should've.' Like he knew he'd said something he'd regret later." She chuckled and raised her empty glass. "Another drink?"

He grinned. "I'd better not. Alcohol doesn't go too well with painkillers," *and I'd hate to say something I'd regret later,* he thought.

A waiter approached carrying a tray of canapés. "Now food on the other hand," he said—his hand hovering over the tiny morsels, "that's an entirely different matter. I'm famished. Now let's see what we've got here." He crammed a handful of assorted savories into his mouth, his eyes still roaming over the tray. He looked at the waiter. "Say, Mac, what time is the real food served?"

"I'm sorry, sir, finger food only is being provided this evening."

"You don't say," he said looking disappointed. He winked at Gloria. "More British hospitality I guess."

She laughed and then looked up suddenly as another waiter scurried over, evidently looking for someone.

"Mr. Carnaby?"

"Yeah, that's me."

"Ah, so sorry to disturb you sir but you have a telephone call."

"I do?"

"Yes, sir. Booth number one out in the foyer."

"Probably my boss checking up on me," he joked. "If you'll excuse me for a moment, I'll be right back."

He followed the waiter back up the stairs and into the foyer. Along the wall opposite the cloakroom was a bank of six phone booths. He went over to booth number one and pulled on the handle. The door was incredibly stiff to open and once inside, it seemed to take an interminable length of time to close again behind him. He picked the receiver up and put it to his ear.

"Hello?"

He heard someone breathing and then a nervous voice. "Mr. Carnaby?"

"Yes, speaking. Who is this?"

"I . . . I'm afraid I can't say over the telephone."

He moved the receiver away from his ear and looked askance at it—*what kind of baloney is this?* he thought. "Is this some kind of practical joke?"

"No. Please don't hang up. It's important. I need to talk to you—tomorrow."

"Why should I see you if you won't even tell me who you are?"

There was a pause. "It concerns Mr. Brice."

He swayed slightly and steadied himself by placing one hand on the directory shelf. He instinctively glanced over his shoulder and turned back again. "Go on."

"Meet me at eleven o'clock tomorrow morning. There is a restaurant called the Parisian Grill in the—"

"Uh-uh," cut in Carnaby at once. "If I'm to meet with you it has to be somewhere out in the open." He thought quickly. "You know Hibiya Park?"

There was another pause. "Yes."

"There's a bunch of discarded statues by the east entrance."

"I know it. Alright. Eleven o'clock by the statues. Please come alone."

"How will you know it's me?"

"I will know."

Click—the line went dead. Carnaby looked at the receiver once again and then hurried out through the door. He took a couple of paces back and looked along the line of booths. The end two were occupied. A man, probably in his sixties, emerged from one of the booths. It couldn't have been him. The caller was a young man, by the sound of his voice at any rate. Frustrated, he strode up to the other booth and peered in through the window, but it was a young woman, dressed in British naval uniform.

He turned around and caught sight of the waiter walking back toward the ballroom. "Excuse me." He waved his hand and caught the waiter's attention.

"Yes, sir. Is everything alright?"

"The caller just now—how did he know I was here?"

"Sorry, sir?" the waiter looked confused.

"When you came out to fetch me, you came straight over like you knew it was me."

"Oh yes, sir. The caller said you were standing by the bar talking to a lady of the press with short hair."

Carnaby stood and stared. "So he was *here*? He called from here?"

"Well, yes," laughed the dim-witted waiter, "I suppose that's right sir."

"Tell me," he said, looking quickly around the foyer, "are there any other internal phones besides these?"

The waiter looked doubtful, and then, as if he'd suddenly remembered, said, "Ah yes, there is a single telephone booth in the entrance hallway."

Carnaby didn't wait for him to finish and took off toward the front entrance. The first thing he noticed was the door—the same type of door, with a strongly sprung hinge, as the others in the foyer. And something else: the door hadn't quite closed fully. He wrenched it open, went inside and lifted the receiver from its cradle. He sniffed at the mouthpiece, and then, as he moved it away from his face, he saw a sprinkling of tiny droplets of condensation. Somebody had definitely used the phone just now.

He came back through the foyer lost in his own thoughts. "Oh, sir?" It was the waiter again. "I just checked with the switchboard girl—the call was placed from the internal telephone by the main entrance."

"I see," he said. "She didn't get the name by any chance?"

"I'm afraid not, sir."

"Okay. Thank you. That's most helpful."

He traipsed back into the ballroom and headed for the bar again. There was no sign of Gloria, and then he saw her—across the other side of the room. She had a British officer pinned up against the wall, giving him a good grilling by the looks of things. Carnaby ordered a double whiskey and slugged it back, his mind working overtime to make sense of the call. The evening was turning out to be pretty interesting after all.

Yet another slow waltz had just started. He checked his watch and thought about leaving when he heard a shriek of protest coming from the fringe of the dance floor.

"Get your hands *off* me!"

"Now come along, dear. Be a good sport now. It's only one little dance. I won't bite, you know."

It was one of the middle-aged duffers, obviously now sufficiently tanked-up with Dutch courage and in the process of physically molesting an extremely attractive young lady. Fortified by the double whiskey, Carnaby launched into action, without a thought as to the possible consequences.

"There you are, doll! I've been looking all over for you. I

keep telling you not to talk to strangers." Carnaby grabbed the stunned girl by the wrist and led her away into the crowd. Her interloper was left dithering on the sidelines, still muttering his confused apologies. "S-sorry old chap, I really had no idea."

He pulled her in close with his arm around her slim waist. She resisted slightly at first, but then succumbed and placed her head on his shoulder. He whispered in her ear, "Sorry I had to do that."

She remained silent, her eyes closed, enraptured by the intoxicating music. Carnaby was in heaven. All his aches and pains and worldly cares seemed to melt away. He could have stayed like that all night, but, like all good things, the music came to an end.

"That was a real pleasure, ma'am." He smiled as the lights came up. He was still holding her gloved hand as if afraid to let go.

She smiled back demurely. "Oh no. The pleasure was all mine. Thank you so much for rescuing me."

"It was the least I could do, believe me. I hate to see a lady in a fix." He paused. "By the way, my name's Carnaby."

She giggled and blushed. "Oh yes, of course. How rude of me." She stepped forward directly under the chandelier, so that the light shone on her perfectly formed features. She held his hands in hers, shook her thick hair back from her shoulders and looked him straight in the eye. "I'm Emma. Emma Forbes. Delighted to make your acquaintance, Mr. Carnaby."

Fifteen

The park was already crowded, and Carnaby suddenly remembered the reason why. There was to be a grand parade, starting at noon from the Imperial Plaza, followed by a friendly baseball game between the Tokyo Metropolitan Police team and players representing SCAP. More proof, if ever more were needed, to demonstrate to the Russians just how well the symbiotic relationship between America and Japan was actually working.

And, as chance would have it, the Japan Communist Party leader, Kyuichi Tokuda, was scheduled to hold a rally at the opposite end of the Imperial Plaza—or "People's Plaza" as they had affectionately renamed it—also beginning, as chance would have it, at noon.

Carnaby vaguely remembered seeing a notice on the office bulletin board a few days earlier recording SCAP's belated decision to allow the rally to go ahead, provided it was held in a peaceful manner. Freedom of speech was, after all, one of the guiding principles of democracy that SCAP was trying to encourage.

He looked at his watch: 10:40—still twenty minutes to wait. It was already very warm and, to add to his discomfort, he had one hell of a hangover from the night before. Why he had felt the need to have that last double whiskey—God only knew. But then, he thought, with a slight smile, the night wouldn't have turned out the way it did if he hadn't. His throat was dry and felt furry. There was a drinking fountain by the park entrance. He wandered over and, pressing down on the worn brass faucet with his right hand, bent over the nozzle and quenched his thirst. He let the cool spray play on his face for a few seconds before drying himself off with a handkerchief.

Suddenly feeling desperate for a cigarette, he pulled a crumpled pack of Lucky Strikes out of his trouser pocket, only to find he had already smoked the last of them for breakfast. Frowning, he turned around and spotted a kiosk across the road, just by the driveway to the Imperial Hotel. He tossed the empty pack into a concrete trash receptacle and strode across the street just as the traffic lights were changing. A helmet-less foreigner with sun-bleached blonde hair jumped the light and buzzed past on his Rabbit motor scooter, narrowly avoiding clipping Carnaby's heels. But he was too preoccupied to have noticed. He approached the kiosk with a fatuous smile—the camouflage he always wore to hide his nerves when dealing with the local people. Clearing his throat he beamed at the vendor. "*Tabako*?"

The vendor, a slightly-built man about his own age and still dressed in his wartime shirt and cap, pointed to the limited selection of brands on sale.

He raised his eyebrows and said, more in hope than expectation, "Lucky Strikes?"

The vendor waved a hand rapidly from side-to-side in front of his nose and smiled back: "No. No. *Kore shika gozaimasen—these are all we have, I'm afraid.*"

He only stocked a couple of brands, Rose and Gion, which were supposedly manufactured locally to cater to the growing GI market. He had tried Rose cigarettes before, and his abiding memory was of smoking something that tasted like a tube of damp straw. He decided on the Gion brand. He also took a copy of the English daily *The Nippon Times*, handed over the correct amount of money and then headed back toward the park entrance.

He was accosted on his way through the gate by a young laborer who was handing out poorly printed copies of *Akahata*, the official organ of the Japan Communist Party. He couldn't read it, of course, but he recognized its distinctive red cover. It had been the subject of endless debate over the last few years—whether to allow it, subject it to the blue-pencil editorial discretion of the censor, or suppress it outright. Censorship was usually rejected as being too much of an administrative burden, although the truth of the matter was that if they went down that route, the entire contents would have to be culled. Publication was currently allowed on an as-is basis, but the suppress-it-outright faction was gaining support almost by the day among the occupation authorities.

He ignored the man and pushed past him and into the park again. It was still only ten minutes to eleven, but he decided to go in through the east entrance anyway and kill time reading his paper.

As he approached the overgrown perimeter hedge, he could hear the shriek of children's laughter. And then, as he came up to the iron gate, he saw them: three scantily clad urchins clambering all over the statue of General Iwao Oyama, hero of the Russo-Japanese War of 1903. The general was one of five statues of military heroes that had been unceremoniously wrenched from their moorings at the end of the war and removed to this secluded corner of the park pending their destruction. As time went on, however, nothing was done about them, so that now, some eight years later, they had become more or less a permanent fixture. Even the one official English guidebook in circulation had devoted a couple of sentences to them under the entry for Hibiya Park:

> 'Entering Hibiya Park from the east entrance the visitor will happen upon a small iron gate set into a tall hedge. There are no signs indicating the way, and it would be easily passed by if one was not aware of its existence. On going through the gate, the visitor will be surprised to find a group of bronze statues depicting five historical persons of note from various periods of Japan's history (in chronological order: Yoshitsune Minamoto, Masashige Kusunoki, Ieyasu Tokugawa, Takamori Saigo, and General Iwao Oyama). The statues, which formerly stood in different parks and public avenues in Tokyo, were dismantled at the beginning of the U.S. occupation as a symbol of America's determination to demilitarize the country. The statues have been there ever since, and, while their fate is as yet uncertain, they have taken on an air of almost defiant permanence.'

This was the only corner of the otherwise immaculately tended park that had been allowed to go to ruin. For the Japanese, it was as if the statues weren't there at all. The hedges were overgrown, and the statues couldn't be seen without first going through the gate. They couldn't be seen; therefore they didn't exist, and neither did the ignominy that went with them. And, as for the occupation authorities, well, inertia had got the better of them at a time when they had much more pressing matters to occupy their time. And in some ways they *had* disposed of the statues by taking them off their grand pedestals in prominent public places and depositing them here—all higgledy-piggledy and out of sight amid the undergrowth—for the children to play on and the vagrants to shelter under.

Apart from the children, there were only two other people in the enclosure: a homeless man lying full length on one of the unpainted benches, a cloth bag—doubtless containing the sum of his worldly belongings—hanging by a cord from his grimy wrist, and, slightly further round the curve, a ruddy-cheeked student who was busily disassembling a rather battered-looking clarinet.

The iron gate sprung back into place behind him with a clatter. He feigned nonchalance, skirted the inner perimeter of the hedge and located a bench on the far side of the enclosure. He brushed some seed pods from the wooden surface with the palm of his hand, hitched his trousers up slightly and sat down. He could just see the lower half of the gate—the upper half being obscured by the bronze tail of the general's horse. He lit a cigarette, inhaled deeply, and then rocked forward, spluttering, with a look of disgust on his face. He took the cigarette out of his mouth and eyed it suspiciously before thumping it to the ground and extinguishing it with the heel of his shoe.

Thinking for a moment he had mistakenly bought the Rose brand cigarettes, he pulled the pack out again and scrutinized the logo: Gion. Different brand, same damp straw taste. And the smell—like animal bedding, only somehow much worse. It was beyond description. He turned the pack over in his hand. There was some English printed in minuscule lettering near the bottom edge: "For domestic consumption only." Huh, he scoffed. Some hope they'd have trying to sell this crap back home.

He looked at his watch, for the umpteenth time: 11:10. Where the hell was this guy? He was starting to become irritated and shook the folded newspaper open and held it by the edges, taut, with both hands. The pages were full of the same old headlines: "War in Korea heats up," "Korean evacuee problem worsens," "UN resolves to provide more support for South Korean people," "Soviets attempt to veto UN resolution," "US tanks roll off production line at Mitsui Heavy Industries' Sagamihara Plant," "Yoshida lambasted in Diet for advocating dispatch of former Japanese soldiers to ease manpower shortage in Korean Peninsula—parliamentary dissolution hangs in the balance."

He breathed out heavily, like an exhausted prizefighter who

had just thrown in the towel. He was sick of it. Sick of the war in goddamned Korea, sick of hearing about it even, sick of his job, sick of Japan, sick of his inability to make a decision about where his life was going. Maybe he ought to pack up and head on home after all. Start up his old law practice again; maybe even settle down with Beth. It wasn't too late. He knew she wanted to, desperately in point of fact.

In the midst of this self-pitying reverie, his peripheral vision registered a movement somewhere over the top of the wavering newspaper. He glanced up and blinked—once, twice, like a camera shutter—and took in the student's legs disappearing through the wrought iron gate before transferring his gaze to the paper again. Then he stopped reading and stared intently for a moment at the same spot on the page while his brain worked to figure out what his mind had already perceived. The iron gate was relatively heavy, and sprung. The student had been carrying a bulky satchel in one hand and his clarinet case in the other. And yet there had been no clanking sound as the gate had banged shut behind him. He slowly lowered the newspaper and peered under the horse's tail. The gate was still open, and in the space where it should have been was a pair of legs clad in beige canvas trousers.

He sat bolt upright and closed the newspaper. Then, feeling ridiculous, he forced himself to relax, eased back a little on the bench, and opened the newspaper again, this time laying it casually across his lap. He bent his head forward and pretended to read the sports column. He heard the gate close—with a low grating sound this time—and then became aware of a lone figure walking slowly, nervously perhaps, around the edge of the enclosure—in the same anticlockwise direction from which he himself had come. His mind searched rapidly through his imperfect memory of the telephone conversation the night before, but nothing came to mind.

He could hear footsteps now—slow and deliberate. He wanted to look up, but kept his head bent over the newspaper—a picture of concentration. For all he knew it might be some completely unconnected individual. A tourist perhaps. He might have spotted the vagrant on the bench and decided to walk this way around. That would be most people's reaction, wouldn't it? The instinctive, natural course of action one would take on being unexpectedly faced with something a little unpleasant.

The footsteps stopped suddenly, just off to his left, in front of the general.

A large black crow fluttered down and landed to the right of his feet. The bird had a disheveled appearance with poor plumage, and it seemed to be speckled all over with a fine gray powder, as if it had been rolling around in the dust. It had a piece of blood-flecked carrion in its beak which it was trying to separate into a more manageable size by pinning it to the ground with its claws and pulling back with short, jerky head movements.

There was a sudden staccato click, and the crow hopped back, cawing raucously, and then darted forward again to retrieve the piece of meat it had dropped. Carnaby started and jerked his head up. It *was* a tourist, he thought. He was probably American, judging from the chintzy windbreaker and beige trousers, and taking snapshots of the statues with his 'Baby Pearl' camera.

He stared at the solitary figure for a few moments longer before returning his attention to his newspaper. A slight breeze came through the hedge, and he felt the sweat on his back go cold.

"Nice day for a parade."

He looked up again. "Pardon me?"

"Nice day for a parade, Mr. Carnaby."

Carnaby froze, his steely eyes unblinking, taking in every detail of the man who stood before him—short, about five six, five seven maybe with sandy-colored sparse hair, a freckled forehead, and a pale, almost nondescript face with a weak jaw line. Thin lips framed a slanted, not quite happy, not quite sad kind of smile—the archetypal misanthrope. He reminded him of a kid he had once known in junior school—the neighborhood weakling, who was always being bullied by the local roughnecks. Bookish, socially inept, no interest in dating girls. His father had been in the army. The poor kid was continually being carted around from state to state. He never stood a chance.

"You are Mister Carnaby, aren't you?"

Carnaby looked him squarely in the face. "And do I get to know who you are this time?"

The slightly-built figure squinted and then raised a hand to shield his eyes from the penetrating glare of the midday sun. "Yes. My name is Boris Chernenkoff. May I?" he continued, indicating the bench with a slight nod.

"Yeah, sure. Why not? Since you're here. Be my guest." Carnaby shifted sideways a little, dragging his feet noisily across the gravel and sending the crow into a spasm of renewed protest.

Chernenkoff sat down and craned his reptilian neck sideways. "I must apologize for being late," he said, emphatically. "I had forgotten all about the baseball game. The crowds . . . " He was suddenly at a loss for words.

"Yeah," sighed Carnaby, rubbing his forehead, "they're quite something, aren't they?"

"It's funny," said Chernenkoff matter-of-factly. "I used to meet my wife for a picnic lunch here sometimes."

"You don't say," said Carnaby, trying without success to disguise his impatience with the small talk.

Chernenkoff chuckled quietly to himself. "Yes. She used to work at the Bank of Japan, before we had our first child that is. Something about this place—the way it's hidden away like this perhaps—made our meetings seem somehow more daring, as if we were having an illicit affair." He chuckled again, adjusted his position and swung one leg casually over the other.

Carnaby looked at his watch and then, wrapping the fingers of his right hand around his left wrist, massaged his forearm and grimaced slightly, as if having just been released from a pair of tight fitting handcuffs. "I don't wish to seem rude, Mr. Chernenkoff, but I don't have a whole lot of free time today. Do you mind getting to the point?"

"Why yes, of course. I am sorry. Please forgive me," he said, pulling out a pack of Lucky Strikes from his trouser pocket. He proffered the pack. "Would you like one?"

"No, thanks. I'm trying to quit," lied Carnaby, who was, in actual fact, desperate for a decent cigarette. He suddenly became aware of the other man's gaze, which had fallen on the cigarette butt at his feet. He cleared his throat loudly and, he realized although didn't care, rather too obviously.

Chernenkoff blew out a trail of smoke and looked up through watery eyes. "I used to work in G2 Counterintelligence," he began, suddenly serious. "Soviet surveillance to be precise. Harvey Brice was a colleague of mine before he was recruited by General Brannigan. We were good friends—had been for several years. We were both involved in Soviet counterespionage after the war—"

"Are you Russian?" interrupted Carnaby.

"No," said Chernenkoff, "although I am often mistaken for

one. I am Polish-American."

"I see. Go on."

"Excuse me?"

"You were saying . . . before I interrupted you."

Chernenkoff took another drag on his cigarette. "Ah, yes. As I was saying, both Harvey and I worked in Soviet surveillance for close to five years. It was quite stressful work at times. In the early days it mainly involved decoding intercepted signals between Moscow and the Soviet embassy here in Tokyo. But as the cold war intensified, we were required to participate in increasingly hazardous covert intelligence operations. You know the sort of thing—clandestine meetings—ingratiating ourselves with the Soviets and allowing ourselves to be 'recruited.' I suppose, strictly speaking, we were acting as double agents. Harvey became quite depressed toward the end."

"Toward the end?" repeated Carnaby. "You mean you kept in touch even after he quit G2?"

"Yes. Sometimes at the church in Chiyoda Ward. Other times he would come by my place for Sunday lunch. And then, of course, I saw him daily once I joined the research project last fall."

"But if he left G2 six months before he died, why was he still depressed?"

Chernenkoff flicked the butt of his smoked cigarette away across the gravel and followed it with his gaze, watching the orange tip fade and then flare suddenly as it was caught and fanned by the breeze coming through the hedge. "Harvey was in debt. Quite badly I fear."

"In debt?" said Carnaby, trying to keep his voice level. "To whom?"

"He wouldn't tell me all the details. He insisted it was not a big deal and he could sort it out. He was stubborn that way. You do know he was going to be married?"

Carnaby remained silent.

"He was trying to save money to buy a house in England and a little extra to see him through the first few months in case he had problems finding a new job. I think he borrowed money, gambled it and lost everything."

"But you don't know that for a fact, right?" Carnaby was starting to become irritated again.

"It is possible I am mistaken," replied Chernenkoff, a little too smugly, "but I knew Harvey very well. Let us just say I have pieced it together from what he told me and from what I know about him. I am ninety-nine percent sure that is what happened."

"And from what you know about him, do you believe he shot himself?"

"Why yes, of course, Mr. Carnaby," spluttered Chernenkoff, barely managing to conceal a smile. "I'm quite frankly surprised that you seem to think otherwise."

"I didn't say that."

Chernenkoff seemed to lose his train of thought and looked at the ground and began making small circles in the gravel with the toe of his shoe.

"Tell me, Mr. Chernenkoff, how did you know who I was last night?"

Chernenkoff fumbled around in his pocket and pulled out his cigarettes again. He shook one out and lit it, drawing deeply on the filter. His hand seemed to be trembling slightly. He forced a smile. "I remembered your picture from the papers a few months ago. And then when I saw you last night."

Carnaby smiled back. "I wasn't aware my picture made the papers. And in any case," he continued, the smile now having evaporated, "that story was totally unconnected with the Brice investigation. What's the matter, Mr. Chernenkoff? I seem to be making you uncomfortable."

"No, not at all. I heard you were asking questions. I was a friend of Harvey's. I just wanted to help, that's all." He looked at his watch, ostentatiously, and then squinted at Carnaby. "I'm afraid I have to go now. I have another appointment."

Suddenly, from the direction of the park, came the sound of excited shouting, interspersed by shrill whistle blasts.

"It looks like our communist friends are in trouble again," said Carnaby, his face expressionless.

But Chernenkoff was already on his feet, stomping his half-smoked cigarette into the gravel. He smiled faintly at Carnaby and said, "If I think of anything else, Mr. Carnaby, I will call you."

Carnaby just looked at him and made no attempt to reply. Chernenkoff stopped smiling, turned and walked quickly toward the gate with the sun shining on his balding scalp.

Carnaby let his arms drop to his sides, leaned back against

the bench and exhaled forcibly. He scrunched his eyes shut and clenched his fists so that his knuckles turned white. He stayed like that for several seconds and then, as if suddenly remembering something, he stood up and walked slowly around the path and stopped in front of the homeless man.

He leaned over, and, much to the bewilderment of the two children, who were now sitting stock still and gazing on from the shadow of Yoshitsune, tugged at the man's trouser leg and said, "Hey, you're taking up the whole bench."

The legs folded at the knees, withdrew and then swung over the edge into a sitting position.

"For a minute there I thought you'd fallen asleep on me," he said, smiling.

Dan Morita smiled back and then stretched expansively. "To tell you the truth, Ralph, I almost did."

"Did you hear any of that?"

"Uh-uh," yawned Morita, shaking his head. He wiped tears from his eyes and looked at Carnaby. "So, did he tell you anything you didn't already know?"

"Nope. Can't say as he did. Except he did his darnedest to convince me that Brice killed himself. Said he was depressed because he was in debt. Said he'd borrowed money and then lost it gambling."

"Well, at least that ties in with the loan shark evidence."

"I don't know, Dan," Carnaby said, folding his arms and gazing into the distance. "Something isn't right. His story was too slick, almost like it was pre-arranged."

"You think someone put him up to it?"

"Yeah, I'm sure of it. Listen, Dan," he continued, glancing at his watch, "I have to go and meet the mysterious Miss Forbes. Do me a favor, will you, and check this guy out? He said his name is Chernenkoff. Boris Chernenkoff. He was working over in G2 up until last fall and then he supposedly transferred to the research project."

"No problem, Ralph," said Morita as Carnaby stood up and brushed the creases out of his trousers. As he strode off toward the gate Morita shouted after him. "Hey, Ralph. Miss Forbes—is she pretty?"

Carnaby stopped dead and looked back over his shoulder with an entirely innocent expression. "She's the prettiest woman I've ever seen."

Sixteen

The first thing Carnaby thought when he saw Emma Forbes again was that she really was the prettiest woman he had ever seen.

They had arranged to meet at the Café Yoshiwara on the ground floor of the Mitsukoshi department store in Ginza, this being a prominent landmark and easily located by even the most geographically challenged visitor to Tokyo.

He bought a spray of roses from a roadside florist that had set up its stall just outside the department store and strode purposefully into the café. He spotted Emma sitting alone at a window table, her head buried in a small book. She looked as though she had stepped out of the pages of *Vogue* magazine—a red velvet pillbox hat perched on top of a cascade of shiny brown shoulder-length hair, and a well-cut red velvet jacket and skirt to match. Her long, slender legs were wrapped in black stockings—probably silk, he thought with a discerning eye—and tapered gracefully into neat little black patent high-heeled shoes.

He beamed. "Miss Forbes. I hope I'm not late."

She looked up and smiled, revealing a row of perfectly formed white teeth. "No, not at all, Mister Carnaby. I've only just arrived myself."

With something of an operatic flourish, he produced the flowers from behind his back. "I think I said it last night, but I'm sorry about your fiancée. I really wish you were out here under different circumstances."

"Oh, they are quite beautiful," she said with a gasp. She paused for a few moments while she admired the bouquet. "Thank you. And thank you for your kind words. Please, won't you sit down?"

"Thank you, ma'am."

"Please, call me Emma."

"Alright, Emma. But only if you call me Ralph."

"Alright, Ralph," she giggled. "You have yourself a deal."

A waiter walked by, and Carnaby ordered two tall iced teas with lemon—the house specialty, he explained, and the perfect refreshment to have on a warm spring day in Tokyo.

They clinked glasses, and he watched her take a measured sip of the light brown liquid.

"That really is delicious. I've never had iced tea before. It's not how we take it in England you know."

He smiled. "No, I don't imagine it is. To be perfectly honest, it's only in the last year that it's really taken off over here. It seems like every café in town has it on the menu now."

She laughed again, easily, he noticed, and gazed thoughtfully at the flowers now resting on their side by the window. He toyed with his napkin, conscious of the sudden awkward silence that had come between them. He took another drink and set his glass down on the coaster. Leaning forward he laced his fingers together and looked at her, his expression suddenly serious. "You know," he began, catching her eye, "I still can't quite believe I ran into you just like that at the embassy last night."

"Neither can I," she replied. "But I'm jolly glad you did. I was beginning to think I would never escape the clutches of those two awful men."

"They *were* pretty drunk I guess," he said with a wry smile.

She suddenly started giggling. "The look on their faces when you came over and whisked me onto the dance floor the way you did—they were at an absolute loss for words!"

"Yeah," he agreed, "but I guess they got what was coming to them. They should know better at their age." He took another sip of tea, leaned back comfortably and said, "By the way, I meant to ask: how's the new job? It must be quite something being governess to the ambassador's children."

"So far so good," she replied. "The children don't arrive until the end of next week. The ambassador is going back for a week to collect them."

"Swell," said Carnaby. "So you have some time to yourself for a few days."

"Yes, that's right. I want to settle in, get to know my way around the city. Do a little sightseeing perhaps."

"Well, I'd be happy to show you around if you like. I'm on leave for a few more days and no plans to go anywhere in particular."

"That's very kind of you." She paused and pressed her hands together, a troubled expression forming on her face. "I was also hoping to make the most of the quiet time to find out what I can about Harvey. . . . " She looked at him and then glanced out the window, momentarily distracted by the squeal of brakes as an Army jeep slewed across the road and pulled up in a hurry at the light by the junction. "It hardly seems like an occupation," she said, dreamily. "At least not the way I had imagined it. It's all so informal—and not nearly as many soldiers as I thought."

"It's been pretty informal from the outset," he started to explain, in spite of himself. "The idea is to allow the Japanese to govern their own people with a minimum of interference from us."

"Oh, I didn't realize that."

"Yeah. Of course, all the important decisions need to be approved beforehand. But it gives them a way of saving face, which is kind of important for the Japanese. It's all designed to encourage a cooperative atmosphere. That way they get to have a say in how their own country is reconstructed."

"That would seem to make sense," she agreed.

"Yeah," he continued, clearly enjoying the opportunity to share with her the benefit of his experience and put off for a short while longer what he sensed was going to be a more difficult conversation for her than he had thought. "Some people call it the 'hearts and minds' campaign. The hope is that when Uncle Sam eventually decides to give the Japs back their independence, they'll be so grateful for what we've done for them they'll want to stick around as our ally. The other benefit to us is that if they do it themselves, it reduces the burden on the occupying force. It's quite different to the occupation in Germany, although over there, of course, there's the added complication of the Russians. Here, we get to call the shots. We run the whole show single-handedly."

"Now wait just one minute Mister Carnaby—"

"Ralph, remember?" He gave her a supercilious grin.

"Sorry, Ralph. Aren't you forgetting the British in all of this?"

He let out a short burst of laughter. "Aw, come on, Emma. You don't seriously believe you guys have any real influence out here do you?"

But Emma wasn't smiling anymore. "The ambassador told me there are almost twelve thousand British and Commonwealth troops stationed in Japan."

"Well, yes, that's probably about right," he admitted, suddenly realizing he had touched a nerve. "Of course, the British force is important. But all I'm trying to say is that in the overall scheme of things, it isn't significant. It's more of a token contribution. That's really why those guys are all based in northern Japan and Hokkaido, where nothing ever happens. The machinery of government is right here in Tokyo. You see what I'm saying?" He appealed to her with a big, stupid grin on his handsome face. But she had turned toward the window, apparently watching the multitude of shoppers coming and going along the wide strip of Ginza-dori. He cupped his hands around his glass and felt the cool condensation trickle through his fingers. He stared at the slice of lemon, stuck to the side of the glass like some translucent golden mollusk. He could tell she was on edge—emotionally fragile. Witness her reaction to his description of the occupation just now. And yet she had seemed so calm and in control before that.

"You said last night that you wanted to talk to me about Harvey," she said abruptly, still gazing out of the window.

"Yeah," he replied, "that's right. Say, would you like a refill?"

"No. Not for the moment thank you."

"Alright. Fine," he said, finding it difficult to conceal his chagrin. He drained his glass and then pulled his chair in closer so as not to be overheard by the eavesdroppers his paranoia had convinced him were sitting amongst the group of old ladies sipping iced tea at the table adjacent to their own. He glanced around one more time, just to make sure, and then said to her, in a confidential tone, "One thing you ought to know before I get into this—I'm not supposed to be investigating this case any more, at least not officially, that is. . . . "

Emma turned her head back, slowly and deliberately, and looked at him quizzically. "Then why are you?"

He felt his shoulders slump, and he let out a long audible sigh. "It's a long story, Emma," he said at length. "I'm not really sure where to begin."

"Perhaps the beginning might be a good place," she suggested.

He ignored the incipient sarcasm in her voice and over the

next thirty minutes or so recounted her, in as much detail as he thought she needed to know for the time being, the circumstances surrounding the death of Harvey Brice.

Throughout his explanation she sat in silence, still as a statue, staring fixedly out the window, as if it was the dullest, most improbable story she had ever heard. And when he had finished talking, she shivered, involuntarily, and said, "I think I'll have that refill now, if I may."

They sat in contemplative silence, avoiding each other's gaze, until the waiter returned with fresh drinks.

Outside, it had started to rain—one of those sudden downpours so typical of *tsuyu*, the rainy season which visits itself on Japan between the end of May and mid-July each year. Everywhere people darted for cover into doorways or hurried along the sidewalk in the direction of the subway steps. The whole scene was suddenly transformed—like a piece of movie house footage that had been speeded up for comical effect.

A G.I. and a young Japanese woman, both soaked to the skin, came in through the café door.

"*Irasshaimase!*" "Welcome!" boomed the waiter.

The drinks arrived and were set down on the table. Carnaby watched her for a few moments, chasing the ice cubes around her glass with the end of a lacquered swizzle stick. The flowers' petals fluttered and danced in the breeze produced by the downdraft from an electric fan, which was suspended from the ceiling. He noticed the goose bumps on her forearms. That was the problem with this lousy weather, he thought to himself—so humid it was impossible to walk ten paces outside without being drenched with sweat and yet the minute you were inside again, the sweat dried cold on your back.

He coughed slightly, and she raised her eyes from her glass. "I guess it's a lot to take in all at once, isn't it?"

"Yes," she said quietly. She bit her bottom lip and stared at the glistening rings of water left by the glasses on the table surface.

He shifted slightly in his chair and coughed again. "Do you mind if I ask you how you came to meet Harvey?"

She lifted her eyes once more. They were red-rimmed he noticed for the first time. "It was back home—in England. In a small town called Bletchley, where I live." She paused and drank some tea.

"So he was on vacation over there?"

"No, no," she answered, wiping her mouth with the napkin. "He was working at Bletchley Park, the government communications center."

"The government communications center?" he repeated, raising his eyebrows. "There was no mention of that in his military record."

"Well, it was only six months. He volunteered for an assignment there—training to use some newfangled decoding equipment they had developed there."

"And he told you all this?"

"Yes. Not at first, of course. I know he probably shouldn't have. It was probably a breach of the Official Secrets Act."

"Emma, let me get this straight. He was based there for six months, and you were working there at the same time."

"No. I mean yes. I mean, yes he was there for six months, but I wasn't working there. I taught in a local junior school just around the corner from Bletchley Park."

"I see," said Carnaby, who didn't really see at all.

"That summer the officers' mess decided to throw a ball, and they invited the mayor and other local dignitaries. I think it was aimed at presenting the military as a friendly organization, with friendly people. There was a lot of secrecy surrounding that place. I think the local townsfolk were suspicious of what went on there. Anyway," she continued, with a sigh, "I ended up going quite by accident really. My aunt Clarice was the person actually invited. She was, still is in fact, president of Bletchley WI—"

"WI?" he said, a little perplexed.

"Women's Institute. Sorry, I keep forgetting you're not English. Aunt Clarice always liked to think she was acting in my best interests. Anyway, to cut a long story short, she thought I might meet a nice young man there."

"I guess she was right about that."

"Yes," nodded Emma, her voice trailing off, "I suppose she was."

"When exactly was this?" he asked.

"Last June," she said without hesitating. She suddenly stared off into the distance, as if in a trance, and said very slowly, "It's funny really. It was a year ago tomorrow that we first met."

"I'm sorry," he muttered, turning his glass around in his hands. "I know this is difficult for you right now. But it's really helping me piece things together. There's so much of the background I just don't know right now."

"It's just like a giant jigsaw puzzle to you, isn't it?"

"Well," he said, sucking in a deep breath and hunching his shoulders, "I'm just trying to figure out for sure what really happened. And, who knows, there might be something in Harvey's past that would help explain all of this." He paused and scratched his arm. "Tell me, when you were together in Bletchley did Harvey say anything to you or do anything to make you think he was in some kind of trouble? Worried about something maybe?"

"No, not that I can recall. We were really happy. Of course, he didn't want to leave at the end of his posting. But we had talked things over—that it would be better if he finished his stint in the army. That way he would be entitled to his annuity payment."

"You were worried about money?"

"No more than anyone else," she retorted, defensively. "It's easy to forget how things were even a year ago. It wasn't like it is now, with the economy booming. Rationing was still in place. There was a lot of uncertainty. We wanted to plan our future together properly—to give ourselves the best start possible."

"How about once he was back here in Japan. Did you talk to him much?"

"He would call usually once every two weeks or so. The telephones weren't terribly reliable, and we were trying to save money in any case. He talked a lot about buying our own house. He said he had saved up half of what we needed already, and once his annuity was paid out we would be able to buy something nice."

Someone on the table behind lit a cigarette, and bluish-gray smoke drifted past Carnaby's face reminding him how desperate he was for a smoke.

"You mean you had already decided on settling back in England?"

"Yes. He loved it over there—loved the history of the place."

"Do you remember when it was that you last spoke to him?"

She suddenly seemed choked up and coughed two or three times into her hand. "It was about two weeks before I received the telegram informing me of his death."

"How did he sound?"

"Oh, you know, fairly cheerful, I'd say. Although, the line was pretty bad that day, and I had trouble hearing everything he said."

"He didn't mention anything out of the ordinary or seem depressed about anything?"

"Depressed?" She leaned back and thought for a second. "No, not really. I've been through this a thousand times myself already. He was frustrated at having to wait now that his discharge date was so close. And he seemed a bit short-tempered—something about his boss not being aware of his discharge date—that he had assumed he was staying on for longer in Tokyo."

"General Brannigan?" said Carnaby, trying to keep his voice level.

"I don't know. Harvey didn't like to talk about his work on the public telephone."

"No, I guess that wouldn't have been wise," he agreed. "Listen, Emma, we're still looking into this, and so there may not be any substance to it, but, well, we have come across some evidence that suggests Harvey may have got himself into debt."

Her eyes opened wide and her face flushed crimson. "What on earth do you mean?"

He raised his hands. "Now don't jump to conclusions. I'm not saying that is what I personally believe. It's just that, well, we came by an accounts ledger for a bogus loan company that was run by the local mob—"

Emma's face had turned ashen.

"Harvey's name was in there. The entry shows he had borrowed a fairly substantial amount of money and that he was in arrears on his repayments."

"That's not true!" she shrieked. "That has to be a lie. He would have told me about it."

Carnaby's hands shot back up again and he appealed to her. "Please, Emma, keep your voice down."

"Don't you tell me to keep my voice down," she hissed.

"Okay, okay. I'm sorry," he said, looking around him at the startled expressions on the faces of the group of old ladies, who were making ready to leave. "All I'm trying to say is that his name was in the ledger, and we are investigating the company concerned right now."

"It could be a mistake, couldn't it?" she said, with a look of desperation in her eye.

"It's possible," he replied, noncommittally. "The only reason I mention it is that, well, remember last night I told you I had that strange call from a guy saying he had information about Harvey?"

"Yes. I had completely forgotten about that. But, anyway, what did he say?"

"The point is when I met with him this morning he also claimed that Harvey was in debt and that he was depressed because of it."

"And you expect me to believe he killed himself because he was in debt? Even if he had been in debt, which I don't for one minute believe, he would have told me. I'm sure of it." Tears were starting to well up in her eyes, and she dabbed at them with the corner of her napkin.

"You know what, Emma," began Carnaby again, "I don't believe it was suicide either. But there are a heck of a lot of loose ends out there, and I'm just trying to tie some of them up. It's a slow and painful process of elimination. But I gotta say, this debt business has got me beat right now."

"What other loose ends are there?" she said, drawing her index finger slowly down the bridge of her nose and sniffing.

"Well," he said, straightening himself, "aside from the ones I've already mentioned, there is one little wrinkle I'm having trouble with."

"Which is what?"

"The landlord."

"The landlord?"

"Yeah. The landlord at Harvey's apartment. He's gone missing."

"I don't understand. What do you mean he's gone missing?"

"We went back to ask some follow-up questions only to find he had been replaced. The management company said he quit, on health grounds. It seems he didn't leave a forwarding address."

"I still don't understand. Why is it so important anyway?"

Carnaby leaned forward again and placed his hands on the table. "Well, you see, he was the one who raised the alarm in the first place. And not only that, in one of your letters to Harvey you said something to the effect that the landlord sounded like a 'real character'—" He stopped suddenly. "What is it Emma?"

She was sitting stock still, staring wildly at him with wet eyes. Her mouth gaped, and her head was moving slowly from side to side. "You read *my* letters?"

"Well, I, er—"

"My personal letters to Harvey? You had no right to do that."

"They'd already been through the censors, and—"

"That's no excuse. That doesn't make it alright to go snooping through someone else's private correspondence!"

She was on her feet now, angry, her voice rising with pure frustration and anger.

Carnaby was flustered. He looked around and directed a weak smile at the group of ladies who by now had paid the bill and were ushering one another quickly away from this embarrassing scene. "I'm just searching for clues, Emma," he said, trying desperately to save the situation. "It seemed to me the landlord may have been phony."

"Phony?" she shouted, pulling her jacket back on. "Let's just talk about who is 'phony' around here. I mean, I don't even know you, and yet here I am telling you my life story. My God, I'm so bloody naïve at times." She put a hand to her hair and brushed it back, melodramatically. "How do I know what you've told me is true? Come to that, how do I know you are who you claim you are, Mr. Carnaby? For all I know, you could be a plant waiting to catch me out. After all, running into you at the embassy 'just like that' is actually unbelievable, when you stop for a moment and think about it."

"Now that's plain ridiculous, Emma—"

"Ridiculous, is it? Well, we'll soon see about that. There's only one way to find out, isn't there? I'm going to go straight to the authorities and ask them to tell me officially what happened."

"Emma, I don't think—"

"Goodbye, Mr. Carnaby."

Seventeen

The sky had gradually darkened and then suddenly turned jet black, throwing the twinkling stars and waxing moon into sharp relief. Below this beautiful firmament, at the northernmost tip of Hokkaido lay a small fishing village—little more than a cluster of fifteen or so *gasshozukuri* thatched houses of the sort that could be found in any part of this far-flung region.

Everything seemed as it had undoubtedly been for the past several hundred years—undisturbed, unhurried, tranquil—*normal.* Except that is, everything was not quite normal. In fact, if one were to listen very carefully on this particular night, strain one's ears above the sound of the sea breaking on the rocks below the cliffs, one would have to conclude that something about this particular village on this particular night was most definitely not quite *normal.*

Rising above the thatched rooftops, carried on the briny sea breeze, were melodious voices. Beautiful voices, singing in Russian:

"Vstavay, proklyat'yem zaklyeymyennyy,
Vyes' mir golodnykh I rabov!
Kipit nash razum vozmushchyennyy
I v smyertnyy boy vyesti gotov.
Vyes' mir nasil'ya, a zatyem—
My nash, my novyy mir postroim:
Kto byl nichyem, tot stanyet vsyem!
Eto yest' nash poslyedniy
I ryeshityel'nyy boy.
S Intyernatsionalom

Vospryanyet rod lyudskoy."

The village folk sat on the compacted ground in the middle of the assembly area, arms linked in a circle of solidarity.

Arise ye workers from your slumbers
Arise ye prisoners of want
For reason in revolt now thunders
And at last ends the age of cant.
Away with all your superstitions
Servile masses arise, arise
We'll change henceforth the old tradition
And spurn the dust to win the prize.
So comrades, come rally
And the last fight let us face
The Internationale
Unites the human race.

Six hundred miles away to the south, in Tokyo, Emma Forbes reclined on the cushioned surface of a luxuriously upholstered Louis XVI chaise longue in the drawing room of the ambassador's residence. Mozart's Violin Concerto No. 4 in D Major [second movement Andante Cantabile] played soothingly in the background. She was sipping black coffee and leafing through a large bound volume titled *Maps of Japan: A Cartographical History.* It was brimming with glossy color plates illustrating the history of Japanese map-making and providing a wealth of detailed information on the cartographers themselves—both Japanese and, more surprisingly for Emma, European.

She marveled at the decorative cartouches, the flamboyant use of heraldic legends, and the colorful vignettes of ships and mythical sea creatures. Turning the page, her eye was drawn to the map illustrated in the top left-hand plate. It looked strikingly familiar, she thought. She glanced over toward the bookcase in the corner of the room, and there it was, set back in an alcove, hanging discreetly from the picture rail. Her eyes traveled back to the page, and she read the description to herself:

"'Isola del Giapone e Peninsola di Corea" CORONELLI, Vincenzo Maria. Venice, 1692. Later color. 30 inches x 40 inches. Typical Coronelli style with a vignette of a boat described as being a Japanese vessel capable of crossing the 220 French miles between

Osaka and Nagasaki in twelve days. Coronelli copied this from Montanus, who had mis-attributed a Korean ship.'

Interesting, she thought, taking another sip of coffee. The crude Italian transliterations of the few place names she already knew made her smile: "Golfo De Iedo"—Edo Bay, or Tokyo Bay as it was now; "Miaco"—Miyako, the old name for the former capital, Kyoto; "Akas"—Akashi; and "Siminaseco"—Shimonoseki, the port city and historical bastion of Catholicism on the southernmost coast of Honshu.

Suddenly, there was a noise from outside. The door opened inwards, and in came the British ambassador, Sir Henry Coaldrake. "Ah, good evening Emma."

"Oh, good evening, sir," replied Emma, who had started to get up, only to find she was not nearly as nimble as usual with a coffee cup in one hand and a large volume of maps nestling in her lap.

"Don't get up, my dear. I told you the other day I'm not expecting any formality. If you are to be at ease with my children, then you will need to be at ease with me also."

"Yes sir," she said, meekly.

"And another thing, Emma, you needn't address me as 'sir' when we are in the informal confines of the embassy. You may call me Henry."

"Yes," she stammered, "Henry."

"Ah," he said, wandering over to the chaise longue and craning his neck down, "I see you've found my favorite book." He sat down next to her with a pleased look on his face.

"Yes, Henry. I was just admiring your Coronelli," she said, knowledgeably, and looked over in the direction of the bookcase.

The ambassador looked stunned. "By jove! I didn't realize you were an expert, my dear. It's a fascinating subject, you know. I actually picked that one up the other day from a small bookshop in Jimbocho. It was a third of the price of London shops. Hardly surprising, I suppose, given the state of things over here."

"The place names are so quaint," she said, turning back a page to the double-leaf illustration of Hondius's 1630 map, also showing Korea as an island.

"Aren't they just," he agreed, nodding his head furiously. "And the other interesting thing about this particular map," he continued excitedly, "is the cartographer's use of footnotes. See—

according to this one, the red spots indicate those areas in Japan which are rich in minerals, gold and iron ore." He sat back and guffawed, exposing a set of heavily stained teeth. "It's absolute rot!" he proclaimed. "Why, it's common knowledge that Japan is entirely deficient in natural resources. And this one is even better." He prodded the illustration with his spindly index finger. "This note would have you believe that those areas marked with a small circle are areas where one may find the best-looking girls in the whole of the Japanese archipelago!" The ambassador rocked with laughter. He was clearly in his element.

Emma smiled, demurely, as he twittered on incessantly about the finer points of the mapmaker's art and the fact that, contrary to popular belief, Japanese maps of the same period were extremely crude by comparison and focused mainly on local districts and prefectures. It was, he explained, the much finer European maps that were to provide the templates in years to come by which Japanese cartographers first mapped their own country in its entirety. Japan had never really been a seafaring nation. At length he stopped and drew in a deep breath. Placing his long fingers on his knees, he levered his lithe frame into an upright position. "Well, I suppose I ought to leave you in peace now. I shall be leaving at an ungodly hour in the morning and need to turn in early I'm afraid. Now remember," he said, wagging his forefinger in a fatherly way, "don't feel the need to do anything too strenuous while I am away. I would far rather you conserved your energy for when the children are here. If I were you, I should use the time to familiarize yourself with your surroundings. Now then, is there anything you would like to ask before I depart?"

Emma pursed her lips, "No, Henry. Everything is just perfect. Thank you."

"Very well. Oh, and remember, if you do need anything, and this applies generally, whether I am here or not, just ask Grace. She has been housekeeper here for the last five years and knows, I shouldn't wonder, all there is to know about this place."

The ambassador reached the door in two great strides and put his hand on the doorknob.

"Henry?" she said suddenly, causing him to reappear through the open doorway.

"Yes," he said, craning his head around the door. "What is it, my dear?"

She held her hands in her lap and looked up at him, a little forlornly and said, "Is it important—what we are doing out here?"

He closed the door again and let his hand fall to his side. In the dim light, the lines on his forehead appeared all the more pronounced. "I'm not sure I understand your question, Emma."

"I'm sorry," she said with a smile. "It's a bit of an odd thing to ask. What I meant to say was is the British involvement in the occupation *important*?"

"You're right," he said, "it is a peculiar thing to ask. But, since you have asked, then I will tell you that I believe it is important. Very important."

"Oh," she said, looking down at the floral bijar pattern on the Indian rug. "It's just that I was talking to someone today who said they thought that while the British contribution was important, it wasn't significant. I just wondered what the official view was, that's all."

The ambassador put his hands in his pockets, wandered back over and hovered in front of her. "I'm not sure I would concern myself too much with the distinction, Emma. To be perfectly frank—and this is my personal opinion you understand—that point of view is probably correct. The number of personnel we have under our command is relatively small when compared with the resources the Americans have at their disposal. So I suppose, in that respect, it can probably be described as 'insignificant'—although I'm not sure I would use that word myself. On the other hand, in the context of the law of nation states, it is important that a number of countries be seen to be participating in the Allied Council. The reality is that it is an occupation dominated by the Americans. But for form's sake, we do need to maintain at least the semblance of a democratic decision-making body in Tokyo." He winked at her and added, "It's all about keeping the Russians happy. Does that answer your question?"

"Yes, it does. Thank you."

"You are a strange bird. I was expecting a question about maps or some such subject. Right-ho." He smiled and then disappeared through the door again.

Emma remained motionless, staring fixedly at the pattern on the rug for several minutes after the ambassador had left the room. She thought about what he had just said, and then she let her mind drift back to the meeting with Ralph Carnaby earlier in the day and what he had told her. Perhaps he was telling the truth, after all. She opened *the* letter from Harvey and read it through again. She couldn't possibly explain all of this to the ambassador—not yet at any rate. It made little enough sense to her. She realized that she had no one else to turn to. It was no use, she decided. She would have to call him. After all, what did she have to lose? She fished around in her handbag and pulled out a small scrap of paper containing the telephone number.

She walked over to the telephone stand in the corner by the bookcase and dialed the number. Her heart was beating quickly while she waited for it to connect. "Hello, Ralph? . . . Yes, it's me, Emma. Listen, I owe you an apology for my behavior today. Pardon? . . . No, no, it's not alright. Listen, I need to see you. . . . When? Tonight . . . Yes, that's right, tonight."

Carnaby met her at the station, and they walked back to his apartment together, stopping occasionally while he pointed out various landmarks along the way: the upturned bucket by the bridge—daytime throne of the 'Kingfisher'; the 'rat run' where, paradoxically, in the quiet dark of the evening, there was no sign of any rodential movement; and, as they turned into his avenue, the serried rows of ginkgo trees, their distinctive leaves illuminated by the silvery light of the full moon.

"Here we are," he said, as they approached the gate to his apartment block. "You can't miss it." He gestured toward the tree in front of them—a larger than average ginkgo with an unusual bifurcated trunk.

As they climbed the stairs, it suddenly struck him that bringing Emma back to his place, albeit at her suggestion, may not be entirely appropriate. After all, he had met her for the first time only the night before. Still, they were here now, and in any case it wasn't as if he could just stop by the embassy without attracting unwanted scrutiny. He opened the door and showed her in.

"Don't you lock your door?" she asked.

He smiled and peeled his cardigan off letting it fall over the back of a dining chair. "I don't usually bother," he said casually. "Japan is a very honest country. People don't tend to steal other people's belongings. Besides which," he continued, "I already had a break-in a few weeks ago—locking the door didn't prevent that from happening."

"But I thought you just said people don't steal other people's belongings?"

He had to laugh at that one. "I guess I did, didn't I? There are exceptions of course, just like anywhere. Fact is I was singled out by some people who took exception to me doing my job properly."

"But that's horrible. Did you catch them?"

"Nope."

"And you're not worried they will come back?"

"Not particularly. I haven't heard anything since. And if they really want me, then they'll find me. Occupational hazard—it comes with the job I guess. Martini?"

She shivered, and looked around the room as if she somehow suspected the perpetrators were still at large, skulking in the shadows. "Yes please. I think I will, just a weak one."

"Have a seat, why don't you?" He poured her drink and a bourbon for himself and brought them over to the sofa.

"It's a nice apartment you have."

"Well, it's not exactly the Ritz, but it works fine for me. I don't make too much mess, and it's convenient for work with the subway being only a couple blocks away." He took a slug of bourbon.

"You don't live with your wife?"

He noticed her looking at his ring finger and answered simply, "She died."

"Oh, gosh. I am sorry. That was rude of me to be so forthright."

"Hey, don't worry about it. It's not an unnatural thing to ask. It was quite some time ago—almost eight years in fact." He stared down into his glass.

"You still miss her, don't you?" Emma wanted to know. It was selfish, she knew, but she wanted to know if *her* heart would still be aching the way it was now in eight years time. She looked over at the photograph of his wife standing on top of the writing bureau.

"Most of the time I don't really think about it too much," he said. "I like to be busy. It takes my mind off it. The evenings are when it sometimes gets to you, especially during the winter months." He looked around at her and seemed to sense what she was thinking. "It does get easier, Emma. There is truth in the saying that time heals all."

"But how long does it take?"

"I guess it depends on the individual and," he said after a brief pause, "the circumstances under which it happened." He cleared his throat and then said in a slightly timorous voice, "If you don't mind me saying, Emma, you must have loved Harvey very much—I mean to come all this way on your own when you could easily have just accepted what you were told. I think it takes a lot of guts to do what you have done."

"Thank you. But for all I know the official version may be correct. This could be just one great wild goose chase."

"But something made you come out here, right?"

"Yes. But like you, Ralph, it was really nothing more than an intuitive feeling. Knowing Harvey the way I did, I simply refuse to believe he would take his own life—not without me knowing something was wrong."

They both sat in silence for a few moments, and then she pulled her handbag onto her lap and opened the clasp. "By the way, I went through my letters again and found what you are looking for. Although to be perfectly frank, I'm not sure it helps." She handed the letter to him. "It's the second paragraph on page two."

He set his whiskey tumbler down carefully on the arm of his chair and opened the letter. There was a faint pencil cross in the margin alongside the paragraph in question.

The new landlord is a really nice guy. I can't believe how fluent his Russian is. I suppose that's something he has brought back from his terrible experiences in Siberia.

Carnaby looked astonished. He leafed through the other pages. "This made it through the censors, intact?"

"Yes. Strange, isn't it? He had included it in a small package, together with a silk scarf for my mother's birthday. Normally he would just send a letter on its own."

Carnaby eased himself out of the chair and walked over to his drink cabinet, humming quietly to himself. "Would you like another one?"

"No thanks, I'd better not."

"Tell me, did Harvey mention anything else about the landlord, or why he was living where he was?"

Emma looked into the distance and thought for a while. "No, I don't recall anything."

He leaned back against the bureau. "The letter is dated November 16, right?"

She looked at the first page and nodded.

"So that means he moved in there right after he switched jobs I guess."

"No," she said, looking puzzled, "he had been at that address for as long as I'd known him. It was the landlord that changed, wasn't it?"

A lightbulb came on in Carnaby's head. Something Gloria had said about Amano Fisheries. He stared at her in silence. A vague suspicion was beginning to form in his mind. He could see a small, bowlegged man in laborer's clothing standing at the docks, amidst a group of other men all similarly attired. And in the background, was a large passenger-cargo ship bearing on its prow in faded white letters the name *Koan Maru*.

Eighteen

Carnaby woke up with a start and glanced across the room at the clock on the sideboard: 17:15. *Shit!* he thought. He was supposed to be at the church in fifteen minutes. He swung his legs off the sofa and scrambled to his feet—too fast. The blood drained from his head, and he had to sit down again for several seconds while the dizziness passed. He waited a moment then stood up, slowly this time, and went quickly into the bathroom.

A ghost's face stared back at him from the mirror. *Christ, I look like death. Of all the days to doze off on the sofa. Why, why, why . . .* He sluiced handfuls of cold water onto his face and then ran a comb through the tangle of his unkempt hair. There was little noticeable improvement. He had a food stain smack bang in the middle of his necktie—egg yolk or something by the looks of it. He dabbed at it a few times with a wet cloth, delicately at first, and then started rubbing it furiously before he lost patience completely and pulled it off with a whipping sound. He flung it into the corner where it landed on top of a growing pile of other variously assorted garments he hadn't quite got around to laundering since Beth left a week before.

His mouth felt as dry as sand. He unscrewed the top to a bottle of mouthwash and swilled a measure around and spat it out again. Bristles pricked at his face—but no time to shave now. He darted back into the living room, looked around quickly for his watch, and spotted the strap sticking out from underneath a newspaper. He fastened it hurriedly and half ran to the door, scooping up his wallet on the way. Kicking his shoes on, he reached for the door handle. He was halfway into the hallway when the phone rang. He stopped dead—undecided as to whether to ignore it and leave. In the end, his sense of duty got the better of him and he stepped gingerly back inside and lifted the receiver. "Yeah?" he said, breathlessly.

"Ralph? You okay? You sound terrible."

"Dan? Listen, I've gotta run. Can it wait?"

"Yeah, sure. But hey, why don't you tell me where you're headed this time?"

"You don't need to worry for once, buddy. I'm going over to the church. The priest called yesterday, said he'd remembered something and could I come over."

"Oh. Okay. Well, give him my regards. I'll call you tomorrow."

"Yeah, sure. I'll be seeing you." He slammed the receiver back down and went out the door, pulling it to behind him. Strange, but since the break-in he hadn't bothered locking it any more—not even when he was alone at night.

He had planned to walk to the church—a pleasant thirty-minute stroll along the riverbank and up through the secondhand bookstore district surrounding the Meiji University campus. He liked the feel of the place—students and old books. It sort of made him feel revitalized, young and carefree again. Anyway, he would have to dash and take the subway now, and then a five-minute walk through a warren of narrow back streets to the west side of the church.

Unusually for that time of day, the train wasn't so busy, although he still couldn't find a seat. He held onto a leather strap for a while and then wormed his way into a slightly more spacious corner near the door. He wished he hadn't bothered. For the next few minutes, an old woman wearing wooden clogs and carrying an enormous basket load of charcoal on her back looked him up and down with ill-disguised interest. He smirked to himself, mildly irritated, and tried to avoid catching her eye, which was difficult given her undivided attention. It didn't seem to matter that *she* looked out of place; on the contrary, it was *he* that seemed to be the object of curiosity. Passengers peeped at him and then averted their eyes, sheepishly, when they realized he had noticed.

He turned his face away and closed his eyes. Opening them a few moments later, he risked a furtive glance, and sure enough the lady's eyes were still fixed in his direction. He looked down at his feet and then peered along the length of the carriage. There were mostly businessmen, and a few students, dressed in their distinctive high-collared Prussian-style school uniforms. And something else he noticed, and couldn't quite reconcile with his Anglo-Saxon Christian upbringing: the seats were all taken by young, fit men while the elderly and infirm, and even pregnant women, were expected to stand and suffer in silence.

A shoeshine boy sat in the opposite corner, his wooden box of polish and brushes wedged under his backside as a make-shift seat. He looked malnourished and exhausted, just like the ones he saw regularly lined up by the side of the HQ building—hoping to earn a little extra and clean the shoes of some well-to-do American officer. Dan had told him they were nearly all orphans, trying to scrape a meager living by working all their waking hours.

Light suddenly flooded the carriage as they came to the surface. There was a sudden lurch as the brakes were applied, and he felt the train begin to slow as it approached the station. It came to a stop, and the doors opened automatically with a hissing sigh. He was half carried out of the carriage by the deluge of alighting passengers. He took a last fleeting glance over his shoulder at the old woman. She opened her mouth wide and smiled, the station lighting glinting off her gold-capped teeth.

He emerged a little ruffled from the subway exit and took a second or two to get his bearings. He straightened his jacket and set off down a narrow side street lined with a whole range of weird and wonderful shops. Everywhere he looked, it was mad busy: commuters crowding the station to go home for the night; people pushing handcarts loaded with all manner of merchandise; and traders taking in storefront displays or replacing the regular price signs on perishables and fresh produce with half price labels as the day drew to a close. And, of course, the ubiquitous hot potato vendor touting his product: '*Ya-ki imo-.*'

He looked at his watch again: 17:40. And then he decided to calm down and take it easy. He was, after all, only ten minutes late, and it wasn't as if the priest would be away; he lived there for pity's sake. And besides, whatever it was the priest wanted to tell him probably wasn't going to add anything to what he already knew.

Another couple of minutes and he arrived at the west gate. The light was fading fast now. He went through and stopped on the other side to take stock of his surroundings. The place seemed deserted, although there was a dim light inside the main building and an external floodlight, which cast a wide swathe of light across the steps at the front. Two smaller lights were embedded in the grass verge, their pale arc washing the trees a spectral white. He noticed the order of service secured to the iron railings on top of the perimeter wall: Weekdays: last service (Russian)—16:00. That at least explained why it was so quiet.

He ran his fingers through his hair and walked up to the main doors. It seemed like only yesterday when he'd first been here with Dan. He pushed with his right hand. The doors rattled slightly but otherwise wouldn't give. He closed one eye and squinted at the sliver of light escaping from the narrow crack between the great double doors. He couldn't see clearly, but it didn't look as though the mortise lock was engaged. There was no door knocker or bell cord, so he hammered on the door with his fist. But the wood was solid and only deadened the sound. He stepped back and peered up at the bell tower and down again past the mullion windows. *Very odd,* he thought. *Why on earth would he jam the door like this?*

He backed up a few paces and looked again. Still no signs of life. And then he noticed a small building off to the right—the priest's house. Of course, the priest didn't actually live in the church itself. He shook his head and sighed at his own stupidity. He hurried across the gravel path with a spring in his step, reached out and rapped the knocker against its brass back plate several times. He stepped back and waited. Nothing.

He knocked again, a little louder this time. The priest was old and likely to be hard of hearing, although it seemed like he was making enough noise to wake the dead. Again nothing. He went over to the window, and, shielding his eyes with his hands to stop the glare from the floodlights, peered into what seemed to be the living room. It was dark inside, but it didn't look as though anyone was there. He quickly went around the side of the building and looked through the small windows, but the curtains were closed. Skirting back along the wall to the front, he looked shiftily about him and tried the door handle. It opened inwards noiselessly. He tiptoed inside and looked around.

"Hello. Anybody home? It's Ralph Carnaby. Sorry I'm late."

Leaving the door ajar, he walked slowly and respectfully through the living room and into the room at the back. Again, not wishing to alarm the old man, he cleared his throat and called out in a firm voice, "Excuse me. I did knock. It's Ralph

Carnaby—you remember, you telephoned me yesterday."

He quickly surveyed the room: a narrow truckle bed on casters was pushed against the far wall. To the left of the bed under the window was a small writing desk with a battered copy of the weekday missal sitting on top. There was a mirror and a plain, unadorned cross on the wall. Otherwise the room was bare—a study in puritanical austerity.

He suddenly felt ill at ease and quickly retraced his steps. He closed the door behind him. And then it struck him—there was likely to be a side door to the church. With the last service of the day finished, it would be natural to close up the main doors for the night. After all, had the priest not said "I will wait for you in the church"?

He walked briskly up to the side of the building, scanning the wall for an opening. Suddenly something moved in the dark ahead. Something small, rat-like. It seemed to be skipping backwards and dragging something. And then he saw it—a large crow pulling a cloth bag in its beak. A little way further up the path a refuse box had been upended and its filthy contents had spilled across the ground. Carnaby breathed out forcefully. He had to admit it he was jumpy as hell. An image from his distant past suddenly flashed before him: a little boy running home late at night and taking a shortcut through the church grounds. Beneath a pewter sky strange, grotesque shapes seemed to rise up and chase him through the graveyard.

He shivered and continued walking. A few feet further on he saw a small depression in the wall, and as he got nearer he saw that it was indeed a side entrance. There was a light fixture, but the flame had not been lit. He fumbled in the darkness for the handle, and his fingers soon located a small rusting latch. He pressed it down and pushed gently. The door opened easily and led him into a narrow, damp passageway. He paused, listening, all the while straining his eyes and peering into the sepulchral gloom. He proceeded down the passageway, his eyes gradually becoming accustomed to the darkness. He couldn't help thinking that something wasn't quite right. To be sure, the priest was old and therefore probably forgetful. Doubtless he used this passageway everyday and did not need to rely on light or landmark to guide his way. But it certainly wasn't very helpful for his present visitor.

The passageway seemed to be getting brighter by degrees the

further on he went. Eventually he saw a chink of light coming from a wooden door set into the wall on his right. He wrapped his fingers around the rough-hewn edge and pulled it fully open. The nave lay splendidly before him with row upon row of pews laid out in serried lines. The pulpit rose out of the floor to his left and obscured his view of the rest of the church's interior.

He walked casually past the stairwell to the pulpit and peered around the other side. He stopped dead in his tracks, dumbfounded, unable to believe his eyes. He broke into an ungainly, panicky run. The priest lay on his back across an overturned pew, his arms bound roughly and held fast under the weight of his own body. His white robes were stained deep red. Carnaby gasped in horror as his eyes took in the handle of a knife embedded up to the hilt in the priest's side. He knelt down quickly and cupped his head in one hand to relieve the strain on his arched back. The old man's sapiential face regarded him calmly. Carnaby's eyes went back to the knife again—he dare not pull it out. He knew full well that without proper surgical equipment, clamps, and instruments to cauterize the wound doing so could well hasten the loss of blood. He leaned forward on both knees, rooted awkwardly in his trouser pocket, pulled out a penknife and selected a blade. He gently rolled the priest to one side exposing his bound wrists. The old man groaned. "I'm sorry," said Carnaby softly as he severed the cord and slipped the bonds off.

Suddenly, the door to the sacristy opened with a grating sound, and a swarthy Japanese man put his head around the door frame. Surprise registered on his face as he saw Carnaby, and he slammed the door shut again. Carnaby's hand went instinctively inside his jacket. *Damn it!* He hadn't brought his gun. He could just see it now, lying on top of his sideboard in his apartment. "Hang in there," he said to the priest, through gritted teeth. He jumped to his feet and ran over to the closed door. Turning caution to the wind, he pulled it open and went straight in. He had his penknife clasped between index and middle finger so that the blade, short as it was, protruded like a knurl on some primitive knuckleduster. He quickly scanned the interior of the sacristy. There was only one other door, set in the far wall. The door had been rudely flung open and Carnaby could hear the sound of running footsteps echoing down the passageway. He ducked under the low stone lintel and gave chase. He was sweating now and felt a knot like a fist deep in his churning stomach. The passageway gave out into a small chamber, itself with a wooden door that was slightly open. He advanced cautiously toward it. He concealed his body behind the stone door frame and pulled the door open sharply.

It led back out into the nave, but at the opposite end this time, by the barricaded front doors. He sidled past the marble aspersorium and went over to an almost identical door on the opposite side of the hall. He pushed it open, his hand cocked and ready to punch. He could see a number of bell-ringer ropes, one of which was wavering ever so slightly, as if someone or something had just brushed passed it. He moved into the room, and then suddenly a gunshot rang through the stone chamber with a deafening crack. He hurled himself headlong across the rough floor. He jerked his head back and looked up to see a dark form disappearing into the belfry. He scrambled to his feet and began climbing thc first set of wooden ladders. They shook under his weight, and for one awful instant he thought the whole structure would wrench itself free of the wall. There was a small square platform just above him, and he put his head carefully through the trapdoor. He could hear his assailant scuttling up the next section of ladders. He jumped through the gap and placed his foot on the bottom rung. Another shot rang out and the bullet chewed its way into the handrail just by his arm. He ducked back into the shadows, just in time to hear a cry of pain, and then a metal object plummeted down the shaft and crashed into the stairs below him.

In his haste to escape, the gunman had run his head straight into a stone protrusion at the top of the last stretch of ladders. Reeling from the impact he had dropped his gun over the edge. Carnaby now realized this and sprang up the ladders in pursuit. He came up the ladders so quickly that he only narrowly avoided doing the same injury to himself. He turned around, his body from the chest down still below the lip of the trapdoor. With a bloodcurdling scream, the Japanese man ran at Carnaby and aimed a vicious kick at his head. Carnaby braced his legs and, while shielding his face with his left forearm, punched the short blade of his penknife fully into his attacker's kneecap. He let out another scream, this time in genuine agony, and reeled backwards. Carnaby leapt after him, meaning to drive home his advantage. The Japanese staggered sideways and stumbled along a narrow parapet leading to the remains of the bell tower.

Carnaby mounted the parapet and followed him. The Japanese stopped, his back pressed up against one of the enormous bronze bells, and regarded Carnaby coolly. He had a purple scar on his left cheek, which lifted the corner of his mouth giving him an oddly sardonic expression. Carnaby came steadily closer and shouted, "Who are you? Who sent you? Do you understand English?" Without warning, the cornered man ran at him, arms outstretched, his wiry fingers formed into claws. Carnaby dipped his head and charged into the man with his shoulder. There was a solid collision, and the lighter Japanese man was flung back against the bell with a resounding clang. Seeing that he was still in the fight, Carnaby grasped him by the shoulders and, using his weight advantage to the full, spun on his heels and launched him through the air against the far wall. Only the wall wasn't there. He looked around just in time to see the man's feet disappear through the belfry window, accompanied by a final, deathly cry.

Forty feet below the broken body lay like a sacrificial offering across the stone steps, his pale, exposed torso, stained with streaks of red.

Carnaby made his way back down the ladders and went quickly over to where the priest lay. The red stain had turned into a pool of blood which lapped gently at the dying man's legs. Supporting his head once again, he looked down at the old man's flickering eyes. His pupils dilated slightly as Carnaby's shadow cut out the light from the altar. The priest let his mouth open slightly. There was a wheezing sound. Carnaby bent lower and put his ear to his mouth to catch the whispered words: "Sacristy . . . look . . . under . . . stone seat." There was a low rush of air as the old man breathed his last. His eyes were motionless now. Carnaby gently closed his eyelids and gripped his hand in his. He stayed like that for a minute, with tears welling up in his own eyes.

Leaving the priest under the watchful gaze of the statue of the Virgin Mary, he went into the sacristy once again. *Stone seat.* He looked around him. Stone wall, stone windowsill, stone bench, *stone seat.* He strode across the room and stopped in front of the stone seat, cut into the wall on the left side of the room like an alcove. He placed his hands on the top and felt its smoothness. He ran his fingers under the edge, which protruded ever so slightly from the wall. He took a short breath, pulled upwards and exhaled sharply, contracting his stomach muscles as he did so. The stone lid gave easily. He levered it off its base and placed it at an angle against the foot of the wall. He took another breath, a deep one this time, and reached both hands carefully into the aperture. His fingers touched a piece of rough Hessian cloth. He moved it to one side and probed deeper into the hole. There was a bag of some sort, lying on its side. He pulled it out and took it over to the stone table in the corner. It was an attaché case, made of good quality leather. He depressed the catch with his thumb, but it was locked. He suddenly remembered the brass key that had been included in Brice's possessions. But no, it was far too big for this lock. He went back over to the stone seat and rummaged around inside but found nothing. He searched his pockets for his penknife, then remembered where it was. He looked around him and then stopped. Licking his thumb and forefinger, he extinguished the flame on a candle and, taking the candle out of the solid brass candlestick, he used the candlestick as a makeshift hammer to smash the clasp off the case. He opened the bag and slid out a large envelope. He tore the envelope open and placed the enclosed sheaf of papers on the tabletop in front of him and stared, stared for a very long time.

Nineteen

Carnaby knelt in the middle of his living room floor surrounded by neatly arranged piles of paper—radiating from the center like the sails of a windmill. He felt like a bewildered child sitting in the middle of a new train set and wondering which locomotive to play with next.

There was a soft knock at the door. He looked up sharply, jumped to his feet and picked his pistol up from the sofa. He padded over to the door in his stockinged feet and, gun raised, shouted, "Who's there?"

"It's me Ralph. Emma."

He lowered his arm and opened the door. "Emma, you're early. I wasn't expecting you for another half hour."

"I'm sorry," she said, sounding cheerfully apologetic. "I haven't quite got the hang of the railway timetable yet I'm afraid."

"Did you find the place okay?"

"Yes. It's quite easy provided you come out of the right exit at the station." She noticed the scratch marks on his neck and, frowning, unconsciously reached out and placed her fingers on the bruised skin. "You're hurt. What happened?"

"It's a long story. Come in," he said closing the door. He turned around to face her, and suddenly the whole room began to shake. An empty glass fell from the edge of the table onto the rug on the floor but luckily didn't break. The windows rattled and vibrated, and the light flickered on and off for several seconds.

"What is it?" shouted Emma, flinging her arms around his shoulders and hanging on as if her life depended on it.

He put his big arm around her and held her tight to his chest. "It's okay," he said reassuringly. "It's just a tremor. They're pretty commonplace in Japan. Usually they're not so big and don't do any real damage. And they don't last very long, like this one. See—it's stopped."

Slowly she released her grip and moved away from him. Averting her eyes, she folded her arms and shivered. "How embarrassing. I'm sorry. I don't know what came over me. I really don't."

"Hey, don't worry about it. When you've been here a while you hardly notice them. Say, can I fix you a drink? You look a little pale."

"Yes. Thank you. That would be lovely."

He walked over to the drink cabinet and poured her a weak martini.

She dropped her bag onto the sofa and then noticed the circle of papers fanned out on the floor. "It's a little late for spring cleaning, isn't it?" she remarked, with a half smile.

He turned, and without saying anything, passed her the glass.

She took it and looked him straight in the eye. The half-smile had disappeared now. "This is what you called me over to see, isn't it?"

He motioned for her to sit down. "I didn't want to discuss it on the telephone," he said, putting his hands in his trouser pockets. "You never know who might be listening."

"But what are they?" she said, nodding toward the documents.

He walked slowly and deliberately over to the writing bureau and leaned his backside against the open desktop. He wet his dry lips and regarded her gravely. And then, trying not to miss anything out, he described to her what had happened the previous day at the church.

She listened attentively to everything he said, her mind working to take it all in and make sense of it. When he had finished his explanation, she looked at him long and hard, as if she somehow expected him to say something cheerful, something to take the sting out of what she had just heard. "That's simply dreadful," was all she could think of saying. And then, suddenly making the connection she added, "So these papers—they are what you found in the attaché case, aren't they?"

"Yeah, that's right." He moved away from the bureau, knelt down and scooped up a set of papers. He sat down next to her on the sofa, took the empty glass from her hand and passed her the documents. "These don't make for very pleasant reading, that's for sure. But I think you need to see them."

She contemplated the documents for several seconds and then placed the first one across her knees. She turned the dust sheet over and began to read.

TOP SECRET
WITHDRAWN FROM TRIAL EVIDENCE [BY ORDER OF SCAP]

International Military Tribunal for the Far East

Pre-trial statement of Major Fumio Kanazawa—September 6, 1946. Doc. 9721. Record Group 143. Records of the Office of the Judge Advocate General (Army), National Archives.

[Official Translation]

I first heard about the Imperial Army's bacteriological and chemical warfare research and development in April 1939 when I assumed my post as a member of the Kwantung Army Quarantine Unit in Harbin, Manchuria. I was 41 years old.

Lieutenant General Shiro Ishii was head of Unit 731, the unit designated to carry out such research, which was also located at that time in Harbin. I first met Lieutenant General Ishii, then Colonel Ishii, when he visited the quarantine unit in September 1939 to ask for volunteers to assist in the research project. We were told that, due to security problems, Unit 731 was in the process of relocating to Pingfang, a sparsely populated district approximately 24 kilometers south of Harbin. To coincide with the move, Lieutenant General Ishii said he had just received authorization from the high command in Tokyo to substantially expand the research facility and recruit more scientists. He told us the work he was doing was of the utmost importance and would contribute to Japan winning the war. He also said that the project had the full backing of the emperor himself and had been granted an extremely generous budget for the coming year.

Since my work at the quarantine unit was relatively mundane, and wanting to do my best for my country, I volunteered for a transfer. At that time, I was unaware of what exactly the research at Pingfang involved. I was interviewed the following week by Lieutenant General Ishii in person. He seemed impressed by my attitude and willingness to work hard for Japan and the war effort. He was also pleased that, like himself, I had graduated from the Medical Department of Kyoto Imperial University.

When I reported for duty in January 1940, I was surprised at the scale of the Pingfang facility, which covered an area of approximately six square kilometers and had its own private airfield and railroad link to Harbin. Already there were more than fifty buildings, including headquarters, barracks, warehouses, a large prison wing, laboratories equipped with the most up-to-date apparatus, power plant and a crematorium containing three large furnaces for the disposal of human cadavers and animal carcasses.

Since the existence of the research facility was secret, word was circulated amongst the local townspeople that the research facility was in fact a lumberyard operated by the Imperial Army's 5th Engineer Group. There was even a fleet of trucks permanently laden with timber, which would drive in and out of the facility at predetermined times throughout the day.

The research subjects were known as maruta *[Translator's note: meaning "logs"]. The* maruta *were mainly Han Chinese, but there were also Red and White Russians, including some Jews who had been long-term residents of Harbin, Soviet prisoners of war captured during the campaign at Nomonhan in 1939, Mongolians, Koreans, and some Europeans. The* maruta *were tried and usually found guilty of theft or the more serious charge of spying. They would be transported by goods train under cover of darkness to Pingfang for experimentation and then extermination. For the most part, the* maruta *were derelicts who served no other useful purpose in life. Prior to being subjected to experimentation, they were treated well and given three good meals a day. It was important for them to be in good health if the results of the experiments were to be relied upon.*

At the beginning, there were approximately three hundred staff and five hundred maruta. *Just before we abandoned the site in August 1945, there were more than three thousand staff and some four thousand* maruta. *From 1941 to 1945, approximately three thousand* maruta *a year were disposed of at the Pingfang facility.*

For the first four months, I was principally engaged in the culture of bacteria, which was a fairly routine task. Although I did not personally take part, I witnessed several bacteriological experiments at this time using live human subjects. The main purpose of conducting such experiments was to develop effective antitoxins and an immunization program designed to protect our troops against the various bacteriological media likely to be employed by the enemy. Scientists engaged in this area produced pathogens, including those for plague, cholera, typhoid and paratyphoid fevers, dysentery, anthrax, glanders, tetanus, undulant fever, cerebrospinal meningitis, smallpox, tick encephalitis, and gas gangrene, in addition to filterable viruses and rickettsiae.

The laboratories were able to produce a large volume of bacteria in only a few days. Each laboratory was equipped with four one-ton boilers for the preparation of the bacteria culture medium and fourteen autoclaves for sterilizing the medium. Each autoclave contained fifty cultivators which, at peak capacity, could produce in the course of one production cycle more than fifty kilograms of cell mass. This meant that it was possible, for example, to produce seven hundred kilograms of plague bacteria each week.

Most of the tests at Pingfang were carried out in the underground testing facilities, directly beneath the prison wing. Maruta *would be brought down and strapped to a wooden bench, where they would be sedated with a dose of morphine. The doctor would then inject the* maruta *with an appropriate dose of a pathogen chosen for the experiment in question. A variety of alternative conductors would be used in order to implant the disease, including chocolates laced with anthrax, fruit and vegetables containing plague bacteria, and liquids such as water, milk and tea contaminated with specific pathogens.*

Depending on the particular experiment, the maruta *was monitored and either vivisected while still alive or, more often, dissected once dead, the disease having run its course. The corpses would be sent to Pathology and then disposed of in the furnaces.*

The most commonly conducted tests were those involving anthrax bacteria. I witnessed an experiment where ten maruta *were administered a course of anthrax spores orally, with the spores being imbibed via milk and other liquids. All ten* maruta *died within a period of six days. The autopsy showed intense degeneration and interstitial edema of the heart; the liver became infected with Hepatitis Serosa III and experienced traumatic hemorrhaging. There was also acute abdominal hemorrhaging.*

Andrew Clare

In May 1940, I was reassigned to the Chemical Development Section at Pingfang, where my role was to work with other scientists in the production, testing and refining of sarin and other organo-phosphorus nerve agents. Research in the area of chemical warfare (CW) was minimal in comparison with that of bacteriological warfare. I had, however, specialized in the development of antitoxins for mustard gas and other airborne toxic substances while teaching and researching at the Tokyo Army Medical College. Although the budget for CW research was limited, Lieutenant General Ishii recognized its potential from the beginning and gave his full support. CW was perceived as being important because, unlike bacteriological media, which took a number of days to make their presence known, the effects were more or less instantaneous.

I was one of a team of, initially, 150 dedicated CW scientists. We also regularly worked alongside technicians from the Okunoshima arsenal, the principal CW facility in Japan.

Although many experiments were conducted locally at Pingfang—for example, exposing maruta *to prussic acid fumes in the confines of the Pingfang gas chamber, the vast majority of experiments took place at Unit 731's proving ground at Anda, one hundred and fifty kilometers north of Harbin. Here* maruta *would be staked out in the open and exposed to mustard gas and, toward the end, sarin nerve agents. The gas would either be sprayed by crop-dusting planes, or by Uji Type 50 bombs detonated statically or deployed by light aircraft. The* maruta *would usually die very quickly, and most of the pathology was necessarily conducted in the field. I observed and recorded the results of many of these experiments, although I had no direct involvement.*

We experienced many problems with the method of delivery of CW agents. The early Uji Type 50 bombs were constructed from either steel casing or ceramic materials. The temperature on impact was usually too great, and the gas would be neutralized. In addition, producing binary shells which would allow the two reactants to mix and synthesize in flight was found to be extremely difficult. In early 1945, however, we achieved a significant breakthrough in design and successfully manufactured a bomb from porcelain with a reduced charge, which was either dropped at high altitude by parachute or fired from mortars.

In August 1945, Unit 731 was ordered to destroy the Ping-

fang facility and return to Japan to assist in preparations for the anticipated Allied invasion of the mainland. I was repatriated before the demolition work commenced. I do not know what happened to the 4,000 maruta *who were still housed in the prison wing. Lieutenant General Ishii returned to Tokyo at about the same time I did, and I understand he was eventually placed under house arrest by the occupation authorities. I do not know the whereabouts of the scientific data and specimens brought back from Pingfang.*

This statement is, to the best of my knowledge and belief, true and correct. Sworn September 6, 1946 in the presence of Colonel T.M. Kennedy, U.S. Army, assistant to Chief War Crimes Prosecutor.

The second document was much shorter, and consisted of an excerpt from the interrogation of one Lieutenant Arai Sasaki.

TOP SECRET
WITHDRAWN FROM TRIAL EVIDENCE [BY ORDER OF SCAP]

Interrogation of Lieutenant Arai Sasaki
NYK Building, Tokyo, March 8, 1946 [excerpt]

Question: What was your status within Unit 731?

Answer: I was a senior technician engaged mainly in research and development.

Question: The research and development of what?

Answer: Preventive medicines for use against chemical agents.

Question: What sort of chemicals were the preventive medicines designed to guard against?

Answer: Mainly mustard gas, but also, toward the end of the war, sarin and other similar nerve agents.

Question: Were human beings used for the purposes of experimentation?

Answer: I personally did not take part in any experiments on human beings.

Question: I did not ask whether you had taken part in such experiments. I shall repeat the question. Were human beings used for the purposes of experimentation?

Answer: Yes.

Question: Describe a typical chemical experiment of the sort that would be routinely carried out at the Anda open-air test-

ing ground.

Answer: Usually a number of subjects—perhaps fifteen or twenty—would be fastened to stakes in the ground in an open area. A bomb or other projectile would then be detonated or sometimes dropped overhead from a light aircraft. The scientists would observe from a distance, wearing protective clothing. In the past, the wind direction had sometimes changed, and our own soldiers were overcome by the gas. Once the subjects were unconscious or dead, the pathologists would remove their internal organs and carry out basic tests in the field laboratory. More detailed tests would usually take place later at the Pingfang laboratories.

Question: What happened to the bodies of the victims following completion of the experiment?

Answer: In the early years, the bodies were buried in waste ground next to a disused abattoir. From 1942 on, Anda was equipped with two large furnaces, and thereafter all bodies were cremated.

Question: What nationality were the victims?

Answer: They were nearly all Chinese—from the Harbin area.

Question: You said they were "nearly all Chinese." What other nationalities were there?

Answer: There were a small number of Koreans and several Soviet POWs captured near the Manchurian border. The POWs were spies engaged in sabotage against Japanese Army installations.

Question: Were any Europeans amongst those sacrificed at Anda?

Answer: I don't recall there being any.

Question: During your initial interview one month ago you stated that experiments were carried out on British and American prisoners of war. Was that not the case?

Answer: Yes, I remember now. There were some Americans and a small number of British POWs involved.

Question: How many American and British POWs were killed?

Answer: I don't remember exactly. Maybe around two hundred.

Question: Two hundred? In total?

Answer: I believe that is the number.

Question: In that case, can you explain what happened to the 1,041 American prisoners of war who are recorded as having been transported by train from Pusan to the Mukden prison-

er of war camp on November 11, 1942, and then on to Harbin, arriving there on November 12?

Answer: No. I do not know.

Question: I find your answer somewhat difficult to believe. Of the nearly ninety thousand American prisoners of war captured on the Bataan Peninsula in April 1942, the 1,041 I have just referred to are the only ones who remain unaccounted for.

Emma finished reading, lifted her head and gazed into the distance with a deeply perturbed expression.

"You finished?" asked Carnaby gently.

She nodded, gripping the documents firmly by the edges, her hands trembling slightly, as if she wanted to rip them to shreds and scatter the fragments across the floor.

"The other affidavits are pretty much the same—one for each of the six doctors listed in the trial bundle index. The one you've just read is a little more detailed than the rest though."

She glanced sideways at him and laced her fingers together. "Could I have one of your cigarettes please?"

"Huh? Oh, yeah, of course," he blurted, mildly amused. He shook one out from the pack that had been lying on the arm of the sofa and handed it to her. He fished out his lighter from his trouser pocket and, as she bent her head toward him, lit the tip and then flipped the cap shut again and extinguished the flame.

She sucked inexpertly on the filter and then coughed violently two or three times like an asthmatic gripped by a sudden seizure.

"Are you okay?"

Still wheezing she nodded affirmatively and said through a haze of tears and smoke, "I just don't understand, that's all. What on earth do these papers mean? And why did Harvey have them at all?"

Carnaby stood up, folded his arms, and began pacing backwards and forwards. He stopped and turned to face her again. "Listen. I don't have all the answers right now, but one thing is for certain: If these documents are genuine, and I've gotta tell you, they look genuine to me, then I can fully understand why whoever is behind all of this would stop at nothing to prevent them from falling into the wrong hands."

"*Wrong hands*?" Her face clouded over. "What are you trying to say?" she said in a voice that was almost a whisper. "That Harvey was killed because of these horrible documents? Is that it?"

He gazed at a spot on the far wall.

She dropped the half-smoked cigarette into her martini glass and looked at him intently. "I mean, if these documents are so *bloody* important, why didn't he just take them to the authorities? Why all this cloak-and-dagger nonsense?"

"But don't you see?" he said, squatting down so his face was level with hers. "Take a look at the stamp on the papers you've just read: 'Withdrawn from Trial Evidence by order of the Supreme Commander for the Allied Powers.' All of the documents bear the same mark. You know what that means?"

She stared at her feet in silence.

"No?" he said, his voice rising a notch. "Well, I'll tell you. It means that these documents were removed from the trial bundle by order of General MacArthur's office. They never even made it to the courtroom. Harvey couldn't take them to the authorities because it was the *authorities* that ordered their suppression in the first place." He stood up with a self-satisfied look and started pacing the room again. And then he stopped suddenly, hands on hips: "Jesus Christ!" He all but spat the words out.

Emma looked up and said, rather lamely, "What is it?"

"This is dynamite! Absolute dynamite. It's starting to become clear now. It explains why my apartment was ransacked. They thought *I* had the attaché case." His eyes were wide with excitement. He ran a hand through his hair and stared about the room like a madman.

Emma's face was a picture of confusion. "But I still don't follow you. The war crimes trials finished a year ago, didn't they?"

He was shaking his head vigorously. "The Tokyo trials, yes. But there's another round, scheduled to open in Yokohama at the end of next month. The list of defendants is still being finalized. That's the whole point," he said, reaching down and picking up the papers from where she had let them fall. He leafed quickly through the pages until he found what he was looking for. "Here," he said, with an air of finality. "According to Kanazawa's statement, the research project had the *full backing* of the emperor himself." He dropped the bundle of papers onto the sofa. "And this document," he proclaimed, picking up and waving the interrogation excerpt in the air with a flourish, "would have us believe that more than a thousand British and

American prisoners of war ended their days in the most horrific manner imaginable at the hands of men like our good doctors here."

Emma was beginning to see what he was driving at: "So, you put two and two together and conclude that the emperor must have known what was happening."

"Exactly," he said, snapping his fingers. "He has imputed knowledge and is therefore fixed with responsibility. Christ! If the press get wind of this they'll have a goddamned field day. It'll be the scoop of the decade. And not only that," he continued, thrusting his hands back into his pockets, "we'd *have* to prosecute. It would be impossible not to with this out in the open. The weight of public opinion back home would demand it. It would play right into the hands of the Soviets."

"The Soviets?" she repeated, momentarily losing the plot again.

"Yeah, the Soviets. The reason why the emperor wasn't indicted as a war criminal in the first place is that we needed him alive. We needed him to stand up there in his emperor's costume and go through the motions. Without him the Japanese would never have accepted the occupation. There would've been a rebellion overnight. It was the only condition to the so-called 'unconditional' surrender. Do you see now?"

He suddenly realized that Emma wasn't listening any more. She was miles away, staring into space. Tears formed in the corners of her pretty eyes and then spilled over the sides and ran down her cheeks. She sniffed, pulled a pink handkerchief from inside her sleeve and blew her nose. "Sorry," she said, her voice muffled through the small square of cotton.

He sat down on the sofa and sidled up to her. "Gee, I'm sorry Emma. It's a lot to take in, I know. I'm still confused by much of it myself."

"No," she sniffed, dabbing at her nose, "it's not that. I was just thinking about Harvey. Poor thing. I can just picture his dilemma now. You see," she continued, turning to face him, "he had a very strong sense of right and wrong. He would have come across these documents—Lord knows where—seen at once the inequity and yet been torn between the patriotism he felt for his country and the moral obligation to make known such a gross miscarriage of justice."

"And so giving the documents to the priest, for safekeeping, so to speak, was the only thing he could do I guess." Carnaby provided what he considered a fitting conclusion and then leaned back and closed his eyes, still muttering to himself, "Christ. This is sensational. Jesus H. Christ."

They both sat in silence for several minutes. And then Emma spoke. "What about the Japanese man that killed the priest? Who was he?"

Carnaby opened one eye, screwed his face up and collected his thoughts. "I got his name from the ID card in his wallet and called it in to Dan Morita this morning. He said he'd check it out and get back to me." He looked at his watch. "Thanks for reminding me."

"What about all of this?" she said dreamily. "You surely can't keep it here. They might come back again."

He rocked forward and placed his hands on his knees. He looked at the mess of papers on the floor and breathed out heavily. "Yeah, I guess you're right. I don't know. I'll think of something."

"I could take them. To my room at the embassy I mean. As far as I know, nobody knows I'm here. It would be the last place they would think of looking."

Carnaby was already on his feet and shaking his head, his hand out in front of his body patting the air, like a traffic cop waving a car to a halt. "Now hold on just one minute. I can't ask you to do that."

"Maybe not. But that's what we are going to do."

Twenty

Dan Morita tripped down the single flight of stairs from his office to the library, which occupied half a floor at the back of the building.

He flashed his ID to the desk clerk, who continued reading his newspaper without looking up, and went on through the turnstile gate. It made a slight clicking sound as he emerged on the other side. He didn't use the library too much these days and found himself stopping halfway along the corridor to check the category markers on the wall. Goddamn, he thought to himself, they were forever rearranging the place. Why couldn't they just put it all in a logical, easy-to-use order and leave it that way? He walked past several racks of steel shelving and spotted what he was looking for on the wall ahead: "Suspects [domestic] Serious crime: Section B3."

He rubbed his chin thoughtfully and carried on to the end of the corridor, turning right into Section B. He moved along past index card boxes for Rows 1 and 2 and presently came to Section B, Row 3. He shot a furtive glance down the corridor to his right and back again the way he had just come. He told himself to relax and stop worrying; he had every right to be down here without requiring additional authorization. He just wished he'd thought of some other suspects he could make out he was investigating just in case he bumped into someone like Aspin, unlikely as that was. It would be awkward, to say the least, to have to explain why he was looking into two people connected with Harvey Brice more than a month after Carnaby had been retired from active pursuit of the investigation.

He opened his file and checked the name again: Shintaro Tanaka. Moving sideways along the narrow space, he soon found the drawers containing family names beginning with "T"—three of them, to be precise—running vertically from top to bottom. He pulled the top one open and flicked past the first few cards: Tabata, Tachikawa, Tada, Takebayashi, Takeuchi, *Tanaka.* It didn't take him long to discover there were literally dozens of Tanakas. Just his luck to have a suspect with one of the most common family names.

Frustrated, he closed the drawer with a bang and roughly pulled out the middle one. He was just about to put his hand in, when suddenly someone appeared from around the corner. *Shit*! He panicked, spun on his heels, and pulled open the drawer directly in front of him—any drawer—he didn't even see what the alphabetical reference was. He started thumbing through the cards with intense concentration, all the while racking his brains for a plausible story. It was the dumbest thing he could have done. He knew full well that nothing attracted attention like fast, jerky movement. No matter. He held his breath and stared into the half-full drawer. His mind had gone completely blank.

A shadowy figure walked silently past him toward the janitor's room at the far end of the corridor. He breathed out loudly, too loudly. The figure stopped suddenly and turned in his direction. It *was* the cleaner. Morita faltered and then recovered himself and nodded. *"Ah, konnichiwa."* The figure returned the greeting and smiled through crooked teeth before continuing on his way.

He could feel the sweat running down his back. He took another deep breath and turned back to the drawer containing the Tanakas. Jesus, there were hundreds, never mind dozens. He slid out the third drawer, his strolling fingers slowing as he came across the cards for Tanaka whose first name began with "S." Satoshi Tanaka, Satomi Tanaka, Shinsuke Tanaka, *Shintaro Tanaka.* He extracted the card and held it close up, scrutinizing the details: "Shintaro Tanaka—disappeared December 1949. Thought to be operating underground with the Yamaguchi-gumi."

He grunted, confusion spreading across his face. His eyes went to the date of birth: October 25, 1918. Jesus Christ—it was the wrong Shintaro Tanaka! Cursing under his breath, he replaced the card and took out the one behind it. "Got you," he smiled. This time, the details tallied with those in his file. He turned the card over to make a mental note of the file index number and gasped. There was a stamp in bold red lettering diagonally across the back: "Removed by order of Counterintelligence Section." His eyes took in the date—today's date! He thrust the card back into the drawer as if it had bitten him and moved quickly away from the bank of index cards.

He waited a few seconds, listening, before moving back to the drawers. He still needed to check the landlord's details. He found the drawer—only one this time—and searched the cards for "Kobayashi." There were only two of them, neither of which was a match. Maybe Ralph's hunch was right after all and it was a bogus ID.

He closed the drawer again and, treading carefully so as not to make too much noise, retraced his steps toward the entrance. He rounded the corner and saw a familiar and very welcome face. The duty roster had changed, and a much more attentive, and certainly more attractive, records clerk was now sitting behind the counter. Wiping his sweaty palms on his trousers, he forced himself to relax.

She spoke first. "Dan! *Shibaraku ne*—it's been a long time."

"It sure has. How are you, Michiko?"

"Oh, just fine. A little busier than usual, but otherwise nothing much changes around here."

"Gee, what I wouldn't give for a quiet life."

They both laughed.

"What brings you down here, Dan? Is there anything I can do for you?" she asked, smiling.

He looked at her archly. "Oh, give me a minute longer and I'm sure I'll think of something."

She blushed and made a show of looking at her watch. "I have a busy day ahead of me, so why don't you come to the point?"

"Only if you let me take you to dinner."

"You don't know when to quit, do you?" She flicked her fringe away from her eyes with a nod of her head, and then smiled. "Okay, call me. Now really, what do you want?"

"Okay," he said, wrinkling his brow and grinning. "There is something you can help me with. The only problem is, well, it's kind of sensitive—if you know what I mean."

"You needn't worry about that," she assured him. "Your secrets are safe with me."

"Seriously, Michiko, I'm trying to find a criminal reference for a certain Shintaro Tanaka. But when I checked the box index just now I found that the file had been removed sometime earlier today."

"What section did you check?"

"Serious Crime—B3."

"In order to remove a file from Serious Crime, you would need authorization from Colonel Aspin or one of the senior officers in Counterintelligence at SCAP HQ."

"General MacArthur included?"

"In name, yes. Although I doubt he actually authorizes things like that any more."

"And where do the files go?"

"Depends on the reason for removal. Sometimes files are reclassified top secret, in which case you will never see them again. Or they may be designated "Authorized Access Only," in which case they will be held in a restricted area over at Kasumigaseki."

"Kasumigaseki?"

"Yeah. In the MPs' building."

"And tell me, do we keep a record here of who actually removed the file today?"

"To be perfectly honest, I'm not sure. It doesn't happen very often." She pulled out a ledger from under the table and ran her finger down the entries column. "Ah, here we go. Oh, but the signature is impossible to read."

"What? Here, let me look." He turned the ledger round and peered at the crabbed handwriting. But she was right. It was nothing more than a hurriedly scribbled line across the signature box. Printed next to it was the file reference: File B3 (a) (iii)—SCAP INT. "I see," he said, staring into space and drumming his fingers on the countertop.

"Are you okay?"

"Yeah," he replied, looking back at her inquiring face. "Sorry, something just occurred to me. Listen, Michiko, I really have to go. Thanks for the advice. I'll be seeing you."

She shouted after him: "Don't forget to call me!"

He looked back. "What?"

"Call me. You know—dinner!" She sat down again, shaking her head and smiling. Morita waved a hand behind him and headed for the stairs.

He took a cab three blocks to the MPs' headquarters. Being

broad daylight, he was more than a little apprehensive. But he figured he might actually blend in more easily during the day when the building was likely to be busy.

His hunch proved correct, and the whole place was a hive of activity. He entered the building and headed along the wide corridor signed for "Records Department." He had been there once before, several years ago while helping to investigate the right-wing assassination of a senior American officer, and, thankfully, it was still in the same location.

He felt more at ease than he imagined. There were proportionately more Japanese and nisei, second-generation Japanese-Americans, working in the building than there were Caucasians. Quite a contrast to his own building.

He headed on through the double doors of the Records Department and noticed, interestingly, no security for the general records section. He sat down on the one free chair and placed his folder in front of him on the large communal desk in the middle of the room. He took out a pencil and made some brief notes. Then he sat back, pretending to think, and quickly scanned the room. There it was, off to the right—a separate entrance manned by two uniformed MPs, both of whom were carrying sidearms.

He watched discreetly for a while. It looked as though everyone going in had the same light green entry pass, probably a pre-approved authority to look at specified documents. He toyed with his pencil while he pondered the question of how he was going to get in. Had it been one guard, perhaps he could be distracted, giving him just enough time to slip by unnoticed. But two . . .

He was just beginning to think it was a hopeless waste of time when he saw his opportunity: the police officer sitting at the end of his table, an overweight individual stuffed into an ill-fitting blue uniform, was dozing, his eyes flickering as he fought a losing battle to stay awake. Every few seconds he would lose control completely and his body would jerk forward. Lying beside the book he had been reading was a green pass.

It was now or never, decided Morita on an impulse. He glanced around the room to make sure nobody was watching him. It looked alright. Most people were engrossed in their reading materials or huddled close, talking in hushed voices. He gently pushed the chair back, being careful not to scrape the legs on the wooden floor, and stood up, picking his file up as he did so. He walked slowly around the head of the table and, as he drew level with the policeman, he placed his file down on top of the pass. He bent down and tied his shoelaces and then stood up again, retrieved his file and proceeded confidently toward the MPs. As he came even with them he nodded and slid the pass out from under the file. One of the MPs took the card and stamped it with the date before returning it and waving him through.

His heart was beating so fast he thought he would pass out. He would need to hurry. There was no telling when the pass's 'donor' would wake up. He went straight to yet another set of box files and searched through the cards. He found it quickly this time: Shintaro Tanaka. He read the description under the name: "Repatriation [via Amano] June 27, 1948. File no: A17."

He closed the drawer and spun around. The files were stacked on wooden shelving in front of him. Standing in front of the first row, he pulled down a buff-colored file which matched the reference. He knew straightaway something was wrong when he felt the weight of it in his hand. It was completely empty, and this time there was no stamp explaining what had happened to the contents.

Suddenly, from the direction of the entrance, he heard raised, protesting voices. He froze for an instant and then thrust the file back onto the shelf. Walking swiftly to the doorway, he fell in line with two other people who were on their way out.

As he passed the entrance, he saw the policeman waving his arms and remonstrating with one of the MPs while the other stood by ready to lend assistance. The man would not be pacified. "Someone has stolen my pass! This is an absolute outrage. What do you intend to do about it? I have to report back to my station commander this afternoon."

People stopped and stared. Staff behind the main records counter put their private conversations on hold and looked over. Even a painter perched high above on bamboo scaffolding stopped mid-brushstroke to peer down at the scene unfolding below.

Morita walked over to the main entrance—not too quickly—and just as he was about to leave the room he turned his head and glanced back. He looked around again as he came out into the corridor and walked headlong into the burly frame of Major General Charles Brannigan. "Jesus! Oh, sorry, sir. Please excuse me."

"What in blazes is going on in there, soldier?" bellowed the general, his face turning an angry red. But he didn't wait for an answer and instead strode into the records room, his fists held in ugly bunched knots, muttering obscenities under his breath.

Morita turned and walked quickly out of the building.

Twenty-one

They met at a coffee shop, close to Kyobashi. Carnaby was there first—early for once. He saw her across the street, waiting for the light to change and struggling under the weight of a large canvas shoulder bag. As she came into the shop he lowered his newspaper and shot a glance at her bag. "Please don't tell me you brought the pouch with you?" His voice was low, but insistent.

"I had to," she said, slumping down in the chair opposite.

"What the hell are you doing, Emma?"

"I had no choice!" she hissed, her voice rising to a strangled pitch.

"Alright, alright." The veins on his neck bulged. He stubbed his cigarette out roughly on his saucer. He began to whisper. "I thought you said you could keep it at the embassy?"

She glared at him. "I thought I could. But the housekeeper, she's a bit of a busybody—likes to come into my room when I least expect it. Helping me settle in—you know, bringing me armfuls of bedding and other useful things. She even came in this morning and watered my plants. I just felt I couldn't take the risk that she might snoop around while I'm out. It sounds awful I know, but well . . . "

He was nodding now in a manner which suggested he understood her predicament. "It's alright. I'm sorry. You did the right thing." He lit another cigarette, blew smoke from his nostrils and looked at her. "What about this friend of yours? Can we trust him?"

"Peter?" She smiled. "Yes, of course. He's an old friend. I went to school with him years and years ago. To tell the truth, I think he had a bit of a crush on me at the time."

"You mentioned he was a reporter, right?"

"Yes, that's right. He's a journalist—with the *Manchester Guardian*."

"The *Manchester Guardian*?"

"Yes," she laughed. "It's not exactly the *New York Tribune*, but he seems to like it."

"And what did he say when you called?"

"He sounded delighted at the prospect of seeing me again."

"And you mentioned me, right?"

She looked down at the tabletop.

"You did tell him I'm coming along too, didn't you?"

"Well, not exactly, Ralph. I just thought there would be a greater chance of—"

"Emma?"

"It's alright. He won't mind at all once we're there. And what's more, he's very discreet. I'm sure he would love to help us."

"Well, I don't know. The more people who know about this the greater the risk of it getting out. And another thing, I've had run-ins with these newspaper types before. If you're not careful, as soon as your back is turned they go and print the whole goddamned story without telling you."

"Oh, don't be silly. You worry far too much. And in any case, it's not as if we have to tell him everything."

"So what exactly did you tell him?"

"Well, I basically said that there is some doubt as to whether Harvey did actually commit suicide and that the police are making further inquiries. Also that I had come by a briefcase containing certain affidavits which Harvey had obviously gone to great lengths to hide—and that the affidavits may therefore have something to do with why he died."

"I thought you just said we don't have to tell him everything?"

She looked at him stony-faced.

"Anyway," he said with a sigh, "what was his reaction?"

"Funny really," she replied, cradling her chin on her hands. "He didn't really say anything. It was as if he was thinking deeply about it. Either that or he simply isn't interested at all. Anyway he said he has some good reference materials and should be able to dig something up to give us something to go on."

They finished their coffee and walked down Ginza in the direction of Shinbashi. It was a pleasant morning, and despite the humidity it was nice to be outside amongst the people of Tokyo.

There seemed to be a new vitality taking hold of the city: construction projects were underway everywhere; the stores were thronged with eager shoppers; and there was a general feeling of renewed prosperity about the place.

They arrived at the Fuji Building just before 09:30 and rode to the fourth floor in a rickety goods elevator. The *Manchester Guardian* occupied the top floor of this none-too-salubrious location. Emma pulled on the door and went straight in. A small and neat Japanese receptionist of about fifty or so and wearing a beautiful green kimono appeared from behind a *noren* dividing curtain and greeted them with a deep bow. Her immaculate appearance seemed incongruous amid the shabby interior of the building.

"Good morning," said Emma. "We're here to see Mr. Peter Farnham."

"Hai, dozo. Kochira e." The receptionist beckoned them into the interior, which turned out to be a small reception lounge with two grubby-looking sofas and a low occasional table. The room was dark and stuffy. An ancient extractor fan set into the outside wall coughed and spluttered as it turned at half speed, the vents being clogged up with months, if not years, of dust and grime.

"Shosho o-machi kudasai," she smiled.

Emma looked confused, but Carnaby explained with a whisper in her ear: "She asked us to wait a minute."

"Dozo, o-kake kudasai." She indicated the sofa and was just about to go into the back office when a tall, ungainly man wearing a cricket sweater opened the door and came striding in.

"Emma!" he exclaimed in genuine delight. "I thought I heard you arrive. My word, look at you. You haven't changed one bit. How lovely to see you."

They embraced, affectionately, with eyes closed. They parted slightly and Farnham held her by the shoulders and looked longingly into her eyes. It was then that he seemed to notice Carnaby hovering uncomfortably in the background.

"Oh, hello." He looked at Carnaby and then transferred his gaze back to Emma and released her shoulders. "I didn't know you were bringing a friend."

Emma smiled. "Peter, this is Ralph Carnaby. Ralph, meet my dear old friend, Peter Farnham."

"Yes, of course," said Farnham, proffering his hand. "How do you do?"

Carnaby shook his hand and smiled warmly. "Good to meet you at last, Peter. I've heard so much about you."

"Oh really? I had no idea."

"Ralph is an investigator. He's helping me look into Harvey's death."

"Oh yes. I am sorry to hear about that, Emma. I really am. How are you bearing up?"

"Oh, you know, it's still early days. But I'm coping quite well enough."

"Good. That's the spirit. Well, shall we go through into the office? It's not very private out here. Would you like some tea, er, Ralph, wasn't it?"

"That would be just great, thanks."

"Lovely, Peter, thanks," added Emma, appreciatively.

"Yoko-san, *o-cha kudasai*."

"Hai, sugu o-mochi shimasu." The receptionist bowed once again and disappeared behind the curtain.

The back office was relatively big and doubled as the library and editing room. They sat down around a small table off to one side. The tea was brought in and the receptionist left them alone, closing the door behind her.

Carnaby broke the silence. "Say, Peter, what is it you actually do around here?"

"*Do*, old boy? As little as possible if I can help it."

Farnham's plummy English accent was beginning to irritate Carnaby, but he did his level best to smile and appreciate the younger man's sense of humor.

"Oh, come on, Peter, for goodness' sake," chimed Emma, "stop being so evasive. Tell us what you do here. I'd like to know too."

Farnham smiled broadly while he rotated a pencil across the back of his fingers. "It's really not that interesting, Emma old girl. I seem to spend most of my time these days wining and dining mid-level politicians and petty bureaucrats in the hope of finding something which will prove to be of earth-shattering importance. Which, incidentally, is very difficult to do on the limited entertainment budget of the *Manchester Guardian*."

"Well, that doesn't sound too dull to me," she said. "You must get to meet some pretty important people."

Farnham suddenly assumed an air of self-importance. "Occasionally. Yes, I suppose I do. In fact," he continued, staring into space with a smile tugging at the corners of his mouth, "I actually managed to interview Shigeru Yoshida a couple of months ago."

"The prime minister?" she asked, looking suitably impressed.

"Yes, that's right. Not that I really learned anything new from him. The few things he did tell me—his views of the opposition party, for example—were so outrageous I wasn't able to publish them."

Carnaby sipped his tea and glanced at Emma pointedly.

She took the hint and said, "Anyway, Peter, as I told you on the telephone, we have something to show you."

"Oh yes, of course." He licked his lips. "It all sounds very intriguing. I like a good mystery to unravel." He rubbed his palms together and rocked forward, giving her his undivided attention.

She lifted her shoulder bag off the floor from where she had been gripping it, pincer-like, between her ankles and placed it squarely on her lap. She untied the plaited cord and pulled out the battered leather briefcase. As she slid the contents out, Carnaby coughed into his hand and looked at Farnham. "Peter, I'm sure I don't need to say this but, well, you do understand that what we're about to show you isn't for the general consumption of your readers?"

"Perfectly, old boy. Don't you worry," he said, licking his lips avariciously and staring at the files in Emma's hands.

She placed the files on the desk. "This one," she said, indicating the top file with her index finger, "is probably the best one to look at. It's fairly representative of the others."

"How many are there?" asked Farnham, scooping up the file and opening the affidavit.

"Six." She reached back into her bag and pulled out a sheet of paper. "I've written the doctors' names down here."

Farnham's brow creased as he began to skim the documents with all the efficiency of a top-class news editor. Occasionally showing signs of excitement, he would raise his right eyebrow a fraction, independently of the other, and mutter to himself, "My, my."

Midway through Carnaby showed signs of losing patience and said, none too subtly, "It's really only the doctors' identities we are after."

Emma had silenced any further protest by mouthing "Stop

it" with a murderous look on her face. She snatched the list of names from Carnaby's hand and put it back in her bag.

At length, Farnham sat back, leaving the last page of the affidavit open in front of him. He looked visibly stunned, but then slowly, almost imperceptibly, a faint smile began to form on his face. Suddenly, without warning, he clapped his hands together with a sonorous crack and jumped to his feet. "I know," he said, and hurried over to one of several large metal-framed book shelves fixed to the far wall. While Emma and Carnaby looked on stupefied, he began pulling dust-covered cardboard boxes down and peering at the dates, which in most cases had been hurriedly scribbled on the lids in pencil. "Nineteen forty-five. Nineteen forty-six . . . Ah, here we go, getting warmer now. February, March, April, May . . . "

Emma and Carnaby exchanged brief glances. Carnaby raised his eyebrows as if to say, "What the hell is your weird friend doing?" and Emma stifled a smile and shrugged.

"June, *July*—bingo!" exclaimed Farnham, not in the least bit concerned about how his behavior was being perceived. He sat down, cross-legged, in the middle of the floor and tore the lid off the box. "Oh," he said, pausing momentarily, "I always wondered what happened to you." He pulled out a small calico square of *gros point* embroidery with "Home Sweet Home" written across the top in neat green cross-stitch. "Present from my sister," he grinned, holding it up for them to see, "from when I first moved out here." He dropped it to the floor and resumed the pursuit of whatever it was he was sure resided in the box. After delving through a top layer of what appeared to be a collection of old postcards and letters, he pulled out two reporter's notebooks. He looked at the first and dropped it dismissively back into the box. The second book, however, seemed to hold his attention.

He cradled it lovingly and then flipped the leather cover over and leafed through the first few pages. The frenetic pace of his activity had slowed now and his powers of concentration took control as he homed in on his quarry. With his shoulders slumped forwards, the deep-ribbed pattern on the back of his cricket sweater gave him the appearance of a lobster-like creature, encased in a long, thin carapace.

There was something quite pathetic, thought Carnaby, about the oddly eccentric behavior of this gangling English bachelor as he sat alone in the middle of the room detached from the world around him, and completely absorbed in the past. He shuddered, the thought suddenly occurring to him that perhaps he wasn't so very different.

Farnham stopped turning the pages and sat staring fixedly down at his pad. Then he stood slowly, still apparently reading, and made his way back over to the desk. With a triumphant smile he sat down again, cleared his throat, and read a short paragraph out to his captive audience.

It was only afterwards that it occurred to me how wrong this all is. Wrong firstly from a moral point of view, in that evidence properly brought to the attention of the court should not be summarily dismissed without consideration and, secondly, wrong from the point of view of coercing the free press by the use of threats and other sanctions.

He looked up, with a self-satisfied expression, as if his reading required no further explanation.

Emma spoke first. "I'm sorry, Peter. I don't really understand."

Farnham crossed one leg over the other and picked irritably at some fluff which had attached itself to his trouser leg. "My first assignment," he began, "following my arrival in Tokyo was to report on the first phase of the International Military Tribunal for the Far East—you know, the war crimes trials."

Emma nodded encouragingly.

"I sat in the press gallery day in day out for the best part of two years, filling pads like this one with shorthand summaries of the proceedings. I had a regular weekly column for the first six months of the trial, but then it was suddenly axed. Readers back home were losing interest in the increasingly convoluted arguments relating to the retroactive application of the new law on crimes against humanity to acts which took place before that law came into being."

There was a pause, and Carnaby interjected, "I still don't get it. Maybe I'm missing something."

"The public wants sensation, not tedium. Tedium doesn't sell newspapers, even good quality ones. Of course, interest was rekindled when the verdicts were handed down and Tojo and his band of cutthroats were given the death penalty. And then there was the appeal, of course."

"Peter, I meant I don't get the relevance of all of that to our doctors."

"I was coming to that." Farnham regarded him with an icy

stare. "My little after-the-fact diary entry here relates to an incident which happened early on in the trial, before everyone understood the 'ground rules,' so to speak." He took a sip of tea and resumed his explanation. "It was during one of the preliminary sessions, at a time when the public were not allowed in. An Australian lawyer, a young fellow, suddenly requested leave of the court to present some new evidence. It was highly irregular, you understand, and with the benefit of hindsight the presiding judge's mistake was to agree to hear him in front of everyone else. Anyway, this chap stood on the stand and explained how he had obtained evidence that a pseudo-military unit attached to the Imperial Japanese Army in Manchuria had conducted a whole range of ghastly experiments on Australian POWs. He said he had a witness, the only survivor from a group of fifty. He also claimed he had a list of names of the senior officers and technicians responsible."

"So what happened?" asked Carnaby, who was beginning to see the relevance of the diary entry.

"Well, for want of a more erudite expression—all hell broke loose. He was asked, in no uncertain terms, to accompany the judge to one of the briefing rooms. I never saw him again. And then all the members of the press were gathered together during the recess for a special briefing by the press liaison officer. It was explained to us that the Australian lawyer had disregarded protocol and attempted to adduce evidence which was improper and unsubstantiated. The liaison officer ordered us not to report what we had heard or make reference to the incident once outside the courtroom. We were also required to hand over any notes or recordings we had taken." Farnham brushed the soft pad of his forefinger over the rough edge of paper where two sheets had been torn out.

"That's simply awful," said Emma. "How could they do that? How could they just sit there and go along with it like that?"

"Oh," laughed Farnham, sarcastically, "it wasn't the first time, and it certainly wasn't the last in my time reporting on that trial. The ostensible reason was that reporting such incidents would only serve to undermine due process and prejudice the outcome of the trial." He looked past his two visitors into the distance as if he was back in the courtroom seven years before, and then he said, as if it had just occurred to him, "Of course, the thing I remember most about that particular incident is the way it seemed to cause a uniform panic among the judges, almost as though some greater authority had already decided that the subject of the Australian's request was on no account to be discussed in public."

"Are you saying there was some kind of cover-up?" asked Carnaby.

"Not just a cover-up, old boy, but a deal."

"A *deal*?"

"Pure speculation. Backroom journalist's gossip. Call it what you will, but word had it that your *friends* in high places had come to an arrangement with the likes of our good doctor here."

"You mean, like freedom in exchange for information?"

"Information, certainly. The Americans would have played high stakes to get hold of the results of experiments like these. But maybe it was more than that. Maybe it also involved a change of identity and a secure job for life."

"But where on earth do we start?" said Emma, a hint of desperation in her voice.

"With educated guesswork," replied Farnham. "We need to narrow down our search field as far as possible."

"Of course," put in Carnaby, "if they have changed their names, you do realize we don't stand a hope in hell of finding them."

"Quite. Let us hope then, Ralph, that they have not." Farnham stood up again and began pacing backwards and forwards, arms folded tightly across his chest. "The doctor is how old now?"

"He would be fifty-five," answered Emma, glancing at the affidavit to make sure.

"And assuming he was threatened with indictment as a war criminal, my guess is he would probably not want to be in too prominent a position."

"Such as?" said Carnaby.

"Such as a scandal-tainted pharmaceutical company like Green Cross, for example. No, my feeling is he will have opted for a much less conspicuous existence—a position that provides a reasonable income and a certain amount of cachet but one that is nevertheless—what shall I say?—a little more removed from public scrutiny."

Emma had both elbows on the desk and was massaging her temples with her fingertips. Suddenly she stopped and sat up. She picked up the affidavit, licked her finger and quickly turned the pages. "Here," she said, with an air of finality. "He worked at Tokyo Imperial University before the war. He says so himself."

"Aw, come on, Emma. He's hardly going to go back there. That would just be plain dumb."

"Not necessarily," said Farnham, coming to Emma's defence. "He would have had contacts there from the past. Provided he hadn't blotted his copybook, then who knows, it might actually have been the obvious place to go." He tapped the side of his nose with his index finger and strolled over to a wooden bookcase against the wall opposite the metal shelves. With his hands on his hips he looked up and down the book titles. He reached out and took down a large volume with Japanese characters on its cover: *The Education Almanac—1953.* He carried the book over and placed it down on the desk.

"You can read that stuff?" asked Carnaby.

"Oh, I get by. There's always room for improvement." He found the contents page and moved his finger down the listings until he came to the entry for Tokyo University—Faculty of Medicine (page 257).

Emma realized she was sweating and wiped her hands on her handkerchief.

Farnham turned to the relevant page. "Damn!" he exclaimed, reading the small print: "Dean: Masaru Oyama." "Oh, but wait a minute," he said, staring wide-eyed at the line below, which read "Associate Dean: Fumio Kanazawa." "Bingo!" He looked elated.

"Thank you, Peter. You're an absolute darling," said Emma, leaning forward and planting a kiss on his forehead.

Carnaby tapped his watch and looked at her. "You know we really should get going and follow up on this while we've got time."

"Yes, I suppose you're right." She turned to face Peter again and smiled. "Sorry, Peter. We really must go. I'll call you soon, promise."

Farnham stretched his arms out, imploringly. "Stay near me—do not take thy flight! A little longer stay in sight!"

Carnaby frowned and glanced at Emma uncomprehending.

"Wordsworth," she said, raising her eyebrows. "Don't worry," she whispered, pushing him through the door. "He's just naturally eccentric."

The day was wearing on, and they had decided to head straight to the university and talk to Kanazawa, leaving Farnham behind to research the names and whereabouts of the remaining five doctors.

When they arrived, Dan Morita was already waiting there in his car.

"Glad you could make it, Dan." Carnaby slapped him playfully on the shoulder as he climbed out of the car. "Dan, this is Emma Forbes. Emma, meet Dan Morita."

"I'm pleased to meet you, Emma." Morita beamed and shook hands.

"It's my pleasure, Dan. Ralph has told me so much about you."

"Nothing bad I hope!"

"No, nothing of the sort," she laughed.

"Sounds like you've got a good lead here, Ralph."

"Let's hope so. We sure could do with a lucky break."

"Listen," said Morita, moving in closer, "I reckon we stand a better chance of getting to see this guy if I go alone. He might get a little spooked if he sees a couple of foreigners headed his way."

"Yeah, I guess you might have a point there."

Carnaby and Emma sat in the back of the car and watched Morita's tall form disappear through the iron gates of the medical faculty.

Fifteen minutes later they were surprised to see him coming back through the gates with a disgruntled look.

He pulled the door open and climbed into the driver's seat. He turned around and said. "We just missed him. Apparently he went on vacation this morning—a fishing trip or something."

"Do we know where?" asked Carnaby.

"Yeah. A place called Wakkanai."

"Wakkanai? Where on earth is that?"

Morita smiled. "About as far north as you can go in Hokkaido."

Twenty-two

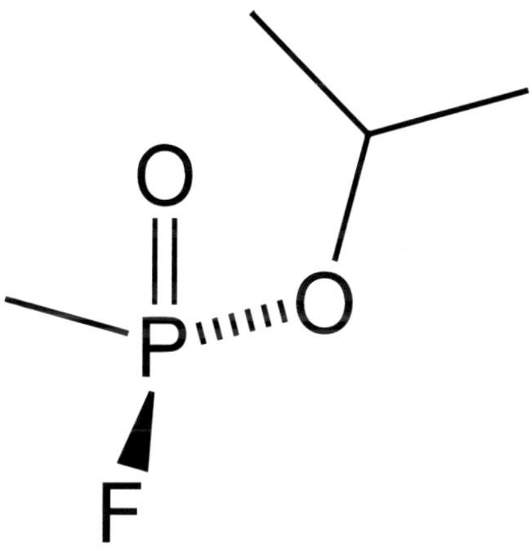

SARIN

Isopropyl Methylphosphorofluoridate, more commonly known as sarin, is a colorless and odorless nerve agent which, in common with all nerve agents, belongs to the group of organophosphorus compounds. First synthesized in 1938 by the distinguished German chemist, Gerhard Schrader, it is twenty-six times more deadly than cyanide gas and twenty times more deadly than potassium cyanide. An amount of 0.01 milligrams per kilogram of body weight is sufficient to kill an adult human being.

Although its effects are instantaneous and deadly, sarin has a low level of persistence and degrades quickly in wet conditions. This is an advantage where the target area needs to be entered and occupied quickly.

The agent may be inhaled through any part of the respiratory tract—from the mucosa of the nose and mouth to the alveoli of the lungs. It can also be absorbed by the iris directly. Droplets of liquid vapor are capable of being absorbed through the skin and mucous membranes as well as by the gastrointestinal tract via the consumption of contaminated foodstuffs.

In the absence of immediate treatment, airway obstruction results from pharyngeal muscular collapse, bronchial secretions, laryngospasm, and paralysis of the respiratory muscles. In all cases where treatment is not given or is not effective, death occurs as a result of respiratory arrest and cardiac arrhythmia.

[Extract from the introduction to A Manual of Chemical Warfare Principles *issued by the Training Wing, Unit 731 Imperial Japanese Army, Pingfang, November 9, 1944]*

Twenty-three

That night Morita had an appointment that would have struck fear into the hearts of most mortals.

Through a combination of persistence, guile and a measure of good fortune, he had managed to secure a meeting with Kenji Maruyama, the notorious *oyabun,* or boss, of the Maruyama-gumi yakuza organization.

The headquarters of the Maruyama-gumi was located in Ikebukuro, not too far, in point of fact, from Sugamo Prison, home to some one hundred Class A war criminals.

Morita arrived at Ikebukuro Station a little after 20:00, armed with the necessary gifts: an envelope containing five hundred US dollars in used twenty-dollar bills, and two bottles of Glenmorangie single malt Scotch whiskey.

It was a ten-minute walk from the station, and it had just started to drizzle. He wasn't familiar with this neighborhood, and he marveled at the myriad of small stores along the roadside—haberdashers, tatami makers, grocers, confectioners, clothiers, *mochi* shops, and a traditional doll maker. He noticed also that the area was more depressed and rundown than most areas he knew in Tokyo. The people looked poorer, somehow less well dressed, and there were many homeless people living in cardboard shelters under railway arches and along the edges of waste ground. Reconstruction had been slow to take place, and there were great strips of ground with incomplete structures sitting abandoned on them.

A mangy dog with one eye came lolloping out of an alley, cocked its leg and urinated on a nearby telegraph pole.

He pulled out a map and squinted at it, using the light from a clog maker's shop window. It looked as though it was the next proper road on the right. Yes, it had to be, he thought, as he watched a small but compact man turn off that way. The man had very short, wavy hair, muscular shoulders, and, the real give-away: the little finger on his left hand was missing, severed just above the middle knuckle. If a yakuza committed a wrongful act, which brought shame on his *oyabun,* or organization, the yakuza was often required to atone for his sins by cutting off his little finger with a samurai dagger. Morita smirked to himself as he recalled the time he had explained this to Ralph, and Ralph's comment had been, "Well, I guess you can't afford to make too many mistakes."

He tucked the map away in his pocket and followed the smaller man down the road, keeping a discreet distance. He paused in the shadows and watched his unwitting guide disappear through the front door of a large building about halfway down.

He took a deep breath and walked on. Coming to the entrance, he took a step back and surveyed the façade of the building. The structure was wooden, traditionally built using beams and pegs, rather like a temple. The roof was covered in expensive-looking blue tiles, and the ridge was decorated with two ceramic '*Shachihoko*'—mythical fish-like creatures with tiger's heads—the age-old means of warding off evil spirits and protecting the building from natural disasters. A discreet sign by the door announced that this was the Tokyo branch of the Nichiren Buddhist Foundation—with registered charitable status. Otherwise there was no indication that it was also home to one of the most powerful yakuza groups in all of Tokyo.

He lingered on the doorstep a moment longer, then, placing his fingers in the recess of the doorframe, he slid one of the large panels back to the right. Climbing up into the *genkan,* the entrance hall, he closed the door behind him. Having removed his shoes, he stepped up onto the polished cedar floor of the reception area and peered about him. There was a row of candles along the back wall, illuminating a wooden wall hanging bearing the characters *jingi,* moral code, but also, Morita knew, the gangster's code of behavior. Clever, he thought, with a smile. Gradually his eyes became accustomed to the gloom. He noticed a small handbell on a shelf to his right and picked it up, shaking it once with a deft flick of his wrist.

Before long, he heard the sound of footsteps hurrying along

the corridor beyond, and a tall monk, wearing a Buddhist cassock, appeared in the inner doorway.

"*O-jama shimasu.*" He bowed. "My name is Morita. I have an appointment to see the *oyabun.*"

"You are welcome. Please come this way."

He followed on behind, for what seemed like an eternity, as they made their way along the labyrinth of interconnecting passageways into the bowels of the building.

As he passed by a bank of tatami rooms, he heard low, whispered voices coming from some and suppressed, vital female voices coming from another. Clearly not noises usually associated with an order of celibate monks. They were probably dormitories for the core band of gangsters most loyal to the *oyabun* and who would need to be resident in order to afford their leader the protection he required.

At length, the passageway gave out onto a large, brightly lit room. Over the far side, a dozen or more yakuza, dressed only in loincloths, knelt on either side of a strip of material, busily playing mah-jongg. Each of them was covered in intricate tattoos, mostly of animals such as tigers or eagles. But there was one man, in the middle with his back to them, who was extremely muscular and had the most splendid tattoo Morita had ever seen. It depicted Yoshitsune, the legendary twelfth-century warrior prince, locked in combat with the giant Benkei with the assistance of the *tengu*—the winged, long-nosed mythical goblins of Japanese folklore.

The whole scene brought to mind the gambling room in the tailor's shop a few weeks back.

He was asked to kneel down on a cushion and wait for the boss to come out. A few minutes later, Kenji Maruyama emerged from the door at the far end of the room wearing full kimono and *hakama*, the traditional split skirt of the samurai. He wore a *kamon* family crest on each breast. It was said he was very proud of his family heritage and could trace his lineage back to the fourteenth century.

Morita rose swiftly, and as Maruyama approached he bowed deeply with sincerity. Then both men adopted the yakuza posture of respect: left leg in front, bent deeply at the knee, body angled forward, and left hand held out, palm uppermost to demonstrate that one was unarmed and had therefore come with peaceful intentions.

Having formally introduced themselves, they knelt down again on cushions.

Morita produced first the envelope and proffered it to the gang leader. “Please accept this gift as a token of my gratitude for the honor of being able to meet with you.”

Maruyama took the envelope, made a slight bow toward it, and slid it inside his kimono.

Morita then brought out the bottles of scotch. “Perhaps you would also do me the honor of accepting these two trifling gifts.”

The greeting having been properly consummated in accordance with yakuza protocol, it was Maruyama’s turn to speak. “I think we can talk more freely in my private room.”

Morita began to get up, but Maruyama spoke again. “But first, I hear you are an accomplished swordsman of quite extraordinary skill.”

“Oh, but *sensei,* I still have much to learn.”

“Nevertheless you *were* runner-up in last year’s first All Japan Kendo Federation Championships, were you not?”

“That is so. But kendo is a sport, and I fear I am not yet of the level where I can truly be described as an accomplished swordsman.”

“I believe, Morita-san, that you are being—how shall I put it?—a little modest. I would like to propose a small challenge. I should like to witness your skill in person. Would you do me the honor of taking part?”

Morita knew full well that he could not refuse, that to do so would result in an unforgivable loss of face for the *oyabun.* “Very well. I accept.”

“Good,” said Maruyama with a smile. He clapped his hands and barked, “Gondo!”

The well-muscled man with the flamboyant tattoo stood up from his mah-jongg board and hurried over.

“You are no doubt familiar with the *bokuto*?” said Maruyama, cradling the long, heavy wooden practice sword in his arms.

“As a training tool with which to strengthen the arms and shoulders, yes.”

“In days gone by, and even now, matches are held using *bokuto.* Of course,” continued Maruyama, gauging Morita’s reaction with a glint in his eye, “one mistake, one slight error of judgment, and a blow from one of these can be crippling and, on occasion, fatal.”

Morita's face was devoid of emotion. He knew only too well that the pre-arranged drills involving attack, parry and counterattack, all with controlled blows, could result in serious injury. He glanced over at his opponent, Gondo, who stood there with an air of arrogance, seemingly unfazed by Morita's kendo prowess. Morita's eyes took in three scars on Gondo's torso and another long, ugly scar, still puckered at the edges, that ran across his forearm. This man, he thought, has fought many times with live blades, probably to the death. It was little wonder then that he looked so confident.

"The match will be decided by *sanbon jiyu kumite*."

Morita shuddered. It was to be the best of three strikes. Controlled in theory, this was the most dangerous form of contest, short of using real swords. He took possession of his weapon and waited in the middle of the room. Gondo squared off against him, sword held in the natural position, on his left side.

The mah-jongg players were now sitting neatly in two rows, waiting with bated breath for the match to begin.

Morita and Gondo exchanged bows, and on the command: "*Hajime!*" both assumed their preferred fighting stance. Morita adopted a conventional position—right leg slightly forward of left, sword tip pointed directly at his opponent, at the height of his throat. Gondo, on the other hand, had transferred his weight to his back foot, and kept his sword low and to the rear. This was a defensive posture—defensive, but one that was nevertheless designed to draw the opponent in to attack.

The two men stayed motionless for the better part of a minute, each trying to gain the psychological advantage. Then suddenly Gondo screamed—an ear-piercing *kiai*. He brought his sword above his head and skipped forward, aiming a deadly overhead cut at Morita's head. The movement was fast and fluid, and Morita realized that Gondo was attacking with all his strength. But it was also telegraphed, and he effected a parry and counterattacked with *kesa-giri*, a long, curving cut aimed at the right shoulder, with the intention of cleaving the opponent in two, the blade traveling diagonally and coming to rest at the opposite hip. Morita expertly stopped the blow short so that the edge of the wooden weapon lay harmlessly on Gondo's shoulder.

"*Yame!*" shouted Maruyama, calling the first exchange to a halt. He indicated a point for Morita, and the bout recommenced.

This time Gondo began slowly circling around Morita, every now and then sliding in and testing his opponent's resolve. Morita attacked—a swift thrust to the throat, accompanied by a deafening, staccato shout—"Yeaaagh!" But Gondo somehow avoided the thrust and jumped in with his own cut to the neck. It connected, but at the same time as Morita's own cut to his opponent's chest.

It was *ai-uchi*, simultaneous strike, and no point was awarded. Morita quickly massaged his pulsating neck; he could feel bruising from the poorly controlled strike to his carotid artery. He looked at Gondo and thought he saw a faintly cynical smile appear on the other's lips.

They faced off again. This time Gondo sprang forward almost as soon as the command was given and aimed a vicious blow at Morita's wrist. Morita pulled back just far enough to avoid taking the full force, but the tip of Gondo's weapon had already found its mark with a sharp thrust under the rib cage. It was a full point, and Morita crouched down low in pain. He realized now that Gondo was making no effort to pull his blows. Why didn't Maruyama stop him?

The next engagement would decide the match. Morita assumed his stance with difficulty. His breathing was erratic, and he had stinging bruises to his neck, wrist and rib cage. Forcing himself to concentrate, he assumed the stance known as *hasso no kamae*, the hilt of the sword held at jaw level with the blade running vertically into the air.

As before, on the shout of *"Hajime!"* Gondo sprang forward with lightning speed, aiming a double blow at the head. Morita back-pedaled furiously and successfully parried both attacks. The two swordsmen froze, each willing the other to make that one vital, all-important mistake which would present an opening for the other.

They were both perspiring heavily now. Rivulets of sweat ran down the face of a long-nosed goblin on Gondo's heaving chest. Then they both attacked at once. Gondo screwed the point of his blade full bore toward Morita's oncoming face. At the last second, Morita dropped to one knee and thrust the handle end of his sword deep into the fleshy part of his opponent's stomach. Gondo folded at the middle and let out a sickening cry as the wind went out of him. In one continuous motion, Morita stood, sword high above his head, and delivered the coup de grâce, controlled perfectly, of course, across Gondo's back.

"As I suspected," said Maruyama, as the two men exchanged bows, signaling the end of the match, "you are indeed an accomplished swordsman of quite extraordinary skill. Now, to business."

Morita followed the *oyabun* across the hall and into his private room. For one of such obvious means, Maruyama's room, though large, was unostentatiously decorated—a simple desk and chair, a hanging scroll depicting a Chinese mountain scene from the ninth-century travels of the Japanese monk Ennin, and a sword rack displaying a *daisho* or set of two samurai swords, both with restrained but nevertheless still beautiful fittings in the *han-dachi* style from Hizen province. A rather crude painting of a snow-capped Mount Fuji hung on the wall behind the desk.

"Please be seated," he said with a wave of his hand.

Morita pulled a chair up and leaned back to face the older man. He felt like he was undergoing a job interview.

"I hope you did not mind too much being subjected to that little test just now. I do not grant interviews lightly, and I need to understand a person's character before I will see them. I also think it is no bad thing for my followers to appreciate from time to time that they are by no means invincible. It tempers their arrogance."

Morita sat in silence and looked Maruyama straight in the eye.

"It is a pity your obvious talents could not be put to more profitable use. I would be inclined to offer you a position within my own organization were it not for the fact that I already know what your answer would be."

"You do me a great honor," said Morita with a sincerity he did not feel.

"Now, I understand you wish to talk to me in connection with a loan made to a foreigner, and the foreigner's subsequent death."

Morita was momentarily taken aback by the abrupt change of subject. "Y-yes. That is correct."

"And what makes you so sure that I know anything about it?"

"With all due respect, *sensei*, I don't think you would have agreed to see me if you did not."

Maruyama smiled. "Go on."

"During one of our investigations, we came across an accounts ledger. The ledger contains an entry recording that a loan of 3.6 million yen was made to the foreigner and," Morita paused, shifting uncomfortably in his chair, "that the foreigner died at a point in time when the loan repayments were in arrears."

Maruyama held Morita's eyes with his own steely gaze. Morita knew that to look away now would ruin his chances of ever discovering the truth of Maruyama's involvement.

At length, Maruyama smiled a knowing smile and looked away, releasing Morita from his ensnaring gaze. Some things did not need to be said to be understood. "My organization is involved in a great many business ventures," he began. "But whatever else we do, I can personally assure you we do not make it our business to murder foreigners." He took out a cigar, guillotined the end, and applied a match. He inhaled deeply and let out wisps of gray smoke from his nose and mouth. "It is true," he continued, "that a loan was made to this foreigner. It is also true that we had discussed various alternative ways of—how shall I say?—encouraging him to settle the arrears. In fact, one of my men was due to pay him a visit to remind him of his obligations. But you must understand, Morita-san, we would not kill for this amount of money, and it is doubtful we would kill a foreigner whatever the price."

Morita spoke frankly now. "I wasn't aware that the Maruyama-gumi, or any other organization for that matter, made loans to foreigners."

"You are right. As a general policy, we do not. And, in retrospect, I wish we had not. It was a mistake on the part of one of my subordinates."

"Do you know why the foreigner was in need of the loan in the first place?"

"Only that he had gambling debts that he wished to clear."

"Gambling debts?"

"Yes. I understand that he gambled regularly."

"Are you able to tell me where he did his gambling?"

"I understand it was a mah-jongg parlor in his own neighborhood."

"An establishment benefiting from your protection?" Morita chose his words carefully, and looked to check the *oyabun's* reaction.

"Yes, since you ask. And to answer your second question, yes, this is one of the reasons why it was possible for a loan to be advanced. We try where we can to assist our clients."

"But on this occasion, you feel it was a mistake?"

"As I have said."

"And you have no idea how or why the foreigner died?"

"None whatsoever." There was a pause, and then Maruyama spoke again in a relaxed, almost friendly tone of voice: "I can see, Morita-san, that there is still an element of doubt in your eyes."

Morita sighed and scrunched his shoulders. "It is just that, well, I do not get the impression that you were particularly concerned about repayment of the loan."

"You are very astute. As I said, it was not a great amount of money, in relative terms of course."

"Was he required to provide some form of collateral?"

He thought he detected a faint flicker in the older man's eyes. Maruyama stood up and stubbed his cigar out. Morita thought he had blown it—asked one question too many. But then the *oyabun* turned, without answering and walked casually over to the picture of Mount Fuji. He lifted it down, and Morita saw that it had concealed a wall safe. Maruyama spun the combination dial backwards and forwards several times and opened the door. He placed both hands in the opening and, with a grunt, lifted out what appeared to be a small, but apparently heavy, wooden crate.

He hefted it onto his desk, released the heavy-duty wire hasp and prized the lid back. Whatever was inside was covered in a piece of dark blue felt cloth. He reached in slowly and lifted out one of three bulky oblong objects, still wrapped in the cloth, and placed it on the desk in front of Morita. Sitting down again, he raised his eyebrows and nodded, as if to say: "*Take a look for yourself.*"

Morita licked his lips apprehensively and very slowly, as if he was about to place his unprotected hand into a viper pit reached out and peeled back the layer of felt.

His senses reeled. He stared wide-eyed. The stamp of the Imperial Bank of Japan was there plain to see. It was the first time and, as he was later to reflect, would no doubt be the last, that he had ever set eyes upon a genuine gold ingot.

Twenty-four

Carnaby couldn't quite believe what he was doing. Later, when he had time to properly reflect, when he thought long and hard about what it was about the Brice affair that had taken such a hold of him, that drove him on with such relentless, unwavering purpose, he decided finally that it must have been the sudden and unexpected appearance in Japan of Emma Forbes.

It was *that* that seemed more than anything to carry him clear of the hurdles his own doubts had begun to place in front of him, so that now, as he sat hiding in a toilet cubicle in the Posts and Telecommunications Building waiting for the secretary to go home, he felt more sure than ever before, in his own mind, about what it was he had to do.

He looked at his watch—20:00. He strained his ears and listened. He knew Brannigan wasn't there. He'd already seen him leave from across the road an hour earlier. He could still hear his secretary slamming things around, opening and closing desk drawers, the occasional cough. Why the hell was she still here at this time of night?

And then he must have dozed off, his head leaning against the partition wall, for when he woke up with a start it was already 10:30. He rubbed his face with both hands and yawned. He couldn't hear anything now, and it seemed much darker over toward the upper windows.

He stood slowly and slid back the bolt. The door creaked slightly as he pulled it back, stopping for a few seconds to listen. Nothing. Nothing that was except for the constant drip, drip, drip of a tap in the corner. He crept out and moved along the wall to the toilet entrance. Again he stopped and listened, and then, when he was sure the place was deserted, he cupped his hand around the edge of the heavy door and opened it a crack. Placing his eye against the slim aperture, he peered out in the direction of Brannigan's office. Only the dim night lights had been left on, and he could just make out the vague shape of the secretary's desk—deserted now, as he had thought.

He came out into the hallway and padded across the floor until he was in line with the desk. He glanced around, his heels squeaking on the polished wooden floor as he turned. He had no idea what time the security guard would make his rounds, but he knew he would have to be quick. Christ, he suddenly thought with a shiver, he would have some serious explaining to do if he were caught snooping around in the dark alone like this. And what if the main entrance was already locked? He could be forced to spend the whole night in the toilet cubicle. But there was no time for thoughts like that now.

He walked straight forward and turned the handle on the door to Brannigan's office. *Shit!* It was locked. But of course it was. He had been a fool to think otherwise. He spun around and went quickly over to the secretary's desk again. He yanked open the top drawer, and, taking out a torch from his jacket pocket, started rooting through the contents, looking for anything that resembled a door key. But it was no use. The drawer was stuffed with an untidy array of stationery—envelopes, rubber bands, paper clips, labels, a tangled ball of parcel string, several pairs of scissors, a packet of stockings and assorted lipsticks. He shut the drawer and tried the one below it, but it was locked and refused to budge.

Without any further delay, he took out his penknife and selected the smallest, narrowest blade. This had worked for him in the past, but, looking at the imposing double doors now in front of him, he had his doubts whether it would do any good at all this time.

But he was wrong. After several minutes of twisting and scraping, all the while stooped in a not-quite-standing, not-quite-kneeling sort of posture, and stopping occasionally to confirm that noises he thought he had heard were simply products of his imagination, the lock gave and he was able to slip into Brannigan's office undetected.

First, he went over to the window on the far wall and peered through the slatted blinds. It seemed quiet enough outside, he thought. He folded his blade away and returned the knife to his pocket. Turning the torch back on again, he scanned the room, being careful to prevent the narrow shaft of light from playing on the windows.

He turned with a start as the beam picked out the Germanic features of the spy, Sorge, staring down at him like some malevolent presence. The bust seemed to hold him in its gaze for a moment, and he felt momentarily paralyzed. He looked away. He was starting to feel ill at ease now and half wished he had thought this whole escapade through a little more thoroughly, or at least discussed it with Dan before coming over here alone like this.

He wandered over to Brannigan's desk—large and vault-like in appearance—and started looking through the drawers. They were, to his dismay, just as untidy as those of his secretary's desk. But at least they all seemed to be unlocked.

He spent ten minutes sifting through what he soon concluded was a pile of junk: old newspapers, out-of-date memoranda, a half-empty pack of Hershey chocolate bars, two or three boxes of different brands of Havana cigars, and, most surprising of all, in the very bottom drawer, hidden under a large telephone directory, five black-and-white photographs, heavily smudged with greasy fingerprints, of a Japanese woman—young, probably in her early twenties, completely naked and adopting a variety of extremely compromising positions.

He shook his head in wonder, replaced the photos and looked around the room again. There was a bookcase next to the door to the adjoining room. He walked over and cast his eye over the titles, but they seemed to be fairly standard military manuals. There was a book on Japanese woodblock prints at the end propped up against a blue glazed pot, from which trailed a bone-dry and apparently dead ivy plant.

Carnaby was starting to think he had come on a wild goose chase. There didn't seem to be anything here out of the ordinary, apart from the photographs that was. He shone the torch back across the room in an arc. It was then that he saw some papers on the desktop. He had been so engrossed in looking through the drawers he hadn't noticed them before. He leaned over and shone the light on them. They seemed to be requisition papers addressed to Logistics for the supply of fuel and foodstuffs. Strange, he thought, and then he noticed a large map spread out underneath. Sliding back the requisition forms, he saw that it was a detailed field map of Hokkaido, and there, marked with a double circle in heavily applied pencil, was the coastal town of Wakkanai. Twice in as many days. Surely this was no coincidence.

Suddenly there was a noise, and the light went on in the corridor beyond the doors. *Jesus H. Christ!* He panicked and started toward the doors but then checked himself. There was no way he could get out that way without being seen, and he had little or no time to try and secure the lock again.

He doused his torch and headed quickly for the interconnecting door, praying that it would be open. It was. But then he remembered the requisition papers and the map. He darted across the room and swiftly spread them out again to obscure the map as they had before. Then he skipped back across the room and closed the door behind him with the softest snick just as the main doors to the room opened.

He froze behind the door as the light came on on the other side. His heart was racing, and he fought to control his breathing. It was then that he heard Brannigan's voice.

"Goddamned bitch of a secretary. Can't trust her to do a damned thing right. If I've told her once, I've told her a thousand times to make sure the fucking door's locked before she leaves."

"Maybe she just plain forgot."

Carnaby strained his ears, but he didn't recognize the second voice. He transferred his weight to the ball of his right foot and put his ear closer to the crack in the door. He heard drawers being opened and slammed shut again and then the sound of a match being struck. A few seconds later the sickly sweet smell of cigar smoke came drifting in under the door. He felt like gagging—he wasn't feeling too great after falling asleep in the toilets.

Brannigan's voice boomed again. "Anyway, you said everything's in place, right?"

"Yeah, Boss. More or less."

"Transports? Fuel?"

"Yep. Requisitions have all been accepted. Your signature worked like a charm. The last of the supplies will be on their way tomorrow."

"All units are confirmed in place?"

"Yes, sir. Confirmed this morning. They're just waiting for the go-ahead."

"Any word from Yamato?"

"Not yet. But he should be there by tomorrow evening."

"Good. And the doctors?"

Carnaby nearly choked. He stumbled sideways and scraped his fingernails across the wooden paneling of the wall as he tried to keep his balance.

"What the hell was that?" said Brannigan.

Carnaby moved swiftly and silently away from the door and behind one of the big heavy curtains which were closed across the sash windows. He held his breath and screwed his eyes shut.

The door opened, and Brannigan's 'acquaintance' put his head through the opening and peered around. He came over to the curtain but, unbelievably, didn't look in Carnaby's direction. He spotted the open top window and shouted back his report. "It's just the wind, sir. Seems like it's coming in through the window back here."

The door slammed shut again, and Carnaby breathed out heavily. His head was throbbing now, and sweat soaked his shirt. There had to be an easier way of making a living, he thought. But he knew full well that he had had any number of opportunities before now to do as he had been told and drop this investigation.

He waited a few minutes and then crept back over to the door. It was quiet now, and the light had been turned off. He breathed out, heavily again, and then tried the door handle. It was locked! Damn it. He swore under his breath and began pacing furiously around the small room. It contained nothing other than a long conference table and chairs.

Taking his penknife out again he backtracked to the door and inserted the blade in the lock. It was a much tighter fit this time, and he found it difficult to get any purchase. Suddenly the blade snapped with a twang, leaving the broken tip lodged irretrievably in the lock mechanism. *Fuck. Fuck. Fuck.* He couldn't believe how the night was turning out. If Brannigan returned and had reason to come in here, he was surely done for.

Then he realized there was really only one way out. He walked quickly over to the curtains, slipped behind them and clambered up onto the windowsill. The window was open alright, but it was quite high up and, he gauged, only just big enough for him to pass through. He pulled on the lower window, more in desperation than genuine expectation, but it was no good. It was locked and sealed with probably a dozen or more layers of ancient paint.

He reached up and opened the small window as far as it would go. Then, placing one foot on the side wall and bracing his left shoulder against the window frame, he levered himself up so that his chest was level with the opening. He could feel the cool breeze on his face. Carefully and slowly he transferred his right hand to the lip of the window frame and pulled his head and torso through the opening. He realized he would have to go through headfirst. There simply wasn't enough room to maneuver his body any other way. With his upper body now dangling from the window, he peered down at the grass embankment some ten feet below. If he could just get his hands onto the outside concrete window ledge, he might be able to do a kind of cartwheel and land feet first on the grass.

Jesus! What the hell was he thinking? He realized, as the pressure began to make his head pulsate, he hadn't done any kind of gym work at all in the last ten years. Just as his waist cleared the window ledge he realized, with horror, that he had lost it. His whole body began to slide downward, slowly at first and then with increasing momentum. He covered his head with his left arm and took the brunt of the impact with his right as he crumpled to the grass in an untidy heap.

He lay there for probably a minute, dazed and nursing his already weakened left arm. Eventually, he pulled himself into a kneeling position and rocked back on his haunches. His head was spinning, and blood dripped from a graze on his left hand where it had collided with the rough surface of the concrete ledge. He got to his feet, using the wall for support, shook his head and made off toward the cover of the trees.

Twenty-five

The languid afternoon sun hung high above the treetops, its hazy light, unimpeded by cloud cover, playing on the still surface of the boating lake.

Dan Morita kicked off with one leg and climbed effortlessly into the stern as the boat moved away from its moorings.

A gull swooped low above the lake and then, as if having determined there was nothing to be had in these shallow waters, abruptly changed direction and headed for the coast and more fertile hunting grounds.

They had decided to meet at Shinobazu Pond in Ueno Park. No longer feeling comfortable meeting at Ralph's place and, since the embassy was out of the question, they preferred somewhere away from the public gaze of central Tokyo. The chances of being overheard while adrift in the middle of an ornamental lake were, they concluded, extremely remote.

Ripples radiated across the surface as the prow of the small craft cut through the calm water ahead of them. A duck, with four ducklings in tow, seeing the wooden object heading her way, altered her course—followed by her obedient offspring.

Emma trailed one hand lazily over the side, allowing her fingers to run through the cool water. The quality of light gave the lake bottom an unearthly, milky-white pallor.

Carnaby cradled his arm, his hand and wrist newly bandaged, and stared out across the expanse of water. Only two other boats—one, closest to them, contained two giggling teenage girls who seemingly couldn't decide which of them was to take the oars and, in changing position, looked set to capsize the boat. In the distance was a much older couple—deep in conversation, oblivious to their precise whereabouts as the boat drifted according to its wont.

It suddenly dawned on Carnaby that, far from looking inconspicuous, their little threesome couldn't have looked odder. Still, he consoled himself with the thought that they would have to be extremely ill-fated to run into any of the people they were trying so hard to avoid.

"Are you sure you are alright?" asked Emma, glancing a little dolefully at Carnaby's bandaged wrist. "I can't believe you just fell out of a window. That really was careless of you, Ralph."

"Yeah. It's just a bad graze, that's all."

"Did you put the dressing on yourself?"

"I sure did. I guess I made a bit of a mess of it, huh?" He laughed again and looked down at the mass of bandages. A loop of material had already unwound itself and hung impotently between his knees.

The boat nosed its way into a narrow channel, which led them around a small ornamental island. A traditional garden, complete with moss-covered stone lanterns, concrete cranes perching on one gracefully bent leg, and torii shrine gates, adorned the middle. As they came around the far side, a heron surprised them as it stretched its wings and, with a powerful flexing of its legs, took off across their bow.

"Look at that!" shrieked Emma in pure delight. "Isn't it beautiful?"

Emma was not a natural city-dweller, and she was finding it hard doing without the birds and other wildlife she so much took for granted back home in Bletchley.

Presently the boat came around the other side of the miniature island, and was now more or less out of sight of the shore and embarkation jetty. Morita slid the oar shafts through the grommets and laid the oars on their sides in the boat, letting the craft come to a gradual standstill.

"Well, I guess this ought to do it," said Carnaby, cupping one hand to his brow in order to shield his eyes from the sun's penetrating rays.

"So, come on, Ralph—let's have it. What did you find out last night?"

"Yes, do tell us," added Emma, her eyes full of curiosity.

"Well, for one thing," he began with a chuckle, "I discovered I'm not nearly as agile as I used to be." He peered down at his arm, and they all smiled. But then he was suddenly serious, and, leaning forward, in a confidential sort of way, he said, "I came *this* close to being caught by Brannigan last night." He held his right hand up and indicated a small gap between the tip of his index finger and thumb. "Brannigan was there, together with another man, don't know who, American by the sound of him."

"And you overheard them?"

"Yeah, that's right, Dan. The first part of their conversation, anyhow. Brannigan is definitely up to something, I can tell you that. He started off by asking the other guy if everything was in place—"

"*Everything?* But what was he referring to?" interjected Emma.

"I don't know for sure, but get this—he also asked if the *doctors* were ready."

Emma and Morita looked at one another, and then Emma turned and spoke again. "I don't understand. Ready for what?"

"Your guess is as good as mine. I was almost discovered and didn't get to hear the rest of the conversation. But you know what I think? Well, I'll tell you—I think they are trying to get the doctors out of the country."

"What makes you say that?" put in Morita.

"There was a map on Brannigan's desk. It was covered with papers, but I caught a glimpse of it just before Brannigan came in. It was a map of Hokkaido. You're not going to believe this, but there was a circle around that place Wakkanai."

"Jesus," said Morita, breathing out forcibly.

"Yeah, that's just what I thought."

"And you think they are trying to get the doctors out of Japan via Wakkanai?" said Emma.

"It's just a hunch."

"But that doesn't make a whole lot of sense, Ralph," pitched in Morita. "Why would Brannigan want to do that?"

"To prevent them from being called before the war crimes tribunal, isn't it?" suggested Emma.

"Well, yes, of course, I understand that Emma. The question is, though, why the hell would Brannigan go to all this trouble to do that?" Morita clenched his fists and stared fixedly at a pure white feather bobbing about in the water. "There is another problem."

"There is?"

"Yeah. You know I called the other doctors before coming out this morning."

"Oh, yeah," said Carnaby, "I meant to ask you about that."

"Well, hold on to your hat and listen to this: they are all away—gone on fishing trips."

"Are you kidding?"

"Nope. And that's not all. They've all taken off to different places—some around Tokyo, others to the west, near Atsugi and Nagoya. One even further afield in Shimonoseki. If they *were* being spirited away, then surely they would all be headed for the same place, wouldn't they?"

"And," began Emma, "Wakkanai would be the obvious place if they were being smuggled out to Russia."

"Exactly," said Carnaby. "I just don't get it. Why would they all disperse to different locations like that? Tell me, Dan, did anyone say when they had gone?"

"Yeah, two days ago. All of them."

"Damn. I guess that rules out pure coincidence."

Emma adjusted her backside on the hard, narrow seat. "Maybe the places they've gone to are just safe houses. You know, somewhere temporary until they know it is safe to travel."

"Yeah, maybe," said Carnaby doubtfully. "In any case, assuming that is the plan, the bigger question is still why Brannigan is putting himself on the line like this for a bunch of former war criminals."

Emma suddenly sat up. "But isn't it obvious? Remember what Peter said? The rumor about a number of former scientists who were supposedly given immunity from prosecution after the war in exchange for the transfer of information on the biological experiments they were involved in."

"What are you suggesting, Emma?" said Morita. "That Brannigan was behind that deal?"

"Yes. Why else would he be going to all that trouble? Don't you see? He's not doing it for *their* benefit, but for his own. He's afraid they will sell him out for failing to keep to the original bargain."

"But why Russia?" said Morita. "I mean, think about it for a moment. The Russians aren't exactly going to welcome these guys with open arms either."

Carnaby stared long and hard into the distance. "You know, I can't help thinking there's something else we're all missing here. What is Brannigan's deal with the Russians? I mean, I know he was a diplomat there before the war, but I just don't get why he's doing this."

Emma's shoulders sagged and she said, "Well, maybe he's telling the doctors one thing, and the Russians something entirely different."

"How do you mean?" said Carnaby.

"Well, perhaps the doctors have been told that they are going to a safe haven, that they can work in a privileged environment with Russian scientists. After all, that was something else that Peter mentioned—that the Russians would also be very interested in getting their hands on data from those experiments."

"I wouldn't have thought the Commies would balk at carrying out their own experiments," said Morita.

Emma ignored his remark and continued. "But maybe the reality is that Brannigan just wants to ship them out of here—regardless of their actual fate."

"Because they could blow his cover, right?" said Morita.

"Yes. It wouldn't be difficult. Presumably Brannigan's signature is on some form of written assurance in their possession."

"Oh, come on, Emma," said Carnaby, "Brannigan's no dummy. He's sure to have covered his tracks. And besides, why would the doctors buy it in the first place? They'd simply be going from one dicey situation to another. This just gets crazier the more I think about it. I don't understand why the doctors are worried all of a sudden. I mean, sure, the second round of trials is about to get underway, but unless someone points the finger at them, and pretty quickly, I don't see how they are in any more danger than they were before."

"You've got a point there, Ralph," agreed Morita.

"Do you think we should row around the lake a little bit," said Emma. "I think we're starting to look a little suspicious."

They had by now drifted back into the main part of the lake and were on show to anyone looking out from the shoreline. Morita took up the oars and struck out for the middle.

Suddenly there was a splash, followed by a short but shrill scream. They all looked over to the right just in time to see one of the teenage girls pull herself into an upright position. She was up to her thighs in water and sopping wet. Both girls were in floods of tears and carrying on as if they were unwilling pawns in some unfolding disaster scenario. There was a commotion on the shore, and two little men appeared from a hut, one carrying a cardboard megaphone. He put it to his mouth and shouted, "Stay calm. Get back into the boat and return to shore immediately."

Morita looked back and sniggered derisively. "Huh. Well, I guess she's in no danger of drowning."

"Dan Morita!" exclaimed Emma. "And I thought you were a gentleman."

Carnaby was staring far off into the distance, almost as if he was unaware of what had just happened.

"You okay, Ralph?" said Morita as he took up the stroke again.

But Carnaby continued staring straight ahead.

"Ralph?"

"Huh? Yeah, sorry—I was just thinking. You know . . . if the doctors are all 'ready,' then whatever it is Brannigan is planning on doing is probably going to happen soon. Wouldn't you agree?"

"Yeah, I guess that makes sense. What are you suggesting we do?"

"Well, maybe we could just follow him—try and see where he goes, who he meets."

"But, what happens if he's already gone?" asked Emma.

"And even if he hasn't," put in Morita, "who would tail him? He knows you, Ralph, so that rules you out. He already bumped into me at the MPs headquarters, although he probably won't remember me—we all look the same you know. And Emma, well, for one thing I think it's far too risky and—"

"I'm not afraid of having a go," retorted Emma defensively.

"That's not what I meant, Emma. In any case, practically it would be too difficult. You don't have any of the passes and authorizations we have. You simply wouldn't be able to access any of the SCAP buildings without attracting attention."

She sighed and looked down at her feet. The sides of her shoes were damp from lying in a small pool of water in the boat.

"I guess you're right," said Carnaby, rubbing his face with his hand. "But I think we need to talk to somebody about this."

"You mean bring it out in the open?"

"Yeah. I guess that's what I mean."

"The problem is, Ralph, for all we know, Brannigan maybe bona-fide. He might be acting on the tacit instructions of SCAP for reasons too secret to make known to the likes of us. Remember, the affidavits were all officially stamped by SCAP. If we bring it out in the open, we may open up a can of worms."

"We might, that's true. But I don't see how else we can move forward now. We've been sitting around waiting for a lucky break, but face it, it ain't going to happen. We have to talk to someone."

"You mean Aspin, right?" said Morita acidly.

"Look, I know you don't exactly see eye to eye with the man, but, well, he's a pretty decent guy underneath. At least if we involve him, then he can make the decision as to whether it goes any further."

"And what if he doesn't buy it? Have you thought about that? What if he says thanks but no thanks? It's off limits, investigation over, period."

"I still think it's a risk we have to take. Emma, what about you? What do you think?"

Emma folded her arms and looked thoughtful. "Well, you know your superiors better than I do. I suppose I am inclined to agree with you. It strikes me that we don't have very much time to do anything. We seem to have exhausted all other options."

"Okay. Why don't I call him later this afternoon and run it by him. I need to see Beth at the hospital later, and I could even drop by the office and see him in person."

Morita gazed disconsolately at the water as it lapped gently against the oars, now motionless in his resting hands.

"Dan?"

Morita sighed, and said, "I guess so. You're the boss."

Later that day, Carnaby had coffee with Beth and then decided to call Aspin just to make sure he was in the office.

"Ralph? Good to hear from you. How are you?"

"Oh, just swell, Mike, just swell."

"Good to hear it. I sure am glad you're coming back to work on Monday. Our experienced operatives are a little thin on the ground right now." Aspin laughed genially.

"As a matter of fact, Mike, I'm only a couple of blocks away. I need to talk to you about something and thought maybe I'd stop by this afternoon."

"Actually, I've gotta dash to a meeting in thirty minutes. Is it anything we can talk about over the phone?"

"Well, I guess I can give you the gist of it, but it may come across a little cryptic. It's basically about Lieutenant Brice."

"Brice?" Aspin sounded winded. "I thought that case was closed. Now please don't tell me that you've spent your entire sick leave running round on some kind of damned fool wild goose chase."

"Look, I know how it must seem. But, the truth of the matter is that this thing has taken on a life of its own."

"I don't think I follow you, Ralph."

"Well, it's a long story, but the thing I want to run by you, Mike, is this. I came by some affidavits signed by a bunch of former military doctors. They had all participated in some pretty sick experiments on live POWs during the war. By rights they should have been tried as Class A war criminals. But someone cut them a deal—freedom in exchange for information. I believe this same person is now trying to arrange for these doctors to leave Japan."

There was a pause on the other end of the line.

"And what has this got to do with Brice?"

"The affidavits were in Brice's possession before he died. He went to great lengths to hide them."

"I see. Listen, Ralph, none of this makes much sense to me. Why don't you come by my office in the morning, say ten o'clock? Maybe if you explain all the background to me we can figure it out."

"Yeah. That sounds good, Mike. I'll do that."

"And, Ralph, why don't you bring the affidavits with you and then I can take a look for myself."

Twenty-six

"Goodnight, Sister," shouted Beth, hitching the strap of her handbag onto her shoulder and smiling.

"Och. Goodnight, lassie. It's high time you were haeme already. You take care of yerself, and I'll be seeing you tomorrow."

She tripped down the two flights of stairs and out through the revolving doors—leaving her day's cares behind her, along with the whiff of hospital disinfectant.

The sky was dark. It was nine o'clock on a Monday evening, but it seemed earlier because of the countless lights illuminating Tokyo in every direction. The main street running alongside the hospital was still busy with automobiles and people. She looked across to the opposite side of the street and smiled. A party of gaily-dressed young office ladies were laughing and joking—out on the town to make the most of the country's slow but steady economic recovery. It was nice to see groups of young revelers out having a good time, and not just the gray-faced ranks of inebriated businessmen that one usually encountered at this time of night.

She had hardly stopped smiling when the physical manifestation of her thoughts appeared on the sidewalk in front of her. Two extremely drunk middle-aged men, their arms wrapped affectionately around one another for support, staggered in her direction looking like ill-matched competitors in a three-legged race. The man on the right was much taller than his colleague, so much so that the shorter man had the appearance of being dragged along on tiptoe with his shirt tails pulled out of his trousers, exposing his hairy navel for everyone to see.

They stopped, suddenly, ten yards in front of her and released each other from the mutual embrace. With the support no longer in place, the taller man swayed and then stumbled backwards against the hospital wall sending up a cloud of chalky dust. He began frantically searching his pockets, first in his jacket, then in his trousers, and at length pulled out a shiny silver cigarette lighter. The shorter of the two was experiencing similar difficulties trying to tuck his shirt back into his trousers without unhitching his belt a notch or two. All the while this pantomime was unfolding, they were both gabbling away to themselves as if engaged in completely separate and garrulous conversations with some fictitious third party.

As Beth drew even with them the short man looked up, and, after several seconds, his blank expression gave way to an impish grin. His eyes wandered over her and took in her nurse's uniform. The grin seemed to stretch even wider and without warning he proffered his arm as if he wanted her to accompany him. "*Issho ni iko.*" The taller man laughed along and then dropped his lighter and cursed under his breath as he bent to retrieve it. She shook her head and laughed too. As she passed them by, the short man raised his voice and pointed at her. "You very pretty! You Ingrid Bergman."

She laughed again, good-naturedly. There were times, increasingly so recently, when she longed to be back home in America. In her daydreams she lived in a large, sprawling farmhouse in West Virginia. She was married to Ralph, and they had a whole baseball team of kids who were being raised on steak and homemade cherry pie. But tonight, she felt happy and content to be in Tokyo. It was vibrant and alive, and yet safe—even for a young woman making her way home alone at night after a busy day at work.

She rounded the corner onto *Eitai-dori*. A line of ten or so charcoal-burning taxi cabs were parked along the side of the road, all primed and smoking, waiting for the evening's first fares. Two of the drivers, both slightly built and wearing grubby headbands, stood up from where they had been squatting deep in conversation and looked at her expectantly.

She smiled cheerfully, nodded and then tried her limited Japanese: "*Konbanwa*"—("Good evening.") They both giggled, appreciative of her efforts, and motioned toward the taxicab. "No, no thank you. *Arigato.*" She beamed before swinging her handbag and continuing on the sidewalk.

She crossed the road at the traffic light and headed under the Chuo mainline bridge in the direction of Nihonbashi, where she planned to take the Ginza Line subway as far as Toranomon, where she lived in the women's army quarters. She stopped, briefly, to take in the culinary delights of a small *yatai*, or street vendor, who was selling freshly made noodles under the eaves of the bridge. She marvelled at his dexterity—the way he seemed to juggle the fresh noodles: untangling and stretching, before plunging them into boiling water for just the right amount of time and then serving them up piping hot in a little lacquer bowl with garnish on top. Two businessmen were already leaning against the temporary counter, heads down in concentration, slurping deliciously. She briefly considered stopping and ordering a bowl for herself, but the night was getting late and in any case, she remembered she had some leftover meatloaf back home in her refrigerator.

She hurried on past the stall and came out the other side of the bridge. In the shadows something moved. A car sped past, its bright headlights picking out in sharp relief a *pan pan*—'woman of the night'—bending down to smooth out her rumpled stockings. Funny, she hadn't noticed anybody there before. The lascivious form edged back into the shadows. She waited until a short convoy of military police jeeps had gone by and then struck out across yet another junction. This time it led to a narrower and altogether quieter road. It was poorly lit and was the only part of her regular walk she felt a little uneasy about.

Reconstruction work had been relatively slow in this stretch of the neighborhood, and off to her left in the darkness were a number of vegetable plots, tended pretty much as they had been since the end of the war. Whenever she came this way, she remembered the poignant words of a haiku poem she had once read:

Small green vegetables
are growing in the rain
along the burned street.

On weekends, when she worked the occasional shift, she often came this way in daylight. It was a different world then—whole groups of family laborers toiling with hoe and spade. This was no idyllic recreation. Many of the 'owners' relied on the produce they grew to supplement their barely subsistence-level wages. She often saw mothers tilling the soil while carrying a baby on their backs inside the flap of a customised kimono. But now, it was quiet, hard to believe she was walking through downtown Tokyo. She could hear crickets in the roadside grass, and the low, rhythmically portentous chirp of cicadas, whose scarab-like forms were hidden from view amongst the dense green patina of foliage somewhere in the distance.

As she walked along, she suddenly became aware of a low, gushing sound—again, something else she had never noticed before. Coming to the end of the unlit portion of road, she saw what it was: A burst drainpipe had forced its way to the surface of the unmade road, rust-colored water seething and bubbling across the camber and flowing into a shallow irrigation ditch on the other side.

And then, for an instant, and it really only was an instant, she could have sworn she heard something metallic somewhere on the road quite a way behind her—back in the direction from which she had come. She pushed the strap of her bag up again and set off at a brisk pace, only to pause a few steps later and look back again. *Must be my imagination,* she thought. And then her imagination caused her to detect, again only very faintly and in the far distance, what looked like the glowing tip of a cigarette as it was lit and flared in the darkness. She shivered, despite the warm night, then turned and half-skipped to the end of the road. Only one more road and she would be out amongst the crowds heading for the same train as she was. But if she was completely honest about her feelings, she wanted to be home now. She had enjoyed her customary walk quite enough for one night. She peered up at the sky. The moon was out—a perfect silver disc floating in the heavens. She squinted and tried to make out the rabbit pounding *mochi.*

She was just about half way along the last stretch of narrow side road when she suddenly decided she was being silly and that there really was no reason to carry on at breakneck speed. She'd had a long day, after all, and the last thing she wanted on a warm evening like this was to have to endure the cramped fifteen-minute journey on the subway in damp, sweat-soaked clothes.

She checked her gait and then stopped to catch her breath. She glanced at her watch: 21:20. Then for some reason, she wasn't quite sure why, she looked back over her shoulder. It was then that she saw *him*. Her heart missed a beat, and she stood frozen, rooted to the spot—paralyzed like a deer caught in a car's headlights. Her pulse raced, and she fought to control the feeling of rising panic and nausea. It was the same man she had seen two nights before, smiling at her from the newspaper stall outside the hospital, and again, the previous morning inside the post office. She hadn't been sure at first. She had thought she was imagining things. But now this. It couldn't be a coincidence. And something about his stance and demeanor—cajoling, chiding almost—left her in no doubt of that.

He stood there, dressed in a well-cut dark blue pinstripe suit and trilby, his body half-concealed behind an abandoned rickshaw, casually drawing on a cigarette and affecting indifference. Smoke escaped from his nostrils in carefully controlled wisps. He parted his ugly lips and smiled urbanely at her. He placed his left hand on his hip, rocked back on the heel of his boot, like a flamenco dancer, and tapped the metal tip on the hard ground.

Come on, Beth Chandler, you must run now, you must, she told herself. From somewhere in the distance a klaxon sounded and seemed to break the trance. She turned around, breathing heavily, and broke into a forward-pitching, ambling run. The strap slipped down her arm, and the bag began to swing wildly from side to side, trapping itself between her thighs, momentarily, until she managed, through sheer panic and determination, to pull it free again. *Come on, Beth, keep going. The main street is busy, surely he wouldn't try anything there—whoever he is.*

Her shoes were killing her. They were sensible and practical flat-heeled shoes, but they were brand new, and the stiff edges dug uncompromisingly into her Achilles tendon and made her eyes water. She put on an extra spurt, the momentum bringing her out onto the main street, just as a nearby subway entrance leading up from the Ginza Line disgorged a trainload of agitated night-shift workers onto the sidewalk—all headed her way. She elbowed and jostled her way through the sea of surging black heads, and when she came out, breathless, on the other side, she could see a bank of public telephones along the fence adjacent to the station entrance. Unbelievably, they were all occupied. She shot a glance sideways. He would be coming round the corner any second now. She hammered on the window of the nearest booth. An angry, florid face turned around and mouthed something abusive. She was close to tears now as she scampered from booth to booth in desperation. The door to the end booth opened suddenly, and she dived in. The young woman who held the door open was saying something to her, but she couldn't begin to guess what. And then she understood: no dialing tone. It was out of order. She shouldered the door open again and spilled out onto the sidewalk. She looked around and saw him on the other side of a crowd of pedestrians. She darted, gazelle-like, for the subway entrance and ran down the steps, taking them two and three at a time, into the bowels of the station.

She ran at full pelt along the platform, right to the far end and up a short flight of steps that led to another long corridor. There was a toilet on the right and a telephone booth. *Telephone booth.* She sprinted forward and pulled the door open with all her strength. Once inside, she crouched down, partially out of sight, and fumbled around in her purse for the coins. Her fingers wouldn't work, she was shaking so much. She finally steadied herself and, pulling the receiver from its hook, dropped in a coin and dialed the number. *Come on, Ralph, please answer.* She looked at her watch. *Come on, please. Where are you?* She let it ring for a full minute before hanging up.

Retracing her steps carefully so as not to make a noise, she went back down the steps to the platform. She could take this line all the way to Toranomon and then walk from there. *Oh, Christ!* The words almost tumbled out of her mouth. He was there, sitting on a bench, one leg crossed on top of the other. Like a scene from a nightmare, he slowly turned his head and looked at her. She took off again up the steps and ran headlong into the toilet. She turned and rested her back against the closed door of the stall, held her breath with her eyes screwed tight shut and silently prayed. Prayed that he wouldn't come in and find her cowering there in the gloom. Several seconds went by. She strained her ears for the slightest sound.

Silence.

She felt the wind first and then a faint electric hum, which gradually intensified and suddenly became a thunderous roar accompanied by a rush of compressed air as a subway train burst out of the tunnel and sped past on the other side of the thin plasterboard wall. She sank to her knees, tears rolling down her cheeks, and out of some almost maternal instinct, drew her bag into her chest and folded her arms tightly around it—as if protecting a newborn baby.

The toilet door swung open with a creak, and she heard two metallic footsteps come in and then stop. A match burst into flame as it was struck roughly across the wall, and then the sulfurous smell of smoke drifted into the airless room. It was *him.* She knew it. She chewed on her blouse collar and stared wide-eyed at the floor. She sobbed silently. A warm sensation enveloped her, and a pool of acrid urine formed under her legs and began to make its way under the door frame.

She must have slept then, for when she opened her eyes and looked down at her watch, it was a quarter to eleven. Suddenly remembering where she was, she kept very still for a few moments and listened. Then, when she was sure she was alone, she carefully swiveled onto her hands and knees and, crouching low, as if preparing to perform a push-up, peered under the door. The room beyond was empty. Picking her bag up, she slowly stood and pulled back the bolt. She opened the door, just a fraction at first, and looked again before coming out. She walked awkwardly over to the sinks. Her pants were wet and riding up her backside. She looked in the mirror. Mascara had run down her cheeks, and her eyes were red and sore from crying. Turning the tap on, she quickly splashed cold water on her face and smoothed down her fly-away hair.

She came back down the steps very slowly, bending from the waist to check he wasn't there. It looked alright. There was a man in a suit carrying a folded newspaper midway along the platform and an old cleaning lady, both apparently waiting for the next train.

She managed to catch the last departure for Toranomon, eventually arriving at the station at half past eleven. She felt utterly exhausted. She kept to the well-lit main road as much as possible before turning off for the short walk to her accommodation. When she got there, she tried her door first before inserting the key. It was still locked. *Thank God,* she thought, breathing a sigh of relief. She went in and locked the door behind her. And, just to make sure, she jammed the back of a chair under the door handle.

She was too tired to eat, and anyway she'd lost her appetite after what she'd just been through. But she was thirsty, her throat felt dry as sand. She went into the kitchenette and poured herself a glass of orange juice from a quart bottle. She wished now she'd caught the train in the opposite direction, to Kanda, and gone straight to Ralph's place. It was late, but she desperately wanted to hear his voice. She was still jittery and surely he wouldn't mind a late call once he heard what she had to tell him.

She drained the glass and placed it on the window ledge. The telephone was on a tall lacquered table in the corner of the room. She switched the standard light on and reached for the receiver.

No dial tone.

Her eyes lifted, slowly, and came to rest on the flex, just where it trailed over the back of the table top. Her hand went out, a little shakily, fingers folded around the thin black wire and lifted. It had been severed about three inches from the base of the phone. A shadow suddenly moved across the wall. She dropped the receiver, turned and screamed.

Twenty-seven

Carnaby awoke early. He hadn't slept at all well—probably on account of wondering how much he should tell his boss. Aspin hadn't sounded too pleased that he was still looking into this, and if he was going to be in trouble over it, he would rather keep quiet about Dan's involvement—especially as Dan was coming up for promotion in the next couple of months.

Beth was also preying on his mind. He'd called her twice before leaving his apartment, but both times it sounded like the telephone was off the hook. It was her morning off, so maybe she was just sleeping in late and didn't want to be disturbed. Strange, though. Hadn't he said he would call in the morning?

He rode the Ginza Line three stops to Kyobashi Station and then walked up *Kajibashi-dori* four blocks, reaching his office just after 09:45. He went to his own room first just to check his mail, but there was nothing of interest. He would have called in at the Ops room, only he knew from Dan that his team was out all day on a surveillance job in Yokohama—suspected drug trafficking, or something like that.

He came out of his room and walked quickly along the corridor to Aspin's office. Then he stopped dead in his tracks. Shit! He'd clean forgotten to take the affidavits from Emma the day before. How could he have been so stupid? He looked at his watch. It was already ten o'clock. No time to get a cab to the embassy and back. No matter. He could get them later if necessary.

He took a deep breath and knocked on the door, thinking it strange as he did so that the door was closed at all. For as long as he could remember, it was only ever closed when Aspin was in conference.

"Come in."

He went on through and smiled warmly.

Aspin jumped up, with a broad smile of his own, moved around his desk and shook Carnaby's hand. "Ralph! It's good to see you. How's the arm shaping up? Hey, but wait a minute," he said, catching sight of the bandaged hand, "I thought it was your shoulder?"

"Yeah, it was. It's a long story, believe me."

"Okay. Well, so long as it's nothing too serious." Aspin's eyes wandered. "You didn't bring the affidavits?"

"No. I'm sorry, Mike. I was in such a rush this morning, it completely slipped my mind. It was stupid of me, I know."

"Hell, don't worry about it. It's easily done. I just hope you've left them somewhere safe that's all."

"Yeah, they're locked up back in my apartment. I can bring them in later if you need to see them today." He amazed himself with the spontaneity of this inspired lie. As was the case with Dan, he really didn't want to bring Emma into the conversation if he could help it.

"Have a seat. Listen, I don't have too much time so, why don't you get straight to it and take me through the whole story, from start to finish. Don't worry if we've already been over parts of it before. It would help enormously if you would refresh my memory."

Carnaby explained everything, with the exception that is of Dan's meeting with the gang boss Maruyama, and he also attributed anything Dan or Emma had done to himself. When he had finished, Aspin coughed hoarsely into his hand and placed his forearms on the desktop in front of him.

"That's all very interesting, Ralph. I have to say I really can't believe you broke into General Brannigan's office just like that. I mean, for Christ's sake, that's a court martial offense."

"Yeah, I'm well aware of that, Mike. But I had to follow it up. And, sure enough, he is up to something."

"Another gut feeling? Okay, but tell me, you really believe these affidavits are genuine?"

"I'm pretty sure they are. It's been a long time since I practiced any law, but, yeah, I'd say they are."

Aspin rocked back and looked him straight in the eye. "Ralph, did you mention all of this to anyone else?"

"No. No one else."

"Quite sure?"

"Absolutely. Why do you ask?"

"Good. It's just that we don't want to cause an unnecessary panic, now do we?"

Aspin casually lifted the receiver from the telephone set and dialed a single internal number: "Please come in, would you?" He replaced the receiver, linked his fingers together and smiled, benignly, at his subordinate.

Carnaby heard footsteps in the corridor behind him. "What the hell's going on, Mike?"

"Oh, don't worry, Ralph."

There was a perfunctory knock on the door and in came Captain Harry Lorimer with two burly MPs at his shoulder. His gun was already unholstered, and his ugly, thin lips were drawn back tightly in a twisted and smug sneer.

Carnaby turned back to Aspin. "You son of a bitch, Aspin."

"Now now, Ralph. There's no need for that. This is for your own good."

"Like hell it is. You're in league with Brannigan, aren't you? It doesn't surprise me that *he* is," he said, jerking his thumb in Lorimer's direction. "But you? I thought at least you had some integrity."

"That's enough, Carnaby! You don't understand what is happening. It's far too big, too important. Oh, you've done very well, I'll grant you that, but you're way off the mark."

"*Way off the mark*? This isn't some kind of fucking guessing game for pity's sake! Men have lost their lives because of this. I don't know why, but I'm sure as hell gonna find out. And arresting me isn't gonna stop me from blabbing once I'm out. Why I'll go straight over and see General MacArthur myself if I have to."

"Oh no, you won't. You've done enough meddling, Carnaby. You're not going to do anything of the sort."

"And what makes you so goddamned sure?"

Aspin smiled and looked over at Lorimer.

"Because," began Lorimer, who looked as though he was really enjoying himself, "if you cause us any more trouble, you'll never see your sweetheart Beth Chandler again."

Carnaby felt like he'd been hit in the chest by a bolt of lightning. His senses reeled. There was a sudden rush of adrenaline beginning in the pit of his stomach and rising with increasing intensity like a volcanic eruption through his entire being until he was seized with a rage. He clenched his fists and lunged at Lorimer. "You bastard!" Both his hands shot out and wrapped around the gun before Lorimer could get off a round. He crushed Lorimer's fingers against the trigger guard and then brought his knee up hard into the older man's groin.

And then suddenly he stopped. An incredible pain knifed through his skull. Behind, one of the MPs raised his nightstick for a second blow. But it wasn't necessary. Carnaby slumped to his knees. And then darkness closed in around him and carried him into the void.

Later that day, Dan Morita stopped by Carnaby's apartment to see how his call with Aspin had gone. The door to his apartment was unlocked, as always, but there was no sign of him, which was odd, he thought, because he had already called the Ops room and they hadn't seen him. And when he put a call in to Emma at the embassy, she hadn't seen him either. Finally he had called Beth's number—three times in fact, and, when each time he was met with an incessant engaged tone, he had finally decided to go round and check for himself. What he found shocked him profoundly.

Events seemed to have overtaken him in the space of a mere twelve hours. No sign of Ralph nor Beth. Perhaps they were together—lying low somewhere. He felt distinctly uneasy. He didn't want to, but he knew he had no choice but to call Aspin. That, unfortunately, was where the trail ended.

He found a public call box five minutes down the street from Beth's.

"Hello. Colonel Aspin?"

"Speaking."

"It's Morita, sir."

"Ah, Morita. I didn't recognize your voice. What is it? Was there some kind of problem with the Op today?"

"No, sir, but—"

"Then why are you ignoring standard procedure? You know as well as I do that information is not to be passed over the public telephone lines unless it is an emergency."

He resisted the urge to slam the receiver back down. "With all due respect, sir, I'm not calling you about the Op. I'll submit my written report tomorrow, as per *standard procedure*."

"Look, I have an important meeting to attend in five minutes.

Would you mind getting to the point?"

"Certainly, sir. I'm trying to locate Captain Carnaby."

"Carnaby? He's on sick leave until Monday. I thought you were aware of that."

"Yes, sir, of course I am. But I just wondered if you had seen him today, that's all."

"No. I have not. The last time I saw him was when he stopped by two weeks ago. I really don't understand what the problem is Morita. Have you tried his home number?"

"Yes, sir." He hesitated, his guard suddenly up. Something wasn't right. "Look, sir, it doesn't matter. I'll try some place else. Sorry to have troubled you."

"Morita, wait. Where are you now? Listen to me. Why don't you come by the office and we can talk—right now, I can wait for you."

"I thought you had an important meeting, sir."

"Yes, but I—"

Click

He replaced the receiver, and stared at his distorted reflection in the window glass of the telephone box. *Aspin,* he thought, *you are one hell of a lousy liar.*

He met Emma at a French-style café on Roppongi-dori, a fashionable district and playground of the wealthy, where Tokyo's *nouveau riche* liked to show off their money. It wasn't that Morita was particularly fond of the area, but that he knew it was exclusive and expensive and therefore of less appeal to the occupation types and that it would be safe to talk there without fear of being recognized. That said, these secret little meetings reminded him of a former operative, long since returned to the United States, who spent half his waking hours figuring out where in Tokyo he could next meet his secretary without bumping into his wife. He managed it for eighteen tense but blissful months, and then finally one day he walked smack bang into her, just as she came out of an expensive restaurant arm in arm with another man. He had been soundly beaten at his own game, by his own wife, right there in Roppongi.

Morita shivered at the thought and ordered a cup of coffee while he waited for Emma to show. The coffee had just been served when he caught sight of her hurrying over the crossing to his front with her by now familiar bag braced under her arm.

They sat together at a table on the sidewalk and soaked up the remains of the late afternoon sun while he told her about his conversation with Aspin. She ordered paté and Melba toast, while he had an enormous open sandwich with chicken and salad.

She was clearly upset and feared the worst. "Dan, this is just awful. What on earth can have happened to Ralph?"

"I don't know. But I can tell you this much, Aspin knows more than he's letting on."

"And what about Beth? You said her phone had been cut off?"

"Yeah. The wire had been cut, deliberately, and it looked like there had been a struggle. A plant stand had been turned over, and there was soil all over the rug."

"But that's just terrible. Did you call the police?"

"No."

"But why not? She could be in grave danger."

"Because if this is all connected, and let's face it, it has to be, then the police won't find anything. Kidnappings are rare in Japan. They just wouldn't know where to begin."

Emma pulled open her bag, rummaged around, and fished out a pack of cigarettes. He watched her with some amusement as she inexpertly struck a match and applied the dancing flame to the tip. She drew on the butt and coughed two or three times. "Do you know," she said, exhaling forcibly, "I've never smoked in my life before I came out here and met your friend Ralph Carnaby."

"Hey, lady, now don't go blaming Ralph. It was your decision to come out here, wasn't it?"

She cast her eyes down to the table and fingered her napkin, wrapping it around her index finger like a small tourniquet.

He frowned. "You know, I wish you'd take this seriously, Emma. This isn't some kind of goddamned game you know. If—"

"I never said it was a game!" She shrieked hysterically and glared at him across the table.

"Okay, okay," he said, rocking back and throwing his arms up in mock surrender. The young couple at the table next along stopped talking and looked around.

"I'm just worried sick, that's all."

"Yeah, me too, Emma."

"They could be in real danger. Now that things are getting out of hand, I think we need to go to the authorities and tell them everything we know."

"The problem is we don't know who to trust. If Aspin is in on it, then who knows who else is involved. We don't even know how all of this is connected, what Brannigan is doing with the doctors or anything."

She blew out another long wisp of smoke and extinguished her half-smoked cigarette, twisting and breaking it in the cheap café ashtray. She lowered her voice, almost to a whisper. "Why don't we demand to see General MacArthur—show him the affidavits and tell him about the sudden disappearance of Ralph and Beth."

Morita felt irritable again. "Tell me this, Emma: If we go to MacArthur with a cock-and-bull story like this, what do you honestly think is going to happen? He probably knew this stuff was withheld from the tribunal. Chances are he even approved it. Besides which, we wouldn't be able to get near him in the first place."

"That's just defeatist."

"That has got nothing whatsoever to do with it," he yelled. "I'm just being realistic. You've got absolutely no idea—"

"How *dare* you speak to me like that in that condescending tone of voice."

He slumped back in his seat and fiddled with his collar. "Look, Emma . . . "

"Don't you 'Look Emma' me." She was still seething.

He decided to change tack. He put the palms of his hands together, placed them between his thighs and leaned forward, hunching his shoulders. He looked up at her and raised his eyebrows like a pathetic dewy-eyed schoolboy about to make an implausible excuse for something he was obviously guilty of. "Friends?"

She looked away and folded her arms across her chest.

He let his head drop and closed his eyes. He had enough to think about without having to placate a hot-tempered and emotional young Englishwoman. He was beginning to wish he had never entertained the idea of meeting up with her this afternoon. But it was too late for such regrets now. She was here, and she meant to stay.

Suddenly a police car roared past, siren screaming as it sped in the direction of Nishi Azabu. Morita followed it with his gaze for a while and then turned back again. Emma was still and pale, her eyes wide and staring. For an instant, her mind's eye could see the police Humber parked outside her mother's house in Bletchley.

"You okay?" he asked, his voice full of concern.

"Yes, thank you," she said, still staring over his shoulder.

An MP wandered past the front of the café, and she instinctively hooked her leg around her bag and drew it in further under the chair. She tried not to look nervous and lit another cigarette. Morita took a bite of his sandwich and nodded at her reassuringly. The MP paid them no attention and crossed the street, stopping briefly to gaze in the window of a tobacconist, before moving off again in the opposite direction.

Morita blew out his breath as pure relief ebbed out of his weary body. "We've gotta relax. There's no reason to think the authorities are looking for us yet."

"But aren't they?"

"I doubt it. Aspin wouldn't put out a warrant for our arrest unless he was sure he could pin something phony on us that would stick."

"And I suppose he doesn't know for sure that we have the affidavits."

"No, but gee, Emma, we have to be the prime suspects once they figure out Ralph doesn't have them. They'll be in a dilemma when they do figure it out, though. It would be difficult to arrest us in public unless they could come up with some false charges. But at the same time, they will know that the affidavits can be verified relatively easily. They couldn't take the chance that someone out there would side with us—believe our side of the story. That would blow their cover sky high."

She swallowed hard. Her mind was awash with possibilities and permutations.

"The problem is," he resumed, brushing crumbs from his lap, "we don't know exactly who is and who isn't working for Brannigan." He took a sip of coffee, gone cold by now, and then suddenly looked up. "Say, what about the British ambassador. He's surely gotta be on the level."

"I already thought of that," she said. "He's in England at the moment. He returns to Japan the day after tomorrow." She balanced her cigarette on the lip of the ashtray and rubbed her hands together. She thought for a while and gazed listlessly along the road. She must have remained like that, lost in her own thoughts, for a minute or more, and then she looked round again, with a twinkle in her eye. "Dan?"

"Huh? Yeah, what is it?"

"Where do you suppose they have taken Ralph and Beth?"

"Your guess is as good as mine. It could be some remote cell at the back of the MPs headquarters. I went down there once. There are dozens of them. The whole place gave me the creeps. Or, it could be some place out of town. Hard to say really." He shrugged and put the last piece of sandwich in his mouth.

"What about that place in Hokkaido?"

"Wakkanai?"

"Yes. Let's just think about this for a moment. We seem to have come to a dead end here in Tokyo. We can't go anywhere or talk to anyone. We don't know who to trust. For all we know, the police may already have warrants for our arrest and be on our trail right now. We are effectively paralyzed in Tokyo. And yet, what we do know is that at least one of the doctors has gone on a fishing trip to Wakkanai. That Brannigan is making some kind of arrangements regarding the doctors. We know from Ralph that there is a map in Brannigan's office with a circle drawn around Wakkanai, and we also know that Brannigan himself was leaving on a trip of his own."

Morita stared blankly back at Emma while he thought about what she had just said. Although he didn't realize it at first, he could definitely feel it coming.

She placed her chin on her bridged hands and smiled at him mischievously. "How long would it take to get there?"

"To get where?"

"Wakkanai, of course."

He guffawed and spat crumbs out onto his shirt. He wiped the spittle from the corners of his mouth with his napkin and said, "About two hours."

"By car?"

He laughed even harder this time. The young couple turned their heads again. "Are you kidding me? Emma, you're so funny, you know that? By *plane*, of course."

"And what about by car?"

The smile started to fade from his face as he realized she was being dead serious. "Why, we're talking more than five hundred miles from here. But it's not just the distance. The roads are terrible. And they get worse the further north you go—and that's just on mainland Honshu. Then you have to catch a ferry across the Tsugaru Strait to Hokkaido. And then, well, you're basically looking at unpaved roads and farm lanes pretty much all the way up to the north of the island."

"We can use your car."

"*My* car? I don't have a car," he protested.

"You were in a car at the university when we met you last week. A nice big black one."

He looked dumbfounded. "Now listen to me," he spluttered, "that wasn't my own car. That car is the property of the government of the United States of America. Surely you realized that."

She laughed, dismissively. "You sound so pompous at times, Dan Morita."

"Maybe so. But the answer is no. Not today, not tomorrow, not any day. Absolutely not."

Twenty-eight

Late that night, Dan Morita eased the gear stick into first and, with headlights doused, drove the black Buick slowly out of the rear gates of the motor pool.

Each time he turned a corner he cringed as the four five-gallon jerry cans of fuel clanged together in the trunk.

He had done some crazy things in his time, but he was forced to concede that this ranked way up there amongst the craziest. He was only too glad that he was not married, and that he didn't have to concern himself with the consequences his present actions may have on his family's security and good name. After all, facing arrest and probably imprisonment for theft of government property would affect no one other than himself.

He picked Emma up at midnight, outside the rear gates of the British Embassy in Hanzomon. She climbed in the front, this time carrying two large bags. She was rosy-cheeked and looked very excited. He began to wonder if she had any idea what she was letting herself in for.

"Hi, what have you got there?" he said, taking the bags from her and stowing them on the spacious back seat.

She slammed the door shut and made herself comfortable. "A picnic hamper. With such a long journey ahead of us, I thought it would be a good idea to raid the larder."

He laughed. "Good thinking. Okay, this is for you as well." He handed her a military-issue ordnance survey map of Japan adding, "There's a more detailed map of Hokkaido on the back."

"Thank you," she said, smiling.

He pulled away from the sidewalk and swung the car around in a U-turn. He pressed down on the gas pedal, and they sped off toward the northern outbound road that would take them in a wide arc around the city and then north through the industrial heartland of Chiba prefecture and on into the rural wilderness of Tohoku and beyond.

He glanced sideways at his passenger. "There's a ferry at 11:00. If we miss that, we'll be sitting around for another three hours twiddling our thumbs." He turned his watch so it caught the light from the street lamps outside. "Midnight, exactly. That gives us eleven hours to get to the crossing."

Emma smiled and pressed her back into the soft leather seat. "Well, with a bit of luck, there won't be too much traffic on the roads at this time of night."

"That's for sure." He beamed. "Anyone with any sense will have been in bed hours ago."

The first few hours were passed in silence as Emma dozed and Morita drove. The further north they went the less traffic there was until, just a little after 04:00, he was convinced they were the only car on the road in the whole country. He stopped once to pour a can of fuel into the car, carefully replacing the empty jerry can in the back again. They would need to find more fuel for the return journey.

Starting the engine once more, he looked over to check on Emma. She was still sleeping soundly, and, although he was dog-tired himself and could have done with the company, he let her be. Instead he turned his mind to Ralph and wondered whether they really would find him at Wakkanai, assuming they ever got that far.

Suddenly he caught sight of a single pinprick of light in the rearview mirror, a motorbike probably, and gaining on them fast. His hand went to his holster, concealed under his sweater and unfastened the retaining strap. Had they been rumbled? Could this be one of Brannigan's outriders? The light was brighter and more insistent now. He realized there was no way of outrunning it; the Buick was heavy and sluggish, built for cruising in comfort, not speed. The bike was ten yards behind him now and starting to pull out. He slipped his gun from its holster and cocked the action. As the motorbike started to overtake their car, he wound the side window down and stared into the wing mirror. The bike sped past with a high-pitched buzz.

Emma stirred slightly, and he breathed a sigh of relief. It had been a civilian machine, and for the moment they were safe.

With one hand on the wheel, he stretched and fumbled about trying to replace his gun in its holster. The muzzle snagged on his belt and he lost his grip and heard it crash to the floor at his feet.

Emma's eyes opened suddenly. "What is it?"

"It's okay, Emma. I'm sorry. I dropped my gun trying to get it back into its holster."

"Gun? Why?" She was still half-asleep and not making fully coherent sentences.

"Relax. I said it's okay, didn't I? There was a motorbike on our tail for a while back there. I thought it might have been someone out looking for us. But it wasn't. It was just an ordinary bike."

She rubbed her eyes, peered around her and looked at her watch—04:15. "Where are we?" she asked, not quite managing to stifle a yawn.

"We've just gone through a small town called Izumi, a little over half the way between Tokyo and the ferry. We're doing pretty well. If we carry on like this then we should get there in time. How are you feeling anyway? Did you get some sleep just now?"

She stared out the window without answering then said, "What will they do when they find out the car is missing?"

"The car?" He smiled mischievously. "Well, I'd signed it out already for a job I was supposed to be doing later on today. I shouldn't think it'll take them too long to figure it out, though. The motor pool guard countersigns the entry book and records the time of departure. He didn't question it. We have assignments going on at all hours usually. But when I don't show in the morning, they'll check back with the log book. Even then it may not register there's a problem. I sometimes take the car straight from work if I'm there late, even though you're not supposed to."

"But Colonel Aspin will know straightaway, won't he?"

"Nope. He left on a trip this morning. The naval base at Nagoya, he said, although I get the sneaky feeling he is going somewhere entirely different. No, they'll finally know something is wrong when I don't show at 10:00 to collect the agent I'm doing the job with. They'll figure I'm stuck in traffic and wait thirty minutes. Then they'll call my place. So, we've probably got until 11:00 before they start to alert the regular cops as well as the MPs."

"Which is just when the ferry will be departing, isn't it?"

He grinned. "Yeah, that's right. We'll be okay until we get off the other side. There's a sizable US Army division garrisoned at Hakodate, just by the ferry terminal. But apart from that, the rest of Hokkaido is quite thinly policed. The Brits have two bases further north. Actually, one of them is pretty close to Wakkanai."

"So, once we are clear of Hakodate we should be okay?"

"Yeah, I should say so. Especially as they will be concentrating on the Tokyo area."

"Dan, I have an idea. Why don't you call the agent you were meeting and tell him you have been delayed? You could say you were sick in the night or something like that."

"That's not a bad idea. It might buy us a little extra time. And," he said, pausing for thought, "I might just get the lowdown on whether or not Aspin actually went on his trip."

"Is the agent someone you can trust?"

"Ted Groves? Yeah. I believe so. We've got each other out of some real scrapes before now." He chuckled and shook his head, like he was remembering a particular occasion.

"It sounds like you work with some nice people."

"*Some.* Yeah. There are always people you don't get on with. But Ralph's team, well, we're all pretty close deep down."

"I expect that's important, doing the kind of job you do every day."

"I never really thought about it. But, yeah, now that you mention it, I guess it is important to be able to trust the person you are with to look out for you."

She hesitated, and then said, "Ralph told me you have quite some history between you."

He looked round, and then put his eyes back on the road. "We go back a long way. I first met Ralph in March 1946. We joined the CIA at the same time—inducted on the very same day in Tokyo. We used to hang around together all the time in those days. I guess he didn't feel entirely at home for quite some time. So I would go places with him on the weekends—shopping trips, sightseeing, that sort of thing."

"Because you speak Japanese?"

"That was one reason. A lot of foreigners do find it difficult to adjust being out here. But I guess the other reason was—" Morita paused, as if he didn't know what to say. "Well, Ralph lost his wife just a month or so before that."

Emma shuddered. “I knew his wife died.”

“He took it real hard for a long time. Blamed himself. I don’t think he’s ever gotten over it, even now.”

“But why would he blame himself?”

He glanced at her again. “She died in a car crash. Ralph had been drinking. He lost control on a tight bend at night. They were on their way home from celebrating the victory against Japan.”

Emma closed her eyes and said quietly, “I didn’t know that’s how it happened.”

“He doesn’t like to talk about it much. But now and again something surfaces, and you can tell it’s still on his mind.”

“But he sees Beth, doesn’t he?”

“Yeah. She’s a nice girl. They get on well together. I keep hoping they’ll get married before it’s too late. He beats himself up about it too much. He feels he’s somehow being disloyal to his wife. I keep telling him its okay—he has to move on.” He suddenly became aware of the silence. “I . . . hope I haven’t said anything improper, Emma.”

“No, you haven’t. I was just wondering whether you do ever get over it, that’s all.”

“If you don’t mind my saying, I think it’s a really brave thing you’re doing out here.”

“Oh, I’m not sure I would agree with you. I haven’t really done anything yet.”

“It still takes a lot of courage to find a job and come all this way out to a country you don’t really know. And to be so determined to find out the truth about Lieutenant Brice.” He paused to collect his thoughts. “You know, it could be dangerous where we’re headed.”

“Yes, I know. You keep telling me that.”

“It’s just that—”

“But I *have* to find out. Do you understand? I’ve come this far and I need to know what happened to him.”

Morita cleared his throat and said, in a sympathetic tone of voice, “You must have loved him very much.”

“Yes, I did. And I still do.” She looked down and then took a deep breath. “And what about you?”

“Me?”

“Yes, what’s your story? Why are you out here?”

“Well,” he laughed, “for one thing I’m Japanese. And I suppose I just like it out here."

"But you are an American citizen, aren't you?"

"Yeah, that's right. I was born and raised in California. My parents emigrated five years before I was born and took US citizenship."

"What did they do there?"

"They bought a vineyard. Nothing very grand. But it was theirs. All paid for out of their own savings."

"That sounds wonderful. Are they still there?"

He fell silent. He seemed to be gripping the steering wheel with all his strength. Presently he looked round again, and said, "No. It didn't quite work out that way."

"Oh," she said, letting her gaze fall to her lap.

"I guess you haven't heard of Executive Order 9066?"

"No, I haven't."

"No, of course not. Why would you have? It was issued in February 1942 by President Roosevelt. It provided for the forcible internment of over one hundred thousand people of Japanese ancestry for the duration of the war. Two thirds of the internees, including my family, already had US citizenship."

"Your family were interned? But that's just unbelievable. How could they treat people like that?"

"It beats me. But they did. After Pearl Harbor there was a lot of paranoia, particularly among people living on the west coast. They thought they might be the next target for attack. So there was very little opposition to the local Japanese population being rounded up. We were among the first batch to be sent. We ended up in a camp called Topaz—a barren, sand-choked wasteland in Utah, close to Delta. My family spent nearly two years scratching out an existence in barrack blocks made of tar paper and wood."

Emma felt tears welling up in her eyes. "And what about your vineyard?"

"It was taken away from us. The government called it compulsory requisition. Oh, they paid some compensation for it, five years after the war had ended, and less than a quarter of the real value of the land. And, of course, no compensation for the loss of produce and earnings while we'd been interned."

"Is your family still over there?"

"My mother and sister are. Living in a small house in Pasadena. My father died two years after the war ended. He smoked heavily and developed emphysema while in Topaz. The authorities claimed they didn't have the resources to treat him properly."

"So you joined the army to get out of there?"

"No. I joined the army to prove my loyalty to the country we had chosen as our home. I figured if I could fight as hard as I could, then they would surely have to let my folks out of that hellhole. I wanted to remove the stigma and clear my family's name. My mother always talked about wanting to remove the 'stain of shame.' I think she really began to wonder why they had ever gone to the US."

She looked round at Morita. "And, do you feel you did what you set out to do—clear your family's name?"

He thought for a moment and chewed on his lip. Then he said, "That's a tough one. I certainly fought hard. And I was mentioned twice in dispatches. My family were among the first to be released in the fall of 1944. So, I guess in that sense, I did clear their name. But . . . well, fighting and killing Japanese soldiers was a lot harder than I had imagined. Before I came out here, I figured that my American upbringing and attitude would keep me from feeling sorry for them. But it was the hardest thing I've ever done. It was the same for all the guys I knew in my unit. There were twenty of us Japanese-American translators attached to a regular unit. And we were highly decorated. But we were all torn between our duty and the feelings we had for our kinsmen. The officers, though, they didn't care at all."

"The officers? Were they Japanese?"

Morita snorted. "No way. Not the ones in charge at any rate. They were all white middle-class Americans and racist as hell. Once, when we were fighting to take Okinawa, I saw one of these guys laughing as he watched civilians leaping off cliffs to their deaths rather than surrender. But we didn't laugh. We all saw in the faces of those people the faces of people we once knew somewhere back home. The caves were the worst. Whole villages would hide in them, and when you got up real close someone would let off a grenade and kill everyone inside. Occasionally you would get lucky and manage to talk to them in their language and some of them would come out. I remember right at the end, a family, or what was left of it, came out of this tiny hole in the ground. You wouldn't have believed anyone could fit in there it was so small. There was a little boy who couldn't have been more than four years old. He came out shivering with fright, even though it was scorching hot. His belly was distended with malnutrition. The poor kid was terrified. It turned out his name was Morita. I was looking at myself as a small boy."

"Is that why you stay? You want to do something to help the people here?"

"I don't really know. I guess I can blend in here, be myself without continually feeling like a second-class citizen."

"Doesn't your mother want to come back?"

"I guess not. All her friends are stateside, and my sister looks after her. I used to send money each month, but she started returning it, so I figured she doesn't need it any more."

"Has she been back here to visit?"

"Yeah. Just once. She came out with my sister one summer a couple of years back. We have a festival called *O-Bon* where we honor the departed souls of our ancestors. She wanted to pay her respects to the graves of her parents. She only stayed four days and then headed back again. Families. I never could work them out."

"Well, if it's any consolation, I think you are wonderful. Your mother should be very proud of you."

He smiled and shook his head slowly. Yawning expansively, he wiped the tears from his eyes with the back of his hand.

Emma looked round sleepily. "Shall I drive for a while?"

He smiled again. "No, it's okay. I'm fine."

"I *can* drive you know."

"I'm sure you can. But honestly, I feel okay."

The car rumbled on into the morning, and when he next looked over a little under thirty minutes later, she was fast asleep again.

One hundred and fifty miles north, in the Tsugaru Strait, the radio operator on board the carrier USS Valley Forge suddenly received a Priority A signal from Naval headquarters in Tokyo.

> Proceed with all haste to Koje-do and await further orders. Maintain radio silence until contacted. Repeat, maintain radio silence until contacted.

The officer of the watch was notified and in turn took the decision to inform the captain, who had been sleeping in his bunk at the time. His reaction on being told the news was rumored to have been something along the lines of: "Jesus fucking Christ. This is it. This is the big one—the one we've been waiting for. It's a couple of days earlier than I expected, but what the hell—Korea, here we come."

Twenty-nine

The car nudged cautiously over the crown of the hill, and the twinkling blue sea, which up until then had been visible only on their right-hand side, rose up and greeted them almost as far as they could see.

Across the Tsugaru Strait, they could just make out the hazy shape of the large port town of Hakodate. From somewhere down in the harbor came the long booming of a foghorn as a ship got under way. The smell of brine filled the air, and a strong northerly wind whipped about them.

The roads were narrow and crowded with commercial traffic—mainly trucks carrying consignments of freshly caught fish, but there were also vehicles hauling lumber, salt, and scrap metal. As they descended the hill that led to the docks, Morita had to slam on his brakes to avoid ramming a lorry loaded to overflowing with huge blocks of ice which had, for no apparent reason, stopped suddenly in front of him.

"Jesus Christ!" he screamed, his hand pressing down firmly on the horn.

"Calm down, Dan. We're almost there now."

"I know, I know. I'm sorry. It's just that we made it all this way without any mishaps, and then this." He held his hands up in frustration and waited for the lorry to restart and move off down a steep side road. He looked at his watch: 10:20. "Forty minutes to find the dock and get aboard."

"Oh, Dan! There's a telephone," shouted Emma excitedly.

He swerved over to the curb and heaved the handbrake on. "I'll leave her running. I don't want to risk stalling before we get across to the other side of the bay." He groped around in his pockets. "Say, do you have some small change?"

"Yes, I'm sure I do," she said, opening her handbag and fishing out her purse. She handed him some coins and watched him disappear into the call box. She peered down at the map and tried to orient herself. The scale was too small to tell with any accuracy, but as far as she could make out they were already on the main road that led down to the ferry terminal. It should be a simple matter of turning right at the bottom of the hill and the dock would be there in front of them. She checked her watch—10:30. Morita seemed to be taking forever. She craned her neck around just as he came out of the call box, stony-faced and muttering to himself.

He climbed back in and slammed the door shut. His hands gripped his knees, and he stared straight ahead for a few moments.

"What is it? What's the matter?"

"I just spoke with Groves. He says Aspin called early this morning, ranting and raving about me. He's issued an official arrest warrant. Apparently, I am wanted for questioning in connection with the attempted sale of classified documents to the Russians."

"Oh, Dan. That's just not true. Did you tell him where you are?"

"Nope. He didn't ask. That's his way of telling me I can trust him and that he doesn't believe a word of it."

"What are we going to do now?"

"Well, there's no turning back, that's for sure. But we do have to lose this car."

"The car?" She looked panic-stricken. "But how will we get to Wakkanai?"

"I don't know yet. But we can't take this car on the ferry. Groves said they've put out a detailed description of it, and not just the license plate number either. It's no good. We'd stick out like a sore thumb. The disembarkation point is likely to be manned by MPs. We'd be picked up right away."

She stared, unblinking. "But we can't just give up."

"I don't intend to. Listen, we have to get moving. We have to ditch this car—somewhere where they won't find it for a while. Then we board the ferry, separately, and meet up on the other side."

"But where shall we meet?"

"There's a café—the Hakodate Royale. It's right on the main road in front of the docks. Go in there and order a coffee. I'll find you."

With only twenty minutes until the ferry departed they had to be quick. He drove the half mile to the bottom of the hill. Just as they spotted the ferry over to the right, he noticed a narrow road off to the left. Without hesitating, he swung the car round and headed for the opening, braking lightly as they went over the rise. The road, they soon found out, was built on a severe gradient, and he could feel the brakes struggling under the weight of the car. They came out at the bottom on a secluded parking bay, fronted by an earthen bank that led, some twenty feet below, to a private dock with a small wooden jetty.

He looked around. The place was deserted. "Quick!" he said, his voice urgent. "Roll your window down. Reach over and do the back ones too."

"Dan, what are you thinking?"

"Just do it. Quickly. Good. Now get out. Here, take the bags. Don't forget the map."

Emma half fell out of the passenger door, bags and other belongings spilling out of her arms.

He shouted through the open window, "Now stand well back!"

"Dan!" she screamed as she realized with horror what he was about to do.

With the door open, he released the handbrake and kicked off the ground with his right foot. The car lurched forward, picked up speed over the fifteen feet or so before the unguarded drop, and plunged over the edge. He hurled himself clear just as the huge car hit the water with an almighty splash. He jumped to his feet, and Emma ran over to his side. The car surfaced again and bobbed around while a great wave gathered momentum and washed its way around the inner wall of the dock.

"*Come on,*" he said through gritted teeth. "Sink. For God's sake, *sink.*"

She clenched her small fists and willed the car to disappear. Then suddenly, with a great rush of air, the car upended and vanished. Pockets of air escaped in clusters of bubbles here and there, and then the surface was calm again.

From the harbor entrance came the high-pitched whine of a small outboard motor, and a launch came around the stone wall and in through the narrow entrance.

As they turned to head back up the hill, they heard a creaking noise, not unlike wood splintering, somewhere above and off to the right. A small window, set in what looked like the back wall of some ancient warehouse, had been pushed open, and an old, toothless crone thrust her bony arm out of the aperture and began waving toward the boat. "Ahoy! Welcome back, Shintaro!"

"Come on." He tapped Emma on the shoulder without being seen, and they walked briskly back up the hill together. They were only just in time, stepping onto the ferry's gangplank as the departure whistle sounded.

He had bought two single tickets. He took the bag containing the affidavits from Emma and, once aboard, they split up and found themselves separate seats in which to spend the three hours it would take to reach the other side of the strait.

Meanwhile, a reserve echelon of the US Seventh Fleet, consisting of the carrier USS Valley Forge, seven battleships, two minesweepers and three supply ships, was sailing at a speed of five knots in a circular holding position twenty-five miles off the west coast of southern Hokkaido. Having set out three hours earlier, in accordance with the Priority A signal, a curious sequence of events had, quite by chance, begun to unfold.

It had all started in the galley when one of the more conscientious naval ratings overheard the radio operator, who was now off duty and tucking into a late breakfast, bragging that he knew where the fleet was headed. Being a talkative sort of person, he also mentioned, to the cook, that the signal was strange in that the sender had started to key in the previous month's initiation call sign before realizing and correcting his mistake. And the other thing that had never, in his experience at least, happened before was that the signal was a Strength Five. Signals from as far away as Tokyo were almost always Strength Three, Four at best. It was, according to the radio operator, almost as if it had originated much further north than Tokyo.

Anyway, to cut a long story short, the eavesdropping rating had mentioned this to the quartermaster, who thought he had better inform the officer of the day, who dutifully took the tale straight to the captain.

Even before the radio operator had finished his breakfast, he had been summoned to give an explanation. The captain, having heard the account firsthand, now took it upon himself to ignore the order to maintain radio silence and instructed the communications room to verify the prior signal.

Dan Morita found Emma, as planned, sitting discreetly toward the back of the Hakodate Royale, sipping a cup of coffee and pretending to read her book. He almost ran across the café floor, he was so pleased to see her. "Emma! You're safe. Quickly now—no time to explain. Come with me."

She started to protest, but he already had hold of her wrist and was pulling her back toward the entrance. They emerged onto the main street just as an MP jeep pulled up outside the café.

"Fancy a quick coffee, Mac?"

"Yeah, sure. But only if you're payin'."

The two men laughed loudly and walked straight past Emma, who put her arm up to fix her hair and conceal her face. She followed Dan along the main street and then right at the junction.

"For goodness' sake, where are we going?"

He looked back over his shoulder and said, while trying to catch his breath, "The station . . . The train . . . leaves in ten . . . minutes." He tore ahead without waiting for her and darted across the road in between an untidy skein of trucks heading for the ferry.

She could see him running up to the ticket office and buying tickets. He turned and waved impatiently for her to hurry up. She hitched her bag up and trotted across to join him. They went through onto the platform just as the Japan Railways train pulled into the station.

"See," he beamed, "trains are never late in Japan. Only early!"

"How long's the ride?" she gasped.

"About twenty hours, give or take. With one change. Still," he added, noticing the look of dismay on her face, "at least we'll be off their radar for a while. Only a madman would go by train."

The train wasn't very full at all, and they found a compartment to themselves. Emma slumped gratefully into the upholstered seat by the window and stared out as they left Hakodate behind them.

"Say, are you hungry?"

"Yes, I'm famished actually. There's hardly anything left of the packed lunch worth eating."

"I'll be right back." He disappeared through the door with a grin on his face. A few minutes later her reappeared, sliding the compartment door back with his booted right foot, and staggered in carrying two metal trays.

"You know," said Emma, her eyes full of childlike curiosity, "you never cease to amaze me. What have you got there? It smells delicious."

"It's an Ainu stew made with *supun,* minced red-bellied dace," he said, setting the trays down and removing the lids from the array of small lacquered bowls.

"How beautiful," she said, feasting her eyes on the food in front of her.

Morita indicated each of the other dishes. "This one is soba—you know, buckwheat noodles. And this one, well, it's fried sea lion steaks."

"Sea lion!" She had turned a peculiar shade of gray. "You really eat sea lion?"

"Yeah. Well, actually, I've never had it myself. But it's supposed to be very popular in Hokkaido."

She was forced to concede that the meal was absolutely first-rate. She wouldn't have missed it for anything.

The journey took them on a winding northerly route up the west side of Hokkaido. The scenery was breathtaking. There were dozens of dairy farms of all shapes and sizes, with scores of cattle out grazing on verdant green pastures. It reminded her somehow of parts of Wales. They went on through the Shikotsu-Toya National Park, with its lush meadows, fields of bright yellow maize, and clumps of beautiful woodland—home to the sacred crane and, of course, the magnificent volcanic Lake Shikotsu, surrounded by the spectacular mountain peaks of Mount Eniwa to the north, and Mount Tarumae and Mount Fuppushi to the south. Here and there alongside the track were great wooden carvings of bears and eagles and numerous totem poles. The carvings looked to Emma's untrained eye more reminiscent of the crafts of the North American Indians. Morita explained to her that these were all sculpted by the Ainu people, the original indigenous population of northern Japan.

She also found the temperature more bearable. It was much less humid than mainland Honshu, and a constant sea breeze kept the temperature at a cool twenty degrees.

The journey passed without event, and Morita, this time, snatched a couple of hours of well-earned sleep.

After the better part of a day traveling, the train pulled in at the station. Wakkanai, they discovered, was a pretty desolate outpost on the northwestern tip of the island. It seemed to have more than its fair share of derelict buildings and boarded-up stores. He explained that a lot of the younger people had gone south in search of better-paying jobs in Tokyo and other industrial conurbations like Osaka and Nagoya.

After walking around aimlessly for thirty minutes, they had the fortune of coming across one of only five working taxicabs in the whole town. The driver was confused at first. Yes, of course he knew where Wakkanai village was, but were they sure that was where they wanted to go? After all, there was nothing there. It was, according to the driver, little more than a near-bankrupt cluster of houses populated by old-timers, which was rich coming from a taxi driver who himself had to have been in his mid-seventies.

Fifteen minutes later, he dropped them at the top of a narrow dirt track, with tractor tire marks baked into the sun-dried mud. They watched him go, his cab bouncing comically over the uneven ground and then disappearing from view behind a cluster of rusting oil drums.

They stood there for a while and looked down the track. At the bottom, they could just see the tops of traditional thatched-roof farmhouses peeping over an embankment.

"Are you ready?" asked Morita.

"I think so," she said. "But what's the plan?"

"Good question. First thing's first. I guess we take a quick look and see how the land lies. There may be nothing here after all."

They wandered slowly down the track and maneuvered themselves into a shallow depression in the embankment. Nearby was a small shrine guarded by two ceramic foxes and a bottle of sake, an offering to the gods. They could see a cluster of thatched-roof farmhouses ahead, each trailing wisps of smoke from their chimneys.

In the foreground, was a wide assembly area of compacted earth. Half a dozen or so old fishermen were busy mending their nets and enjoying the warm early morning sun. A warbler flitted from branch to branch of a nearby tree, singing its beautiful summer song.

Morita turned to Emma with a pensive look on his face and, in hushed tones, said, "I hate to say it, but maybe the cabdriver was right after all." He peered at the old men again.

She sighed and closed her eyes. She couldn't help but smile at the irony of the situation: Here they were, at the northernmost tip of Hokkaido, with no car or other visible means of getting home, on the run from the authorities, and spying on a perfectly normal, if slightly rundown, fishing village.

"Here," he said suddenly, "take this." He handed her the bag with the affidavits and map inside. "I'm going to get a little closer. Since we're here, we may as well make sure."

"Dan?"

"Yeah?"

"Be careful."

He nodded, smiling, and began to edge his way along the perimeter of the embankment. She lost sight of him briefly, and then he reappeared further around the curve and on the other side of the embankment. She could see him crouching low and moving over toward the back of a large hayrick. He had just come to the end of the hayrick and was about to cross the open ground ahead when, from her hiding place behind the embankment, Emma suddenly caught sight of a group of at least a dozen young men, dressed in camouflage fatigues and carrying an array of machine guns.

Her heart was in her mouth, and she desperately wanted to cry out and warn Dan of what was coming his way. But her mouth wouldn't form the right shape, much less produce any sound. All she could do was stare in disbelief. The column rounded the corner and saw him at once. A shout went up as they ran over to him, guns at the ready. Morita sprinted toward a low wall and hurled himself bodily over it. A brace of startled chickens flew into the air and scooted noisily away up the embankment.

One of the soldiers ran straight into the gully behind the wall. Emma heard a sickening crack and then saw the same soldier stagger backwards in a daze, holding his blood-soaked head in both hands, his weapon discarded. Morita leapt out after him, a length of wooden planking gripped tightly in his hands.

A staccato burst of machine-gun fire volleyed over his head—a warning shot fired harmlessly, but menacingly, into the air. Morita knew then that it was no use.

Please, she thought, *please don't resist anymore, Dan. Give in and save yourself.* She crouched low and watched them haul him off in the direction of one of the houses. Then, ever so carefully, she lowered herself down from the embankment and eased herself out of the hollow and back onto the track. She paused for a few seconds, listening, and, when she was quite sure she was alone, she made her way quickly up the track.

When she reached the top, she had to stop for a minute to catch her breath. Her mind was racing, despite her fatigue. What should she do? The taxi had long since gone. She staggered on along the track and out onto the top road. She realized that if anyone from the village were to come by now, she was done for. Then she remembered her scarf in the bag. She pulled it out and, with her fingers working frantically, fastened it around her face. She couldn't disguise the shape of her eyes, but at least this way she was a little less conspicuous.

And then she saw the corner of the map sticking out of the bag, and she remembered what Dan had said about there being two British bases in Hokkaido, one of them "quite close to Wakkanai, in fact."

She pulled the map out frantically and opened it, spreading it out on the grassy verge. Being standard military-issue, all the bases were marked. *There it was!* She snapped off a stem of grass and, using it as a crude measuring stick, placed it against the scale in the margin and tried to gauge the distance on the map. It was about eight miles southeast. She folded the map carefully and shouldered her bag. There was nothing for it, she thought, and she set off at a brisk pace, even though her shoes were cutting into her ankles. She simply had to find help.

She had just rounded the next bend in the road when she heard a faintly familiar purring noise. Approaching the corner carefully, she looked round and saw a tractor, engine running, parked at the side of the road, driver-less.

As she came alongside it, she caught sight of the farmer as he disappeared through the door of a narrow wooden shack, perched on one of the thin strips of ground between two rice fields. Without thinking, she clambered up onto the seat, released the brake and sped off down the road. With the wind in her hair it was exhilarating, and for a fleeting moment she was back in Blighty during the war years, driving her tractor across the plow-furrowed fields of Buckinghamshire.

Emma was concentrating so hard on driving with one hand and holding the wind-torn map on her lap with the other, that she almost failed to notice the young British sentry who stood in front of her, flailing his arms frantically above his head.

Having convinced the soldier that she was dead serious about seeing the base commander and that yes, thank you very much, it was imperative that she be put in touch with the British ambassador in Tokyo, she was escorted from her agrarian chariot and given an audience with Major Peter Gladstone, of the 2nd Battalion, Royal Welsh Fusiliers. And, after a further twenty minutes of questioning, Emma, who later felt justifiably proud of herself for keeping her temper under control, managed to persuade the major to call the ambassador.

As luck would have it, the ambassador had arrived back from England with his family just two hours before.

"And this is all absolutely true, Emma?"

"Yes, sir, all of it. I know how it must sound, but please believe me, I beg you."

"Alright. I want you to put Major Gladstone back on the telephone. And, Emma?"

"Yes, sir?"

"You stay where you are. I don't want you to put yourself in any further danger. Do you understand?"

"Yes, sir. Perfectly. And thank you."

Later that same day, as a result of a highly confidential telephone conversation between the British ambassador and certain military chiefs in Tokyo, two missions were carried out.

The first, involving three Panther jets from the carrier USS Valley Forge, confirmed that there was an unprecedented build-up of Russian troops on the southern tip of Sakhalin Island, just sixty kilometers from the northern seaboard of Hokkaido.

And the second, which took place, by necessity, after nightfall (by certain crack soldiers from the British base near Wakkanai), confirmed that there were at least fifty heavily armed soldiers in the vicinity of Wakkanai, and that they appeared to be wearing gas masks and protective suits, and handling large steel containers—rather like oil drums.

Thirty

"You son of a bitch!" screamed Morita as his head bounced off the hut wall for the second time. He spat blood and eyed his antagonist with contempt. He struggled violently but to no avail. The two thugs by his sides had pinned his arms savagely, and effectively, behind his back and held him firmly in place as the "interrogator" approached again.

The "interrogator" was short but broad and extremely muscular, with hands of iron. Not—one could be forgiven for thinking—characteristics normally attributed to one whose recent occupations included that of landlord.

"Tell us what we want to know, Morita, and I will go easy on you. Now, where is the briefcase? Who else knows you are here?"

"Fuck you!"

The interrogator closed in again, his brows knitted, a brutal look on his face. He struck Morita with his right fist, low, in the pit of the stomach. Morita slumped, prevented from falling onto his face only by the "helping hands" of the interrogator's assistants. He was dragged roughly into an upright position again. The interrogator shook him violently by the shoulders. "Wake up, you stupid bastard!"

Morita's head stopped bobbing around and a defiant grin settled on his face. The interrogator slapped him hard across the face and kneed him in the groin. He bent double—no longer supported by the two accomplices—and dropped like a stone to the floor, groaning as the air went out of his lungs. The interrogator crouched low and scampered after him, pinning him in place with his knees. He raised his right hand, with his calloused index and middle fingers protruding like two steel prongs on a pitchfork. "Now, you piece of shit," he rasped, "either tell me where those papers are or I'll drive my fingers into your eye sockets as far as they'll go."

"That's enough, Kobayashi!" A voice rang out, in English, from the doorway behind. Morita's head was spinning, but he thought he recognized the voice. He blinked sweat away from his eyes and stared, with difficulty, through the arc of light that had been trained on him.

"Lorimer?"

"We meet again, Lieutenant Morita. And how are you enjoying our hospitality so far?"

The chieftain's house, traditionally the biggest and occupying a plot in the center of the village, appeared tranquil from the outside. To its left was a raised storehouse, used for surplus rice or fish, to help see the chieftain's family through the harsh winter months when snow drifts on this exposed western seaboard typically grew to twelve feet or more in height. And, to the right, was a sturdy bear cage, vacant at present.

Bears featured prominently in the mythology of the Ainu and were both a source of meat in the spring, when the half-starved animal emerged weakened and vulnerable from hibernation, and as a creature to be venerated and even worshiped as a *kamui* or divine being.

Inside the house, Ralph Carnaby sat with his back against the supporting pillar of the house, his face bruised and swollen. He was bound to the pillar with a length of coarse rope which was looped tightly twice around his torso. His wrists and ankles were similarly fastened. His captors, evidently worried by his achievements to date, were in no mood for taking unnecessary risks.

He had been in the village a whole day now, having been transported from Tokyo in the hold of a light cargo plane the night before. Apart from a brief period early that morning when he also had been subjected to interrogation, he had been pretty much ignored. He had spent the day trying to figure out what was going on around him. There was no sign of Brannigan, only the comings and goings of Japanese in military garb.

And where was Beth? Was she here in the same village? Or were they keeping her under lock and key somewhere back in Tokyo? Anything was possible, judging from the events of the last few days. Nothing he saw made any sense: men wandering around with reels of telephone wire, lighting equipment, rifles, mortar tubes, wooden crates. If they really *were* smuggling the doctors out, why didn't they simply fly them over to Sakhalin? They could even use the plane that he had been bundled into.

He stared vacantly up at the wall, which was decorated with the paraphernalia of the hunter: a small bow, a variety of spring traps, snowshoes and, of course, a bearskin. Mugwort arrows protruded from the underside of the thatched roof, left where they had been shot thirty years earlier when the house had been rebuilt—an age-old custom designed to satisfy and quieten the spirits of the felled trees.

God, his head ached. His face felt like a side of raw beef, and it itched like hell. He relaxed his hands, tried to make them smaller, and pulled slowly. But once he realized the ligatures were not going to yield, he started to struggle furiously. But it was useless. Carnaby couldn't have known it, but his hands had been tied by an expert huntsman. The cords were strong enough to restrain the powerful and desperate movements of a fully grown male brown bear.

He slumped forward. Delirium was taking hold again, and he could feel himself slipping into unconsciousness. He had the strangest of dreams. At one point he could have sworn that creepy guy he met in Hibiya Park was in the room laughing at him. Boris, wasn't it? That's right—Boris Chernenkoff.

When he came round two hours later, Brannigan was sitting directly opposite, poring over a map and chewing on one of his big fat trademark cigars.

He blew out a dirty pall of smoke and smiled expansively. "Welcome to the land of the living, Captain."

Carnaby's eyes opened wide, and he found himself shouting, "Where's Beth? What have you done with her?"

Brannigan held his gaze and kept smiling.

Carnaby shifted position and squinted through the smoke. "If you've laid one finger on her Brannigan, I'll—"

"You'll what, Carnaby? Exactly what will you do? Teach me a lesson, is that it?" He chuckled at his own mirth. "If you don't mind me saying so, you're not really in a position to be making threats right now."

"I want to know how she is. I want to see her."

"All in good time, Carnaby. All in good time." He folded his map and tucked it back inside his jacket. He leaned forward and smiled again. "But in return, I need you to tell me where you have hidden those documents."

"Like I told that gorilla of yours this morning five times already, I burned them."

"You know," said Brannigan, stubbing out his Havana on the wooden armrest of the chair, "you disappoint me. I would have thought a man of your obvious talents would make a more plausible liar."

"Are you worried, General?"

Brannigan dropped his cigar butt to the dirt floor and ground it in with the heel of his combat boot. "Worried? Not at all. Why the hell should I be? I'm just trying to tie up some loose ends, that's all."

"Seems to me it's more than that. I'm sure you wouldn't be going to all this trouble just for the sake of tying up some loose ends."

"You're out of order, Carnaby."

"Am I, General?" He smiled. "You know what I think? I think you're worried shitless. Worried that maybe I showed those affidavits to someone who knows what they're about. Worried that half the US Army is on its way up here right now and they're going to put a stop to your little game. Those doctors aren't going anywhere, General, except to prison where they belong."

Brannigan jammed another cigar in the corner of his mouth and began clapping slowly and methodically. "You have *no* idea, do you?" He was starting to get excited now, his voice rising a notch. "You think you're so smart, don't you? You think this is about the doctors?" He looked up at the rafters and laughed out loud. "Oh boy, I overestimated your intelligence, Carnaby. You obviously don't get it at all, do you? Do you know, you're absolutely right. The doctors aren't going anywhere. They are a means to an end. Period."

Carnaby stared, unblinking, and then grimaced suddenly as his leg was seized with a cramp. "Means to an end? You mean you saved those guys from the gallows seven years ago so that they could help you with whatever it is you're doing now?"

Brannigan laughed again and rocked back in his chair. "I may be brilliant, but I'm not that goddamn brilliant. Sure, I knew about the deal that the State Department cut back then. The US simply couldn't afford to lose that data, and to get it the doctors' safety needed to be guaranteed. But what it also meant was that the doctors would never be completely free. The threat of further tribunals has meant that the specter of the gallows has always been with those poor bastards. And now, when we need them most, it has played right into our hands."

"So what are you doing with them?"

Brannigan stared at Carnaby, his expression suddenly serious. "You really wanna know, huh? I assume you actually read the affidavits before you . . . *burned* them? Tell me, what is it that doctors do best?"

Carnaby sat in silence.

"Ah," said Brannigan, "not prepared to play along, eh? Okay, just for your benefit, I will give you the questions *and* supply the answers. Happy?" He took out another cigar and lit it. He took a draft and stared at Carnaby.

"Question: what is it that doctors do best?

"Answer: they kill people, lots of people, using a variety of deadly nerve agents.

"Question: assuming one of the doctors is staying here with us, how many doctors does that leave?

"Answer: five doctors.

"Question: Excluding the large British army base down the road from here, how many significant bases are there in Japan?

"Answer: five.

"Do you see where this is going yet, Carnaby?" Brannigan winked, provocatively, and puffed out three neat little rings of smoke. "Question: how are nerve gases most effectively deployed?

"Answer: by mortar.

"Question: what have my men been unloading from the truck outside under cover of darkness?

"Answer: mortar tubes.

"Shall I go on?"

Carnaby was aghast. He could feel his heartbeat quicken and that all-too-familiar knotting in the pit of his stomach. He could taste bile in the back of his throat. He screwed his eyes shut, blinked a few times, and finally looked Brannigan straight in the eye. Very deliberately and slowly, he spoke. "Are you trying to tell me that you and your doctor friends, together with a bunch of mercenaries, are going to drop nerve agent on US soldiers? Your own soldiers?"

"Now you're finally getting it. But don't worry yourself too much. Most of those bases are operating at ten percent strength right now. As you know, Uncle Sam's boys are dug in over in Korea, and the way things are shaping up over there they ain't likely to come back."

Carnaby gazed past Brannigan, as if looking off into the distance. And then he said, in a quiet, almost contemplative voice, "And Lieutenant Brice was killed for this?"

"Unfortunately, yes. He was a brilliant linguist and cryptanalyst."

"But why?"

"Because he decided he didn't like what we were doing. And not only that, he was going to blab to MacArthur. The affidavits he took were the proof he was looking for. All he had to do next was find a way of proving what I was doing. We couldn't allow that to happen. Months, no, years, of work would have been ruined."

"It was the landlord, right?" said Carnaby, still staring into the distance. "He came in through Amano, didn't he? Befriended Brice, took him into his confidence. Arranged the loan for him and then murdered him in cold blood."

Brannigan sighed. "He has his uses."

"Yeah, I experienced one of them this morning." There was a long pause as he mentally dropped the missing pieces into the metaphorical jigsaw puzzle. "And, so once the bases have been knocked out, let me guess, you telephone old Ivan across the water there and let him know the coast is clear and—"

"And tomorrow night history will be rewritten. Japan will at last become Russian sovereign territory."

Carnaby and Brannigan jerked their heads toward the doorway and the figure who had just spoken, his face still hidden in shadow.

"Ah," said Brannigan, his voice faltering slightly, as if he knew somehow he had told Carnaby more than he should have. "I'm sorry, Yamato, I didn't see you there."

The tall figure moved forward a pace so that the light from the crude oil lamp shone on his face.

Carnaby's heart all but stopped. In the doorway, dressed completely in black, stood a handsome man with dark curly hair and strangely Germanic features. "*Sorge.* But you're dead! They hanged you!"

Sorge seemed amused and came further into the room, smiling, genially. He stroked his neck with his fingers and said, "Well, if they did, they didn't make a very good job of it."

"I don't understand." Carnaby's voice had trailed off almost to a whisper.

"It was a substitute. He died in my place, so that I might carry on my work for the greater good of Comintern and the Motherland. My work is too important for me to die. He was a very brave man."

So the rumors were true, he thought.

Sorge positioned himself squarely in front of Carnaby, hands placed ostentatiously on his hips. Tilting his head slightly to one side, he said in soft tones, "I believe you are Mr. Ralph Carnaby. I am pleased to be able to meet you at long last. I have heard so much about you."

"I'm flattered," muttered Carnaby.

"Oh no, please—it was not meant as a compliment. On the contrary, Mr. Carnaby, you have caused us a great deal of trouble. You have been, how do you say, a thorn in our side for quite some time."

"Well, I wish I could say I was sorry," he said cynically.

"I can understand your frustration."

"Oh, I *bet* you can. I'd say it was a little more than frustration, wouldn't you? Sitting here helpless while you and your band of cutthroats plan to massacre thousands of innocent Americans."

"It is a regrettable but nevertheless necessary task in ensuring victory for the socialist movement against the canker of Western capitalism."

"You sound like a two-cent propaganda sheet, for Christ's sake."

"It is easy to scoff, Mr Carnaby. But our beliefs are firm, and we *will* win. You mark my words."

Carnaby looked past Sorge and fixed his eyes on Brannigan. "And tell me, General Brannigan, how does it feel to be selling out your own country like this?"

The general shifted in his chair and folded his great meaty arms across his chest. "My conscience is clear. I have absolutely nothing to be ashamed of."

"Nothing to be ashamed of? You don't think plotting to kill thousands of innocent people in cold blood and facilitating the illegal invasion of a country is anything to be ashamed of?"

"I don't expect you to understand, Carnaby."

"So why *are* you doing it? They must be paying you one hell of a pile of money for your mercenary services."

Brannigan was shaking his head. "You know, Carnaby, you're just making one wrong assumption after another. You're really not so smart after all. I thought you'd done your homework. You must have known I spent close to ten years in Moscow in the '20s. I've been a communist ever since."

The words hit Carnaby like a blow to the stomach. "How the hell did you manage to keep that quiet for so long?"

"I am a very patient man. Besides which, it was easy during the Pacific War. We were all fighting the same fascist enemy. And since then, well, I have been waiting to be called."

"You're a goddamned lousy traitor, Brannigan. You'll hang for this."

"I should be more concerned with your own fate, Carnaby, rather than worry about mine."

"Do you honestly think the Japanese are just gonna sit there and take it? There'll be a frigging uprising."

Brannigan smiled. "I doubt that very much. The Japanese on the whole are a pretty apathetic bunch. They've had enough of war and hardship—"

"Hardship?" repeated Carnaby, his voice loaded with incredulity. "You think turning the place into a Russian satellite will make things better? Communism's just about bankrupted that country."

"I think you are missing the point, my friend." Sorge spoke again. "The Motherland is overcoming its problems—problems, I might add, that any country experiences following a long war. And it will emerge from it all the stronger. What matters now is the ideological battle. We must and will win it."

Carnaby noticed Brannigan had wandered over to a telephone in the corner. He picked up the receiver and made a short call.

"And," continued Sorge, "there is another factor you are overlooking: There is within Japan already a large and growing base of support for the Communist Party. It is these communists who will be leading the glorious attack tomorrow evening."

This man is dangerously mad, thought Carnaby. Suddenly there was a noise at the door. He looked up. His eyes opened wide. "Beth!"

Two guards, one with a pistol in his hand, escorted her into the room.

"Oh, Ralph!" she screamed, and ran over to him, throwing her arms around his shoulders and showering his neck with kisses. "What have they done to you?" she said, examining his bruised face.

"It's okay. I'm fine, really. How are you? I was so worried about you."

Tears ran down her face, and she whispered, "I'm okay. They've been kind to me. But this . . . " She turned to face their gaolers. "Can't you please untie him, General? These ropes are cutting into his skin."

"I'd like to help, Miss Chandler, I really would. But you understand I can't let a man like Captain Carnaby wander around here at will. And we don't have sufficient resources to guard him properly unless he is immobilized." Brannigan smiled a crocodile smile and eyed her figure up and down.

Sorge looked at Brannigan and tapped his wristwatch. Brannigan took his cue and said, "We have things we must attend to now. I didn't think you'd crack easily, Carnaby. But I'm going to give you one more chance to help yourself. Now, tell me where you have hidden those affidavits?"

"I told you I burned them, and that's the truth."

"You know, Carnaby, you're really trying my goddamned patience. Guards!"

"What are you going to do? Leave him alone!" Beth shouted.

The guards sprang forward, and the shorter of the two, a hunting knife already in his hand, cut the rope that bound Carnaby to the pillar and together they hauled him into a standing position.

Beth screamed again, and Brannigan grabbed her arm and twisted it behind her back.

Carnaby started to protest. "You hurt her, Brannigan, and I'll break your fuck—"

A scrunched-up scarf was stuffed forcibly into his mouth and secured by a length of material, which was deftly tied behind his head. Like a roll of carpet, the guards upended him, and, one at each end, they began to carry him toward the door.

"Oh, Carnaby," said Brannigan with a sneer, "it's now a little after midnight. It will be high tide in approximately six hours. I hope for your sake that you will tell me what I want to know before then. And," he paused while he ran his eyes down the front of Beth's blouse and licked his greasy lips, "in the meantime, we will do our best to entertain Miss Chandler here."

Beth screamed again. "Ralph!"

Carnaby writhed and grunted, but the guards held him fast and manhandled him out of the door, banging his head hard on the jamb as he went through. The last thing he saw before he blacked out again was Brannigan's lecherous face staring down at Beth's terrified form.

In the sky above the fishing village, the Great Bear kept watch over the vast wilderness. And across the Sea of Okhotsk, a mere sixty kilometers away, another bear was beginning to stir. Black silhouettes moved around purposefully on the horizon as a red star above a hammer and sickle fluttered in the wind behind them. Final preparations were under way. All now waited for the signal.

Thirty-one

"Tomorrow night history will be rewritten" . . . "But you're dead. They hanged you" . . . "It was a substitute . . . he was a very brave man . . . my work is too important for me to die . . . what matters now is the ideological battle—we must and will win it . . . "

Memories crowded Carnaby's head. His legs were cold, and a numbing sensation seemed to be climbing its way agonizingly upwards, clawing at his limbs, trying to pull him down and submerge him.

"We will do our best to entertain Miss Chandler here" . . . "Ralph!"

He jerked awake and promptly retched all down his side.

"Ralph! Jesus, are you okay?"

For a moment he thought he was still dreaming, that Dan Morita's voice was just more white noise flying around his head. But when he looked round, Morita was there in the flesh, smiling back at him.

"Dan! They got you too, huh?"

Morita was nodding and smiling. His right eye was almost closed, with just a narrow slit to see through, like the split skin of an overly ripe orange.

Carnaby looked about him. They were both bound to large wooden stakes that had been driven deep into the sandy floor of the cave that was to be their tomb. The tide was on its way in, no doubt about it, and water lapped teasingly about their thighs. He struggled, as he had done before, but the knots had been tied by the same expert hands. He stopped abruptly and looked around again. "Emma. Where's Emma, Dan?"

"It's okay, I think. They didn't see her. She got away."

"From here? You mean you guys made it all the way here on your own?"

"Yeah. It's a long story, but we took a car and drove through the night. I got caught snooping around the village. But Emma, she hung back and hid behind the embankment."

"Where is she now?"

Morita shrugged. "I don't know. Hopefully she went to get help."

"There's supposed to be a big British base close by."

"Yeah. Plus she had a map, a military one. The base was marked on there. But that's a day ago now. Surely they would've been here by now."

"Maybe they did catch her after all," said Carnaby dejectedly. He hung his head and closed his eyes. The water had risen almost to waist height now. "You know what the bastards are planning on doing, Dan?"

"Uh-uh." Morita shook his head slowly.

"They're going to drop nerve agent on thousands of US and British troops throughout Japan, and then the Russians are going to invade from southern Sakhalin."

Morita laughed, in spite of himself, and peered at Carnaby through his good eye. "If that's some kind of joke, Ralph, then it's not one of your better ones."

"I'm not laughing. I'm dead serious."

The smile hung on Morita's face for a second longer and then evaporated. "You're not kidding, huh?"

He shook his head and snapped his neck back, smacking his head against the stake.

"And just how the hell are they going to do that?"

"Easy," said Carnaby flatly. He licked salt and blood from his lips. "Communist villages."

"Say again?"

"I said, communist villages. Remember when you called the doctors?"

"Yeah, sure I do."

"Do you recall where you were told each of them had gone on their 'fishing' trips?"

"Vaguely. I made a note somewhere. What are you getting at?"

"I guess if you checked it out on a military map, you would find that each of those locations is in the vicinity of a significant

US or British base."

Morita thought for a minute. He started to reel them off, one by one: "Two near Tokyo—Sagamihara and Yokosuka, then there's Atsugi and Nagoya, and Shimonoseki in the west."

"And Wakkanai, up here, close to where we are now." Carnaby completed the list.

"But that's a huge undertaking. It couldn't be done."

"Yeah," laughed Carnaby. "But they do have the resources. Hundreds of avowed communists. The doctors have spent months producing and refining the agents in the comfort of their cozy little university labs, all the time operating well under the radar. And tonight it all begins."

"Tonight?" Morita looked panic-stricken.

"Do you realize how serious this is? It could trigger another world war."

Morita suddenly started writhing, twisting his body backwards and forwards, grimacing in pain as the ligatures cut into his wrists and ankles.

The water continued to rise. It was up to Carnaby's chest now.

Morita broke into a coughing fit; he had taken in a mouthful of salt water as he struggled to break free of his bonds. "What time do you suppose it is?" he gasped.

"Brannigan said high tide is at six. It must be near that now."

Just under the rock canopy they could see the first signs of daybreak—a faint, very faint, difference in the quality of light, difficult to make out properly because of the dancing flame from the oil lamp behind them.

"We've got to get out of here, Dan, or we're done for. I thought Brannigan would have been back before now to continue his questioning."

"What did you tell him?"

"About the affidavits?"

"Yeah."

"I told him I burned them."

"And he didn't buy it, right?"

Carnaby nodded. "Come to think of it, where are they? Does Emma still have them?"

"Yeah, they were in her bag." Morita stopped suddenly; a shadow seemed to fall across his face.

"What is it?"

"I was just thinking, if she has been captured, and they now have the affidavits—"

"Then there would be no reason to come back and see us."

"Shit!"

They both started struggling again. Morita sucked in a deep breath and plunged under water, trying desperately to work the rope down so he could untie his ankles. But the rope caught fast halfway down the rough stake—trapping him below the surface.

Carnaby's face was starting to disappear in the foaming sea. He wondered for a fleeting moment whether it was true that people on the verge of death see their lives flash before their eyes. He was not normally the panicky type, but the situation seemed to call for nothing else. He screamed at the top of his voice: "Help! Somebody, please help! For God's sake, help!"

The water covered his mouth so that all that emerged was a succession of bubbles. He stretched as far as he could. His wrists felt like they were dislocated, and he fought to stop his feet sinking further into the sand. Just as his eyes were about to be consumed by the voracious water, he saw a torchlight float, seemingly unaided, under the rock canopy. A dinghy paddled swiftly into the cave, riding on the crest of a small wave. Hushed voices echoed around the cave interior, and then a miracle happened. A lone figure slipped silently over the side and swam underwater, slicing first through Morita's bonds and then his own.

Helping hands reached out, and Carnaby and Morita were hauled from their watery cell and laid on the sand at the top of the cave, next to the steps cut in the rock.

Morita was on his hands and knees, vomiting seawater into the sand.

"Who are you?" asked Carnaby, looking up into the blackened face of his rescuer.

"Captain Denning, sir. I'm with the Royal Welsh Fusiliers."

Emma, thought Carnaby, smiling. *Good girl. You did it.*

Suddenly, from somewhere at the top of the cliff steps came a loud and continuous report.

"It's started," said Denning, signaling to his men with short chopping motions.

The boat had been pulled up onto the sand. The soldiers, eight in all, unslung their weapons and began to run gingerly up the steps.

"I have to leave now. Can you both manage?"

"Yeah," gasped Carnaby. "Thanks a lot, Captain. You saved

our lives."

"Here—you may need this. Sorry. It's all we can spare." Denning smiled, patted Carnaby on the shoulder and handed him a Browning pistol. He turned and took off up the steps after his men.

"You okay, Dan?"

Morita rocked back on his heels, coughing and wheezing. He wiped his tear-soaked eyes and said, "I guess so. I really thought we'd had it then, Ralph."

"Yeah, me too. Come on, I've gotta find Beth."

"Beth? Jesus, I'd forgotten all about her. Was she okay?"

"Kind of. That son of a bitch Brannigan was all over her when I was dragged away."

Carnaby checked the action on the pistol, and they made their way slowly up the steps to the top. When they got there, all hell had broken loose.

From somewhere over to their right flank, a heavy machine gun chattered. Explosions rocked the village. Frantic shouts came from all directions.

Suddenly, through the smoke, Morita caught sight of Lorimer making a frantic dash for the perimeter embankment. His arms were pumping like a couple of pistons on a two-stroke engine, and his head was bent low into the wind, like a sprinter diving for the tape. A split second later he was somersaulting through the air, caught in a grenade blast. A cloud of smoke and vaporized body parts blew over the thatched roof of the chieftain's house. His body landed in a heap of mincemeat, and his head shot across the rough ground like a bowling ball, only stopping when it hit the side of the bear cage with a resounding thud. Carnaby looked down and closed his eyes. Dawn was coming on fast, and a strange purplish light seemed to be growing in intensity on the horizon.

A crack rang out from the building to their left, and he realized they were being sniped at.

"Duck!" shouted Morita, pushing him down behind a low wall. Another shot screamed overhead and shattered a window in the building next door. They cautiously edged around the wall and moved toward the rear of the building. "I wish to hell we had another gun," whispered Morita, frowning.

Carnaby moved toward the door just as a rifle barrel came probing out of the broken window. Without hesitation, he thrust his pistol through the opening and squeezed the trigger twice in rapid succession. Morita dived in from the other side, the momentum carrying them both through the flimsy door. Morita caught hold of the gun barrel as its former owner collapsed onto the floor, two bullet holes in his heart. It was only then that he realized who it was—the interrogator. His eyes were limpid, even in death.

Morita clapped the rifle into his hands. An M1 Garand. It would do, he thought.

They began to move through the house, senses alive to the slightest movement.

Another explosion shook the house. They were both thrown to the floor and covered in shards of glass and timber.

"Goddamn," spat Carnaby, "don't these Brits realize we're in here?"

"Ralph," spluttered Morita, spitting out bits of splintered wood, "where was Beth?"

"The next house along—the big one out front."

They pressed themselves up against the wall and peered out the window. A flash illuminated the sky, followed by a hail of machine gun fire.

"You know," said Carnaby, crouching low, "if those Brits don't kill us first it'll be a goddamned miracle."

Morita jumped first through the smoldering opening where the wall used to be and zigzagged across a short stretch of open ground to the side wall of the chieftain's house. He waved the all-clear, and Carnaby joined him. Pushing the door open, they slipped into a small room used for storing fire wood. Logs, cut lengthways into quarters and bound with string, were piled up in neat stacks all around the room. A pungent, almost cloying resin-like smell filled the air.

Suddenly there was a noise from the next room. Throwing caution to the wind, Morita charged the door. He came crashing through and staggered, dropping his rifle. He bent to scoop it up, straightened, and took a shot in his upper thigh. He collapsed in agony as Brannigan started to take aim again.

A loud bang shattered the air around them. Carnaby stood over Morita's writhing form, his arm and gun in perfect alignment, a thin wisp of smoke trailing out of the muzzle of his pistol and curling up toward the ceiling.

Brannigan seemed to stay on his feet much longer than he

should have done. A thin stream of blood ran down the middle of his face from the blackish red hole in his forehead. He keeled over, still clutching his pistol, and fell untidily into the ash-filled base of the cooking hearth.

A noise came from the back of the house, and the door opened. A voice shouted, "Brannigan!" Sorge came through, his forearm locked around Beth's neck, a gun gripped in his other hand.

"Beth!" Carnaby shouted.

Sorge quickly took in the scene and pulled his hostage back through the door, shouting, "Don't follow or she dies!"

The door slammed to, and Carnaby leapt forward.

"Ralph!" Morita beckoned from the floor, where he sat cradling his leg in a slowly spreading pool of blood. "Be careful. But get the bastard for me."

"Don't worry, Dan." He cautiously pushed the door open and realized instantly that Sorge had already left the building by the back door. He dived through and heard an engine kick into life from somewhere behind the house. Taking a run at the door, he smashed it open with the heel of his shoe, flinging himself bodily outside just as the jeep roared past him. Lying on his stomach, and thinking this situation looked uncomfortably familiar, he took aim, nice and low, and squeezed off two more shots. He jumped to his feet and gave chase. He rounded the corner as the jeep bounced across the open ground of the assembly area, weaving around the bodies of fallen soldiers, and headed for the field on the far side of the village.

The shots were more sporadic now, and he could see more British troops filing along the gully by the perimeter wall, making safe one small area of the village before moving on to another.

Suddenly there was a shout. Carnaby turned his head and gasped. It was a middle-aged Japanese man dressed in overalls. *The doctor*! he thought. He was running toward a group of British soldiers, screaming hysterically. In his hands he carried a small sphere. A cord trailed from one end and fastened around his wrist. Two of the soldiers ran to meet him, alternately running and covering one another—so-called "pepper-potting."

Oh my God, thought Carnaby, *they're going to be too late*! "Stop!" he screamed, waving his arms frantically. "Stop! There's going to—"

Boom! A dull explosion, of the sort made by a reduced charge, sent the container up in smoke. The doctor lay on the ground, hands around his own throat, making strange shapes with his mouth, like a beached fish.

The two soldiers were on their knees by now, enveloped in the deadly mist. They tried to turn tail and crawl away. But the doctor's invisible nemesis pursued them, and they lay there writhing in agony, slowly suffocating. And then they were still.

"Don't go near them!" screamed Carnaby. "It's poisonous gas!"

Taking a wide berth, he ran over the embankment and spotted Captain Denning reloading his rifle by the wall. "Captain, I need a vehicle. The ringleader, Sorge, got away over the fields in a jeep. He's taken a woman hostage."

Denning looked around him. Two jeeps were out of action—a gaping hole in the hood of one, and the other riddled with holes, looking more like Swiss cheese. "There's only one vehicle—the reserve ambulance at the back." He pointed to a spot a little way up the road. "But we're going to need that here soon, by the looks of things."

"I'll bring it straight back," said Carnaby. He ran up the hill and pulled open the door, climbing in with a grunt.

"'Ere, what's your game then?" A medical orderly turned to face him, a look of surprise registering on his thin face.

"It's urgent, son. Captain Denning gave me his permission."

"Ralph!"

He nearly jumped out of his skin. He turned around and found himself face to face with Emma.

"Emma! Thank God you're okay!"

They embraced, at which point the medical orderly decided he'd had enough and promptly got out of the ambulance.

Carnaby turned the key in the ignition.

"Ralph, what on earth's happening? Where's Dan?"

"He's been hit, but he'll be okay. I can't explain now, but someone's kidnapped Beth. They're in a jeep. They've got a bit of a head start on us. Listen, I want you to get out here and wait by the wall over there."

"I shan't."

"What?"

"I shan't. I'm coming with you, Ralph Carnaby."

"Use your eyes, Emma. There's a pitched battle going on down there. People are dying all over the place."

"Which is all the more reason for coming with you, wouldn't

you agree? And in any case, I've already had this argument with Major Gladstone."

"Who?"

"The commander of the British camp."

He realized he was no match for her verbal fisticuffs. He slammed the vehicle into gear and took off down the hill. Heading along the back of the perimeter wall, he braked as the wheels went off the hard surface of the road and into the field. The ground was deeply rutted and full of depressions, but he could just make out the remains of a track and guessed the ground would be firm enough to take the weight of the long-wheelbase jeep. The vehicle rocked and bounced. At one point, he took his eyes off the trail and gazed out to sea, and they hit a huge hole, sending the stretcher and a whole box of medical supplies sailing through the air and crashing into the back doors.

"I hope they don't need the ambulance too soon back there," said Emma.

They emerged on the other side onto a narrow but more level track that took them up onto the cliff-top road.

They were just approaching the highest point when she pointed and screamed, "There! Over there, look!"

About a hundred yards ahead and parked right in the middle of the track was a jeep.

"Wait here." He opened the door and climbed out. He pulled his pistol out of his pocket and slid the magazine out into the palm of his hand. Shit! Only one round left. He knew there was something else he should have done back there. No matter. Crouching low, he moved quickly up the track, all the time keeping directly behind the abandoned jeep. As he came closer, he noticed a faint trail of liquid on the surface of the track. Gasoline! Reaching the side of the vehicle, he saw a hole punched in its side—just level with the fuel tanks.

Pressing his back against the side of the jeep, he surveyed the ground around him. He took a deep breath and moved off, hugging the ground as he came to the top of the rise. He looked over, and there they were. Sorge was shouting and cursing at Beth to walk faster as he led her roughly by the wrist dangerously close to the cliff's edge. Carnaby swallowed hard and took off down the slope after them.

A plane screamed overhead. *Russian probably*, he thought as he put on a spurt and raced up behind Sorge. *Don't turn around now, not yet. Just a little farther.*

Another plane flew past, and Sorge turned slightly to look. It was then that he saw Carnaby, almost on top of him. He grabbed Beth viciously by the throat and reined her in. Wheeling about, he brought his arm up and leveled his gun at Carnaby's chest. He took a step back toward the edge of the cliff.

A cluster of four pure white seagulls chased one another just below the edge of the cliff top. Sorge grinned at Carnaby and then started to laugh maniacally.

Carnaby stood still, leaning slightly into the wind, his face expressionless, pistol at his side.

Sorge stopped laughing and tightened his grip on Beth's throat. "Congratulations, Mr. Carnaby. You have succeeded in ruining a lifetime's work."

He remained motionless and stared into Sorge's crazed eyes. "Let her loose, Sorge."

"But, Mr. Carnaby, I need to salvage something out of all this. I may have lost the war, but I need to win at least one of its battles."

"It's over, Sorge. Give up while you can."

"Why? So they can hang me all over again. I cannot die yet. My work is too important."

"Let her go."

Sorge increased the pressure on Beth's throat. She whimpered and screwed her eyes shut.

Carnaby felt his fingers tighten around the pistol grip. He tried to keep the anxiety out of his voice. "Listen to me. If you let her go, I'll see what I can do. I'll talk to the authorities on your behalf. I'll—"

From the distance a deep booming sound came across the sea, carried on the strong wind. From around the promontory came a neat line of ships in battle formation. The US Seventh Fleet!

Sorge seemed transfixed. He stared toward the sea like a blind man, vacantly, his eyes devoid of all hope. His dreams had disappeared in an instant. More planes flew overhead. Not, Carnaby now realized, Russian, but F9F-2 Panthers from the flight deck of the USS Valley Forge.

Sorge's grip seemed to loosen, and in that instant Carnaby saw his chance. "Beth, move!"

She let her body go limp and dropped to the ground. Carnaby's arm shot up to shoulder level, and he made his bullet count. It hit Sorge in the shoulder and spun him around. Sorge dropped his gun and staggered backwards, making no attempt to retrieve it. He teetered on the edge of the cliff, the salty wind playing with his dark hair.

There was a pitiful look of resignation in his eyes. He glanced out at the sea, and then slowly turned his head back again and smiled. "I bid you farewell. Long live the Motherland!" He stepped off the cliff, still smiling, and plummeted two hundred feet to the rocks below.

Beth screamed, and Carnaby embraced her, pulling her into him, and caressed her hair with his hand.

Behind them, on the track, the ambulance had pulled up, and Emma had jumped down and was running across the strip of grass, arms outstretched, crying and laughing. The three of them stood there, arms around one another, embracing. The Siberian wind rolled in from the north, drying their tears. They collapsed to the ground, locked in silent communion, and gazed out to sea—out toward Sakhalin and beyond.

Epilogue

Carnaby sat in his worn leather chair sipping strong black coffee and staring out into the night.

A storm was brewing, and droplets of rain started to streak across the windowpanes. He removed his gaze from the mesmerizing lights of the city and let his eyes come to rest on the telephone in front of him as if he half expected it to ring. Hadn't it all started out this way some six months ago?

He leaned forward, placed his coffee cup on his desk, stood up and walked slowly over to the window. He rubbed his tired eyes and peered out. The rain was heavier now and produced a distorting effect on the lights, like an imprecise, blurred memory. He closed his eyes and cast his mind back to the events of the last few days and felt himself shudder involuntarily. It all seemed so unreal now he was back in familiar surroundings.

But it was all real enough. Witness the changes the last forty-eight hours had brought:

His boss, Colonel Aspin, had been arrested en route to Atsugi Air Station, where he had planned to fly to Wakkanai and join the ill-fated General Brannigan and his band of disaffected cutthroats. He now languished in a Tokyo prison, his career, if not his future, effectively over.

Brannigan, Lorimer and all six doctors had perished in the firefights—an end which, as far as the occupation authorities were concerned, was not only fitting, but also extremely convenient. Phase Two of the Tokyo War Crimes Trials would proceed, with the list of defendants' names unchanged.

The Russians, of course, denied all knowledge of—let alone

involvement in—this apparent grand scheme, and seized upon the opportunity to criticize the Americans for failing to root out these traitors in their midst. The Soviet ambassador to Tokyo went on record as saying, "This latest allegation concerning the appearance or should I say, 'reappearance,'—of Richard Sorge, is nothing but a fictitious product of the capitalist propaganda machine. What more proof do we need of America's predilection for conspiracy theories? Sorge was hanged nine years ago. If you do not believe it, then ask his widow." (Which the press naturally then felt duty-bound to do). The unprecedented military build-up on Southern Sakhalin was characterized as a routine training exercise, something the Soviets were well within their rights to do on sovereign territory, in much the same way as the US Seventh Fleet apparently felt within its rights carrying out maneuvers in Japanese territorial waters. The whole incident served only to strengthen Russia's demands for a greater role in the administration of the occupation.

Emma Forbes, that plucky little English schoolteacher, had decided to stay on and see out her new position as governess to the British ambassador's children until she decided what she really wanted to do with her life. She had, after all, achieved what she had come all that way to do.

As for Carnaby's friend and colleague Dan Morita, he had received a long-overdue promotion and yet another citation for bravery. He was convalescing in the Roosevelt Memorial Hospital, his recovery no doubt being speeded along by the care and loving attentions of Staff Nurse Beth Chandler.

Carnaby smiled at the thought and brushed the backs of his fingers across his cheek. In his mind's eye he could see Beth skipping lightly down the steps in the hospital's entrance hall, that infectious smile and sheer joy of life radiating from her pretty, youthful face.

He sighed and opened his eyes again. The rain had stopped momentarily, and he caught sight of his own dark reflection staring back at himself. And what of himself? What had he learned over the course of the last few months? Well, for one thing, he felt he had come of age and finally stopped blaming himself for Laura's death. In the past he had treated his own well-being with reckless abandon, feeling that without Laura, life held no meaning for him. But it was more than that, he now realized. He was in love with Beth. He had been, in point of fact, ever since he first laid eyes upon her some four years ago. He could finally admit it to himself without feeling ravaged with guilt. All along he had been afraid of falling in love again, of having something, someone, so precious in case he lost that too. Little wonder then that Beth had been so confused by his mood swings these last few years. But seeing her in the clutches of that madman Sorge, and knowing just how close he had come to losing her, made him realize finally just how much she meant to him. Quite why it had taken him so long to trust in his feelings was beyond him. Not that it mattered now. He only hoped he wasn't too late. He resolved there and then to ask her. He would go to her apartment this evening. If she were willing, then he would take her back home, and they would live their lives together, come what may.

He smiled again, turned and wandered back to his desk. He drained his coffee cup and pulled his coat on.

He looked round once more at his room. *This occupation would get along just fine without me,* he thought as he turned the light off and closed the door.

Historical Notes

While Yamato is a work of fiction, some of the characters portrayed are based on real people, and many of the events are based on actual events.

Major General Charles Brannigan

Major General Charles Brannigan was in real life Major General Charles Willoughby. Willoughby, referred to affectionately by General Douglas MacArthur as 'my lovable fascist,' was MacArthur's intelligence chief both during the Pacific campaigns and the occupation where he was head of G-2 (Intelligence). Unbeknown to MacArthur, Willoughby recruited Lieutenant General Seizo Arisue, former chief of military intelligence for the Japanese General Staff. Using Arisue's contacts, and operating under the guise of G-2's Historical Section, Willoughby put in place a secret organization whose aim was to create a nationwide network of former Japanese soldiers who could be easily mobilized against communist insurgents in Japan. Willoughby bordered on the fanatical in his loathing of the communists and encouraged the fight against what he termed the "grimacing face of the red Medusa." The extent of Willoughby's spying and other 'unauthorized' activities has been the subject of a great deal of speculation over the years.

Richard Sorge ('Yamato')

Richard Sorge, a German national, was once described as the most over-qualified spy in history. He worked for Comintern until 1929, when he was transferred to Department Four (Intelligence Section) of the Red Army. As a highly respected journalist in Tokyo he fraternized with some of the most influential politicians in the Japanese government, as well as with leading figures at the German Embassy. He was known for his heavy drinking, his appetite for extra-marital affairs, his reckless eccentricity and, above all, his apparently flagrant indifference to the dangers of his position. Sorge was a communist, albeit an unconventional one, who felt an overwhelming sense of personal involvement in the destiny of Japan. Like his Japanese acquaintance, Hotsumi Ozaki (also hanged), Sorge believed passionately that Comintern would provide a framework for international cooperation in the form of a communist community of nations. At the end of the War, rumors circulated that Sorge had not in fact been executed by the Japanese and that a double had been hanged in his place. However, Sorge's mistress, Hanako Miyake, refuted such rumors (having identified his body following his execution).

Repatriated Imperial Japanese Army soldiers

In the final days of the Pacific War the Soviet Union captured nearly three million Japanese soldiers. Half a million of those soldiers were transported to labor camps, many of which were located deep in Siberia. All captives were systematically subjected to a course of indoctrination for the duration of their captivity (which, in extreme cases, lasted for eight years or more). There are many newspaper reports from the time describing how repatriated soldiers sang communist songs, such as the '*Internationale*' and the '*Communist Youth Song*,' from the decks of the ships as they entered Japanese territorial waters. Although screening centers were set up to 'debrief' the repatriates (or *aktivs* as they came to be known), it is thought that a large number subsequently joined the Japan Communist Party and actively spied on behalf of the Soviet Union.

Japan Communist Party

There seemed to have been a genuine fear in the early 1950's that the communists in Japan would bring about a revolution. Although the activities of the Japan Communist Party were severely repressed by the occupation authorities, the Party continued to enjoy a great deal of support, particularly in the rural districts of Japan. Communists openly talked about the inevitability of armed struggle in Japan. The concern was so great at one point that several prominent politicians, including Tokutaro Kimura, Prime Minister Shigeru Yoshida's outspoken minister for justice, voiced their alarm on a number of occasions. On the eve of the signing of the Peace Treaty in 1952, Kimura reportedly said:

'It is clear as day the communists will rise in revolt all over Japan and a bloody revolution will begin. I already have information that a standing government of the Communist Party would be formed in Nagano Prefecture. There is information that the police is infiltrated by the reds, and there are many Communist Party members among high ranking officers of the Reserve Corps. Furthermore, there are many who are not regular members of the Communist Party but have pledged loyalty to the Party. If so, we cannot depend on the police, and there is a strong possibility that the Reserve Force will become our foe.'

Unit 731

Unit 731 was a division of the Imperial Japanese Army tasked with carrying out bacteriological warfare research at secret installations in Manchuria throughout the 1930s and early 1940s. Most of the experiments were conducted on live Chinese guinea pigs (known as '*maruta*' or logs). It is estimated that in excess of ten thousand *maruta* died as a direct result of such experiments. Although no hard evidence has come to light, there have been claims that a small number of British and American POWs were included in this number. It is well documented that the American government provided immunity from trial for the scientists and military doctors who were former members of Unit 731. Had these people faced trial they would almost certainly have been sentenced to hang as class A war criminals. Instead they were allowed back into Japanese society (in exchange for transferring the data from the experiments). Many of the doctors were subsequently appointed heads of science departments in prestigious universities. Following their capture at the end of the war, the doctors swore affidavits testifying their involvement in bacteriological experiments. None of the affidavits were ever adduced as evidence in the proceedings of the International Military Tribunal Far East.

Yakuza

The Yakuza, Japan's peculiar crime syndicates, flourished during occupation Japan. Japan was a bankrupt country by the end of the war and it took another decade before the recovery started to be felt. Black markets thrived throughout Tokyo and the Yakuza fought with the 'Sangokujin' (groups of Chinese and Koreans) for control of the markets. Although the occupation authorities suppressed many of the Yakuza's activities (including the forced closure of clubs and brothels), generally speaking the Yakuza were tolerated and even encouraged by certain US officials. Elements within the occupation authorities found it expedient to live with the status quo (and some sources suggest that America actually funded certain Yakuza groups for the specific purpose of disrupting leftist activities). The Yakuza gangs were almost without exception vehemently anti-communist.

The Occupation Army

Although overwhelmingly American, the occupation army was multi-national. The British Commonwealth Occupation Force (BCOF) in February 1946 comprised some thirty-six thousand men and women drawn from the armies of Britain, Australia, New Zealand, Canada and India. The BCOF sector in reality was southwestern Honshu (the western part of the mainland), together with the island of Shikoku to the south. Although their role was of only minor importance, it was considered to be more than mere token involvement. The BCOF was also charged with two additional and significant tasks: first, the dismantling of Okunoshima Arsenal and disposal of over eighteen thousand tons of poison gases and vesicants and, second, the management and operation of the largest repatriation screening centers in the country.

Contributors

About the author

Andrew Clare served five years in the Royal Marines, first with 42 Commando, and then with 3rd Commando Brigade, based in Plymouth. A keen cross-country skier and marksman, he spent four winters on exercise in northern Norway with the Mountain & Arctic Warfare Cadre.

He left the armed forces in 1987 to read Japanese at Sheffield University and went on to take a Master of Political Science degree at Kobe University in Japan. Subsequently training as a lawyer, he now works for an international law firm in Tokyo.

He has translated several Japanese novels into English, including Junnosuke Yoshiyuki's *Toward Dusk and Other Stories* (Kurodahan Press, 2011), which in the original won the 1978 Noma Prize, Japan's highest literary award.

About the Artist

Mike Dubisch can see into other dimensions, they say.

His art and subject matter are pulled from pulp science-fiction, EC comics, *Heavy Metal*, fantasy art and horror fiction, and he cites his greatest influences fantasy and comics illustrators Frank Frazetta, Richard Corben, Bernie Wrightson, Moebius, Barry Windsor Smith, Wally Wood, Greg Irons, Alex Niño and Jack Kirby.

In recent years Dubisch has become a figure in the world of Cthulhu Mythos fandom, publishing his Cthulhu Mythos space fantasy *Weirdling*, a graphic novel collecting his independent comic books, and releasing the limited edition collectible artbook *The Black Velvet Necronomicon: Black Velvet Cthulhu*.

Dubisch paintings are usually created in mixed media, utilizing pencil, colored ink, gouache, and colored pencil.

In his work, he strives to put human into the inhuman—to render the unreal as real—to make a static image appear full of movement, and to render shadow as full of light.

Mike can be reached at dubisch.com and facebook.com/MikeDubischArt.

Printed by BoD™ in Norderstedt, Germany

9 784902 075533